SONS OF THE PROMISED LAND

The Land Shall Not be Sold in Perpetuity, For the Land is Mine

DEREK WACHTER

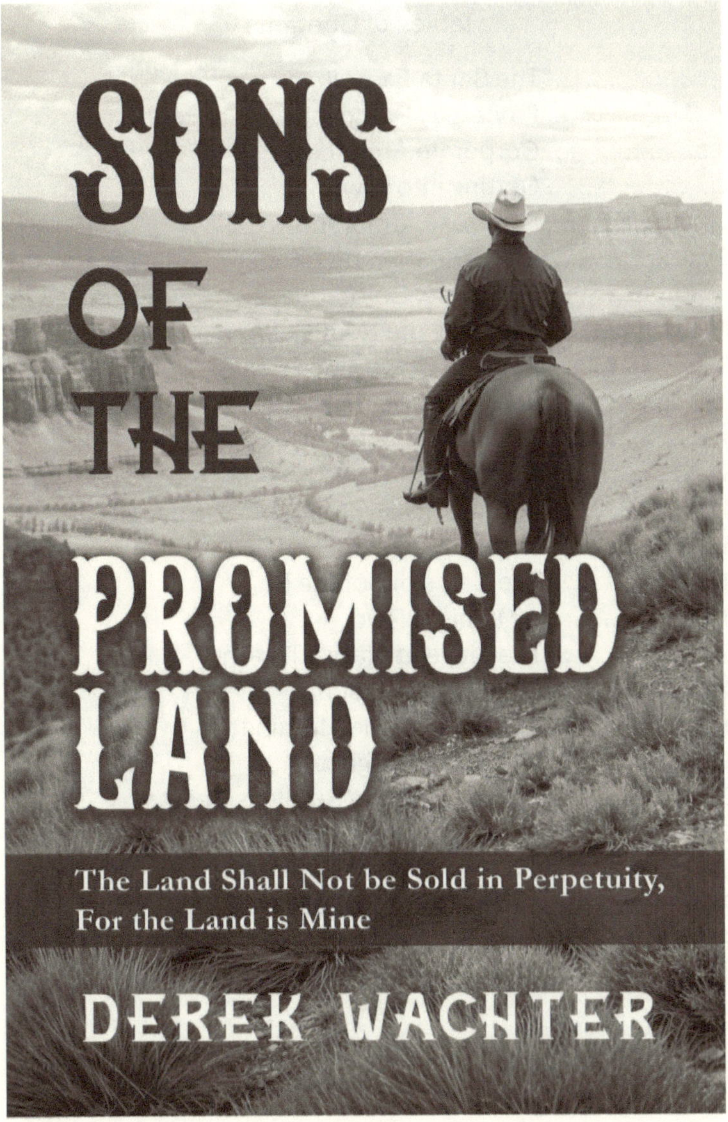

Sons of the Promised Land edited by Mark Becker, LLC

Cover Designer: Cindy Michaels

Tables of Contents

Chapter 1...................... The Santa Fe Trail
Chapter 2...................... Forcefully Removed
Chapter 3...................... Corporate America
Chapter 4...................... Getting into Town
Chapter 5...................... Montrose, Colorado – 1887
Chapter 6...................... Hackenberry and Sanderlin Real Estate Located in Montrose, Colorado
Chapter 7...................... Finishing the Root Cellar
Chapter 8...................... Ain't No Grave Can Hold my Body Down
Chapter 9...................... Vengeance is mine, sayeth the Lord
Chapter 10.................... Thieves in the Night
Chapter 11.................... Sheriff Walt Jones
Chapter 12.................... Economic Development
Chapter 13.................... Taking a Prisoner
Chapter 14.................... The Cat is out of the Bag
Chapter 15.................... A Midnight Raid
Chapter 16.................... The Siege at Mary's Tavern
Chapter 17.................... Ladrón en la Noche
Chapter 18.................... A Red Sky in the Morning
Chapter 19.................... The Ides of August
Chapter 20.................... George Holt the Ruthless Bastard
Chapter 21.................... The Dark Night of the Souls
Chapter 22.................... On Their Wrongs Swift Vengeance Waits
Chapter 23.................... Saying Goodbye is Hard to Do
Chapter 24.................... The Final Chapter

The earth provides enough to satisfy every man's needs, but not every man's greeds.

-Mahatma Gandhi

Chapter 1: The Santa Fe Trail

"Papa, how much longer will it be until we get there?" asked a young girl, who was barely a few weeks over ten years old.

"Oh, not too much longer. You see those mountains off in the distance up ahead there?" said the coachman, steering the horse-drawn wagon carrying his family and everything he owned.

The wagon was larger than what other folks would normally have, but the Ashberger family had a little more than the normal family after having owned a smaller, but profitable orange farm in St. Augustine, Florida for the past twenty years. Folks in the area knew them as the citrus family. After having moved there two decades ago from Philadelphia, Pennsylvania, where John had met his wife, Martha, while he was working in Philadelphia as a farm hand for a cornfield. John Ashberger had always dreamed of owning his own farm. And in this case, an opportunity to grow oranges in Florida opened to him shortly after his union with Martha, and the young couple then set off for Florida to try their hand in being the owner of a farm. Their oldest, Anna, was born a few years after they had lived in Florida and subsequently, Margaret was born thereafter, followed by Ida, who was the youngest of the three.

"We're getting closer to the San Juan Mountains. Those mountains are in southeastern Colorado. Once we get over those mountains, then it's down into the valley of Montrose and onto our new property," said John.

"This ride is bumpy," said another one of the man's daughters, sticking her head out the flap of the wagon canvas that covered the back, protecting the contents of the wagon from the elements.

"Well, it is a dirt wagon trail," said the coachman.

"Excuse me, child. I'm going to sit up front with your father for a bit," said a middle-aged woman, crouching down and making her way through the front of the canvas. She sat down next to the coachman, giving him a kiss on the cheek.

"Okay, John. Be honest with me. How much further do we have until we reach our new property in Montrose?" said the woman.

"Oh, from where we are, I'd say about two or three days through the mountain trail," said John. "It'll go by quick. How are the kids doing?"

"Restless," said his wife, Martha Ashberger. "Margaret is wanting to be done traveling. Anna is still upset that we left her friends back in St. Augustine. And Ida is currently occupying her time playing with her dolls Ollie, Ellen, and Kelly in the back corner of the wagon."

"Well, it has been a rather long trip. Just glad nothing bad has happened along the way to us. How are our food rations?" asked John.

"Fine, after the buffalo you shot a couple of days ago. But the kids are getting tired of eating meat and oranges."

"Well, I hope they like apples."

"How about our home? Is it built for us yet?"

"Well, from the last telegraph I received before we left Florida, it sounded like the wood was delivered not too long ago and they were working on cutting the logs and setting them up. But we just need to try to get the home finished before the winter months set in. That gives us nearly six months to get everything ready and prepared for winter. We'll need to do that, while having the Mexicans get the fields ready for planting in the spring months, too."

"Is Guadalupe there already?" asked Martha.

"He is. Him and Roman got there about a month ago, along with a group of men who came up from Sinaloa with them."

"I'm not so sure about these men from Mexico. We haven't met them before."

"We haven't, but I trust Guadalupe and Roman. They have our best interests in mind, Martha. Guadalupe personally has been a close friend for a number of years."

"Papa," said a young girl's voice from the back of the wagon.

John turned around and saw his youngest daughter, Ida, with her head sticking out through the opening in the flap of the canvas.

"Papa, how much longer until we are home?"

John smiled and turned to face the horse.

"Not much further, sweetheart. Go back inside and continue playing with your dolls," said John.

"Yes, Papa," said Ida, listening to John. She turned and went back into the wagon, leaving John and his wife alone in the driver's seat of the wagon.

"When we get to Montrose, you can send out a post to your brother Robert in Philadelphia. Letting him know we made it okay," said John.

"Oh, that's a good idea. I'll be sure and do that."

"How is he doing?"

"Oh, the last I heard he's doing alright. Still choosing to live in Philadelphia."

"How is he handling your mom's death?"

"Sounds like he's okay."

"How are you handling it?" ·

"I'm fine."

"Are you?"

"I think so. I don't know. I have days I go back and forth. Today is a good day," she said, smiling at her husband as she grabbed hold of his hand.

"When do you want to stop for dinner this evening?" asked John.

"I think soon would be good. It'll take time to make a fire and cook some buffalo meat."

"What about those strawberries that the girls found the other day?"

"They're still good. We could have those too."

"Sounds like a good dinner. Buffalo meat, oranges, and only a day-old wild strawberry."

"Could be a lot worse than that."

"Yeah, it could be. How about the next flat space of land along the trail? We'll stop then and get a small camp set up."

"Sounds good to me. I'll head back and tell the girls we're stopping for the evening."

Martha stood up and went into the back of the wagon, disappearing behind the canvas. The wagon rolled down the Santa Fe Trail, moving up and down the hills as the four horses pulled on. Finally, John came to a spot along the trail that was relatively flat and a good place to stop and camp for the evening.

He stopped the horses and got off the driver's seat, jumping down to the ground. Unhitching the horses, John walked them both over to a fallen tree, tying them up to the log by their bridles, allowing them enough room to move about and graze in the grass there in the area. The kids were the first to jump out of the back of the wagon. The two youngest girls ran off into the brush to relieve themselves, while the oldest daughter helped her mother unload some cargo for the evening.

"Ida, Margaret, don't wander off too far. There are cougars and coyotes out there," said John.

"Yes, Papa, we won't," said Margaret, as she grabbed Ida's hand, leading her off into the brush together.

"John, can you get the fire started, please?" said Martha.

"Oh, yes. Just a moment and let me gather some wood from the back of the wagon," said John as he walked to the back of the wagon.

He pushed the canvas back some and pulled out some wooden logs and made a small pile of wood along the trail. John then grabbed some hay, stuffing it under the logs and taking a flint with steel, he struck the stone with the steel. Sparks flew from the strike and landed in the dried hay, lighting it on fire. In no time, the hay was on fire and caught the dried wood on fire, too.

"Oh, you got the fire started already," said Martha, who was walking some buffalo meat over to the fire.

"Of course. Starting fires is what I can do," said John. "That and hunting."

"Where did the girls go?" asked Martha.

"They went off into the brush to relieve themselves just a few moments ago. Anna, can you take two of the jugs down to the stream and fill it with water? One for drinking and one for cleaning up," said John.

"Yes, Papa," she replied, walking to the back of the wagon to retrieve the water jugs. After she had left, both girls came back to the wagon.

"Papa, Ida found a yellow flower in the bushes back there."

John looked down at his daughter's hand and saw the flower. Inspecting it closely he came to an answer as to what type of flower it was.

"Golden banner. They do bloom this time of the year here in the wild."

"Can we eat it?"

"Girls don't be silly. Of course you can't eat them."

"But we could eat the calendula pedals back home."

"That's a different kind of flower. Don't eat the golden banners."

"Yes, Papa."

"Your sister is going to the creek to get some water for us. Please help us out and gather some wood from the brush, too. So that we don't have to use any more of our supply in the wagon."

"Yes, Papa."

"And be careful of the wild animals out there."

"We will, Papa."

John turned and walked to the side of the wagon. Reaching in, he grabbed his rifle. He checked to make sure it was loaded, then went back over to the fire as Martha kneeled down to start cooking the meat over the fire.

"I sent Margaret and Ida to gather firewood," said John, sitting down on a log nearby.

"That sounds good to me. Anna should be back soon, too. That creek isn't too far away from us."

"Want me to go out and try to find some sage and thyme for the meat?"

"No, it's fine. We still have some sage from the other night I can use."

"What about the oranges and strawberries?"

"Anna got them out before she went out to get some water."

While cooking the meat, Anna came back with jugs of water in each hand.

"Here is the water for drinking, Papa," she said, setting the jug in her right hand down by her mother. "And here is the water for washing."

"Thank you, Anna," said John as the two youngest girls brought back an armload of sticks and limbs.

"Thank you, girls. You can set the wood down by the fire. I'm sure we'll use it all this evening. Are you girls going to get your tents out and sleep on the ground tonight? Or are you sleeping in the wagon?"

"Preferably in the wagon, Papa. We've slept on the ground the last two nights and would very much like to sleep in the wagon tonight," said the girls, sitting by the fire to warm up.

"That is fine. I'd prefer that too. I don't trust the wild animals around here, anyway. Anna, can you please help clean the strawberries and prepare the oranges while your mother cooks the meat?"

"Yes, Papa. I will."

"John, could you put some more wood on the fire for me?" said Martha, picking up the meat from the fire.

John stood up and placed some more onto the fire.

"It's supposed to be cold tonight. At least it looks like it won't be snowing or raining again," said John.

"Like it was the last couple of nights? Yes, I do appreciate that. Not saying our makeshift bed in the back of the wagon isn't warm enough," she said, putting the meat back onto the fire.

"Papa, the fruit is ready for dinner," said Anna.

"Thank you, Anna."

"The meat is almost ready, too. I would imagine this may be the last night we have buffalo."

"Papa?"

"Yes, Ida."

"Papa, I miss home."

"I know, Ida. But Colorado will present a lot of new opportunities for us. We came to own a lot of land there for a good price, thanks in part to Mr. Chase. It'll be worth it."

"But what about my friends?"

"You can make new friends in Colorado."

"Alright."

"Papa."

"Yes, Anna."

"What are you going to do with twenty acres of land?"

"Your mother and I talked about this before we left St. Augustine. We're going to plant apples."

"Apples?"

"Oh, I love apples!" said Ida.

"Yes, apples. It's the next big thing. People are starting to love apples more than they love oranges. So, it's time to make some changes for us to survive and make a living. Like adapting."

"I don't like how cold it is here," said Margaret.

"It won't be cold year-round. It's just this time of the year it's cold at night around these parts."

"Papa, what kind of apples are you going to grow?" asked Anna.

"Colorado orange," said John.

"That sounds tasty!" said Ida.

"Is Guadalupe going to be working for us again?" asked Anna.

"He is. He and Roman both are. They also have a group of men they know in Mexico that are going to come up and work the farm with us."

"A group of men?"

"Yes."

"Have we ever met them before?" asked Anna.

"No. But I trust Guadalupe and Roman. If they think these men are good to have around the farm and family, then they are good to be around the farm and family."

"Meat is ready. John, would you cut it into pieces for us?" asked Martha.

"I will. But let it cool for a moment. I need to wash my hands first, too."

John stood up and walked over to the jug of water used for cleaning. Pouring some out into his hands, he washed and then took a knife out from the sheath attached to his belt. Walking back over to the fire, he cut pieces of meat from the larger piece of meat and handed it to each child, then to his wife, taking what was left behind for himself.

"My meat is tough," said Margaret.

"Mine is too," said Ida.

"It's buffalo, you guys. It's not tender meat like chicken," said John.

"Can we have chicken tomorrow night?" asked Ida.

"Yeah, chicken," said Anna.

"Sounds good to me. We can slaughter a chicken from one of the crates in the back of the wagon for dinner tomorrow," said John. "We also have oranges and those wild strawberries that Anna found yesterday."

"Are they still good to eat?"

"They certainly are."

The family finished their dinner by the fire as the sun set into the San Juan Mountain range. After dinner, all three kids went out into the brush to retrieve more wood, while John and Martha stayed behind with the fire.

"So, John, twenty acres is a lot of land," said Martha.

"It is."

"We had a good thing in Florida. People bought oranges, and we were living comfortably."

"We were, but this is a wonderful opportunity, Martha. This is four times as much land as we had before with the oranges. We can grow and sell more fruit and afford to pay the farm hands while living comfortably. And apples are a fruit that is in demand now. On top of that, there is a gold rush out here, too. The trains are running out west. There is a lot of opportunity for us to grow and expand our family here."

"I understand. I just hate the change when we were living comfortably back in Florida."

"Martha. I understand that you're nervous about the change. I get it. I really do. But this is an opportunity to own land out west, and a lot of it. Twenty acres. And we acquired it cheaply from the government for only $800 dollars. Martha, do you realize that with one good harvest that we would recoup all our payment for the land by almost a hundred times?"

"Where did they get the land from that they're just giving it away like that, then?"

"They got it from the Utes. Local native tribe. A couple of years back, a group of Utes retaliated against their treatment from the government, resulting in the Meeker Massacre. As a result of their retaliation, they lost most of their remaining land out there in the Montrose valley, and they were all confined to reservations."

"So that is how the government came to own the land?"

"Own it and sell it for a profit."

"And you don't think the local tribe is going to have resentment over that?"

"Why would they? We're putting the land to good use. We farm it and produce fruits and vegetables with the land. Mining gold from the hills, no less. They can only stand to benefit from it all if they just allow us to do what we need to do and cultivate the lands."

"I see."

"So yes, this is an opportunity for us, Martha. One that we would be wise to take advantage of."

"What about the girls, though? I know they don't like the idea of moving out to Colorado. They liked it in Florida."

"They will get used to the change. It will be good for them, too."

"Well, whatever you decide on doing, I do trust you, John."

"And I don't take that lightly, Martha. I really don't."

"Papa."

John turned around and saw Ida and Anna coming from the brush.

"We found more wood for the fire. Margaret will be coming shortly with more wood, too."

"Thank you, girls."

The two girls dropped the wood next to the fire, while the third came out from the brush, dropping her pile of wood onto theirs too.

"Are you guys warm enough?"

"It's cold, Papa. Can we put more wood on the fire?" asked Margaret.

John stood up and picked up more wood the girls brought out of the brush, setting it into the fire.

"I want to get an early start on the day tomorrow. Cover some extra ground and see if we can get to the property quicker."

"Yes, Papa."

"I mean it. By the first light in the morning, we are going to get ready to move out. You guys can sleep in if you would like, but I will be up and hitching the horses back to the wagon, and then we're leaving first thing."

"Yes, Papa."

"Do you want fruit for breakfast tomorrow?" asked Martha.

"How many oranges do we have left?"

"We still have a box that hasn't spoiled yet. Plus, some strawberries if they are still good, too."

"And eggs?"

"Yes, the chickens laid six eggs today."

"Perfect. Sounds like a good breakfast to me. I'm going to go to bed for the night then, if I'm going to get up early tomorrow to start traveling. Here, Martha. Take the rifle. Shoot to kill anything if you need to."

"Alright," said Martha, who took the rifle from John.

"Goodnight girls."

"Goodnight, Papa," said all three girls.

John climbed inside the wagon through the back flap and lay down on a pile of hay with a blanket over the top of it. Taking the second blanket that was there, he covered himself to stay warm while Martha and all three girls sat by the fire and stayed warm outside for a little while longer. John lay there on the bed of hay, staring up at the top of the wagon. His thoughts raced through his mind as he wondered if he was making the right choice for him and his family. Was moving them from Florida, where their roots were settled down and living comfortably the right thing to do? Was it not? Was he making a mistake? Or was he doing something that was going to set up his family for success in the future and give his three girls the best chance to succeed in life?

All that mattered to him was that his family was safe and secure. Not just physically, but financially as well. And this was going to be what did just that, building an empire on agriculture in the new and fertile lands of Montrose, by the San Juan Mountain Range. John smiled to himself, knowing he was doing the right thing, then he shut his eyes, soon falling into a deep sleep.

*   *   *   *

Morning was slow to arrive the following day. Clouds loomed in the sky with the feeling of rain in the atmosphere again. John rose from his bed, his wife Martha fast asleep by his side. All three kids were still asleep near the front of the wagon, too. Moving the covers off himself, John rolled off the bed of hay, got out of the wagon, and tied the heavy canvas on the back of the wagon cover together again.

He walked over to the horses nearby and checked on them. They were grazing from the patch of grass next to the wagon, where they were tied up. John took them one by one back over to the wagon, tying them to the neck yoke of the wagon, then to the reins. Next, John reached into the side of the wagon and checked the rifle that they had with them. It was still loaded and ready to fire if needed. He holstered the rifle into a special section by the driver's seat, somewhere he could quickly grab it and defend himself from wild animals, or even worse, other human beings like bandits or, God forbid, Indians.

After everything was ready to go, John made a quick fire in the fire pit, cracked some eggs, scrambled them in the skillet, and then peeled an orange for himself. After breakfast, John used the rest of the water gathered yesterday by Anna for cleaning and then put the fire out with it before putting the empty clay jug back into the wagon. He took the drinking water, drank from the jug for a moment, then put the rest of that water in the back of the wagon as well. Before leaving, he went into the bushes to relieve himself, and as he was, John looked out into the valley and admired the beauty of the Colorado countryside. When he was finished, John walked back to the campsite and climbed up into the driver's seat of the wagon coach, putting his hat on and then grabbing the reins. Looking around himself and the area, he gave a tug of the reins, and the horses knew what to do after that. Both animals pulled the wagon and walked back onto the trail, towing the wagon behind them, taking the family to their new home in Montrose, Colorado.

A short time after leaving the camp, it rained hard. The trail got muddy, and the wagon struggled to get through the mud, but the horses continued to pull and move on. John reached into the back of the wagon, grabbing a blanket to do his best to stay warm and dry. He wrapped it around his shoulders to keep the rain off himself while the horses continued to pull the wagon down a hill along the trail. The trail then leveled out some, which was good because the rain and mud made it very difficult to traverse up hills. Later in the morning, John's first daughter Ida had woken up, as she came and sat out with John in the driver's seat next to him.

"Honey, you're going to get wet and cold out here," said John, opening the blanket up and allowing his youngest daughter to snuggle in with him.

"I'll be fine, papa," said Ida. "Papa, how much further do we have to go?"

"Not much further. We'll be close to the end of the trail here by the end of the day, I hope. Then we'll be in the Montrose valley, on our way to our property."

"Papa?"

"Yes, Ida?"

"I'm hungry."

"Try having an orange? Or even some strawberries from the back?"

"The strawberries aren't any good anymore."

"Well, the oranges still are."

"Kinda."

"We can stop and make some eggs for breakfast this morning when everyone is up. Maybe I can find some more wild strawberries along the trail, too."

"Okay. Papa?"

"Yes, sweetheart?"

"How much further until we're home?"

"Alright, get to the back and wake your sisters up," said John, with a smile on his face as he pushed Ida into the back of the wagon.

"Yes, Papa."

Ida crawled back through the opening in the canvas to go wake her siblings, while John steered the coach down the muddy trail through the San Juan Mountain range of Colorado, looking for a dry place to start a fire. After driving the coach for a while, John came to some splits in the tall rocks along the side of the mountain, where he stopped the wagon for a bit.

"Thank you for stopping. The girls need to relieve themselves and they're hungry, too," said his wife, Martha, sticking her head out through the front opening of the canvas.

"There's a small cave here it looks that we can use to build a fire and stay out of the rain to make some breakfast this morning. Are you hungry too?"

"Starving."

"How many eggs do we have left?"

"It looks like the chickens have laid six more eggs since the last I checked. So, we have eight in total it looks like. Did you have some this morning? I thought they laid six yesterday?"

"They did. I had two before I started this morning, along with an orange. But I'll make the rest for you guys and then for dinner this evening we'll butcher a chicken and have meat for dinner if I can't find anything along the way."

"That'll mean we'll only have five chickens left."

"We'll be fine. We're almost there anyway, Martha," said John, jumping off the wagon and down onto the ground. "Besides, the one chicken I'm thinking of is old and not producing eggs anymore for us."

"Is that what you're going to do with me when I get too old, John?" smiled Martha.

"Actually, yes. That was my plan," said John, hugging his wife as the two shared a laugh together.

"How long has it been raining for?" asked Martha.

"Ever since we took off this morning."

"Papa, do you want me to get the wood out of the back of the wagon?" asked Anna.

"Yes, I do. Grab an arm full of wood and take it into that split in the rock there," said John, pointing out the place he was talking about to Anna.

Anna got out of the wagon, grabbing firewood and doing what she was told. Martha got out the back of the wagon and grabbed the eggs from the blanket she kept them in, and took them with her into the small cave as well. Both Ida and Margaret grabbed some oranges and took them with them.

"Papa, we don't have that many oranges left," said Maragret.

"I know, my dear. We'll be in Montrose soon enough. Then we won't have to worry about not having food."

The family walked into the small cave and John started a fire with the wood that Anna brought with them. Inside the small cave, there were drawings carved into the side of the walls, depicting what looked like humans hunting buffalo, riding horses, the sun rising, and humans standing on top of a mountain.

"What are these, Papa?" asked Ida.

"Cave drawings from Indians," replied Margaret.

"Your sister's right, Ida. More than likely Utes," said John.

"How do you know?" asked his wife.

"The men who look like they're standing on top of the mountain, with the sun rising next to it. The name Ute means the people of the sun."

The children continued to check out the cave drawings as Martha now was interested in looking at all the different drawings too. Martha then went out to the wagon as John started up a fire in the cave. The fire quickly warmed the space in the rock, but most important to them, it was a dry spot to stop for a bit.

Martha came back in the skillet with her, setting it over the fire with the eggs in it. She scrambled the eggs while the kids peeled the last of the oranges. When everything was cooked and prepared, the family ate while John kept an eye out on the trail, making sure no one would come to their spot along the trail and try to take anything from their wagon. When the family had finished eating, they packed their things up and put the fire out. On the way back to the wagon, Margaret looked across the road and saw cherries growing in a couple of trees along the side of the road.

"Papa, look! Cherries!" yelled Margaret.

The girls ran across the road to the two trees and pulled red bing cherries off the limbs, one by one. Martha joined them, reaching some of the cherries that were higher off the ground that the kids couldn't get for themselves. After gathering a sack full of cherries, Martha and the kids came back to the wagon, where John was getting ready to leave.

"You guys get some cherries over there?" asked John.

"Look how many!" yelled Margaret, showing the bag to John.

"That's a lot," said John, reaching in, grabbing a cherry and popping it into his mouth.

"Sweet too," he said as he chewed and then spit the seed out onto the trail.

Margaret handed the bag of cherries to Martha while the kids crawled into the back of the wagon. Martha then climbed into the wagon herself, and John kicked the horses with the reins and all four horses started to move, pulling the wagon back onto the trail and the family was again on their way, after their short stop for breakfast, to their new twenty-acre property in Montrose, Colorado.

Chapter 2: Forcefully Removed

The Utes were proud people. They were the great warriors of the southern Rocky Mountains. As the American West was settled by white European gold prospectors and colonialists in the mid-1800s, the Utes were increasingly pressured or killed and then eventually forced off their lands that were promised to them by their ancestors. They entered treaties with the United States government to preserve their lives and some of their land, but were eventually forcibly relocated to the government-created reservations designated for them.

However, the treaties heavily favored the new settlers in the area, removing the rights of the Utes who were there before them, leaving them with minuscule parcels of the land they at one time owned outright. These lands were also infertile, and void of the great animals they once hunted such as deer, elk, and the buffalo.

A few of the key tribal land defensive conflicts during this period included the Walker War, which occurred when the religious sect of Mormons arrived around 1853, the Black Hawk War where other Native Americans went for treaty talks, but were slaughtered by American forces from 1865 to around 1872, and the worst of them all, the Meeker Massacre in which the Utes tried to regain control of their lands with warring tactics in 1879, but were defeated again, losing more control over their lands as a result of their actions.

Ignacio Black Hawk, whose father was one of the Utes leaders in the rebellion during the Black Hawk War over fifteen years ago, sat in the corner of a shack-made into a bar in the small Utes settlement just outside the town of Montrose. Some other Utes tribal members would spend their time drinking liquors that procured by pawning and bartering with rich white gold prospectors in the area. They traded with the gold they had found in the mountains for liquor from the white men.

On his seventh drink of the evening, a large glass of whiskey, Ignacio drank intending to pass out for the evening, just to wake up the next day and do it all over again. Picking up the freshly served glass, Ignacio took a drink when the door to the shed was opened, and a Ute man walked into the small shack. He looked around the group of Ute men who were there and saw Ignacio sitting in the corner of the shack at a tilted table. The man walked in, leaving the door open behind him.

"Close that door when you come in here," said one of the men in the shack.

"Why? So, we can keep the smell of piss and body sweat in here? Leave it open," said the man as he walked toward Ignacio's table.

"May I sit down?" said the man.

"Did the whites give you permission to?" said Ignacio, taking another large drink of whiskey. "Because if they gave you permission to, then it's alright."

"I take no orders from no white man, and I only ask you because at one time I had a shed of respect for the man that sits before me here today, deep into that god damn whiskey," said the man, who pulled up a chair.

"Ahiga, I appreciate you coming here, but you weren't invited."

"Ignacio, you could have at least offered to buy me a drink, too."

"With what money? What little I earn from selling buffalo, deer, and elk hides to white prospector families goes into my drinking. You know, all they are interested in is the gold up in the mountains."

"Ignacio, you can't sit here every day and continue to drink yourself to death," said Ahiga.

"Why not?" said Ignacio, taking another large gulp of whiskey.

"What more do we have left? My father was killed in the Black Hawk War. My mother was marched off these lands by white men on horseback. Probably raped and killed by the white men that took her captive. We don't have our promised lands to hunt and live on anymore. You want to know where I live now, my friend? In a fuckin' pile of sticks down by the creek. And why do I drink myself to death, you ask? Isn't it fucking obvious, Ahiga?"

"Your father would look on you with disapproval by how you handle yourself now," said Ahiga.

"I suggest you leave my father out of this conversation. At least his spirit finds itself in better lands now than the ones we find ourselves left with."

"Do you think your father would be proud of how you are going about your life, then? Like some drunk piece of shit wasting their life sitting in the darkness of a shack?"

Ignacio stood up, shoving the table into his friend Ahiga. He took a swing with a balled-up fist, but clearly missed and tripped over the table, falling at the feet of his friend. He landed hard on his face in the process.

"Shit!" he said.

"Ignacio, if you could only control your anger and direct it towards the ones who deserve it," said Ahiga, picking him up by the arm. "Sit down in the chair for a moment and listen to me, my friend."

Ahiga helped Ignacio back into his chair and took a seat in front of him.

"Ignacio, for how long have we been plagued by the white men? Those prospectors who came to our lands for the precious minerals?"

"Long enough."

"Indeed. But for nearly twenty years now, we've been bullied and pushed around by the white prospectors. By their leaders. By their farmers. By their white colonials. And for twenty years, we fought back. Our finest warriors, dying in battle to fight for our lands. Including your father. As the white men just kept taking and taking and taking from us."

"What is your point, Ahiga?"

"God damn it!" said Ahiga, standing up and grabbing Ignacio by his shirt.

Ahiga dragged him out of the shack, and then around the corner, behind the small building. He pointed over the land and the small river that ran from north to south.

"Do you see that, Ignacio? Do you see that land out there? That water? The animals? The birds of the sky? The trees? The plants? All of it. We fight for all of it. Not just for us. The spirits of all living things. Even the spirit of the rocks on the ground cry out for us to stand up and do something to defend the world around us. Your father knew that!" Ahiga shoved him back. "Our fathers knew that. And that is what they fought for. These lands that our loved ones and ancestors fought to preserve. Where we have called home for generation after generation. And you sit here, giving up, drinking in a poorly made wooden shack that would fall over from a gentle wind, killing yourself. And the source of your whiskey? The white man, Ignacio. If you could only be the leader that your father knew you could be—that I know you can be. We need hope and optimism, not abandonment and surrender."

Ignacio sat down in the long grass there along the hill, overlooking the valley in front of them. Ahiga sat down next to him.

"Do you feel that breeze? Blowing through the long grass, the spirits of the world flow all around us? All of that will cease to exist if we give up now."

"But what can I do? What can anyone do? The lands my family owned, lived, and hunted on are all but divided up and sold to individual white families. Our people, the Tabegauche, are a dying people."

"Then die with some fucking dignity. Not at the bottom of a bottle of whiskey!"

"We've tried and time and time again we were defeated. The land is lost."

"The land is ours, Ignacio. It always has been, and it always will be. Nothing will ever change that."

"We lost those lands when Walkara died nearly twenty harvests ago."

"Walkara believed in something and did something about it. Just like what you could do."

"I can't think about this right now."

"Then sober up and stop drinking yourself to death. Be proud of who you are. Your ancestors before you wouldn't approve of the man that stands here before me today, drinking himself to an early grave. I want you to go see the pö' rat in our village. They will see the course of your future and then you will know more of what I talk about."

"They will see me in my rightful place. At the bottom of a glass of drink."

"They will show you what you are missing out on. Don't be a fool, Ignacio. Much of our future will rest on your shoulders. You just are too drunk to see it for yourself."

Ahiga stood up from the long grass and walked away, leaving Ignacio sitting there. He stared out into the evening as the sun set over the lands. The view was beautiful, and for a moment, Ignacio remembered how life was so much better when he was a young boy. When he wasn't worried about the land and losing it to anyone. The times he went out with his father and hunted the buffalo into the late evening hours. He then leaned back into the grass and fell asleep, watching the stars dot the early evening sky one by one.

*   *   *   *

Ignacio woke up inside a wickiup shelter—a structure made from brush supported by four poles. They were effective in protecting its occupants, and protection it did provide to Ignacio, as he lay in a bed of hay. Sitting upright in the hay, Ignacio looked and saw the pö' rat of the small village sitting cross-legged on the floor in the center of the room. He wore a headpiece and traditional hides made from elk and deer. Adorning his neck was a necklace of small animal skulls on a leather strap.

"They say you have been having much of the drink, Ignacio," said the pö' rat.

"Not nearly enough. Who are you?" asked Ignacio.

"You know who I am, Ignacio. Your fathers are disappointed in you."

"I'm disappointed in myself. There's no fighting back anymore. We lost everything that we had."

"And you're willing to accept that?"

"What can I do?"

"Listen to your heart, Ignacio. You know what your fathers have fought for? The hard work and effort they put into these lands? Giving up their lives for it and all living things within it. And you are going to let that go to invaders without fighting for it? This is why your fathers are disappointed in you. Not because of the drink, but because you don't stand up and fight."

"Did Ahiga send you to tell me that?" asked Ignacio, trying to rise to a standing position.

"The spirits share with me what they see. For the future. You know this."

"I can't fight them all by myself."

"Young fool. If you only made the effort and stand for what is right for our people, you will see that they would follow."

"Who is they?"

"Our people."

"What do you see, pö' rat? What does my future hold then?"

"Mmmm. You have conflict in your heart, Ignacio. In your heart, there are two bucks fighting with one another for control of the herd. One buck fights for laziness, submission, weakness. While the other fights for leadership and resistance against the white men that have invaded our world. The buck that fights for weakness is winning. And until you stand up for yourself and be the leader you are capable of being, then this buck will win. And you will live a life of servitude and despair. Then one day you will wake up and realize that the wrong buck won."

"What does my future hold then, pö' rat?"

"That entirely depends on you, young buck," said the pö' rat, as he removed an old wax candle from his leather vest.

He stood up and walked over to a group of lit candles, lighting the one he carried with him before walking back to the center of the room where he sat bow legged onto the ground. He gazed into the flickering flame from the candle's wick and took a moment to gather his thoughts. He stared into the fire and Ignacio could see that he was transcending his own mortal body into a spiritual vision that only he could see.

"If you choose to let the buck of weakness win Ignacio, then the path that lies before you will be one of self-isolation. A path of loneliness. You will die, but you will die as a weak man. A vanquished man. Lost to your own evil spirits. However, if you choose to let the buck of leadership win, then you will die in battle. Fighting and making your family and fathers proud of you. Those here and those that have gone before you will be proud of the man you have become. The leader they know you were born to be."

"So, either path will result in my death."

"We all pass on to our next lives one way or another, Ignacio. The only thing you can control is how you make it to that point in your life when your spirit is ready to cross over. Will you get there as a coward? A drunk who never knew his own true potential? Or will you get there as a warrior? A leader who will be talked about in our children's stories?"

"How do I get there as a warrior?"

"You know how, Ignacio. Your fathers and their fathers laid out the map to get you there. To get there as a warrior, redeem your people. Bring them back to our lands. Return to your home and take it back."

"I can't do it on my own, though."

"You are right. You need to make the change. Only you can do that. If you choose to lead, though, you will have the support of the men that will follow you all the way to our next life, when our spirits return to the winds of the earth. Believe in your brothers."

Ignacio stood up and walked over to the candles by the side of the wickiup they were in.

"What do I have to do?" he asked, turning to look back at the pö' rat.

The pö' rat looked down into the small dancing flame on the wick of the candle. Staring into the flame, he transcended reality again. It took a moment, but he shared the vision that he saw.

"You must gather the men together. The warriors here in this village. They will follow you when you stand up and lead. And you will take them to the white settlement of Montrose, the valley that was your home before the white men came from the east and took it from you. And you will get your land back. By any means necessary, Ignacio."

"I understand."

"Ahiga will follow you and help support you along this journey. Listen to him. He is both wise and experienced."

"I understand."

"There, in Montrose, you will find the family that took your very own home. Not just the home of our people, but the land your fathers owned that is rightfully yours. Their name is Ashberger. He travels from the east with his family—a wife and three children. One is fourteen, one is ten, and the youngest is six. They will enter Montrose on this very day by a wagon drawn by four horses. The people from the south are there, constructing a white wickiup for them right now."

"Ashberger?"

"Yes. You will find them living on your father's land."

Ignacio stood up and was ready to leave the tent when the pö' rat stopped him.

"Ignacio, wait!"

Ignacio turned and looked back at the pö' rat.

"What is it?" he asked.

"I see other white men coming to the valleys as well. They too, are from the east. They have malice in their hearts, and greed for wealth. They don't have friends, nor do they have love for their family. They only have love for their wealth. They too, will try to take the lands from our people. The white men will eat one another, though. They will not be friends. However, just because they won't be friends doesn't mean they will be friends to you either, Ignacio. Do not trust the white men from the east."

Ignacio scowled, then turned and left the pö' rat's wikiup. Walking through the camp of multiple wikiups that surrounded the small area they lived in. It was a decent sized encampment. There were nearly a thousand people of the Uncompahgre band of the Utes tribe there, forcibly contained in a small plot of land forced to live together in the southeastern corner of Colorado. They did their best to grow corn and vegetables on the land, but the grounds weren't fertile, and the Uncompahgre found it difficult to get water up the hill they lived on without carrying it to their gardens in buckets one by one. They ultimately grew dependent on the United States government for food, which no one liked to be dependent on the white men from the east for anything, especially food.

Ignacio walked through the camp, over to Ahiga's wikiup.

"Ahiga!" he yelled.

Ahiga opened the flap of his wikiup and walked outside, meeting Ignacio by the entrance.

"We need to talk," said Ignacio.

"Come into my wikiup then," said Ahiga, opening the flap for him.

Ignacio walked in and saw that his wife and child were in the wikiup with them.

"Would you like for me to ask them to leave?" asked Ahiga, as he stooped down and entered the wikiup, too.

"No. It is fine. They can stay. They need to hear this as well, Ahiga. My friend, I am sorry for what happened last night. I had given up hope but have found it again."

"You visited the pö' rat here in the village, yes?"

"I did."

"And?"

"She explained my future to me in detail. That it was my choice of what happens from here to the end of my life in this world."

"Ignacio, it has always been your choice. It's why I get so disappointed in you. You have chosen to drink the drink from the white men, rather than fulfilling your future that was laid out before you by your fathers."

"That will change today, my friend. We need to take back the land that we once owned. We must do it for our fathers, who fought and gave their lives for it, for us, and the spirits of the land around us."

"You know I will fight with you as hard as I can for as long as I can, Ignacio. I will be by your side. You will be my leader."

"We can't do anything with only two men, though. I need the support of the men here in the village, too."

"It's going to take some effort to gain their trust."

"I know this. I worry about this."

"You don't need to worry about that, Ignacio. I know the men here in this village will support you. So long as you are truthful about being a warrior leader."

"I am being honest with you, Ahiga."

"Come, follow me then," Ahiga said, leading Ignacio out of the wikiup.

The two men walked out towards the edge of the village where the creek water ran by down into the river.

"In this wikiup here, you will meet five men. Ahote the restless one, Jaanesh the Lord of men, Liwanu the growling bear, Makya the eagle hunter, and Miakoda who has the power of the moon with him. They are five very influential warriors here in the village and among the Uncompahgre. Among the five, you only must worry about speaking to Jaanesh. There is a reason he is called the lord of men. He will speak on behalf of the other four. If you can convince him you are being serious about being a leader, then you will have success, young one."

"Alright. Lead the way," said Ignacio, motioning with his hand to Ahiga to lead them into the wikiup.

"Jaanesh!" yelled Ahiga.

A few moments later a tall, strong Ute man walked out the wikiup and met them outside. He was a stoic man, and a battle proven warrior. Scars adorned his chest like tattoos, and a single long scar ran from the top of his face down to his lower jawbone, from an attack by a Comanche obsidian knife a few years ago when the warring factions happened to accidentally come across one another out in the Utes wildlands.

"Jaanesh, my friend. I want you to meet this man," said Ahiga.

"I know who this man is already, Ignacio. He is no warrior. Nothing but a drunken fool in that wooden shack in the village, where they serve the white man's drink. He has had his part in making us all look like fools among the white men. Desperate to give up his life to the drink."

"Be that as it may, Jaanesh, this man wants to change his ways. He wants to lead and take back our lands with us. We need help to do this though."

Jaanesh laughed. "The day that I go to war with this piece of bull's shit, is the day I will drown myself in that creek, Ahiga. This man is no leader. He is not like his father and never will be."

"We need to work together, Jaanesh. The reason we lost our lands is because we didn't fight together. We fought separately. This is a chance to come together and take back our lands."

"Forget it, Ahiga. This squaw isn't interested in fighting back against the whites. He's more interested in just sitting around his wikiup with a bunch of other men," said Ignacio.

"What did you call me?" asked Jaanesh.

"I called you squaw," said Ignacio.

"Big talk coming from a man who has committed his life to the white man's drink, speaking to a true warrior."

"I said what I said, and if you want to do something about it, stop being a squaw bitch and do something about it."

Jaanesh quickly shoved Ignacio to the ground, taking a couple of steps towards him.

"Your drunk mouth is going to get you into trouble. I suggest you pick up your spear and defend yourself," said Jaanesh, who walked back into the wikiup.

"What the hell are you doing?" asked Ahiga. "You could have handled that in a more respectful way."

"Trust me, I know what I'm doing," replied Ignacio.

"Are you still drunk?"

"No, I'm fine."

Jaanesh then walked out of the wikiup with a spear in each hand and tossed one to Ignacio, that landed at his feet.

"Pick it up. Prove to me you're not just a pile of horseshit and are actually the leader your father thought you would turn out to be." said Jaanesh.

Ignacio leaned down to pick up the spear when Jaanesh took a swipe at him with the handle end of the spear. Ignacio quickly avoided the swipe, picking the spear at his feet up off the ground, and the two sparred with one another. Some of the men in earshot who heard the clacking of the wooden spears with one another came over to the wikiup to see what the commotion was about. Back and forth the two young men went, trying to gain the advantage on one another without killing each other. Ignacio then landed a blow with the shaft of the spear, striking Jaanesh in the bottom lip, splitting it. Blood ran down the chin of the Ute warrior.

"You fuckin squaw!" yelled Jaanesh, as his pride got the better of him.

He started swinging harder at Ignacio, nearly cutting him with the sharp end of the spear. Jaanesh took one more big swing of the spear, striking Ignacio's spear. The two instantly snapped in half on contact, and the two men then dropped their broken weapons and went into a wrestling fight. They grappled with one another for minutes and dust was being kicked up from the ground as some of the men watching cheered the two on.

Finally, Ignacio got the upper hand on Jaanesh, placing him in a headlock until finally the Ute warrior started to pass out from the lack of blood flow to his brain. Just before he completely passed out though, Ignacio let him go, and the two disengaged from the fight. Some of the men watching helped the two up to their feet.

"Stop fighting, Jaanesh!" yelled Ignacio. "There is no point in fighting with one another."

"You don't understand, Ignacio. I have been fighting all my life. I've seen wars with the white men and among our people and the people of other tribes. Fighting is what we do!"

"Then direct the fight against the ones that we need to fight against, Jaanesh! Fighting amongst ourselves only helps them and hurts us. And that's for the rest of you!" yelled Ignacio. "What will you do? Do you enjoy not having a place to set your wikiup down and call your own? Do you enjoy having to always be on the move? Look around yourselves! The lands we once owned and what we once had, all taken from us on account of those damned white men! Well, I have had enough, and I will no longer run and be confined like an animal to a reserve. The white men have disrespected our land, our people, and our way of life long enough! They don't respect the spirits of the world around us, nor do they respect our ancestors or your fathers. Or my fathers. They only want wealth and prosperity and what they can get their hands on for themselves. They are greedy and eventually will take everything we have built for ourselves at the expense of our lands and our own lives. Have you not seen it happen with your own eyes!?"

Silence fell over the men standing around him. Ignacio walked around the group, looking at each man in the eye as he walked by them one by one.

"Will you give up your wives and mothers? Your children? Your horse? Your weapons? Your land? Your homes? Your spirit! Or will you come with me and get back what we once had? What rightfully belongs to us, to our people."

"And how do you expect us to do that, Ignacio?"

"We take back what was taken from us, by any means necessary, Jaanesh. Will you join me in taking our world back?"

Silence again fell over the group of men standing by, watching Ignacio speak. Finally, a voice spoke up from the group of men standing there.

"I will," said a man, stepping out from the group.

Ignacio looked up and saw that a man named Pallaton separated himself from the group of men. He walked up to Ignacio and stood mere feet away from him.

"I will," he said. "I acknowledge you as my leader."

"As do I," said another voice from the group.

This time a man named Tadi walked out from the group, who was followed one by one by other men. The first being Naakesh, followed by Napayshni. Wanikiy then stepped out and eventually the friends of Jaanesh, Liwanu, Makaya, and Miakoda also stepped forward. Ahiga was the last man to walk forward after some others, such as Utah and Rowtag, who were helping hold Jaanesh up, joined Ignacio as well. They all walked over to Ignacio, declaring their allegiance to him and acknowledging him as a leader.

"So, what does the drunken master suggest that we do then?" asked Jaanesh, stepping forward as the last man to join him.

"We take our land back. What rightfully belongs to us and to our people. We don't let our history die. We start in the white settlement of Montrose, just over the hill, and we take back what belongs to us."

Chapter 3: Corporate America

"Rain. Rain today. Rain yesterday. Rain the day before that. It's a wonder the fucking horses can get up and down the streets of Baltimore in this mess," said James Hackenberry, as he stared out the pane glass window of his realtor business.

He was a prominent business owner with a beautiful view of the harbor in the newly established business district of Baltimore, Maryland. Other successful business owners, trade investors, and salesmen owned shops along the dirt road that ran the length of the harbor.

"Horses be damned. It's hard to even walk the streets right now with all that mud," said his business partner, Charles Sanderlin.

He was a short and stocky man. His hair was thinning in his older age, and he wore a silver-colored goatee on his portly face. He always dressed in a nice suit when he was in the office working alongside his partner, James. James was more of a slender man and a bit younger than the more experienced Charles, yet he had just as much knowledge and the cutthroat attitude needed to be successful in the business world.

The two men had met one another nearly ten years ago during a poker game at The Sovereign Hideaway, just down the road from where they set up shop. Real estate was their game and still was to this day, as they grew to know one another through poker games and finally established a business partnership with one another. Hackenberry and Sanderlin soon would grow to become a wealthy real estate tycoon group in the Baltimore area. They'd own nearly 112 different properties in the city, along with land they used to develop more business offices, and they were also the first to develop golf courses in the area, bringing the game of golf from overseas to the New World.

Some of the properties they owned and sold were to prominent figures in society, including the mayor of Baltimore, governor of the state of Maryland, Benjamin Franklin's son, and even the family of John Hancock. Business to say the least, was booming for the two men. Each day, they would collect hefty rent pay for the land and property they owned at their office located at 14 Magnolia Heights.

"You think the city would do something more about the roads."

"Well, we should make them."

"Come now, James. Did you speak to the Smith family yesterday?"

"Which one?"

"Marvin and Darlene."

"Oh, yes. The home over on Baker Avenue. I did."

"And?"

"They aren't able to come up with the rent they owe us," said James, sitting down at his desk there in the office that sat opposite the open room concept of Charles.

"God damn them."

"God damn them indeed. I went ahead and took the luxury of submitting an eviction notice as well."

"They did so well to pay every month for the past seven months in that building as well. I wonder what befell them?" asked Charles.

"They said the business hadn't been good for the past month now. On account of the weather, no one wanting to come out in the rain we've had, and on top of that, a lot of folks are moving out of the city."

"Well, that's not really our problem. You did well in serving them the eviction, James."

"I thought so myself."

James reached over to grab an envelope from off his desk and began opening it when the front door to their business opened and a middle-aged man, with shortcut red hair and a clean-shaven face, entered. He wore commoner clothing but dressed as nicely as he could for the office. He quietly entered the room, taking his raincoat off and hanging it up on the coat rack by the front door. Turning around, he walked around the corner of his desk by the front door and sat down.

"Well, good morning to you too, John," said Charles.

"Good morning, gentlemen. I hope you are both doing well this rainy, wet morning," said John Marshall, the treasurer and secretary of the business.

"Indeed, we are. Another day, another ten thousand in our business accounts," said James.

"Did you receive the letter yesterday from Marvin and Darlene over on Baker?" asked John as he opened his desk drawer and pulled out a stack of files to work on for the day.

"I did. I visited them yesterday."

"And?"

"I served them their eviction papers."

"But James, they were diligent in paying the last seven months," said John. "You need to give folks a fair chance at making amends. I'm certain they would have come up with the money if you would have given them the chance to next month."

"John, this is why you sit by the front door in our office. In this world of land marketing and management, you need to be more ruthless. Being nice and giving them a chance to recover next month will only mean you won't get rent the following month as well. And at that, one more month of no payment," said James as he stood up and walked over to his desk by the front. "The day you learn to do that, and the day you stop having a bleeding heart for these Almains, might be the day you become a partner here with us?"

"I'm not sure I would like that very much," said John.

"You will. If you love money like I know you do," said Charles from the other side of his desk.

"But how will you build a loyal following to your business if you are evicting everyone who struggles for a few weeks in their work?"

"That is neither his, nor my problem. Nor is it yours, John. Your only job is to collect rent from them. Your only concern is to ensure that the properties we own sell and that they sell for above market value. These renters and buyers will take advantage of you the moment they get the chance to. It's best you take advantage of them first. For example, Marvin and Darlene," said James, walking back to his desk. "If I would have let them slide for even a month from paying rent, what do you think they would have done the very next month?"

"Not paid rent?" said John, questioning the response.

"Indeed. Not paid rent. They would have skipped paying rent then. And then the following month. And the month after that. Until I finally grew the balls to do something about it. You, John, need to let your balls grow out. You, John, need to be harder on these folks. Or else you won't make it in this world. We have what they want. And if they want it bad enough, they will find the money to pay for it from somewhere. Whether they pick up more hours to work or they whore their wives out for extra pay," said Charles.

"I just think you have to build some sort of brand loyalty somewhere," said John, as he opened yesterday's mail. "Least whoring their wives out."

"Brand loyalty is for losers, John. Weak, pissants, who could never do the work that we do. There is a reason why we are nearing close to a million dollars in earnings as a business. And it's not because we've built a brand loyalty first business," said James.

"Indeed," said John as he continued opening letters.

He grabbed the next letter, seeing it was addressed from the governor's office of the state of Maryland.

"Interesting," said John.

"What is it?" said James, looking up at John from his desk.

"This letter is from the governor's office."

"William Hamilton?" asked Charles.

"Yes. Governor Hamilton," replied John.

"What does he want? We already sold him the parcel up on the hill overlooking the harbor for his mansion. Sold it at a pretty good price as well, so that coffin dodger better be happy with what he got from us."

John opened the envelope and took the letter out and began to read it.

"Well, what does it say, John?" asked James.

"It says, dear honorable James Hackenberry and honorable Charles Sanderlin. Your efforts in helping the city of Baltimore grow over the years by conducting appropriate business within our district have been much appreciated. Equally, your assistance in helping the, at the time governor James Groome, in developing the governor's mansion here in the city for himself and other future governors was instrumental. As a reward for your consistent efforts to improve the city and culture around us, we have a business proposition for you gentlemen and would like to invite you to the governor's mansion located at 14 W. Harborview Street on Friday, April the third at eleven in the morning. We hope you are able to attend and listen to our proposal. Signed, Edward League."

"Edward League? The treasurer?" asked Charles.

"I would assume so. Unless there is another Edward League working for the governor."

"Why would the treasurer want to see us?" asked James.

"Your guess would be as good as mine, James. The bastard didn't give us much time, though, having to meet today."

"Indeed. Fortunately for him, we are free around that time. I see we do not have any business to attend to until two o'clock today when the Pulliams come over to inquire about that property on Prince Edward Street."

"Oh yes, the two-level mansion. Well, I suppose we can go to the governor's mansion this morning and see what the proposition is."

"It'd better be worth our time," said James, as he walked over to the window at the front of the building.

He stood there, watching the rain fall from the sky and people moving about the streets. One man just happened to turn off the side walkway and up towards their front door.

"Oh, Christ," said James.

"What is it?" asked Charles.

"That damned William Riddle is coming up to our door."

"Riddle? The man that is renting out the home on Harbor Avenue?"

"With his wife and child, the same."

"Settle down, James. Probably just coming to pay rent is all. In fact, his rent was due yesterday."

"Yesterday?"

"Yes."

"John, why don't you pay attention and learn a lesson in business here?" said James, as the door to the business opened and in walked a man. His clothes were soaking wet from being out in the rain and his hair unkept and wet lying flat along the sides of his head, resting on his shoulders.

"Good morning, Mr. Hackenberry, Mr. Sanderlin. I've come to make a rent payment for our home."

"That's good. I hope your home over on Harbor Avenue is to your liking?" asked Charles.

"It is. Everything is good, but Mr. Sanderlin, Mr. Hackenberry, I've not just come to make a rent payment, but also to ask a favor of you."

"Oh?" said James.

"What is it?" said Charles.

"Well, you see, my wife had broken her leg this past month, stepping awkwardly off the front walkway step at the house. We had to spend some extra money that we didn't have for the town doctor to set her leg and cast it to make sure it healed in the proper place again. We couldn't come up with all the rent for the month this month, but I will pay the rent next month. Plus, what I missed this month."

"How short are you this month?" asked James.

"Short by $20 dollars."

"And how much is your rent for?" asked Charles.

"$35 dollars."

"So, you mean to tell me that you will come up with $35 dollars for next month's rent, plus an additional $20 dollars?"

"Yes, sir."

"Alright. I tell you what, you come up with $55 dollars for rent next month, plus an additional $20 dollars. So, you come up with $75 dollars for rent and then you and your family can continue to stay in the home. If for whatever reason on the first next month, if you don't have the money, then perhaps you can whore your wife out as I'm sure she won't be able to do anything but just lay there anyway," said James.

"I understand, sir. Thank you," said the man with an angry look on his face as he turned and left the building.

John noticed his expression as he was leaving, and saw that the man was not only angry, but was also questioning how in the world he was going to come up with $75 dollars to make rent by the first of the following month. James stood by the window and watched the man walk back out into the street, stepping into puddles of mud. He then turned around and looked at John at the front desk.

"There. You see? Brand loyalty, Mr. Marshall," said James.

The morning went on, business as usual. Tenants and prospective property buyers came into the realtor's office and conducted their business with James and Charles. Finally, the grandfather clock that's ticking echoed throughout the office chimed ten times, indicating it was now ten in the morning.

"Gentlemen, you should consider making your way to the governor's mansion soon," said John.

"Damn it, it's still raining outside," said Charles.

"Of course it is. It rains all the time in Baltimore," said James. "But John is right, we should think about going soon. John?" said James.

"Yes, sir?"

"Can you go out and ensure that the horses are tied to the carriage and ready to go? I would care to not spend any more time out in the rain than I must."

"Yes, sir," said John, who stood up from his desk and left the office.

He went outside to make sure the horses were tied to the carriage for James and Charles.

"Why don't you wrap up what you're working on, James? Do you have your umbrella?"

"I do. It's in the closet, over by the front desk. Would you grab it for me?"

"Consider it done."

James finished writing a note and stood up from his desk while Charles walked over to the closet. Opening the door, he reached in and grabbed two umbrellas out from the closet. James set his quill down in the ink jar, then walked over towards the front where Charles was.

"Don't forget your raincoat as well, James," said Charles, handing him the coat. At that moment, the front door opened and in walked John, who was soaked from the rain.

"The horses are ready, and the carriage is prepared, sir," said John.

"Thank you, Mr. Marshall. James, after you sir," said Charles, opening the front door and allowing James to walk out the office building.

Together, they left the office and climbed into the carriage. Once inside, John shut the door and got up in the driver's seat. Grabbing the reins, John kicked the horses and off they went. The horses struggled to pull the carriage through the muddy street of the Baltimore city business district, but their destination wasn't very far. It was dry inside the carriage, however, where James and Charles sat. James reached over and lit a small oil lantern on the side of the carriage.

"There. We can afford a little bit of light on a dark and stormy day," said James.

"Indeed, we can," replied Charles.

"So, what do you think this meeting is about?" asked James.

"Knowing Governor Hamilton, more than likely, it has something to do with another land purchase. Although, I'm not sure what this one would be for now. He already has the mansion. We sold him that 55-acre tobacco farm just west of the city out in the Monroe district. And got his wife a nice home overlooking the water by the beach on the south side of the city, away from all the Polacks. I don't know what more he needs. Does he have children, do you know?"

"Not that I'm aware of. And perhaps it's not even Governor Hamilton. The letter was addressed to us from the treasurer for the Governor, Edward."

"Perhaps he is looking to purchase land at an affordable price as well?" asked Charles.

"I wouldn't think so. He already owns that large mansion on the north side of town, over on Garver St," replied James.

"Oh yes, Garver St. A nice neighborhood. Did I tell you that we acquired a property over there just recently?"

"Oh yes, you did over lunch the other day. 267 Garver, yes?"

"That's right. The two-level home."

"Excellent. That property should fetch a good price and quickly for us, too."

"Indeed."

The carriage shifted as it hit a pothole in the street, knocking James off balance in the carriage.

"God damn it, Mr. Marshall! Keep the ride as smooth as possible, please!" yelled Charles out the side window.

"I'm sorry, sir. I certainly am trying. The streets aren't in the best of condition from the rain," replied John from the driver's seat.

"Streets aren't in good shape," muttered Charles, disgusted as he leaned back in his seat inside the dry carriage cabin, stroking his silver mustache.

"Perhaps we should contribute some funds to fixing the street, then?" said James, laughing.

"Fucking nonsense. It's not our responsibility to keep the streets in good order at all. Perhaps we will speak with the governor about it today during our visit, then," said Charles.

"Excellent idea," said James.

"Mr. Haceknberry, Mr. Sanderlin, we are pulling up to the mansion now," said John.

"Well, it is about time. James, would you douse the light, please?" asked Charles.

"I will," said James, reaching over and blowing out the light from the lamp, as the carriage turned down a long cobblestone driveway that led back through the trees towards a large, three level white colored house surrounded by large maple trees.

Coming to the end of the cobblestone driveway, the carriage pulled in front of the double-sided entryway doors up front. The doors opened and out stepped two men, workers of the home. They stepped out into the rain while John was dismounting from the driver's seat of the carriage. He opened the door to the carriage, and Charles and James stepped out onto the cobblestone walkway. Opening their umbrellas, they were met by the two workers of the home.

"Gentlemen, thank you for coming today. I'm sorry about the weather we are having. However, rest assured, it is far more comfortable inside the governor's mansion. We are serving warm tea for your meeting with Mr. League, who is awaiting your arrival in the west wing of the mansion."

"Thank you, gentlemen. Mr. Marshall, please stay with the carriage and tend to the horses. James, after you," said Charles, using his hand to gesture to the entryway of the home.

The two workers escorted James and Charles inside the mansion. Beautiful architecture adorned the home, along with clay sculptures that were imported from Italian artists, as well as a multitude of paintings and sculptures from Europe. James stopped and admired one painting in the large great room on the side of the wall by the door. While he was admiring the painting, he heard footsteps behind him on the hardwood floor.

"It's a beautiful piece, isn't it?" said the voice behind him.

James recognized the voice without having to turn around, as the man walked up behind him, just to his left side.

"It certainly is," said James.-

"It comes from the Baroque period. The infant Hercules, strangling serpents in the cradle. Governor Hamilton loves this room."

"Indeed. It's rather a unique piece, Edward."

"It's a pleasure to see you, James," said Edward League.

Edward League was a young prominent politician in the Baltimore area, serving currently as a treasurer to the governor of the state of Maryland. He was a tall, lanky man. He grew a short stubble beard and wore a full head of reddish-brown hair. He dressed professionally and carried himself with a sense of pride and arrogance that even the governor's administration team could see.

"The pleasure is all mine. Where is your colleague, Charles?"

"Your workers took him over to the west wing. Tell me about this other piece," said James.

"This?" said Edward, pointing to a painting on the wall in the hallway leading to the west wing.

"Yes. It's sad. Why is the man crying in the chair?"

"Some new artist over in Europe, named Van Gogh, I believe painted this. Governor Hamilton said he is the next great artist that works in oils of this generation. This is one of his earlier pieces. I believe it's titled 'At Eternity's Gate.' In the piece, the man's soul is being judged by God."

"Judged by God. He doesn't appear to be happy; I imagine it's not going so well for the poor chap?" said James.

"I don't know. From what I see, it certainly doesn't look promising, but I don't know much about this Van Gogh yet. Nevertheless, let us go to the west wing and meet with your colleague. I have tea all ready for us to warm you on this cold, dreary day."

"Thank you, Edward. How have you been?" asked James, as the two men walked to the west wing.

"I've been well. Just business as usual."

"Is the governor here today?"

"No. No, he is traveling on his way to Boston to meet with the governor of Massachusetts at the moment. He left yesterday, around noon."

"What's his business up there?"

"He's meeting with Governor Long, who just took office after what happened to Talbot."

"What happened to Governor Talbot?"

"He simply declined to run for re-election, and this will be the first meeting that our illustrious governor of Maryland will be meeting with Long."

The two men walked into the west wing together. It was a larger room surrounded by windows, allowing natural light into the room. In the corner of this room was a large table with a decanter on it, filled with whiskey. In another corner of the room was a large bookshelf, filled with old books that sat behind an old oak desk. The walls that weren't taken up by windows were painted a white marble color. In the center of the room was a large marble carved coffee table, surrounded by old European furniture of couches and chairs. On one couch sat Charles, who was taking a sip of tea from his teacup.

"Mmm. James, Edward," said Charles, finishing his sip of tea as he stood up.

"Please don't stand on my account. James, would you like a tea?" asked Edward.

"Yes, please."

"Cream in yours?"

"No, thank you. Just straight black tea, please."

"Straight black tea it is," said Edward.

By the corner of the door was a woman, who Edward motioned to with his hand and the woman turned and left the room.

"James, please have a seat with your colleague. I need to go to my desk here and grab a file for us to look over. There is something I wish to speak with you both about."

James walked over to the couch and sat next to Charles, who was picking up his cup of tea from the marble coffee table again.

"It really is good tea, I'm certain you will enjoy it, James," said Charles.

Edward walked back to his desk in the corner by the bookshelf. Opening a drawer, he pulled out a file filled with paper documents and then walked back over to the center of the room where James and Charles were. As he was sitting down, the woman walked back into the room with a couple cups of tea on a silver platter for Edward and James. While Edward was sitting down on the chair opposite the two men, the woman slid the silver serving tray on the table with the teacups on it.

"Oh. Thank you, Emma. This tea is rather delightful. It's called Duke of Earl, and it's imported directly from England," said Edward, picking up one of the cups on the tray and taking a sip from it. "Go ahead, James. Take the cup."

James leaned over and grabbed the last cup from the tray and took a sip.

"Mmm. Yes, it is rather delightful. Perhaps we'll import some for ourselves as well."

"Indeed. Well, gentlemen, I didn't call you here today to drink tea. I called you here today for a purpose, and a reason that I'd much rather the governor didn't know about either," said Edward, setting the folder down on the marble coffee table.

"Edward?"

"Please. Let me explain why you are here. I have a business proposition for you, gentlemen," said Edward, taking another sip of tea from the cup and setting it back down on the table. "A proposition that our governor doesn't need to know about."

"A proposition that the governor doesn't need to know about seems like it could come back and cause a problem in the end, Edward," said Charles.

"Nonsense," replied Edward. "He doesn't have to know about it because it doesn't concern the state of Maryland."

"So, what is it if it doesn't concern Baltimore or anything here in Maryland?" said James.

"Have you gentlemen heard of Colorado?"

"Colorado?" replied Charles.

"Yes. The state of Colorado."

"We have. It's one of the newer states out west in recent years. Fools leaving the east and going to look for gold out west hoping to strike it rich, all while not being butchered and devoured by native savages of the lands out that way."

"That's a fairly accurate representation of Colorado, Charles," said Edward.

"But what does that have to do with us and why we are here today?" asked James.

Edward set the teacup back down on the table and leaned in to speak with both James and Charles.

"The United States government recently came into possession of owning some land out that way. Seems Colorado is too young of a democracy to know how to efficiently manage their lands, leaving the federal government to seize land from those fucking Utes back there."

"Utes?"

"The Utes. Indians."

"A native tribe?" asked Charles.

"Indeed. So now we have their unused land in our possession. A man named Edward Chase, a real piece of shit if you ask me, but for some reason he thinks that we're best friends, went back to Colorado from Washington. Took down information of the lands back there, subdivided plots, and sold some land while he was there, pocketing the money for himself. In turn, he came back to Baltimore just this past week and notified me of his land acquisitions. He gave me a couple of the plots of land back there, as I have the drawn-up deeds to the land right here in this folder that sits on this very table," said Edward, pointing out the folder that rested on the marble table.

Edward stood up from his seat and walked over to the windows to have a look outside, sticking his hands into his pant pockets.

"Now gentlemen, I have no desire to move out west with the wild animals and those fucking savage Indians. I am quite satisfied with making my wealth and living here in Baltimore on the east coast where there is still some level of civility. However, this means I need to find something to do with the land that is out west, and preferably before our charmed governor Hamilton returns from his recent trip to Boston."

"So, what are you proposing, Edward?" asked James.

Edward turned and smiled. "Gentlemen, I'm proposing that you fine men take advantage of this opportunity. Imagine yourselves owning land out west, surrounded by the photogenic mountain ranges of the Uncompahgre Plateau to the west and snow-capped San Juan mountains to the south. You can start a mining business for gold in the hills there. Start your own real estate business. Divide the land and sell to other men who travel to live there. The possibilities are endless. The state and territory are so young. Imagine controlling all the real estate on the entire western parts of the country."

"How much do you propose to sell the land for, Mr. League?" asked Charles.

Edward walked back to his seat and sat down in his chair.

"Three dollars an acre," said Edward.

"That's all?" asked James.

"That's all," replied Edward. "Four hundred acres, three dollars an acre. Twelve hundred dollars and you gentlemen can become the business moguls of the west. A twelve-hundred-dollar investment today will make you the two most financially powerful men in the west."

"Can I have a moment to speak with my colleague, Edward?" asked Charles.

"Most certainly," said Edward, standing up and walking away.

Before he left the room, however, he stopped and turned back to the two real estate tycoons.

"Oh, and gentlemen, do make the decision quickly. I have another interested buyer coming at noon today, and it's almost noon and I won't have a lot of time to hear your decision here shortly," said Edward, smiling, turning and leaving the room.

"So, what are you thinking, James?" asked Charles.

"This seems to be normal behavior for Edward. Doing deals like this behind Hamilton's back."

"Mmm, yes. However, in this case, do you feel we benefit from it?"

"Have we personally seen the land?" asked James.

"Not even a picture of it. How do we even know there is land out there? I don't trust Edward. As long as I have known him for, he's been crooked. Perfect for a political figure," said Charles, standing up and walking over towards the window. He looked out the window as the rain fell in the side yard of the west wing.

"But what if he is being honest with us?" asked James.

"And that's a big what if," said Charles. "It is quite beautiful land we sold them right here to build the governor's mansion on."

"It is."

"Twelve hundred dollars."

"Twelve hundred dollars," said James.

"There are gold miners that are heading out to the hills out that way. We buy the land, and perhaps we could invest in the mining business."

"Fuck the mining business, Charles. I say we build."

"Build what though, James? Mining would be a verifiable business. With land prices that could potentially go up in value over time as well."

"Indeed, mining could be a means to have the land pay for itself, but what if we built a resort?"

"A resort?"

"Indeed, Charles. A resort. With four hundred acres of land, we could build the first golf course out there, a private hotel, a bar. We could sell prostitutes to the miners. We wouldn't even have to hire men to mine the hills. We can just pawn women off and take from the miners what they harvest from the hills."

"Mmm. It's quite a risk, James. What of our work here in Baltimore?" asked Charles.

"What of it? We can have John run the day-to-day operations here while we build an empire there. Give John some of the profits, to convince him to stick around and manage. Then we can be out west, building our opulent resort. We could invite the wealthy from the east coast to come out and vacation there. And eventually, we can even start gobbling up more land around the area. We could own the town, before the town even is a dot on the map."

"What about the Indians out that way?"

"Fuck those savages. They lost the land fair and square to us."

"That's not what I meant. They can be savages. I'm certain it's quite dangerous getting there, and then staying there. And how do you propose to build this resort, James? Create the golf course, build the buildings, and hire enough manpower to bring your ideas to life?"

"Let me answer your second question first, my friend," said James. "The answer to your second question is we can hire men from here in Baltimore to come out. Then also hire men from the town of Montrose to build as well."

"Alright."

"And second, the answer to your first question is that I know a man here, in the city."

"Great, James. I know many men here in Baltimore as well. Many of whom I have done business with."

"No, no. This man is different. Robert Steele—a hard-nosed son of a bitch. Him and his friends will take care of any Indians that give us shit out there, while working on building a resort plantation. They're the kind of men that don't care one way or the other."

"Alright. So, what are you saying out of all this, James?" said Charles, turning to face James, who was standing behind him.

"What I'm saying is, twelve hundred dollars is twelve hundred dollars. But let's take the risk. We buy the land today. Edward has the papers drafted up already. The skinny little fuck already had a plan today if you couldn't already tell. However, trust me on this. I'm going to negotiate the price with him. We'll get it knocked down to a thousand."

"Well, I do like the sound of that," said Charles. "Alright, if you can make a business deal, then let's do it."

"We'll make a business deal. Let me go out and get Edward. Oh, by the way, he's full of shit, too. He doesn't have anyone out there waiting to buy land from him," said James.

"Indeed. I know he doesn't either," replied Charles.

James sneered as he turned and walked out of the room, on his way to ask Edwards to come join them. Charles took one last look outside, then turned and walked back to the couch in the center of the room. As he was sitting down, James and Edward entered the room.

"So, have you gentlemen had a moment to discuss your plan? My other buyer is very interested in purchasing it for twelve hundred dollars, but I like you two and I'd rather sell it to you. Especially for all the good you've done for me and the governor's mansion here," Edward said, sitting down in the chair opposite James and Charles.

"Cut the bullshit, Edward," said James. "Do you really think that Charles and I got into the business by making friends?"

"We have not," said Charles. "We got into the business by being shrewd and cunning, taking advantage of moments and opportunities as they came, using our position to manipulate buyers. The same thing that you yourself are doing right now. The truth is, Edward, you don't have another buyer out in the other room, you fucking asshole. So, I suggest you listen to my business partner, as he gives you our offer for the land, because we are somewhat interested. But remember, we have a lot of success here in Maryland. Especially here in the city limits of Baltimore. We don't need this for ourselves, but because we both are fucking stupid enough to like you somewhat, we would like to give you our offer to outright purchase the land from you directly. We won't be buying for twelve hundred dollars though, no."

"But we will offer you eight hundred dollars for the land," said James.

"Eight hundred?!" replied Edward in disbelief.

"Eight hundred. And you're going to take it. And you know how I know you're going to take it?" asked Charles.

"How is that, Charles?" said a frustrated Edward.

"Because your boss comes home tomorrow. Did you think that I don't really know where the governor is always? I knew that fat son of a bitch was going to Boston well before you did. And you work for the motherfucker. So, aside from not having another prospective buyer. And the fact your boss is coming back to the mansion tomorrow, whom you are trying to keep this a secret from, means if you don't sell this land today, it goes to the governor when he finds out about it tomorrow. Which means you don't see a fucking penny from it when the governor goes and sells that land to us, anyway."

Edward sat back in the chair in disbelief, frustrated. His eyes rapidly switched back and forth to the table, the paper documents in the folder, and the empty teacups. He scratched his brow nervously, knowing that both Charles and James were right. If he didn't make this sale today, then he wouldn't see a dime of the sale when the governor got his hands on the land.

"So let me be very up front with you, Edward. Like I said, I like you. Call me a fucking fool, but I do like you. I always have. Which is why I'm making you the offer. Not your boss. Eight hundred dollars is my final offer for the land. This is your one and only chance. Nonnegotiable. Take it or get nothing and lose your control of it tomorrow."

"Fuck you!" said Edward.

"Come now, Edward. Is that any way to talk to your business guests?" said James as he picked up his teacup. "My tea is empty, by the way."

"Alright then. Eight hundred dollars," said Edward.

"You're a smart man, Edward. You will be a fine businessman someday," said Charles, reaching into his coat pocket and pulling out a wallet.

Opening the wallet, he took out a wad of cash and slowly counted each one-hundred-dollar bill until he counted eight hundred dollars' worth.

"Now then. I believe that there is eight hundred dollars," he said.

Edward leaned down, picked up the folder from the table, and carried it over to his desk. He took a seat, opened the folder, and took the documents out as he grabbed a quill from the inkwell and began signing documents.

After he had finished signing his name on two documents and filling them out, Edward dipped the quill back into the inkwell, then slid the papers to the two men.

"Here is the deed of sale. If you sign the papers, I can have them filed at the county courthouse before the end of the day and the land will be yours," said Edward.

"And the eight hundred dollars here is yours. You've earned it," said James, laying the money down on the table.

The two men each signed the papers, then set the quill back into the inkwell.

"I believe a handshake will seal the deal, gentlemen," said Charles, extending his hand out to Edward.

Edward reluctantly grabbed it, shaking Charles' hand. In turn James shook Edward's hand as well.

"It was truly wonderful doing business with you. As always, I thank you for thinking of us," said Charles.

"The second copy is yours for your record. I appreciate the business, gentlemen," said Edward, handing the second deeded copy to Charles, who took the paper and folded it into thirds, stuffing it into the inside of his coat pocket next to his wallet.

"Until we meet again, Edward," said James.

"The pleasure will be all mine, gentlemen."

The two men turned and walked out of the governor's mansion together, outside to the carriage that was waiting for them. John stepped out of the carriage's cabin and kicked the steps down for James and Charles to get in.

"Well, how was your visit to the governor's mansion?" asked John in the rain.

"Just fine. Get us back to the office," said Charles, who was the first to step inside, followed closely by James.

John shut the door to the cabin, kicked up the steps, and locked them into place. He then got up into the driver's seat and kick started the horses into leaving the mansion.

"That was a shrewd way of doing business, Charles," said James.

"It wasn't shrewd at all. I just knew the situation and made an offer that I knew he would have to take, but was also good for us. It's not my fault he didn't have the upper hand, and yet acted as if he did."

The horses dragged the carriage through the rainy streets of Baltimore, as they continued to discuss their deal they made, taking the two men back to their office at 14 Magnolia Heights.

Chapter 4: Getting into Town

The sunrise peaked over the top of the San Juan Mountain range in the early summer morning, lighting the way for a lone wagon entering the south end of Montrose, Colorado. Four horses pulled the wagon into town as a man sat in the driver's seat, steering the coach with his family in the back with all of his possessions. In the streets of Montrose, the men and women who were up early stopped and watched as the lone stagecoach rolled by.

John Ashberger waved at folks as he rode by, tipping the brim of his hat to greet the folks that were awake already in the early morning hours. While riding into town, John could hear someone stirring in the back, waking up. Moments later, a small head poked its way out of the opening of the wagon tarp right behind him. It was his youngest daughter, Ida.

"Daddy?"

"Yes, sweetheart?" replied John.

"Are we there yet?"

"We are. We're in town. Why don't you try to wake your mother for me? Have her come up front."

"Okay, daddy," said Ida as she ducked back into the tent.

Her calls for her mom, Martha Ashberger, were audible even among the loud sounds of the horses drawing the wagon through the streets of the town. Moments later, his wife exited the wagon and came up front and sat next to him.

"We're here," she said.

"We are," said John, turning towards her and smiling.

"This is so exciting."

"Isn't it?" said John.

"Where is our property?"

"On the southeastern side of town."

"John Ashberger!" a voice yelled from the street.

John looked around and saw a familiar face standing on the wooden sidewalk, waving him down from the front of an old stick building.

"I'll be goddamned! Guadalupe? Is that you?" said John, slowing the wagon and horses down.

The man walked out onto the dirt road and up toward the stopped wagon.

"Yes, sir. That it is. You made it!" said Guadalupe.

"We did. How are your men doing? How was your travel from Mexico?" asked John.

"Everyone is doing just fine. We escaped Sinaloa more so than left. But we made it here safely, nonetheless. Working on your home at the moment."

"How is the home coming along?"

"Much better than anticipated, John. I predict we will be done within the month."

"That is wonderful news."

"The men I brought with me are hard working. They're nonstop around the clock."

"What about Roman?"

"He's back at the house right now. Keeping an eye on the crew in building your home. I'm here in town to negotiate a decent price for more lumber. If we can get some more lumber here soon, then getting this home finished up by the end of the month is very possible."

"That's good. Then we can start planting apples in the fields around the property," said John.

"Fucking hell, that is going to take a long time to do, John. Twenty acres you were telling me before?"

"Yes, that's right. Twenty acres. You want a ride? You can show me exactly where the property is then, and I won't wander around the dirt roads looking for a new home being built by a group of Mexicans."

"I'm going to head to the back with the girls. It's good to see you, Guadalupe," said his wife, Martha.

"As always, the pleasure is all mine, Mrs. Ashberger," said Guadalupe as he walked around the front of the horses and over to the driver's seat of the coach.

Martha went through the front flap of the wagon canvas and sat in the back with the children.

"So, I brought up thirty-two men with me from Sinaloa," said Guadalupe, removing his hat and wiping his brow with the back of his shirt sleeve.

"Thirty-two men! God damn it, Guadalupe! How the fuck am I going to pay that many men?" said John, kicking the horses with the reins to start moving again.

"You worry too much. These men were just grateful to get out of Sinaloa. All the violence and shit they have had to deal with down there, they were glad to get out. Plus, I may have told them that they can have a place to stay here in Colorado, too."

"A place to stay?"

"Sure, at your farm."

"God damn it, Guadalupe."

"Well, you wanted farm hands for cheap. Plus, they're good workers. They will do a good job. They're also excited about trying to mine some gold on their downtime from working on the farm. I told them all about the gold up in the mountains of the San Juan. So, there is an incentive for them to live here. They hate President Diaz down there anyway, that fucking tyrant. So, believe me, they were glad to get out of Mexico and jumped on the opportunity to be here."

"Well, I suppose we can build them a large building to sleep in. Or small, individual ones, I suppose. Hell, I don't know Guadalupe. Whatever you all decide. Just as long as they work the fields when the fields need working," said John.

"They are good workers. I wouldn't have brought them with me if they weren't. Turn here," said Guadalupe, as he pointed down an old dirt road that was barely carved out, which cut through pine trees on each side of the dirt trail.

"Interesting road to the home, Guadalupe," said John.

"I figured you would like the privacy, John. We had to cut some trees down through here, but we split and put them to good use on the home, so it's not like we wasted anything."

After a few minutes of riding the wagon down the long dirt trail that at some points it looked as if it wasn't a trail anymore, but the horses kept pulling and eventually they pulled the wagon out of the small, wooded area and out into a wide opening. The expanse of land contained a large stick wood home being built nearby, and an open field that stretched out along the hillside as far as the eye could see. Along the side of the hill, a small river flowed from the north end of the property to the south.

"Kids, do you want to see your new home?" yelled John as he stopped the horses just as the wagon pulled out of the clearing.

All three kids poked their heads out of the back flap and saw the forest behind them as they were exiting the wooded area.

"Papa?" said Ida.

"Yes, honey?" replied John.

"What kind of trees are those?"

"Those are pine, Ida."

"I've never seen such big pine trees before."

"Well, now you have," said John, stopping the horses and wagon around a large pile of lumber by the house.

He stood up and jumped off the driver's seat, along with Guadalupe. John walked around to the back of the wagon, while his wife Martha was climbing out the back. Ida then popped her head out the back of the wagon, jumping into her father's arms and causing him to stumble backwards for a couple of steps.

"Jesus, honey. Those oranges are making you bigger," said John, setting her down feet first onto the ground.

The other two girls, Anna and Margaret, each came out the back one by one with their father's help. Once all three girls were on the ground, they sprinted to the large stick building that was going to be their home now.

"Kids, be careful around the house while the men are working, please. Don't get in their way!" yelled Martha, who walked over to the house, following them.

John laughed and then turned around and walked around the other side of the wagon. Standing there waiting for him was Guadalupe. John walked up next to him and stood there, looking out into the open land and the hills. He removed his hat and spat on the ground.

"The river out there along the side of the hills will make for good irrigation," said Guadalupe, pointing out to the open valley land. "We can dig trenches and bring the water out into the field."

"I suppose. How long do you think it will take to prep the land?" asked John.

"Months," replied Guadalupe.

"Ahh, fuck," said John, spitting on the ground and taking a couple of steps forward. "Thirty-two men, yes?"

"Si."

"I want to see each man getting out there, working around the clock to break soil out there. We've got to get the saplings into the ground before the ground freezes in winter."

"We got another problem though, John."

"What is that?"

"Mice. I went out there and saw mice holes scattered all around the field. There are probably hundreds of nests out in that field. They certainly will be a pest if we don't take care of them now."

"God damn it. We just can't catch a break, can we? Alright, go back into town and see if you can find some cats. Look all over. I'll try to convince Martha that we need them. But find as many as you can and bring them out here. Take a couple of the men with you, too."

"I can do that."

"Is there anything else?" asked John.

"No, not yet. But John, what about the building for the men?"

"Well, you guys have some down time if you're working around the clock. Some take the first 12-hour shift and others take the second 12-hour shift. Find time in-between your shifts and build yourselves a building or smaller buildings, too."

"Where?"

"Just find a place down there by the field or by the river. But don't take long. Remember, we've got twenty acres of apple saplings to plant out there. Plus, we need to grind up the soil and we must do it all before the ground freezes. Or else we're waiting for an extra growing season, and I don't know if I got the time or the resources to do that just yet."

"I understand, John. I'll go find the cats. How do we chew up the field, then?"

"You'll need pickaxes, spades. I can see if I can find someone who can lend us some ox in the town along with a plow. If worse comes to worse, we can always use the horses we got to start tilling up the field."

"I think that may be the way to go, John."

"Yeah. I'd prefer not to. These horses just dragged a wagon for days on end across the country to get us here. Now I got to ask of them to till up twenty acres of more than likely rocky field too?"

"It's better than nothing. Plus, there are no guarantees you will find someone selling or even renting out oxen."

"There's no guarantee I'll even find a plow to tie up to them, either."

"Indeed, John."

"Try anyway. Like I said. The saplings need to be in the ground before the ground freezes, or else I'm going to find some other Mexicans to work in the field."

"Yes, John. We'll certainly do what we can."

"I know you will, Guadalupe. I know you will," said John, smiling at him, then placing his hat back on his head and walking away, out from around the side of the cabin and into the newly constructed building on the property.

Guadalupe followed close behind and went over to a couple of men working in the home. Speaking in Spanish to them, he asked them to come with him to the town to fetch stray cats for the field. John removed his hat and walked around the building and began to assist where he could with the home's construction.

Meanwhile, the girls and his wife walked around the grounds of the house, finding different plants and berries along the way. The grounds were green and fresh. The trees swayed in the gentle Uncompahgre valley breeze while the girls wandered around the trees that surrounded the newly constructed home. Martha stayed behind at the house to help where she could.

"Look at the pretty yellow flowers," said Ida.

"Oh, yeah. They're so pretty. And look at the purple ones too," replied Margaret. "I wonder if there are any fresh berries growing around here?"

"There could be, but before you try them, ask father. You don't know what's okay to eat and what isn't around here," replied Anna.

"Ouch!" yelled Ida, as she sat down, grabbing her foot as her eyes began to tear up.

"What's wrong? What happened?" asked Margaret.

"I hit something on the ground with my foot," said Ida through the tears that were now streaming down her face.

They made their way down to the corner of the property, where a small patch of trees and bushes were. They entered a small grove of low-lying pine and maple trees. When they entered the grove, Anna looked down and saw a square stone sticking out of the ground halfway. She kneeled and used her hand to brush away some of the dirt from the stone.

"This is a big stone," said Anna.

"Anna, look. There are more," said Margaret, looking around the crude makeshift rows of the trees.

Ida stood back up off the ground, wiping away tears with her shirtsleeve as she looked around the area, too.

"This one has a feather necklace draped on it."

"And this one has a blanket set on it."

"It doesn't feel right being here," said Anna.

"What do you mean? This is our home," said Margaret.

"No. Something feels wrong. We should tell father."

"I think we should, too. Everything here looks too uniform to be natural," said Anna.

"What do you mean?" asked Margaret.

"It feels like these stones were placed here and have been here for a while," replied Anna. "Ida, go get Papa and bring him back here."

"Okay," said Ida as she ran back up to the house.

It wasn't long before Ida returned with her father and a couple of the Mexican workers' right behind him.

"What is it, girls?" said John.

"Papa, do you see all the stones here on the ground?"

"Yeah, I do," said John as he walked around the area, looking at the stones, analyzing them one at a time.

"Rodrlgo," he said. "Go back to the home and grab a shovel."

Rodrigo nodded, went back to the home, grabbed a shove and brought it back to John.

John took the shovel and walked over to one of the stones in the soil. He drove the spade into the soil, attempting to dig up the rock.

"The damn thing is big," said John as he removed soil from around the rock.

He kept digging down into the dirt when he hit something solid that wasn't a rock anymore.

"What the hell is that?" he said to one of the other men standing there beside him.

John got down on his hands and knees and began using his hands to dig away dirt from the solid object he hit with the shovel. The more dirt he removed from the spot, the more this white rock was revealed. The more he kept clearing dirt from this white rock, the more he realized it wasn't a rock at all.

It was a human skull.

"What the fuck is this?" he muttered, freeing the skull from the soil and pulling it up to investigate.

In the ground, with it, was a necklace of an arrowhead made of flint mineral. John dropped the skull back into the soil without regard to care. Then he used his hand to push the dirt back over the skull. He went over and dug around another rock about the same size as the first and when he got down far enough, saw that there was another skeletal body in the soil. This time there was a dull and rusted knife in the soil with the body.

"It's a Native American burial site," said John. "Girls, why don't you three go back up to the house where your mother is and stay with her for a bit?"

The girls listened to John and turned to walk back up the trail, back to the house. John and the two Mexican workers followed him back to the house. John carried the shovel in hand. Once the three men got back to the house, he approached Martha, who saw the look on his face and knew he had something to say to her, without the kids present.

"Children, why don't you go run and check out the river out in the field? See if you can find some colorful stones in the river," she said.

The children acknowledged her and ran out into the field toward the small river.

"There's a Native American burial site out in the trees," said John.

"Oh? What do we do about it?" asked Martha.

"Nothing. I don't give a fuck about it. It's our land now, and we bought it. Just leave it be, I suppose. We'll never use anything over there other than maybe a tree or two for firewood or lumber. But we'll never dig there, and we'll never grow anything there, so why waste the effort in digging anything up to move it?"

"I don't know if I feel comfortable having a cemetery a couple hundred feet from the back of the house," said Martha.

"What difference does it make? They're dead anyway. There aren't any natives coming around these parts anymore. Seems more of a waste of time and energy to dig them up and move them. We must finish building the house, then planting the apple saplings into the field before the ground freezes. I'm not interested in wasting my time on Indians around here."

"Alright, well, I'll take your word on this one, then. I'm going to see if I can go into town and find us some food at the market."

"That's fine. I told Guadalupe to take a couple of men into town to find us some cats."

"Cats?"

"For the field. They found some mouse holes out there and we could use the cats to keep the mice away."

"Whatever works. I'm unhitching the horses and going to ride into town."

"Sounds good to me. I'm getting back to working on the house. And no more thinking about the cemetery in our woods. Don't worry about it."

"Okay," said Martha, heading towards the front of the house.

When she got there, she unhitched a horse and mounted it. Then she took off for the market in town to get ingredients for dinner. John went back to working on the house with the men there, in hopes that the home would be built soon, and they could get to work on preparing the field for planting.

Chapter 5: Montrose, Colorado – 1887

Five years later...

It took work. Lots of work. Hard work, no less, from digging trenches to planting the apple tree saplings. Then all the work after that to maintain the orchard, too. Trimming. Irrigating from the small river next to the property. Removing rocks from the soil to clear room for the tree's roots. Not to mention the buildings that were built: finishing the Ashberger's home, and the small shacks for the field crew to stay in, the equipment building and barn for the horses, and the chicken coop.

Even five years later, they still weren't completely done building up the property. In those five years' time, John even wanted to have a fence built around the native American cemetery that his daughters had found when they first moved in, yet there hadn't been enough time for that project either. From the time the Ashberger family arrived five summers ago, to the present spring of 1887, it had been more work than what they were accustomed to while living in Florida.

However, the reward was about to be worth it. This was the first growing season for the newly established twenty acres of Colorado Orange apples grown on the Ashberger farm in Montrose, Colorado. The soil was fertile and the apples trees, with proper care, had grown in substantial size. This was the first year that the family was expecting some fruit to show. Which meant that the family was about to get rich. The fruits of their labor were about to pay off.

John Ashberger walked out the back door of his home in the early morning hours on that day in early May, out onto the wrap around deck that was built on the home three years ago. He sat down in an old wooden rocking chair that overlooked the apple fields. His life's work poured into the soil. The sun had yet to rise over the hills, yet it was still light out enough to be considered dawn.

Out in the field, an older Mexican man walked up to the house, while John was rocking back and forth in the chair. The man walked up to the deck and removed his straw at as he sat down.

"All the trees look like they are doing well. Healthy and flourishing. Blossoms are being worked by honeybees, too. You can tell the blossoms are being pollinated," said Guadalupe, as he leaned back in the chair and started rocking with John.

"That is good news, Guadalupe. How about the river?"

"River is pushing water into the trenches up and down the rows too. So, irrigation is working well."

"And no dead trees?"

"None that the men or I can see so far."

"Good. If we can get some good fruit this year, we could become rich, Guadalupe. This could be our year. We can give the men something to look forward to at the end of the season."

"I hope so, John. They're growing restless. Panning and mining for gold in their free time isn't making this worth their while. Some are considering moving back to Sinaloa."

"Then let them. But they will miss their share of the profits if they do."

"How many apples do you think we could get in harvest this fall if they do produce?" asked Guadalupe. "Twenty acres is a lot of production."

"It is. And we'll probably need more men for the work. You have any more friends around town?"

"Not here in Colorado. We can find some help in town, but I won't know who they are. Who knows if they'll be honest workers or not?"

"To answer your question, Guadalupe. We could end up with 200,000 pounds of apple from the harvest this fall. Granted, some may rot or may not make it, but we could end up with close to $80,000 dollars in profits just this year alone."

"Jesus Christ. $80,000 dollars. Year after year."

"If there's a market for it. And there certainly is one right now. Let's hope there always will be too. If that's the case, you Mexicans will be the richest Mexicans north of the border," said John.

"I'm sure the men will appreciate that."

"You're goddamn right they'll appreciate that. Money talks, my friend."

"I'm going to head into town to grab some equipment for the root cellar. We need to get that project finished this year before the harvest to keep the apples cool before shipping them out."

"Did you get a chance to talk to Tim Brown while he was up here from Texas this past week?"

"I did. He's interested in purchasing our crop this season if we have a good production."

"You have any way to ship them out to Texas?"

"The trains leaving south from the terminal are our only option. There's too much fruit to ship back using horses and buggies. We can load a large supply of apples and let the trains take them down south to Dallas."

"Sounds like a plan to me, John. How you gonna keep them fresh, though?"

"Ice. We'll need to get some snow and ice from up in the mountains. That's why it's so important to get that root cellar dug out, so we can store the fruit in a cool environment until the snow and the cooler weather come."

"That'll surely take some work, John."

"Just remember, for the money, it'll be worth it when we're done."

"I'll take your word for it. What time you gonna be back today?" asked Guadalupe.

"Oh, I'll head out later this morning when we get some eggs scrambled. Should be back around noon, I'd think."

"What do you want the men to do while you're gone?"

"Nothing. Tell them to take a day off. Go mine some gold if they so desire. But when I get back, we need to get started on that root cellar. It'll take time to dig it out and we need it up and operating by the fall for this harvest."

"They should be happy about that. Francisco thinks he's close to hitting some gold up in the cave he's mining in during his free time, too."

"Well, good for him. The real gold however, is going to be out in that field in about five months though."

"Alright, John. I'm going to walk the field some more. Make sure the bees are pollinating things like they are supposed to," said Guadalupe, standing up from the rocking chair and putting his hat on.

"And what if they aren't?"

"I'll have a talk with them?" he said, walking away.

"You speak bee?"

"When there's eighty thousand dollars on the line, I speak whatever language you need me to speak, amigo."

John laughed. "Alright, Guadalupe. I'll see you later."

"See you later," said Guadalupe, walking down the steps of the deck and back out into the field.

"Come in and get some breakfast when you're done talking to the bees!" said John.

"Gracious, John," said Guadalupe, waving his hand at him as he walked away.

The sun crested the top of the hill, lighting the small valley where the Ashberger home and orchard were located. Warming light slapped John in the face as he rocked in his chair. He stood up and walked back into the house and was just about to make coffee when he heard his wife walking down the stairs to the kitchen area from the kid's bedrooms.

"Good morning, John. How did you sleep?" she asked.

"I slept well. Thank you. How about you?" he replied, as he started the burner on the stove and began boiling coffee.

"Alright. I had nightmares again last night."

"I'm sorry to hear that. Same nightmares from before, too?"

"They were. Being trapped in a house together with the kids. Some man dressed in black walking around the house, shooting the children, shooting you, shooting me."

"Well, that will never happen, dear."

"I certainly hope not. Would you like some breakfast?"

"Yes, please."

"Eggs?"

"Scrambled."

"I'll go out and see if I can get some eggs from the chicken coop, then."

"Sounds good, dear."

"Coffee?"

"Working on it right now. Is Anna still asleep?" asked John.

"She is, along with Henry, too," said Martha.

"You know it's been a year now, but I'm starting to actually like the bastard," said John as he stepped away from the stove and sat at the dining room table.

"It only took you a year?"

"That's all. When are they headed home?"

"This afternoon. Sometime this morning Henry is going to ask you about fixing the hay loft flooring in his barn. We discussed that last night after you had gone to bed."

"Goddamn it, can't he do that himself?"

"He can, but he wants you to watch and make sure he's doing it right," said Martha, as she reached up into the cupboard and grabbed a coffee cup for John.

Pouring a cup, she brought over a cup of black coffee and set it down on the table in front of John. He reached out, grabbed the handle and drew the brim of the mug to his lips, and sipped.

"Will Margaret and Ida want to come along today too?" asked John.

"Margaret, I don't know about, and Ida, I'm sure she would. She loves to play out by the creek at their house and look for the crawdads," she said as she turned and walked back to the sink.

"Well, this better not be an all-day thing. I need to run into town," said John.

"What do you need in town?"

"Getting some supplies for making the root cellar."

"How is Guadalupe doing on that project?" asked Martha.

"Slow. Considerably slow," said John, taking another drink of his coffee. "Some of the guys are going to dig some more on the cellar today. If we stay steady on the project, then we might be done come harvest."

"How many apples do you think you'll get from this harvest?"

"Oh, it's hard to say, being the first harvest we'll have. Maybe with a little luck, close to two hundred thousand pounds."

"That's a decent amount," said Martha.

"Biggest harvest west of the Mississippi, I would imagine. We'll need a lot of hands out there picking fruit this fall."

"Maybe you can find some folks from town who would help for a little extra pay?"

"Yeah, maybe. Guadalupe might know some more Mexicans that can come up from Sinaloa and help us out, too."

"That would be good," said Martha, setting a washcloth down in the sink. "I'm going to run out and grab us some eggs from the coop. I'll be right back in."

"Okay, dear," said John, as Martha walked out through the back screen door.

John sat in silence for a moment, listening to a crowing rooster from the backyard while he watched the sun through the dining-room window rise from behind the San Juan mountains. Drawing his coffee mug up to his lips again, he took another drink and heard more footsteps coming down the stairs to the first floor. He looked over and saw that it was his middle-aged child, Margaret, coming down the stairs to the kitchen.

"Good morning," said John in a stoic tone of voice.

"Morning papa," said Margaret.

"You sleep alright?" he asked.

"Fine. Mom said she was going to talk to you about going over to Anna and Harry's house today on the other side of town."

"She did. If I have time. Did you want to go too?"

"I guess."

"What about your younger sister?"

"She always wants to go. She can catch crawdads there in the creek by their house."

"Your mother went out to the chicken coop to gather some eggs for breakfast. You should go out and help her."

"I'll go out in a bit."

"How late did you guys stay up last night?"

"Not too late. The clock in the living room said ten."

"That's a good two hours after I went to bed."

"Yeah, and I bet you were up a good two hours before everyone else, too."

"I was. Out in the field."

"How do the apples look?"

"They look good. I'm certain we will have a harvest this year."

The back screen door opened, and Martha walked back into the house. Using the front of her apron to carry the eggs, she brought back over twenty eggs from the coop. John stood up from the table, carrying his coffee with him over to the counter where Martha was carefully setting eggs down into a bowl.

"That's a decent number of eggs," said John.

"There were still more out there."

"Margaret, why don't you see about waking up your sisters and your oldest sister's husband?" said John.

Margaret stood up from her chair and walked back upstairs to the bedrooms.

"Did Guadalupe or anyone else want to join us for breakfast too?" asked Martha as she unloaded the last of the eggs from her apron into the bowl.

"I told Guadalupe that we were having breakfast this morning, but he wanted to go back out into the field to make sure the bees were pollinating."

"He's such a loyal man to you, John," said Martha, as she reached up in the cupboard and pulled out a large bowl.

"He is. He's a good man. I'm lucky to have him," said John.

The two stood by the counter, cracking eggs together into the bowl. While they were cracking eggs, the rest of the family made their way downstairs, one by one, from the bedrooms. Harry followed behind Anna as the two newlyweds came down together.

"Good morning you guys," said Martha.

"Good morning," everyone groggily replied.

"I'm just doing some scrambled eggs for breakfast this morning, so I hope that works fine," said Martha as she stirred the eggs together.

"Yes," everyone replied again, as John started a fire under the second burner on the stove.

Taking a large skillet that hung on the wall, he set it down on the burner and went back to sit at the table with his coffee as Martha began pouring the eggs into the skillet.

"Mr. Ashberger?" said Harry.

"Harry, we've known one another for well over a year and we're family now. You don't need to call me Mr. Ashberger," said John.

"Oh, I'm sorry, sir."

"Dad, Harry was going to ask you if you would be willing to come over to the house today and look at the floor of the hayloft for us?" said Anna.

"I can. I need to go into town today to get some supplies for the root cellar. Then later this evening we can work on your barn some."

"Thank you, John," said Harry. "I think we may need to replace some of the floor."

"No problem," said John. "You want a coffee, Harry?"

"That sounds great. Thank you."

"Margaret, can you get a cup from the cupboard for Harry?" asked John.

Margaret moaned quietly to herself as she forced herself up from her seat and walked into the kitchen. Opening the cupboard, she took out a cup and, with her mom's help, poured a cup of coffee from the coffeepot on the stove. She walked the cup back over to Harry, sitting the cup down in front of him.

Martha then finished making breakfast for the family. With the help of the three girls, they set the table while John and Harry were talking about the project that Harry and Anna needed help with at their new home. Martha then served eggs to the family, who all sat down and ate breakfast together.

"Mom, do we have any fresh strawberries growing on the plants outside?" asked Ida.

"No, we don't yet, Ida," replied Martha.

"Okay," she said, sighing in displeasure.

"John, are you sure Guadalupe didn't want to come in for breakfast?" asked Martha.

"I don't know, dear. He's out doing his work and getting the crew ready for their work and tasks for today, too. While I'm out in town, some of them are going to go up to Miller's cave and continue mining."

"Have they found any gold yet?"

"Not yet, but apparently, Francisco thinks he's close to a vein of gold."

"Well, good for him. Hope he finds something," said Martha.

John stood up from the table, taking one last drink of coffee from his cup.

"Alright, I need to go," said John.

"Can I come?" asked Ida.

"Sure, if it's okay with your mother?" John replied.

"Can I go to town with papa, momma?"

"Yes, but make sure you stick with your father. Don't get lost."

"I won't."

John walked over to the screen door in the kitchen, grabbing his hat from the counter and putting it on. Ida quickly got up from the table and followed close behind him.

"Like your mom said, you gotta keep up with me and don't get yourself lost while in town. No running off," said John as he walked out the door, holding it open for his daughter to follow him out.

The two then walked to the barn where the horses were kept on the property.

"Where are we going, papa?"

"We're going to the general store. I need to find some wooden boards, nails, and equipment for the root cellar that we're going to dig out this summer."

"I love the general store! That's where I found Ollie!" exclaimed Ida as she held up her doll, a small gray knit doll that resembled something you would find from a voodoo witch doctor. With big black button eyes and a sewn in smile.

"You're very fond of that doll, aren't you?" asked John with a smile as he opened the barn door.

"I am. I love Ollie. I love Ellen and Kelly too."

"Your other two dolls?"

"Yes!"

"Well, which horse do you want to take today?" asked John.

"Can I ride one myself too?"

"No, we're only taking one horse. You can ride with me. But I'll let you pick which one we take to town."

"I want to take Bella."

"Alright, now what do we do before we take the horse out?" John asked.

"We need to check the horse for injuries. And scratches."

"That's right. So what do we do after we check the horse for injuries?" asked John, as the two walked around Bella, a beautiful black and white quarter horse.

"We make sure that the saddle fits the horse and isn't loose. Then tack up the horse, papa."

"Very good. Which saddle are we going to use from the wall here?"

Ida pointed to the one she thought they would use for Bella. "This one, papa?"

"No, that one is a little too big for Bella. It's for the Clydesdale, my dear. For tilling up the ground," said John, laughing. "Let's go with one that is a little smaller and more comfortable for Bella."

He picked up the saddle off the hook and set it on the quarter horse, securing it in place. "Okay, now what do we do?"

"Secure the straps of the saddle. Then warm the horse up, papa."

"That's right. And how do we do that?"

"Walk him out of the stall for a little bit."

"I should almost let you take us into town. You're doing great Ida," said John, as he opened the gate to the stall and walked the horse out by the reins.

Ida followed close behind her father, careful not to walk directly behind the horse. The two walked the horse outside the barn and around the grounds for a few minutes.

"Now what do we do, Ida?" he asked.

"We get on and ride, papa."

John picked up Ida and set her on the saddle. Ida giggled and smiled as she was set on top of the animal.

"Now hang onto the pommel, Ida."

"Aren't you going to get on too, papa?"

"Not yet. I'll walk for a bit," he said as he led the horse up the road, off the property, and back to town.

"How long until we're in town, papa?"

"Only about ten minutes. It's not too far when we take one of the horses with us. So have you thought about what you're going to do this summer, Ida?"

"I think I want to stick around home this summer."

"You don't want to go visit your aunt in Philadelphia like last year?"

"No, not this summer."

"Well, I don't blame you. Pennsylvania is a long way away from home here in Colorado."

"Are you excited for school to be out at least?"

"Kinda. I like school. I'll miss my friends," said Ida as she sat Ollie down on the saddle to make it look like her stuffed doll was riding the horse too.

"Well, why don't you go visit your friends this summer some, then? Or invite them over and play in the small river out back?"

"Yeah, I suppose I can do that."

"Sure, you can."

"Papa, look!" said Ida, pointing over to the side of the road up ahead, where a squirrel was stopped and resting comfortably on the ground among the grass and flowers.

"Yup. Those things are everywhere around here. Hopefully, they won't be an issue with the apples this summer."

"Papa, that's why we have the cats in the field."

"You're a smart young lady. That is exactly why we have the cats. Alright, I'm going to get up on Bella," said John as he stepped up, placing his left foot in the stirrup and carefully climbed up on the back of the animal and into the front of the saddle.

"You and Ollie hold on to the back of me. Let me know if you need to stop along the way, okay?" said John.

He spurred the horse, and the animal picked up some speed. The two rode together until they made it into Montrose. The town was a small community with a population of nearly 400 people who lived in the town and outlying communities. As with most western towns, Montrose had its fair share of saloons and brothels, as men and women looked to barter their services. The women sold their bodies for a little taste of the gold that many of the miners in the area were bringing back to town from up in the San Juan mountains.

More importantly, to John now, though, Montrose had a decent number of general stores that carried farming and building supplies, too. The general store they were going to wasn't far into town, which was good because John hated taking the kids by the saloons and brothels. Once they were in front of the general store, John got off Bella and tied her reins to the hitching post. He then helped Ida off the back of the horse.

"I'm going to go check out the toys, papa," she said as she ran into the store.

"Alright, just remember we're not here to get any toys, and don't set Ollie down and forget about him over there," he replied as he walked into the store behind her.

"Okay, papa."

"Sam, how the hell are ya?" said John to the shop owner.

"John Ashberger. What do I have the pleasure of seeing you in here today for?"

"I need lumber, Sam."

"Oh? What do you need that for?" said the shop owner, grabbing a towel from underneath the counter and wiping the glass countertop with it.

"We're digging out the root cellar on the property, and I'll need some lumber to help the cellar not cave in on itself."

"Fair enough. You are single-handedly keeping me in business around this town. I appreciate you and your family ever since you moved in, John."

"Well, I like to shop locally, but especially in your shop. You're alright, you son of a bitch."

"Alright, John. I can get you some lumber. What exactly are you looking for?" asked Sam as he laughed, set the towel down on the glass and picked up a pencil and paper.

"Railroad ties. Then four by four lumber, eight feet in length."

"Any type of wood in particular?" he asked as he started writing.

"Oak, if you can get it."

"What are you thinking as far as how many railroad ties you'll need?"

"Twelve."

"And the four by fours?"

"Twenty. I have some stored in the barn that are still in good condition I can use from the home build."

"You need some nails too?" asked Sam.

"I will. Probably two pounds' worth."

"Iron? Or Steel?"

"Iron, preferably."

"Anything else you need?"

"No, that should do. We have the tools we need."

"Right," said Sam, calculating a price for John.

"Looks like an order like that would run you close to $120.00 dollars. I can get the order in through the telegraph at the courthouse this afternoon. Probably get it here on the train from the sawmill in Philadelphia sometime next week. Will that work out okay for you, John?"

"Fine by me. It'll take some time to get the ground dug out, anyway. So, I'm not in a rush. Let me pay you now, though," said John, getting his wallet out from his back pocket of his pants.

"I'm never opposed to taking money from anyone," said Sam as he walked over to the cash register and totaled out the order.

"Hey, new machine?" asked John.

"Certainly is. Just came in from Ohio a couple weeks ago. Oh, John, that reminds me. Speaking of coming from the east coast, there were a couple of men that just got into town a few days ago. They stopped by the shop to grab a couple of supplies for themselves, but they were asking about you."

"Asking about me?"

"Yeah, damned if I can remember their names at the moment. Big wigs from Baltimore or Boston are what I remember them saying."

"And you don't remember their names?"

"Just give me a minute and I'll remember who they are. Jesus, John, I'm too goddamn stupid to do two things at once."

"You're right, Sam. I'm sorry."

"Alright. How the fuck did this thing total out to $115? Fuck it, I'm not punching the numbers back in. How's about $115, John?"

"Whatever you say, and I'll buy you a coffee the next time I'm in town to make up the difference. Now, Sam, try to remember their names. Who are they exactly?"

"One of them was named Charles—some sort of real estate owner back on the east coast."

"Why is he here? And what does he want to do with me?" asked John.

"Said something about buying land out here. I'd imagine because you bought land out here five years ago and moved out here. Probably wants to know your thoughts about the Utes and how you dealt with them."

"Papa, look at the toy logs!" said Ida, running around the corner aisle in the store, with toy building logs in her hands.

"Oh, Ida. I didn't notice you come in," said Sam.

"That's great, honey. Put them back. We're going to leave soon. And don't forget to grab Ollie too."

Ida turned around and ran back to the toy section of the general store.

"I've never had any interactions with the Indians around here. Although there is that burial ground up in the forest around my property."

"Maybe that's what they're talking about? Are you going to dig them up and move them out?"

"Fuck it. I don't care about it being there. They aren't harming anyone in that spot on the property. Haven't seen any Indians since I moved out here five years ago, anyway. If I ever must move the damn thing, I suppose I will. For now, though, I've got more important things to tend to at the place."

"Well, you should go pay Charles and his friend a visit."

"What do you mean, a visit?"

"See that shop across the street with the writing in gold paint on the window?"

"The one that says Hackenberry and Sanderlin real estate?" asked John.

"That's the one. I don't know who Charles is of the two, but those are their last names on the glass."

"I'm too busy today, and I've got Ida with me. It'll have to be a different day when I stop by. Are they over there right now?"

"You know I haven't seen anyone go in and out today, but they were there yesterday. A couple of different men went in to tell you the truth. Big guys too. Farm hands maybe?"

"Mexicans?"

"No, not the Mexicans. White guys. Looked like pissant Irish, and covered in dirt, but what do I know?"

"Right. Okay, Ida. Time to go," yelled John to the back of the store.

Ida came running up to the front counter to meet her dad with her doll, Ollie, in hand.

"Hold on, little lady. Everyone who comes to my shop always must take a free piece of raspberry taffy."

"Thanks Sam," said John sarcastically.

"She'll wear off that extra sugar energy throughout the day. You'll thank me later when she's passed out and you're ready to get some rest in the evening yourself."

"Alright, thanks for the order, Sam. I'll be back Wednesday next week with the wagon to pick up the lumber."

"Alright, John. And remember, stop by and talk to Charles in that office over there," said Sam as he pointed at the newly opened real estate office across the street. "He was very interested in talking with you for some reason."

"I'll come into town in a couple of days again and visit with them."

John opened the shop door, while Ida ran out to where Bella was tied up to the hitching post. She started to pet the horse's face as Bella leaned down. John walked up from behind Ida, grabbed her, and helped put her back in the saddle.

"Are we going home now, papa?" asked Ida.

"Yes, we are. We have some work to do around the house today," said John as he untied the reins from the hitching post. "Well, at least I have work to do today."

John stuck one foot in the stirrup and then mounted Bella in one jump up onto the horse. Once he was seated comfortably and Ida was hanging on, he spurred Bella on, heading back to home.

"Papa?"

"Yes?"

"What is fuck?"

"What?!"

"Fuck. Sam said it a couple of times at the counter when you were talking. What does it mean?"

"Goddamn you, Sam," muttered John under his breath. "It doesn't mean anything, Ida. But you repeat that word around your momma and she will tan your hide. Best not to say that to anyone, understand?"

"Yes, papa. I'm sorry."

"It's okay, honey. Do you have Ollie with you?" he said, quickly trying to change the subject.

"Oh yes, he's in my pocket."

"Did Ollie have a fun time playing with the toys in the shop?"

"He did!"

"Tell me what you guys played with while we were at the store."

Ida spent the next fifteen minutes sharing with John what she and Ollie played with while in the store while Bella meandered her way back to the Ashberger farm on the outskirts of Montrose, Colorado.

Chapter 6: Hackenberry and Sanderlin Real Estate Located in Montrose, Colorado

"Orlando, you dig like a dog. Carelessly flinging dirt all around you. How are we going to dig when we aren't moving the dirt away from the pit?" said Guadalupe, reprimanding one of the Mexican crewmen who was digging out the root cellar on the property of John Ashberger.

John, too, was working on digging out the cellar. He, along with his workers, used pickaxes to break up the rocky soil while the work crew, led by Guadalupe, shoveled out dirt. They were making a decent amount of progress after a couple of weeks had gone by, digging into the ground by almost ten feet. Another couple feet and John would feel good about the depth of the cellar.

Now, the question was how wide to make the cellar? Aside from being roughly twelve feet deep, John was having the crew expand while they were underground, digging out to a diameter of 50 feet. However, the goal was now to dig down. Then, once the lumber had arrived at the general store in town, they could start fixing the wooden supports in the cellar. Soon they would have a perfect storage space for their harvest while they prepared the fruit for transport.

It was late in the morning, and the summer sun was heating up the day. John swung the pickaxe deep into the soil, prying up rocks and stones with it. Sweat poured from his brow, staining the front of his shirt with dirt mixed with his sweat. He stopped for a minute and took a step back while the other crew members continued breaking up the soil.

"Guadalupe," said John as he removed his hat and wiped his brow with the back of his forearm.

"Yes, John?"

"Have the men dig down about another foot or two. Level out the ground as best as you guys can," John said. "It's been about a week now, and the lumber should be here from the sawmill in Philadelphia by now."

"We stopping to take a meal break today?" asked Guadalupe.

"Of course. Hungry men don't work as fast as satisfied men. Have Martha get the children together, and butcher one of the cows out there in the cow field. We will have meat for supper tonight."

"That sounds pretty good, John. Are you headed to town, then?"

"I am. I'm going to pick up the lumber from Sam. Then tomorrow we can start digging outward and setting up the support structure for the cellar, too."

John handed the pickaxe to Guadalupe, who took the axe and started swinging it into the ground alongside the other men. John worked on climbing up out of the hole in the ground, using the makeshift ladder they had made to get in and out. Once at the top of the surface, John sat on the ground for a moment to compose himself.

"Papa, are you okay?" said a faint voice behind him.

John turned around and standing behind him was his daughter, Margaret.

"Oh. Yes, I'm fine Margaret. Just not as young as I used to be. I remember when I worked in the cornfields in Pennsylvania, where I met your dear mother, I could work all hours of the day. Even the night. Long have those days come and gone. How are you doing?" he said as he caught his breath.

"Fine. Momma wanted to know what you wanted to make for supper tonight?"

"One of the cows in the field out back. We're going to slaughter it and cook meat for supper. The Mexicans are going to join us."

"Are they going to cook?"

"I wasn't planning on having them cook."

"But that's what you wanted was one of the cows in the field?"

"Yes. The black and white cow in the backfield. It's good for meat, not milk. In the next couple days, I'll go out and see if I can't find some deer to get for us too."

"What about some fish?"

"Fish is good too. But for now, tell your mom we'll slaughter the black and white cow in the field this evening. Go help her clean and prepare it. And make sure your sister helps too," said John as he stood up off the ground.

"I'm going to head into town and get the lumber from Sam at the general store. I shouldn't be too long," said John.

"A couple hours?" asked Margaret.

"Probably a couple hours, yes."

"Okay, dad."

"Which horse are you taking?"

"Probably Boone. He's big enough to haul the wagon and all the lumber back to the home here alone."

"Okay, papa. Be safe."

"Thank you, sweetheart."

Margaret turned and ran back to the house. Meanwhile, John walked over to the barn and found Boone—a large draft horse that was used to pulling the wagon and was one of the horses that helped pull the wagon from Florida to Colorado for them five years ago.

John grabbed the saddle and strapped it on Boone, who grunted when the heavy seat was placed on his back. Petting the face of the horse, John then affixed the bridle onto Boone, who fought it as he always had before. Finally, John got the bridle put on effectively, leading Boon out to where a small wagon was along the side of the barn. He finished strapping the harnesses to Boone and tied him to the wagon.

Once everything was set up, John climbed up on the back of Boone and started to go. Boone began pulling the wagon, and they were on their way into town.

"You're a good boy, Boone. Thank you for your help again," said John, petting the large animal's shoulder.

Just before he left the property, John saw Martha coming out of the house to meet with him.

"Hey honey. I'm headed to town to pick up the lumber," he said.

"Can you pick up some salt while you're there too?"

"Salt?"

"To season the meat."

"Oh, alright. Yes, I can do that."

"Thank you," said Martha, as she turned around and went back towards the house.

"Hey," said John, grabbing her attention. "I love you."

With a smile on her face, she replied, "I love you too, John. Stay safe in town."

"I will."

With that, John kicked the reins, and Boone took off, towing the wagon behind him as the two went to town. John noticed the mosquitos were out in full force again today. Every year for the last five years, the "blood sucking bastards" as John called them, were out in full force and would continue to be until the early part of October. It didn't help that some places by the small river had pooled and formed small still water reservoirs for them to lay their eggs in, too.

John slapped at these nuisances as they landed on his exposed arms, neck, and shoulders before they could bite him. The bugs made the ten-minute ride feel like an eternity. Riding into town, John towed the wagon to the general store and parked it out front. He got off Boone and tied the reins to the hitching post in front of the store and walked in. Sam stood behind the counter, looking as if he had little to do. He looked up and saw John walking into the store and greeted him.

"Oh, John. Thank you for coming today. Your shipment actually came yesterday," he said, leading John around to the back of the building, past the front counter. "It'll be nice to clear up some space in the back now that you're gonna take this wood out of here."

"Well, that was early then," said John as they went out a back door, behind the building where the lumber was piled on the ground.

"Indeed. Got everything that you need here too, your nails, and railroad ties, all twelve of them. And the twenty, four by fours, too."

"Great. Do you want me to bring the wagon around to the back here, Sam?"

"Don't worry about it, John. I've got a couple of young men who are looking for some work to do. Caught one of the little fuckers trying to shoplift a candy bar from my store. So, as their punishment, they are going to do some work for me. I'll have them load your wagon up so they can be done with it and get the hell out of my life."

"Are you talking about the two kids in the store?"

"Sure am. Caught them no more than two days ago. They've been working in the shop nonstop ever since. This way, I don't turn 'em in to Walt. You know how our sheriff is around town here."

"Yeah, I know the bastard. Worthless and lazy until it's something that he wants for himself. Then he will get up and do something."

"Regardless, I'll have those two do this and send them on their way. That'll be good payment for their crime," said Sam, as the two walked back into the general store from the back door of the building.

"Thanks Sam. I'm going to wait out front then with Boone."

"The horse?"

"Yeah, that's the horse."

"Hey!" yelled Sam to the two teenage boys who were helping dust shelves in one of the food aisles.

"Yes, sir?"

"I'll make another deal with you two little bastards. This man here is John Ashberger. He's got a wagon out front that needs that wood behind the building here loaded into it. You load all that wood into his wagon for him. Then leave and never come back in here. Understand?"

"Yes, sir."

"You boys go find some other store to fuck around in."

"Yes, sir."

"Mr. Ashberger's gonna go wait out front, but bring the wood around the side of the building, through the alley and out front here piece by piece and load it up."

The two teenage boys handed the towels they were using to dust the shelves off back to Sam, then both proceeded to walk out the back door to help start loading wood for John.

"Sam, I appreciate your help. Thank you very much for getting this order in for me."

"Hey, it's no problem at all, John. I appreciate your business. How is your root cellar coming along?"

"It's good. The Mexicans are digging right now," said John. "Fuck, I need to get salt while I'm here."

"Salt?"

"Yeah, we're going to butcher one of the cows in the field out back for supper."

"Sounds good. I got some rock salt here. You want ground up salt though?"

"I'd prefer pre-ground up salt. Well, I'm sure she would prefer pre-ground up salt."

"You should have the Mexicans barbecue the meat. You said they love to barbecue and do a good job with their spices and shit," said Sam, walking over to a shelf with glass bottles of salt.

"They do, but the kids don't like the spices they use."

"Goddamn kids," said Sam as he picked up a bottle of powdered salt and handed it to John.

"Right," said John, laughing. "Salt is fine, though. Meat is meat, Sam. How much do I owe you for the salt?"

"Twenty-five cents."

John fished twenty-five cents from his pocket, handing it to Sam.

"Alright Sam, I'm going to get out there and make sure the kids load the lumber up right."

"Wouldn't be a bad idea to keep an eye on them. These two are pretty fucking stupid."

"Have a good day, Sam," said John, as he opened the front door to the shop and walked out, holding the door open for a nicely dressed man who walked in past him.

"You too!" yelled Sam, just before the door shut.

Once outside, John watched as the two teenage boys carried another railroad tie and loaded it up onto the wagon. They had loaded up three so far, and nothing else.

"Jesus, it's going to take you two all day to load wood up like that. Move quicker, please. I don't got all day."

"Sorry, mister. We'll try to move faster," said one of the boys.

John stood by Boone, looking out into the street while the teens went to the back to get more lumber. He watched folks come and go up and down the sidewalk, crossing the dirt road from one side of the main street to the other.

John looked across the street and saw the business with the sign painted on the glass in gold paint:

Hackenberry and Sanderlin Real Estate of Montrose, Colorado

John remembered what Sam had told him not that long ago. That the two men who just moved there from Baltimore wanted to meet with him for some reason. Albeit; Sam didn't know why, as the man named Charles and his associate didn't share their business outside of the office with just anyone.

The door to the general store opened and out stepped the man dressed in a fancy white suit. He was holding a Dr. Pepper in his hands—a new revolutionary soda that just came to town only a few months ago. The man took a big drink of the soda from the opened bottle, then looked at John.

"Mister, have you ever had a Dr. Pepper before?" asked the man.

"No, sir. I can't say I have," replied John.

"Don't get me wrong. I generally like whiskey, hard ciders, and even rum sometimes too. But this new Dr. Pepper, goddamn, that is a tasty drink."

The man walked up to John and shook his hand.

"My name's Charles, Charles Sanderlin of Hackenberry and Sanderlin Real Estate from across the street."

"Oh, I'm John Ashberger."

"John Ashberger... John Asherbeger...." said Charles as he took another drink of soda.

"You're the gentlemen that has the apple orchard here in town, yes? Twenty acres on the southeast side of the town?"

"Twenty acres. That's right."

"Twenty acres? Boy oh boy, that's got to be quite a lot of work to keep that up and running."

"I have a good crew of men from Mexico that work the land, and a good farm lead. They know what they're doing. We've spent the last five years preparing the orchard and getting everything set and ready to produce this summer for a fall harvest."

"Well, that's a real good thing for you. A real good thing indeed. All that hard work gonna pay off soon, I see. Listen, I want you to come with me for a minute. I want you to meet my colleague, James."

"Sir, I really don't have time at the moment. I need to get this lumber loaded so that I can get back to the property and continue making my root cellar."

"That's a good idea to have a root cellar," said Charles. "A real good idea."

He took another large drink from his soda, emptying the bottle and tossing it onto the side of the road by the wooden sidewalk.

"It looks like those boys will take a little while to get you all loaded up. I insist you join me for a drink of whiskey. Or, I also have some old scotch that needs to be used, and I couldn't think of a better person to have a drink with."

John was hesitant, but at the persistence of Charles, he walked with him across the street to Hackenberry and Sanderlin Real Estate.

"Here, let me grab the door for you, my friend," said Charles, opening the door for him and allowing John to walk inside.

The inside of the realtor's office was organized and decorated sophistically, with fancy furniture, chairs, and desks, along with a phone resting on one of the desks. John walked over to the phone and picked it up, testing it out as he heard a dial tone on the other end.

"Isn't that fancy as shit?" asked Charles. "That was our original phone we had in our first office together back in Baltimore."

"I've never seen a phone in town here before. Or where we come from, for that matter."

"It's the only one in town. Has its own special wire hooked up outside to the building."

"You come from Baltimore, you say?"

"We both do, yes. We had real estate and properties in the greater city area, rentals, lands, and homes for sale."

"Sounds like you both had it good back there."

"We had a lot of success in Baltimore," said Charles as he walked over to the countertop and grabbed two glasses.

He poured scotch from an old glass decanter, filling both glasses halfway with the drink. He then grabbed the glasses, walked back over to John, and handed him a drink.

"Some of the finest scotch, John. Made in Wales and imported specifically for James and me. This specific drink spent 81 years building character in a seasoned cask. Only 142 decanters were filled with it. We happen to own 34 of those decanters.

John took a drink from the glass. "Tastes just like scotch to me."

"Well, not everyone's palates are attuned to the finer drinks in life. And that is okay. John, would you like to have a seat on the couch?"

John walked over to a large open room with fancy loveseats and chairs facing one another. There was a beautiful stone fireplace in the room with wood placed on the grate in the firebox. John picked a seat and sat down, followed by Charles, who sat across a beautiful marble coffee table with carved flowers on the side of the table, painted in bright gold.

"Do you like the furniture in this room, John? A lot of what you see here came from Europe. Generally, furniture like this is made only for the house of royalty in England."

"So, how did you come into possession of it all?"

"Well, let's just say that I happen to know some folks in Europe who managed to secure some pristine pieces for our office here in the new world, John."

"Congratulations on that."

"My partner, James, should be back soon. He had stepped out for a moment to go meet with some folks this morning. He was supposed to be back by noon," said Charles, checking his pocket watch. "And according to my watch, he should be back in the next ten minutes or so."

"So, what brings you to Montrose, Mr. Sanderlin?" asked John.

"Well, opportunity, I suppose. How about yourself?"

"I suppose the same thing. My opportunity is obvious, though. I'm a farmer, Charles. Apples are what I grow and how I will make my living. Oranges were how I made my living in Florida. And corn put food on my plate in Pennsylvania. However, you are a real estate mogul. Why come out here to Montrose?"

"Why not, John? There's gold out here. Gold and untouched land left behind by the natives. Land, prime for the taking. Land that can be developed and sold."

"So, is that what you are here for, then?"

"For the most part it is," said Charles as he sipped his scotch. "We happened to come into ownership of a large piece of land southeast of the town here. Just up against the mountain range, no less."

"Well, that is interesting. We own land out that way."

"How do you like living out there, John?"

"It's beautiful. Definitely different from Florida," said John.

"Different here from Baltimore too."

"I would imagine so.

"So, why did you come out here?" asked Charles.

"There was an opportunity in the apple growing business."

"Interesting. Who did you buy from?"

"Edward Chase. He was a realtor hired by the state of Colorado to sell some of the lands that the Indian treaties gave to the state. Sold it for a cheap price too."

"How much? If you don't mind my asking, sir?"

"The twenty acres of land was sold to me for five thousand dollars."

"Five thousand. I see. And you own the land down there by the small river, yes?"

"That's right. The San Juan River runs along the side of my property. It borders some open land on the opposite side that hasn't been used since we started living on the property five years ago."

"Beautiful land out there, with the San Juan Mountain range and that small river that runs through the valley there. I suppose sunrises and sunsets are rather majestic, wouldn't you say?"

"I suppose you could say that. I've made our family burial plot in the corner of the property where the sun's first morning light hits the land as it rises over the San Juan Mountain Range. Sometimes I just enjoy going out there and watching the sunrise, to be honest with you."

The front door to the office opened and in walked James Hackenberry. He removed his jacket and hung it on the coat rack by the door, along with his hat. He walked into the office and turned the corner to see Charles sitting there with a guest.

"Oh, my apologies. I didn't know we had company here," said James.

"It's no concern, James. No concern at all. Please come in. I would like for you to meet someone," said Charles as he stood up. "John, this is James Hackenberry. He is my colleague and partner in the business here. And James, this is John Ashberger."

James walked in and extended his arm while John stood up. The two shook hands and greeted one another.

"John, it's a pleasure to meet you. Are you here for business?" asked James.

Charles laughed. "Oh, no. Not at all, we are just having a conversation. John owns the twenty-acre orchard out by the San Juan River, in the valley southeast of town."

"Oh, yes, the apple orchard. You seem to be in a good position to strike it rich with a healthy crop this year."

"Yes, sir. So long as everything goes according to plan."

"Well, you're going to make a lot of people around here happy. There'll be apples abundant for us all."

"Of course, but the majority of our harvest is going to be shipped to Texas to sell to a distributor from there."

"I see you're a businessman."

"All farmers have to have some sense of conducting business, Mr. Hackenberry."

"James, would you like a glass of scotch?" asked Charles.

"Oh, yes. Did Charles tell you about the scotch, John?" asked James.

"Yes, he did. Came from somewhere in Europe."

"Wales, to be specific. A very rare cask that had been sitting for over eighty years."

"Well, it tastes like scotch to me. So, you guys are into real estate here in Montrose now. I would assume that you know everything there is to know about the area here. Something I've been wondering for quite a while now is who owns the land on the opposite side of the river from my farm?"

"John, that is a good question. And we would like to know just as much as you. Perhaps my colleague has explained to you that we came from Baltimore, where we had a very well-established reputation for being successful real estate agents. We're coming into ownership of some land around here, but we are also trying to figure out who owns that land on the opposite side of the river from you, too."

"Well, it's beautiful land. At some point I would like to buy it myself if I could. Expand the apples on that side of the river too."

"Why, you would have the largest apple orchard operation this side of the Mississippi river."

"I believe I might already have it, Charles," said John. "But it certainly could expand. Then it could be an operation that I could leave in my family for generations to come. That's my version of an American dream, giving my girls and their husbands an opportunity to have a sense of pride in ownership."

"That right there sounds like the American dream to me, John. I can't argue with that," said Charles.

John looked out the window across the street and saw the boys finish loading the last of the wood into the wagon.

"Gentlemen, I thank you for the scotch. However, it appears to be time for me to go. The wood is loaded, and I need to get back to the farm to continue working on the root cellar."

"Of course, please don't let us hold you back from conducting your business. John, it was a pleasure to visit with you for a bit. You are always welcome to come back and visit us anytime."

John stood up and took one last drink from the scotch, setting the glass down on the coffee table in front of him.

"You know what? That does taste like superb scotch after all. Thank you for the drink," said John as he turned and walked out of the office.

After John had left and the front door was shut, James started talking to Charles.

"It was good not to tell him that we own that land," said James.

"Indeed. We can't let him know that yet. When we start building the resort and golf course there soon, the cat will be out of the bag, though."

"It will be. But by the time he figures out that we own it, we will already be deep into building the resort plantation," said James, who stood up from the couch and walked over towards the window.

He looked out the window and watched as John mounted his horse while one of the teenage boys brought out a bucket of nails and placed it into the wagon, too.

"We need to find a way to obtain his property as well. How much did he purchase it for?"

"Five thousand dollars," said Charles. "Bought from Edward Chase."

"Fucking Edward Chase," said James, turning to look back at Charles, then back out the window. "I'd wish he would fall into the deepest of pits in hell, never to be seen from again."

"Well, regardless, he sold the land to Ashberger and now he owns that twenty acres legally. And I'm not sure we can convince him to sell us the property. Sounds as if he plans on owning that property for life and passing it down to his nasty daughters."

"Perhaps not. Or perhaps we can find alternative ways to obtain the property, Charles?"

"Indeed, James. Perhaps there are alternative ways that we can explore to help us obtain the land. I would say the first thing we need to do is make some new friends here in town."

Chapter 7: Finishing the Root Cellar

John steered the horse back down the long dirt road that led to his home in southeastern Montrose, Colorado. Swatting bugs along the way, he steered the horse through a small patch of forest until he came into the clearing where his two-level home was located. Out in the front yard of the property, sitting under an apple tree, his youngest daughter Ida was playing with her favorite doll, Ollie.

Ollie reminded John of a small, plush voodoo doll he had seen back in New Orleans. Along with Ollie, Ida had an elephant doll named Ellen, and a plush cow named Kelly. John steered the wagon past the front of the house, waving at Ida as he rode by. Ida looked up and saw him approaching. A smile dawned on her face as she watched her father ride in on the horse.

"Hi papa!" she yelled.

"Hi Ida."

John steered the horse around the back of the house where his crewmen were working on digging out the root cellar. John parked the wagon next to the hole in the ground, got off the horse, untied him from the wagon, and led him back into the barn.

"Thank you, Boone," he said, giving him a pat on the side of his face and neck.

John turned and walked out of the stable, closing the gate behind him. He leaned over and took a chunk of hay and tossed it into the stable where Boone was. He then left the barn, shutting the door behind him, and walked back out to where his men were working on the root cellar still. When he got there, Guadalupe was crawling out of the hole and up to the wagon that John had parked there.

"You need a hand?" asked John, walking up to the edge of the pit as Guadalupe neared the top.

Guadalupe reached out his hand and John took it, pulling him up out of the pit.

"Thanks."

"How's the digging going?" asked John.

"Well," said Guadalupe, removing his straw hat from his head. "We've dug down deep enough and started digging into the side of the dirt. But these goddamn bugs! What kind of wood did you get?"

"Four by fours and railroad ties to support the top of the cellar."

"How many railroad ties?" asked Guadalupe.

"Twelve. Plus, the ten we have in the back by the barn should be more than enough."

"I would imagine so. What about four by fours?"

"Twenty-four of those," said John.

"That should be plenty, too."

"We have some two by fours in the barn too, but I don't think we will put those to use."

"We may. Just for a little extra security or reinforcement, too."

"You think so?"

"There's a lot of earth on top of the cellar, John. One heavy snow or wet winter and the whole fucking thing could cave in. Best we reinforce it with everything we got."

"Alright, Guadalupe. You make sense. Have the men taken a break yet?"

"They have."

"Where's Martha on the cow?"

"Butchered. She and the children are working on cutting it up. A couple of the men helped them bring the cow up to the house and slit its throat over by the corner of the house."

"Okay. I'll take her the salt I got and then I'll be right back out. Tell the men to take a break and get some water. Stay hydrated, it's getting warm out. Don't need anyone passing out from the heat like what happened last year."

John then turned and walked away from Guadalupe, back towards the house. He heard Guadalupe giving the orders to the men in Spanish that it was time for a break. John walked back into the house through the back door and into the kitchen area, where Margaret and his wife were preparing meat from the butchered cow. Martha held a knife in hand, apron bloodied from cutting chunks of meat from the animal.

"Oh, hi John, did you get that salt?" she asked him as he walked into the house.

"Yeah. Got it right here," John replied as he walked over and gave his wife a kiss.

"You can set it down on the counter."

"How is the cow coming along?" asked John, setting the jar of salt on the counter.

"Fine. I forget how much work it is to butcher. Domingo and Segundo helped, though."

"That was nice of them," said John.

"They offered to butcher too, but I told them I could do that."

"You want me to send them back in here to help?"

"Would you?"

John laughed. "No problem. Margaret, how are you two doing?"

"Fine," she replied as she sliced the meat that Martha was giving her.

"I appreciate you helping your mother out like this."

"It's fine, papa," said Margaret. "Hey after we're done cleaning the cow, can we go into town for a bit?"

"By the time you're done cleaning the cow, it'll be close to suppertime. But why do you feel the pressing need to go into town?"

"The general store has kites now. They always get kites in early June and I'd like to get one this year."

"I see. Well, if not today, we can always go into town tomorrow, too. I need to get back out there and keep working on that root cellar, honey."

"How's it coming along so far?" asked Martha.

"Looks to be good to me. They've dug down far enough now, so we're starting to expand and dig into the side and under the ground."

"Be careful out there. Don't let the ground cave in on you all out there."

"We won't. I got the lumber we need and then I'll have some of the Mexicans go down to the river to grab some river rock to stick into the ceiling above the wooden boards to help reinforce the ceiling."

"Well, just be careful doing all that."

"We will, dear," said John as he walked out the back door.

At this time, all the men were out of the pit and sitting in the shade of a beautiful willow tree. John walked up to the men as they rested.

"Domingo, Segundo, would you please go back inside and help Martha with carving up the meat for supper?"

Both men smiled and said, "Si," as they stood up and walked towards the house.

"Guadalupe, we need to unload the wood from the wagon and toss it down into the pit. Then I'll take Boone and hook him up again and take some men with me down to the river to gather river rocks for the ceiling."

"Sounds good."

"You guys keep taking your break, though. I'll work on unloading the wood myself."

"I can help too, John," said Guadalupe.

John took Guadalupe's hand and helped him up. While the rest of the men rested in the shade, drinking water, the other two went back to the hole where the wagon was parked and unloaded it piece by piece, dropping boards down into the hole.

"While I'm taking the wagon by the barn, we can grab the rest of the wooden boards and bring them back over here. We may as well put them to use in the root cellar, too."

"Sounds good, John. I certainly think we can have this dug out in the next month, no problem. It'll be ready well before the harvest season."

"Have you seen some of the trees are starting to shoot out apples on their branches, too? And the bees are working the rest of the blossoms that are left too. So, whatever you told them, they're doing a great job pollinating."

"We should have a good harvest then. Thank God," said John, tossing another four by four into the hole. "So, while I was in town, I met the realtors."

"The realtors?" asked Guadalupe.

"Yeah. Two realtors from Baltimore, or somewhere on the east coast. I can't remember where they said they were from."

"What were their names?"

"Hackenberry and Sanderlin?"

"What was your first impression of them?"

"Snooty. Sophisticated. Higher and mightier than thou."

"Well, most folks who sell land are. What do you think of them besides all that?"

John dropped a board into the pit, then turned around and leaned his arms on the side of the wagon. He thought for a moment before he answered that question. "I don't know if I trust them, to be honest. I just got a strange feeling about them. Like they were trying to be my friend or something, after I had just met them."

Guadalupe laughed. "Well, you never trust a fucking realtor, John. You know this."

"It might not be a bad idea to know realtors. Especially if they can find out who owns that property on the other side of the river from us. I'd like to try to buy it someday, plant some apples over there. Maybe something different from the Colorado Oranges."

"Whatever you say, but I wouldn't put my trust in them," said Guadalupe as he tossed the last four by four into the pit. "Alright, that's the last of it."

"Good. I think I'll take Rito, Hipolito, Bartolome, and Basadilo with me down to the river and gather some rock for us."

"Sounds good. Are Domingo and Segundo going to stay inside and help Martha and the kids with supper, then?"

"Yeah, I'm planning on leaving them in there for the rest of the day. There's a lot of work left to be done with the cow meat. Martha is too proud to accept help, but I know when she needs it and doesn't need it, and this afternoon it looks like she needs it."

"You're a great husband, John. I'll go have the men get ready to start working in the pit again," said Guadalupe, patting John on the back.

"You want to come along too?"

"To the river? No, I'll stay here and make sure the men keep working on the cellar."

"Alright," John said, turning and walking towards the barn to go get his horse.

After retrieving Boone, most of the Mexicans had gone back to work and, one by one, were descending the ladder into the hole. Once at the bottom of the pit, the men organized the lumber piece by piece.

As John started securing Boone to the wagon, he turned and saw Domingo and Segundo walking back from the house.

"What's going on, you two?" asked John.

"She asked for different seasoning," said Segundo.

"Different seasoning?"

"Si."

"Goddamn it," said John, frustrated. "I don't have time to go back to town and get more seasoning. I trust you two. Take a couple horses from the barn and head to town and grab some more seasoning for her, then."

"We can do that," said Domingo, as they both turned and walked to the barn to each grab a horse to take to town.

John finished securing the wagon back to Boone. He walked up to the edge of the pit and called for Rito, Hipolito, Bartolome, and Basadilo to come with him to the river. The men ascended the ladder and jumped into the back of the wagon.

John spurred Boone, coaxing him into pulling the wagon. Domingo and Segundo were leaving the barn as John was riding by with his wagon.

"When you two get back, help Martha and the kids in the kitchen to get supper ready for this evening," said John.

"Si, sir."

The two men kicked their horses and galloped down the road, on their way into town.

John rode on, down to the river, with Boone towing the wagon.

*   *   *   *

The two men made it into town in a short amount of time. The two horses they took to the general store were two of John's best horses. They were the two thoroughbreds that Ida and Margaret were going to learn to ride on. Because of that, one of the two horses had some early summer wildflowers picked from the apple field and tied into the mane of the reddish-brown animal. Segundo and Domingo approached the general store, got off their horses, and tied the reins to the hitching post.

"Do you remember which seasoning she wanted?" asked Domingo.

"She asked for rosemary," replied Segundo.

"What the fuck is that?"

"It's a seasoning you puta," said Segundo as they entered the store, and walked up to the counter where Sam was standing.

"Excuse me, mister. Mr. John sent us here. His wife needs rosemary," said Segundo.

"Rosemary? The seasoning?" asked Sam.

"Si. For cow meat."

"Oh, I think I got some here. Why didn't John come in?" asked Sam as he walked around the corner of the counter out into the aisles of the small store.

"He's busy getting river rocks down by the river in the field."

"How's your cellar coming?"

"It's fine, sir. Our friends are working on digging the cellar out."

"Well, I'm sure it'll take some time, but you boys should be able to clear it out before your harvest, I'd imagine. John was saying he thinks you guys should have a good harvest this year too," said Sam as he thumbed through the glass bottles of spices he had on the shelf.

"That's the plan, sir," said Domingo.

"I'd guess it should be dug out with the group you have in about a couple of months' time. Ahh, here we go. Rosemary," said Sam, picking up the glass bottle from the shelf.

"How much is it, sir?"

"Nah, just tell John he owes me thirty cents the next time he comes in," said Sam, handing the jar to Domingo.

"Thank you, sir. We will let him know."

"Anything else you boys need?"

"No, sir. That was all."

"Alright then, you two have a good day. Tell John I said hi too," said Sam as he turned and walked back to the front of the store.

"Thank you, sir," said Segundo, as the two men also turned and left the store.

They walked out onto the sidewalk and back to the horses. While they were unhitching their horses, they looked out into the street and saw a native American man standing beside them, admiring the colors and the health of the animals.

"These two yours?" the man asked.

"Si, sir. They belong to our boss."

"Beautiful animals. What the fuck is in the mane of this horse?" said the man, laughing to himself.

"Flowers. That one is our boss's younger daughter's horse," said Segundo.

"Who is your boss?"

"A man named John Ashberger."

"John Ashberger?"

"Si, sir."

"How long have you worked for him now?" asked the Indian man.

"Oh, the better part of five years now," said Domingo, as he opened the side saddle of the horse and stuffed the jar of rosemary into it.

"Five years. Where are you two from?"

"Sinaloa, sir."

"Down in Mexico?"

"Si."

"You two got names?"

"I'm Domingo. This is Segundo."

"Domingo. Segundo."

"You have a name, sir?"

"Ignacio. Ignacio Black Hawk."

"You from around here, sir?"

"I am. Lived in this area all my life. Along with my father, and his father."

"We like it here. On our down time, we go up into the mountain range and mine for gold, too. One of our friends is finding gold up there in his free time."

"Oh yes, I know there's gold up there. I've mined for it myself before, too," said Ignacio, petting the side of Segundo's horse.

"So, do you live around here still, then?" asked Domingo.

"I used to. I plan to again someday soon."

"It's beautiful here."

"It is."

"Why did you leave in the first place, sir?"

"Well, let's just say because of opportunities that were forced upon me," said Ignacio.

"Opportunities?"

"Yes. Opportunities," said Ignacio, smiling at the two men. "So, what did your master send you to town for?"

"He's not our master, sir. We're free men. Can come and go as we please. He just employs us to work for him. Gives us a place to stay. Feeds us. Gives us drink. Treats us just like family. But he sent us into town because his wife needed seasoning for cooking meat."

"His wife?"

"Si. He has a family. Two girls, a wife, and then John. He also has a third daughter that lives in town here."

"Where does she live?"

"We don't know, sir. We just know she lives here in town with her husband, somewhere just outside the city. We live out in the worker buildings with our friends—shacks by the river that we built nearly five years ago for ourselves."

"Sounds like you're well taken care of, then."

"We are, sir."

"Where is the farm?"

"In the southeast corner of town. He has twenty acres of land. Apples planted that should be producing this summer, it sounds like."

"Southeast corner of town?"

"Si."

"Next to the mountain range?"

"At the foot of the mountain range, si."

"Tell me. Does the river bend where the trees begin?"

"What?"

"The river. Does the river bend where the trees begin around the fields there?"

"Si. The river bends a little into the property. We spent time one summer digging out canals from that point as water seemed to flow better into the apple field from there."

"I see."

"It's a beautiful area. The sunrises over the mountains there are hermoso. Sometimes, John will spend some time out in the corner of the field. There is a small, lifted patch of land overlooking the property where he says he is going to have his family's burial plot. He likes to go up there from time to time, sit on a boulder and watch the sunrise."

"Sounds like he appreciates the land and what it's worth, then," said Ignacio.

"I suppose you could say that, sir."

"Has your master cut down any of the forest on the corner of his property? By the bend in the river?"

"No, sir. He has not. Not yet, anyway."

Ignacio slapped at a large horse fly that landed on the flank of the horse, killing it and knocking it to the ground, where he promptly stepped on the insect.

"These fucking flies," he said. "Well, don't let me hold you up any more than I already have."

"It's alright, sir. But we should be going. His wife is expecting us back with the seasoning."

"Of course she is," said Ignacio, smiling and stepping back from the horse. "Of course she is."

"It was a pleasure meeting you, Ignacio," said the men as they unhitched the horses and mounted them. "Perhaps we'll see you around again."

"The pleasure was mine, gentlemen," replied Ignacio as he stepped back into the street.

The two men turned their horses, tipped their straw hats to Ignacio, then rode off. Ignacio watched from the street as the men slowly headed out of town.

The two men rode for a few minutes as they left the town limits. The mid-summer day sun was warm, beating down on them both.

"It is goddamn hot," said Segundo.

"Si, it is," replied Domingo.

"When we get back, we need to—"

Segundo was interrupted by the sound of two horses galloping up behind them. The two men looked back and saw Ignacio, along with a second man, riding up to them. When the two horses had caught up, they stopped a few feet away from them.

"Oh, Ignacio. What is it you need, sir?" asked Segundo.

"I'm curious to ask you two one more question I forgot to ask back in the town," he said.

"Well, what is it?" asked Domingo.

The two men drew pistols from their holsters and shot each horse between the eyes, dropping the beautiful animals dead on the road. Domingo fell off the horse and his head struck a rock on the ground. Segundo's horse fell, pinning his right leg between the ground and the animal's abdomen. The weight of the horse easily broke his leg as he screamed in agonizing pain.

Domingo opened his eyes and saw the world with blurred vision. He heard his partner screaming in terrible pain next to him.

The two native men jumped off their horses. Ignacio walked up to Domingo, who was still stunned on the ground and drove the butt of his pistol it into Domingo's skull as if he was hammering a nail into a board. Only a thin layer of flesh barely held Domingo's brain in his cracked skull when Ignacio was finished.

Meanwhile, the second man tied a rope around Segundo's neck, mounted his horse and rode back into town. Segundo's neck instantly snapped while his lifeless body was dragged across the ground.

Ignacio mounted his horse again and followed the Native man back to Montrose. They dragged the body back through the town as some townsfolk watched in horror.

"Ahiga! That's enough!" yelled Ignacio.

Ahiga stopped the horse and dropped the rope tied around Segundo's neck in the street. Most of Segundo's skin had been ground off from the road, including one eye that was hanging out of its socket. His clothing was torn and tattered as his body lay motionless in the street while the two Native Americans took off and rode fast out of town, heading north.

Some men from the town came out with rifles in hand to see what was happening. When they found the dead body lying in the street, some of the men vomited, while one man turned and ran to get the county sheriff.

A few moments later, the sheriff came out and approached the body in the street.

"What the fuck happened here?" asked the sheriff.

"I don't know," said one man. "I heard a commotion. Two Indians were riding through town. I thought they were dragging a sack of something. One of them dropped the rope, and then they took off out of town."

"There was a second man with him. They were at the general store like twenty minutes ago."

"Where the hell is he?"

"I don't know, sir."

"Where the fuck did those Utes go?"

"They went north. Out of town," said one of the men.

"Up towards Olathe?" asked the sheriff.

"Yes, sir."

"Who saw the two men when they were in town?"

"Well, Sam at the general store would have, sir."

The Sheriff pointed at two men standing there in the street.

"Get this goddamn body off the road before anyone else in the town sees it. I'm going to go talk with Sam and find out what happened to that other man. Fuckin Indians are getting crazier and crazier each day," said the sheriff, as he turned and walked away towards the general store on the south side of town.

Chapter 8: Ain't No Grave Can Hold my Body Down

The door to the general store opened and in walked the sheriff of Montrose, Colorado. He was a stoic man in his late 40s, with a handlebar mustache and a noticeable limp in his right leg—the result of fighting in the Civil War. In a brash move on the battlefield back in 1864, he had charged the field to attack the Union army in Prairie D'Ane, Arkansas, where he took a stray musket ball from a union soldier's rifle square in the shin.

He became county sheriff in the newly established county of Montrose in 1883. He was the first sheriff the county ever had. His office sat in the town limits of Montrose, too. Some folks in the town liked him, but he was disliked more by most. He carried a reputation for hating anyone other than the white folks in town, and even then, some of the townfolk thought he was even taking bribes by some landowners to turn the other way when it came to securing more acreage for their properties from the last of the Indians who owned anything.

The sheriff walked up to the counter, where Sam was sitting in a chair by the register. He placed his closed fists on the top of the glass, bracing himself on the counter.

"Sam," he said.

"Yes, Sheriff Jones?" said Sam, standing up from behind the counter.

"Two men were in here no more than half an hour ago. Two Mexicans."

"Yeah, what about them?"

"You see where they went when they left?"

"No? Why do you ask, Sheriff?"

"You know who they are?" asked Sheriff Jones.

"Two of John Ashberger's boys. They came in and got some rosemary for their dinners tonight."

"What the fuck do Mexicans use rosemary for? Don't they like that hot spice shit? Jalapenos, or something?"

"It was for John's wife, from what I understand."

"Where does John live?"

"He owns that apple orchard, the twenty acres down there in the southeast part of town, just ten minutes down the road that leads south."

"You think he's there right now?"

"Well, I don't know where else he would be? Him and his wife and workers."

"I need to go pay him a visit. Let him know what happened to his Mexicans."

"Sheriff, what happened? Why do you care?"

"His two Mexicans got killed. Sounds like they were killed by the goddamn Indians around this area too."

"Killed?"

"That's right. The townsfolk say a couple Utes killed 'em. They dragged one body into town behind them on their horse and I would assume the other Mexican is up lyin' dead in the road, too."

"Jesus, that's terrible. I don't think John would know, sir. They were just here half an hour ago."

"Well, I'm gonna go talk to John myself, then."

"Alright, sheriff. If you need any more information, just stop by. I'm here until sundown."

"Thank you, Sam," said Sheriff Jones, tipping his cap, then turning and leaving the store.

Sheriff Jones walked out to where his horse was when he was approached by another man.

"I saw it all happen," said James Hackenberry. "Our office is right across the street from the general store."

"I'm sure you did. What did you see?" asked Sheriff Jones.

"My partner and I, we were in our office, working on some real estate loans and applications we were going to go file at the courthouse today. I looked up and saw a couple of Indians talking to the two Mexicans that left this very store."

"Did they leave together?"

"No, they didn't. The Mexicans left first. Got on their horses and took off. Then, maybe like three or four minutes after the Mexicans left, the Indians followed in the same direction they went."

"You see them ride back into town, dragging one of those Mexicans behind them?" said the Sheriff, as he took the reins off the hitching post and mounted his horse.

"No, sir. I didn't see that. But I wasn't really paying attention. I was organizing a filing cabinet, getting papers organized."

"Sounds like these two boys come from a farm southeast from here."

"Apple farm?"

"Yes, sir."

"John Ashberger probably," said James.

"That's what the shop owner was saying," replied Sheriff Jones.

"He owns that twenty acres of Colorado Orange out there on the opposite side of the river from our property."

"When you two gonna build that golf course you been talkin' about since you got into town here?"

"Soon. We'd like to acquire more land out there, though. Preferably that orchard across that small river from us," said James.

"Sounds like it's gonna be pretty god damn difficult if someone else legally owns property out that way."

"Of course."

"Unless you can talk whoever owns the land into selling it legally to you. I suppose you could come into acquiring it in different ways, too."

"Well, if you have any way of helping us out with that, sir?"

"I may have my own ways and ideas on how to convince someone to give me something. What are you thinking?" asked Sheriff Jones.

"We'd like to buy the land from John if it's at all possible. Maybe get some more land to the south of the land we already own too. All the way up to the foothills of the mountain range there."

"I know who owns that land to the south of your property. It's a man named John Murdock. Old bastard lives in a shack on the south side of thirteen acres. Has no family. Wife died about a year and a half ago. No one would miss him if he just ended up missing. To be honest, I'm not sure anyone would even remember him either."

"Whatever we need to do to get a deal done, sheriff."

"Won't be a problem. However, John might be a different issue. You talk to him about acquiring the land from him?"

"We briefly did the other day, but didn't have much time to actually sit down and talk in depth about it."

"So, what can you two do for me if I help you out with this? Chances are good if old man Murdock goes missing by accident, no one's gonna know it. That land is good for the taking. It's Ashberger I'd be worried about. Sounds like he's got family and a group of Mexicans working for him. He owns the biggest apple orchard this side of the Mississippi it sounds like. Fucker's gonna be a hard one to take care of," said the sheriff, stepping out of the realtor's office, followed by the two realtors close behind him.

They walked across the road to the general store. He mounted his horse and prepared himself to leave for John's property.

"You got a minute to hear us out before taking off, sheriff?"

"Depends on what you got for me. So far, I'm hearing a lot of 'I need, I need, I need,' and not enough, 'we can take care of you, Walt.' Those that need my services don't get it for free around here. I'm pretty damn good at what I do, and if you need some work done on the side, apart from my sherif duties, of course, I'll be your man. But you gotta make it worth my while."

"Don't worry about that. I got you something along the Uncompahgre River you might be interested in," said Charles, as he handed the sheriff a folder he had brought outside with him. "Prime land. Close to our property and everything. Quiet. Peaceful. Fish the river any time you want. Be surrounded by the elite and upper class who will come out and stay in the resort and golf on the course we're going to build."

"How about a claim up in the mountains?"

"A claim?"

"A claim on some gold. You throw that pretty little riverfront property in the deal you're talking about; you've piqued my curiosity. You throw a claim for gold up in the San Juan's, now you've sparked my interest in a business partnership."

"Then please, come back into our office. And let's talk business then," said James.

"Well, I suppose I can hear what you and your partner have to say. Those Mexicans aren't gonna get any deader than they already are. At least the one."

With that, Sheriff Jones got off his horse, tying it back to the hitching post in front of the general store. He followed the two realtors back to their office to discuss the piece of land along the Uncompahgre River with them—a deal to acquire some free riverfront property, with a beautiful view of the San Juan Mountain Range, followed by the possibility of owning a claim for a gold mine up in the mountains, too. All Sheriff Jones had to do was dispatch the old man to the south of their property and then get some help to make sure John Ashberger and his family made the right choice to sell their land to Hackenberry and Sanderlin by any means necessary.

*   *   *   *

"Pick up that river rock there, Rito," said a frustrated John Ashberger, as he tossed another rock from the river onto the back of the wagon.

"Which one?" asked Rito.

"That god damn gray round one to the left of your foot," he said, pointing out the rock.

"Oh," replied Rito, as he bent down and picked up the rock John was talking about.

He brought the rock back up and walked it over, setting it in the back of the wagon.

"Sir, don't we have enough rocks yet?" asked Hipolito.

"Almost. Let's grab more rocks for about five more minutes, then we'll head back with what we have. Fucking back is killing me right now, anyway."

The five men continued to pick up rocks from the riverbank, setting them in the back of the wagon until John said that it was enough and that it was time to head back to the house and to the root cellar to unload their cargo. The wagon was full, and John mounted the horse while the four Mexicans piled into the back of the wagon. Boone struggled to pull it back up to the house, but eventually the horse accomplished the job, and the wagon was back at the edge of the root cellar.

John got off the horse, while his men jumped out of the back of the wagon and unloaded river rock from the wagon. John looked down into the pit and saw the men were making some progress digging into the side of the pit as they began to form the inside of the root cellar.

"Guadalupe!" yelled John down into the hole.

Guadalupe came out of the gap they were cutting into the side of the pit.

"John, you're back," he said from the bottom of the pit, looking up.

"I'm going to have the men start dumping some of these rocks into the pit. We'll dump behind you guys. Make sure you move the rocks and stack them away from where we're dumping them down there."

"You got it," said Guadalupe, as he went back into the hole in the side of the pit to dig some more. "Oh, John! We need to devise a method to get this soil out of this pit, too."

"I can send a large bucket on a pulley down there. Let me figure out how to make it work," said John.

"Okay, John!"

John turned around and spoke with the Mexicans who were unloading the river rock from the back of the wagon, instructing them on where to toss the stones into the pit. When he finished talking with his crew, John looked up and saw a lone rider on a black horse riding down the dirt road onto his property. The man was dressed in black with a black hat on.

"Who the hell is this now?" he said to himself, as the mysterious rider rode past the side of his home and up to him by the wagon.

"You, John Ashberger?" the rider said.

"I am. If you don't mind my asking, who do I have the pleasure of welcoming onto my property?" asked John.

The man in black removed his hat to greet John.

"My name is Walter Jones. I'm the Sheriff of Montrose County."

"Sheriff? What can I do for you, sir? My name is John Ashberger by the way," said John, who walked up and shook the sheriff's hand.

"You the owner of a couple of Mexicans that went into town?" asked the Sheriff.

"I wouldn't say owner. My men aren't slaves, sheriff. They work on this farm as freemen, making an honest living. But yes, there were a couple of my men who went into town to the general store to get spices for my wife."

"Well, I regret to inform you they are both dead."

"Dead?"

"Yes, sir."

"How? What happened?"

"Fucking Indians around here. God damn Utes will get a wild hair up their asses and do things like that from time to time. Looks like they picked your two men to go get this time. Trust me, we've been having a problem with those fuckin Indians for the longest time now."

"Hold on one moment, sir," said John, who walked over to the pit.

"Guadalupe! Please come up here. I need you for a minute," yelled John.

"What are you working on here?" asked the sheriff.

"Digging out a root cellar for our crop this year. Okay, I'm sorry. Explain to me what the hell happened to them, please. What do you know?"

"Well, the first man I found was dragged into town by his neck. I had a couple of men back in town get his body and some of the pieces of his body off the street. Limbs and an eye, no less. Chunks of skin, too. On the way here, I found the second man dead along the side of the road with his head caved in and part of his brain splattered on the road. Fucking Indians even killed the two horses your boys had."

"Son of a bitch," said John under his breath.

"Indeed. You live in this area, you gotta be aware of the Indians around here and what they're capable of. God knows they have some sort of issue with us trying to make their lives better for them," said the sheriff.

"John, who is this? What's going on?" asked Guadalupe, who just got out of the pit, brushing himself off.

"Guadalupe. Domingo and Segundo are both dead?" said John.

"What?"

"They're dead."

"How? What happened?"

"Indians killed them is what the sheriff is saying here."

"I don't believe it."

"I need you to tell the men. Let them know that we need to be more careful around here. Keep an eye out for Indians while we work the field," said John.

"It would be a good idea," said the sheriff.

"We've never had an issue with Indians around these parts before."

"Doesn't mean they aren't out there. Maybe even watching you right now from the rocks up in the hills there, too."

"Can we have the bodies back, sheriff?"

"The fuck you want the bodies back for?"

"I would like to bury them on the property, down by the bend in the river. In the place on the property where the sun first hits the ground on the new day in my family plot."

"You want to waste a couple of spaces in your family plot on a couple Mexicans?"

"They are family to me. They would give their lives for me and I for them. They all would be welcomed in my family plot."

"Well, I suppose you can have the bodies back. Ain't gonna do me or anyone in the town any good to have them lying around and rotting, anyway."

"And the horses too?"

"Hell, you do what you want with those, too."

"Fuck. We've never had an issue with the Utes people around here. We have a god damn tribal burial ground down in the woods on the end of the property and even then, in five years here, we've not had one problem with them," said John, pointing down on the edge of the property where the burial ground was located.

"They come and go as they please. Haven't seen them in a while around here, but lately there has been a group of men from their tribe that's been hangin' around town and causing problems. Think I'll send out a telegram to the governor letting them know we have an Indian problem around here in Montrose again when I get back into town."

"Well, thank you for letting me know. I will take care of the bodies of the two men and two horses personally."

"Alright, John. You folks been out here for the last five years now, you said?"

"Yes, sir. A little over five years now."

"And you got twenty acres of apples out here?"

"Yes, sir. Twenty acres of Colorado Orange."

"Well, isn't that good for you? You gonna have a harvest this year?"

"Yes, sir," said John. "Planning on harvesting close to 200,000 pounds of apples from this orchard."

"Jesus Christ, that's a hefty number of apples."

"It'll be a decent amount for sure."

"When you gonna harvest?"

"Probably September. Maybe early October."

"Looks like you got a pretty smooth operation going on here. What the hell is a root cellar for?"

"To store the apples until they are shipped out to a distributor in Texas."

"I see. That's a good idea, John. But this certainly looks like a lot of work."

"The payout will be good. You want to come inside for some coffee, sheriff?" said John, gesturing to his home.

"You know what, if it wouldn't be too much trouble?" said Sheriff Jones. "I could use a break today."

"No trouble at all. Guadalupe, Sheriff Jones and I are going to go into the house for a bit. Can you please take the men and go take care of Domingo and Segundo, and the two horses on the road? We'll talk later, but for now, please go pick them up and bring them all back here."

"Alright, John. I will," said Guadalupe, who turned and spoke to two men in Spanish.

"Come with me, sheriff. I'll introduce you to my family," said John, as the two men walked up to the back door of the home and walked inside the house.

Inside the house, Martha was working in the kitchen, while his daughter Margaret was helping her mom prepare dinner.

"Hey John, have you heard from Domingo and Segundo yet? It's been a while since they left to town," asked his wife.

"Yes, I'll have to talk with you here in a bit about them. Martha, this is Sheriff Walter Jones."

Sheriff Jones removed his hat and extended his hand out to shake Martha's hand.

"Ma'am, the pleasure is all mine."

"Oh, welcome to our home. I'm sorry, I would shake your hand, but they're covered in blood at the moment. We're butchering one of the cows from the field for supper this evening," said Martha. "No disrespect, of course."

"None taken," said Sheriff Jones, with a smile on his face. "I like a woman who knows her way around a kitchen and isn't afraid to slice up some cow, too."

"Sheriff Jones came in for some coffee. We're going to talk a bit in the living room," said John.

"No worries. We're just going to be here working on the meat. You can get your own coffee?"

"Yes, I can pour us both a cup."

John reached into the cupboard and pulled out a couple of coffee cups, set them down on the counter, and poured some coffee from the stove into them.

"It's not fresh, but Martha makes coffee so good it lasts all day," said John as he handed the sheriff a cup.

"Thank you," he replied.

"Would you like to follow me into the living room?" asked John.

"After you."

The two men left the kitchen and walked into the adjacent living room, and sat down on a couch beside a coffee table. Before setting his cup down, Sheriff Jones took a sip of coffee.

"That's some damn good coffee, John."

"Martha has always made pretty good coffee for as long as I known her," replied John.

"Lucky man."

"So, I don't think I've ever had the pleasure of getting to know you, sheriff. How long have you been sheriff for in town?"

"Well, I became sheriff in the county in 1883. My seat was up in Grand Junction for a year. Then south in Durango. And just recently, they moved me here to Montrose."

"Sounds like you were moved around a lot here in the county, then."

"I go where I'm told to go. I serve the people, John."

"Where you come from, Sheriff?"

"Lynden. Lynden, Alabama. Born and raised."

"Southeast corner of the state."

"Right you are, John."

"We come from Florida. Traveled through the Lynden area on our way to Colorado a few years back."

"You come from Florida?"

"Pennsylvania actually. But when we married, we moved down to Florida and owned a small orange farm until this opportunity came about here in Colorado five years ago."

"Why leave Florida then? Especially when you're having some success down there?" asked Sheriff Jones, as he leaned over and picked up his coffee cup from the table.

"Well, this opportunity to own land out here came along for us. We had a friend that told us that apple growing was going to be the future of farming. We plan on harvesting about $80,000 dollars' worth of apples this fall and shipping those down to Texas for distribution."

"$80,000 dollars' worth of apples?"

"That's right, sir. A pretty penny's worth," said John, taking a drink from his cup and leaning back into the backrest of the couch.

"Well, that's real nice for you. Real nice indeed. So, you wouldn't be interested in selling this beautiful piece of land, then I take it?"

"I haven't thought about it, and really, I'm not interested in selling it either. We have the chance to make $80,000 to $100,000 dollars each year from the number of apples we have out there on the trees. As it is, we have so many that I may ask my farm hand out there if he knows any more friends back in Sinaloa who he can invite to come work for us here. Especially now, after Domingo and Segundo are gone."

"Twenty acres is a lot," said the sheriff.

"So, have there been issues with the Indians around here? We've been here for five years now, and we've never had a problem."

"Fuckin' savages they are. So around here there hasn't been too much of an issue with them. I've had some encounters with them down south in Durango. The county seat funded a sheriff and two deputies. Because of those fucking Indians, though, I'm looking for two new deputies. Believe me, John. Kill an Indian, save a man, I think is how the old expression goes."

"I didn't know they were an issue like that here."

"Oh, they are. Make sure your wife and children aren't out there alone these days. And arm your Mexicans if you can. So, you said that there is an Indian burial site out there on your property?"

"There is," said John, taking a drink from his coffee cup. "Down in the woods on the end of the property."

"How many graves are there?"

"The fuck if I know. They're crudely marked. No names. Just rocks of different shapes, sizes and colors to mark where bodies are laid. Indian shit scattered everywhere: blankets, clothes, stone pendants. All valueless things."

"Well, that sounds exciting, John," said the sheriff, taking a drink of his coffee.

"Sheriff, do you know who owns the property across the river from us here?"

Sheriff Jones looked out the window and onto the property, overlooking the apple orchard and the small river beyond the trees.

"I'm not too sure who owns that land," said Sheriff Jones. "Someone from outside the area owns it legally last I heard. Bought two years ago is what I heard. Fuckin Indians are pissed that they don't have their land here anymore. I'm sure they owned your property at one time, too. Especially if there is an Indian cemetery out there. They probably value this land very highly. Well, tough shit for them. Fuck 'em, right John?"

"I suppose so. Further south of us, there is a small shack by the river. It's off our property, but I've never met the man who owned that property."

"You're referring to old John Murdock. John used to work the railroad back on the east coast when he got a wild hair up his ass one day years ago to come out here to Montrose out of all places to make a living on the gold up in the hills here. Think if he would have wanted gold, he would have kept going to San Francisco. Well, for years he was up there digging around, never found a goddamn thing. He ended up building a shack along the river. He comes into town from time to time and gets drunk off his ass at the saloon in town. But he's never amounted to anything in his life. In fact, I'm certain he has no family. None that I ever heard of, anyway."

"Think he would ever sell his property and move back to the east coast?"

"Shit, not old John. He's not going anywhere. I could see him dying in that shack, to be honest with you," said the sheriff.

"So, if he dies, who does the property go to?" asked John.

"Well, I suppose it would go to the county and the county decides on what to do with it from there."

"Goes to auction then?" asked John.

"More than likely."

"Sheriff, have you met the realtors across the street from the general store?"

"No, can't say I have yet. Sounds like they are new in town, too."

"Charles Sanderlin and James Hackenberry."

"Those names don't sound like folk I met in town before."

"Possibly. They had said they came from Baltimore."

"Baltimore? In Maryland?" asked the Sheriff.

"That's right."

"Well, I can't say I've ever met them, nor have I talked to any realtors in the town." Sheriff Jones drank the last of his coffee and set it down on the table. "Well, John, I appreciate you welcoming me into your home and property. Thanks for the coffee, but it's time for me to get back to town and get to work."

"Is there anything else I can do for you here?"

"Nope, your hospitality is much obliged, though," said the sheriff, who stood up from the couch and walked towards the door in the kitchen.

"Well, you are welcome to come back anytime," said John, standing up and grabbing both cups from the table.

The two men walked back to the kitchen, and the sheriff tipped his hat to Martha and Margaret.

"Ladies, thank you for having me in your home."

"Pleasure is ours. Have a good day, sir," said Martha.

John set the two coffee cups down on the counter and both men walked out of the house together, out to where the sheriff had tied his horse to the side of John's wagon. When they got to the wagon, sheriff Jones untied the reins and got up onto the back of his horse.

"John, remember what I said. Make sure your crew has some way of defending themselves out here. You can never trust these Indians around here. For that matter, anyone or anything else around town here."

"I appreciate the advice, sir. I'll make sure my crew collected the two bodies as well, and I'll have them buried on the property."

"Well, you do what you want with them. The county of Montrose does not acknowledge their existence here in the county, anyway. Especially if they ain't no citizens of America. If you want to put them in the ground, you put them in the ground yourself. If not, leave 'em out for the wolves and maybe the wolves won't bother you too much out here if you give them a steady supply of Mexicans."

With that, Sheriff Jones kicked his horse with his spurs, and the horse took off, back down the dirt road that led to the Ashberger property, headed back to the town of Montrose, Colorado.

Chapter 9: Vengeance is Mine, Sayeth the Lord

Guadalupe and some of the men returned later that afternoon just before dinner with Boone, pulling the wagon, carrying the dead bodies of Segundo and Domingo and their two horses on it. A tarp was laid over their lifeless bodies so that the children didn't see as they brought the men and horses back in.

John had pulled his wife Martha to the side shortly after the sheriff had left earlier in the day and informed her of what had happened. It was her job to keep the children inside while the men took the bodies out to the family's burial ground—a beautiful part of the land that was on the south side of the property.

This would be his first burial on the property. John met Guadalupe on another one of his horses, then rode with them to the burial grounds. With the horses, the men took the dead animals to the edge of the property and dumped them off for the wild animals of the area to find them and feed from. At the burial ground, though, the men dug the graves for Segundo and Domingo, putting their bodies to rest in the ground there. When the dirt was put back in the graves, the men erected wooden crosses up as tombstones to identify the graves. The men carved their names into the crosses. When their work was done there, some men said prayers to commemorate the graves.

John turned around to look at his men, some of which had somber looks on their faces.

"Guadalupe," said John, summoning Guadalupe to come over to him. "Interpret what I'm about to say to the crew."

"Alright, John," said Guadalupe, who interpreted for John as he spoke to the group.

"Gentlemen, we live in a difficult world. Whether it's wild animals, famine, disease, or, in this case, our own fellow man. From now on, I want everyone to carry a weapon to defend yourselves with. Whether that's a pistol or a knife, that's up to you. Do you understand?"

The men agreed with John and acknowledged that they understood what he was telling them.

"We'll also defend this land from any outside threats. This land belongs to us. It is our livelihood. We put the work into making this land prosperous for the past five years now. The land must be defended at all costs too."

The men nodded in understanding.

"Do they understand, Guadalupe?"

"Si, John. They do."

One of the men asked Guadalupe a question in Spanish, which he translated back to John.

"He says, what if they don't own weapons, John?" said Guadalupe.

"I have rifles, pistols, and knives. Hell, even use your farming tools if you must. But you are all welcome to what I have for guns and knives, too. I'll get some more ammunition from Sam at the general store."

Guadalupe interpreted this message to the men, and they all understood.

"Alright. Let's go have dinner together then. Each one of you here is like family to me. I am grateful for all of you being here, working at this farm and orchard. You all have sacrificed, and this year the fruits of your labor will finally pay off. Without you, all of this wouldn't be a possibility," said John as he turned and mounted Boone.

The men all got onto the back of the wagon, with Guadalupe joining them lastly. Together they went back to the house where they had dinner prepared by John's wife, together, as a family.

*   *   *   *

The Utes tribe for years had been taken advantage of by the invaders from the east, better known to them as the white man. A broken people, pushed down first by new white Mormon settlers who exploited them for their land and resources. Ignacio, his men, their families, and their fathers, began to be impacted by European-American contact with the 1847 arrival of Mormon settlers. After the initial settlement by the Mormons, the Utes were pushed off their land. Wars with the Mormon settlers began in the 1850s when some Ute children were captured in New Mexico and Utah by Anglo-American traders and sold in New Mexico and California. The rush of Euro-American settlers and prospectors into Ute country began with an 1858 gold strike in the San Juan Mountains of Colorado.

Mormons, however, continued to push the Utes off their homelands, which escalated into the Walker War that started in 1853. By the mid-1870s, the U.S. federal government forced Ignacio's father and all their people onto a reservation. The reservation amounted to less than ten percent of their former lands acreage. Their families found the small piece of land they were forced to live on to be very inhospitable as they tried to continue hunting and gathering off the reservation. Because of this, Ignacio's band of Utes caused concern among other Ute tribal members, as many other bands were still in fear of the white men and what they were capable of. With the weapons, horses, and immense manpower, the white men had the advantage, and the Utes knew it. The only band that refused to believe this was Ignacio and his men.

Two horses rode back into a small, makeshift camp of wickiup tipis with what light was left in the closing of the day. The riders rode into the camp and dismounted their horses, tying them to a log at the entrance to the camp.

"It was a successful day, my friend," said Ignacio.

"Indeed, it was," replied Ahiga. "And we only used two bullets, too."

"How was your trip into the town?" asked a man, walking up to Ignacio and Ahiga.

"Ahote, it's good to see you. Our trip into town was successful. We learned who owns the land where our families are buried."

"You have?"

"Yes. We have."

"Well, share with me."

"All in due time, Ahote," said Ahiga. "First, we need to make plans. Go and gather the men and tell them to meet up at the firepit in the center of the camp. There, Ignacio and I will address the men together."

"Are we finally going to do something?"

"The time is coming that we will do something soon, but we can't be reckless about it. Now go gather the men. We need to talk."

With that, Ahote turned and went back into the camp of wickiups.

"We are so close now, my friend. I feel like I should make plans on what I will do with our land when we get it back."

"Don't outrun the rising sun, Ignacio. Be patient. Take your time. The man who acts impatiently, the man who acts recklessly, the man who doesn't think before their actions, is the man that finds their life taken away. Be careful, Ignacio," said Ahiga, as the two men walked into the camp.

One woman in the camp saw the two men approaching and stood up from the ground. She leaned down and picked up a basket, carrying it with both hands and bringing it over to the two men.

"Blackberries from the stream nearby," the woman said.

"Thank you," said Ignacio, as he took his hand and grabbed a handful of wild blackberries that were picked just that morning.

Ahiga took a handful of blackberries too.

"Ignacio!" yelled a voice from within the camp.

Ignacio turned to see another one of his friends stepping out of a wikiup and walking up to them.

"Jaanesh, how are you feeling?" he asked.

"Fine. The medicine from Liwanu broke my fever this morning," said Jaanesh.

"That is great, my friend. I'm glad to hear that. Has Ahote come to tell you yet?"

"Tell me what?"

"We are meeting at the fire in the center of the camp. Ahiga and I have news to share with the men here. The time is coming."

"I hope it is good news. I am tired of moving from place to place, never settling down in the land that rightfully belongs to us."

"All in due time, my friend. Come with us. We will address all the men together."

The three men then walked through the encampment together until they reached the center of the camp, where a large fire was blazing strong. Some children were playing nearby, while some women in the camp worked on cleaning food and stitching together clothing. They sat on a log by the fire together. A few moments went by, and the men of the camp started to come, one by one. Each man approached the logs that surrounded the fire and sat down.

Joining Ignacio, Ahiga and Jaanesh were Ahote, which means the restless one. Liwanu, that means growling bear. Makya, whose name means eagle hunter. Miakoda whose name means the power of the moon. Naakesh; The Lord of heaven. Napayshni; Courageous/Strong. Pallaton, whose name means warrior. Rowtag whose name means fire. Tadi, who was named after the wind from the prairies of the lands they once all owned. Utah, whose translation means the people of the mountain. Finally, Wanikiy, whose name means the savior.

When all the men were there, seated with Ignacio and Ahiga, Ignacio spoke up and addressed them all.

"My friends, Ahiga and I have come back to you with good news. The land that was taken from us, and given to the invaders, will once again be ours. The land where the golden light of the morning touches the blades of grass and the graves of our fathers and their fathers."

"What have you found, Ignacio?" asked one of the men.

"I found who is living on our lands. A man named Ashberger. He is using our land to grow apples."

"What of our burial ground, Ignacio?" asked Pallaton.

"I do not know what has become of the burial grounds. With some luck, the white men haven't found it yet. Besides Ashberger, two other white men control the land on the other side of the river there. The land your fathers hunted on, Miakoda."

"Who are they?" asked Miakoda.

"The two white men I found are named Sanderlin and Hackenberry. They are selling our land in the area, making a profit from stolen property. They, too, must pay for their sins. Such as Ashberger. Ashberger has people of brown skin working the land with him. He also has a wife, children, and animals."

"What of the other two white men?" asked Liwanu.

"I do not know if there are more that work for them right now. Then the white man who dresses in black. He continues to hunt our people relentlessly. He shot and killed Tocho not that long ago from the Uncompahgre camp, then while he was still alive and watching, cut the throat of his wife."

"He must die, Ignacio," said Naakesha.

"Be calm, Naakesha. We need to be careful with the man in black. When he dies, there will be more like him, those who are greater than the stars in the night sky, and they will carry with them rifles and swords. They will march us off the land again and into parts of the land they call reservations where we will only continue to lose more and more of our land until we have nothing left. We have come a long way, my friends. Now is not the time to lose our progress, because we lose control of our emotions."

"So, what do you suggest, Ignacio?"

"I suggest that this evening, we go to the apple farmer and kill his brown men who live on our land. Then it's just Ashberger and his family left. We then kill them too and take back our land."

"How do you suggest we enter the land unseen tonight, Ignacio?" asked Ahiga.

"We travel by water, down the river that runs along the side of the mountain. The sound of the running water will mask the noise as we move into the camp. We'll kill the brown men quietly."

"We are ready, Ignacio, and will follow you wherever you lead us."

"Then come, my friends. Sharpen your knives and let's take back what belongs to us. Be prepared to leave in the next hour."

Ignacio stood up, followed by each of his men, who all stood up from the logs and returned to their own wikiups, except for Ignacio. He instead walked through the wikiups to the outside of the camp to a lonely wikiup that stood by the river on a small hill overlooking the water and the valley. When he got there, he reached out and moved the blanket that was covering the front entry to the shelter. There in the center of the room was a man, sitting bow-legged by a small fire in the center of the wikiup.

"I knew you were coming, Ignacio. You rallied your men this evening to attack the white men," said the pö' rat.

"We will attack the white men this evening," said Ignacio, walking into the center of the wikiup and sitting by the fire with the pö' rat, crossing his legs, mirroring the pö' rat.

"And you come to hear what the result of your work will be this evening."

"I do."

"Ignacio, prepare your soul for what I have to say," said the pö' rat, reaching over to a clay pot on the ground and picking it up.

He reached in and took out a handful of pure white sand that he threw directly into the fire. Instantly, the fire burst into green flames and purple smoke billowed out of the fire. The pö' rat stuck his face into the purple flame, inhaling the smoke as he held his breath and kept it in his lungs. He exhaled and purple smoke blew out of his mouth like a fire-breathing dragon.

"Listen to my words, Ignacio. Heed what I have to say. You will have many fights with the white men. You will slay white men. You will slay brown men. But you will lose many friends in the process. There is evil around us all."

"I can accept the loss of my brothers."

"Can you?"

"For the cause we fight for."

"Your heart and will are strong, Ignacio. But you fail to think of others. Namely, those that will follow you to death. This will ultimately be your own downfall."

"I will not fail."

"You will. What has been done cannot be undone. The moment the white men came onto our lands, killed our buffalo, stole our crops... It has set in motion events that cannot be changed."

"What are you saying?"

"You and your men will die, Ignacio. You fight valiantly for our cause, but what I see is nothing but death. Blood stains the ground of your fathers. Fire burns the crops of our people."

"I don't deny that I won't die, nor will my family. But it won't be today. Nor will it be tomorrow."

"You're right. But you will die under the hand of a white man. It will not be old age that takes your life. The future of our people will be torn up by the roots. Forced from our lands. And there will be no going back. No amount of fighting will ever change that."

"You see wrong! Look again into the future!"

"Ignacio, do not be angry with me for showing your future to you. Go and have your war. Just know that in the end it will not matter, and you will lose more than what you started with. Your family. Your people. What you have owned and what little we have will all be destroyed."

"It's better than sitting in a dark corner, drinking white man's water."

"Your father is proud of you, though, Ignacio."

"What?"

"He has spoken to me. He sits to your right. Senawahv has permitted his spirit to come and give you a message," said the pö' rat.

Ignacio looked to his right and felt an icy presence against the right side of his body. He reached out his arm and what felt like tiny pins and needles sticking into his skin ran up and down the length of his arm.

"What is his message?" asked Ignacio.

"He says that when your physical body dies, that he will come back for you to guide you to the temple of our spirits. He is proud of the leader that you have become, Ignacio. He is proud that you gave up the white man's drink."

"When does he say I will die?"

"Only Senawahv knows the exact day and time, Ignacio. Not even I can see that. He also says that when you go to fight, be prepared to lose everything. You will lose everything here in our world. But you will one day again gain everything with which you have lost here."

"What else does he say?"

"He says he loves you, Ignacio. He is proud of you."

"Tell him that I'm not going to let him down."

"He sits to your right. You tell him that," said the pö' rat.

Ignacio turned to his right side and spoke into the air. "Father, I will not let you down."

"Now be gone from me, and do what you feel is right to do, Ignacio."

Ignacio stood up and started to walk out of the wikiup, when he stopped, then turned and faced the pö' rat again.

"Bless me," said Ignacio.

The pö' rat stood up from the fire, walked over and grabbed a clay jar from a wooden shelf. He opened the jar, grabbed a handful of fresh huckleberries, and crushed them in his palm. The pö' rat swept the huckleberry juice over his index and middle finger and spread it across Ignacio's forehead.

"May you be blessed with intelligence, knowledge, and leadership. May you make wise choices in battle."

Then the pö' rat took his two fingers and applied more huckleberry juice to Ignacio's chest.

"And may your heart continue to show courage and fight for as long as it beats."

Ignacio thanked the pö' rat, then left his wikiup. He went back into the camp and sat by the fire for a bit until his men showed up, one by one. He then stood up, and they followed him out of the camp. They all left armed with their knives to kill the working crew of John Ashberger.

Chapter 10: Thieves in the Night

"Thank you for the dinner, Martha," said Guadalupe. "The men needed the break tonight after having to bury Domingo and Segundo today."

"I'm sorry for your loss," said Martha. "I know you all are very close to one another."

"Thank you. Yes, we are all close. We come from the same area in Mexico. Many of our families back home are close. Today was especially difficult for some of us."

"Guadalupe, go take the men and get some rest. We'll start again on the root cellar tomorrow," said John.

"Alright. Thank you."

"Don't forget to take the weapons with you, too. You take the rifle. Have Roman and Romulado take the pistols. And make sure each man takes a knife or machete with them. Just in case, Guadalupe."

"Alright, thank you, John."

Guadalupe stood up from the dining room table and spoke in Spanish to the men. Each man stood up from around the table and took their plates to the sink in the kitchen. Setting the plates down on the counter, they walked out the back door and into the darkness of the night. Each man was armed with some sort of weapon. Guadalupe was the last to leave the house. He took two torches with him that he lit from the fire in the fireplace. Handing one torch to one of the men, Guadalupe led the group out into the orchard where the men's worker shacks were located on the property down by the river.

The men talked with one another as they walked to their housing out in the field around where the river ran. They had built the worker's housing there so that they could use the river for a water source and to bathe and wash their clothing in. While walking back through the orchard, the men made random talk with one another. They also tried to decide on what to do with the gold that Segundo and Domingo had mined on their time off from the San Juan Mountain range that they had collected for themselves.

It was decided that the men would divide the gold up equally among themselves and give themselves an even share of the mined minerals they had gathered. When they passed the last row of apples in the orchard, they arrived back at their buildings. Each housing unit held four men per unit in them. Each man went to their respective buildings while Guadalupe looked around the area. It was a quiet night tonight. A full moon was out that lit the grounds around the worker's shacks in a blue iridescent color. All seemed quiet this beautiful evening. Many of the men lit candles in their shacks to light the rooms up temporarily to get ready for sleep. After walking around the area and securing the grounds, Guadalupe retired to his shack for a rest, too. One by one, the lights when out in each shack, and the men slowly fell into a deep sleep.

*   *   *   *

The river's current slowly brought Ignacio and his men in their canoes down the river and onto the property of John Ashberger. The canoes held three men a piece, to the exception of one that held two men: Ignacio and Ahiga. Their canoe was in the front, while the other four floated behind them.

"Ahiga, where do you think we should pull the canoes off and onto the bank?" asked Ignacio.

"We will pull off soon, Ignacio. I can see the apples in the moonlight now."

"We should walk from here, then."

"I agree," said Ahiga.

The two men grabbed their oars, then paddled their way through the river to an open sandy spot along the bank of the river. They beached their canoes into the side of the river, one by one. Ignacio and his men got out and checked the weapons they had with them, knives and hatchets. A couple of men had brought bows and arrows with them as well.

They met together for a moment and Ignacio told them the plan. They'd walk up the side of the river, look for the worker's shacks, then kill as many as they could quietly as they slept. When the men understood what the plan was, Ignacio led them down the bank of the river, downstream, as they walked in the darkness of the night. They kept an eye out in the orchard, seeing the silhouettes of the apple trees and, on occasion, a cat darting across the field as they hunted field mice. It didn't take too long for them to finally come up to the shacks where Ashberger's men were sleeping.

Ignacio stopped his men and used the light of the full moon to watch the camp for a moment. They didn't see any movement around the shacks as they watched silently.

"Are they even in there?" asked Ahiga.

"Of course they are. I can smell them upwind," said Ignacio. "Prepare your knives and remember, we kill as many as we can quietly."

"Did you all hear that?" whispered Ignacio. "Kill as many as you can."

The group of young Ute men understood what they were told, and together they all slowly crept down to the shacks along the river where John's crew slept. When they got to the small shacks, the men looked in through the dirty thin glass windows, where they could faintly make out the shapes of bodies lying in the beds. Ignacio slowly crept around the side of the shack.

He turned the corner of the building, preparing to find the door and enter one of the shacks when he was met face to face with one of John's men, who was getting up to relieve himself. Ignacio quickly took his knife, jabbing it into the man's torso before he knew what had happened. The man let out a loud grunt as the knife penetrated his body. He fell back into the shack, causing a loud thud against the wall. Ignacio took the knife out of his stomach, then jabbed the blade firmly into the side of the man's head and twisted the blade, causing a sickening cracking sound as the skull split under the knife's churning pressure.

The commotion outside woke a couple of the men in the shack that the now dead man had fallen into. Guadalupe opened his eyes and saw the silhouettes of men passing by the front window of the shack. He slowly pulled out his rifle from underneath the covers in the bed, aiming it at the door to the shack. He watched in the moonlight that was shining through the front window as the doorknob to the shack slowly turned. The door slightly cracked open, causing more moonlight to flood the room. A head popped in through the crack in the door and looked around before he entered.

Guadalupe watched as a second man started to come into the room. Both men were carrying what looked like knives that shimmered in the blue moonlit night. Guadalupe aimed his gun at one of the two men and pulled the trigger, shooting the second man who entered the room in the side of his head. The bullet went through the man's head, lodging itself in the wall behind him.

The first man panicked and tried to run out of the shack when one of the other men sleeping in the shack aimed his pistol, shooting him in his lower back, causing the man to stumble and fall to the floor. The sounds of the gunfire caused the rest of Ignacio's men to run away and hide in the night's darkness. They ran up the bank of the river, then a short way up, jumped into the river, and swam to the other side. Meanwhile, back in the shack, the Mexicans woke up one by one. They came out of the shacks with their weapons in hand when they saw their fallen friend laying up against the side of the shack.

"Librada!" said one of the men, grabbing him by the face.

The man then saw the wound on the side of Librada's head. When the man moved his head, some of his brain matter poured out of the wound, falling to the ground.

"Guadalupe!" yelled the man, as by this time everyone had come out of the shacks.

Guadalupe ran out of his shack.

"Librada is dead," said the man as he stepped back from Librada's body.

Guadalupe looked down at the wound on the side of his head, seeing that he was, in fact, dead. He went back into the shack where the two Ute Indians were. One of the Ute's was dead, with a gunshot wound to the head, laying still in a pool of his own blood. The second man, however, was still alive, but in obvious pain on the floor. Guadalupe looked at the gunshot wound and saw the man had been shot through the center of his back, likely causing a spinal injury.

"Roman! Refugio!" he yelled back through the open door as the two men walked back inside the shack.

"Quickly, run and go get John from the house. I need him here, now! Take one of the pistols with you just in case there are more Indians out there hiding in the darkness. Kill any that you find," said Guadalupe to the two men.

The two men then turned and left the shack, running back to the house. While the two men were on their way to get John, Guadalupe tried talking to the paralyzed Indian lying chest first on the wooden floor of the shack.

"Senior, who are you?" he asked.

The man grunted in pain but did not answer him.

"Rito!" he yelled out to the men, and Rito came into the shack.

"Light the candles and then have the men check around the area and see if you can find where those Indians went. I guarantee there were more than just two of them here tonight," said Guadalupe.

Rito stepped over the top of the dead Indian on the floor and lit the candles on the shelves in the shack to light the room. When the last candle was lit, he went outside and took a couple of the men who, at this time, had lit torches to help light the surrounding area. They walked around the area, looking for any tracks, and then found footprints leading up the river that they tracked to their destination.

A short time later, John arrived at the shack after he had run there with Romand and Refugio, armed with a pistol of his own in his hand. When he approached the shack with the two men, he saw some of his crewmen outside the front of the shack, looking into the shack through the front door. He then noticed the dead body of another one of his workers, lying propped up against the shack with brain matter coming out of the large gash in the side of his head, dripping down the side of his head and onto his chest. He entered the shack where he saw Guadalupe, with one dead Indian and a second, writhing in pain on the floor, unable to move his body from the waist down.

"What the fuck is going on here?" John asked Guadalupe.

"They came during the night while we slept. Killed Librada outside," replied Guadalupe. "Drove a knife into his stomach, and then into the side of his head."

"Goddamn it!" said John out of frustration, kicking the dead Indian in the side of his head.

The force of the kick caused some of the blood from the open wound to spray onto the side of the shack wall.

"What's this one's problem?" asked John, pointing his pistol at the wounded man, who was convulsing on the floor in pain.

"Roman shot him in the center of the back. I think the bullet hit his spine and paralyzed him," said Guadalupe.

John lifted his gun up and aimed it at the back of the man's head, with the intention to end the Indian's life right then and there. Before he pulled the trigger, though, he lowered his gun.

"Bring him outside, now," said John.

Guadalupe called for Roman to come and together the two men picked him up by the arms and dragged him outside of the shack. The man squirmed in pain as they dragged him from the shack to the river. John told the two men to turn him over, but only submerge his head into the water, leaving the rest of his body on the riverbank. The men did what they were told, turning the Indian around and setting him down on the bank of the river, where his head was submerged in the water momentarily. The Ute man lifted his head up to keep his face from being submerged in the icy river water.

John holstered his pistol, grabbing the man by his long black hair and forcing his head down into the river water. The man struggled to get his head above the water when John pulled his head up from the water.

"You speak English?" John asked the man.

"Yes!" gasped the Ute, trying to catch his breath.

"Who are you?" asked John.

"My name is Rowtag," he replied.

"Who the fuck is that friend of yours lying dead in the shack, with a hole in the side of his fuckin head?" said John, shoving Rowtag's head back under the surface of the water, then bringing him back up.

"Miakoda! We call him Miakoda," said Rowtag.

"Who is we?"

Rowtag gasped to catch his breath.

"Our men."

"Who is that? Don't you jack me here, you goddamn fuckin Indian!"

John shoved the man's head back under the surface of the water as Rowtag struggled against him. John then lifted his head back up out of the water.

"Utes. Utes men."

"Local Indians?"

"Yes."

"Why are you here?"

"For the land."

"For the land?"

"Yes."

"I own this land, you goddamn savage. You come onto my land and do this to my property and to my family and to my workers?"

"No. No, you don't own this land. We do. We always have. It's ours, white man."

John shoved the man's head back underwater with force, driving Rowtag's head back into a submerged river rock. He struggled again, trying to use his hands to break John's grasp on his hair, but he could not. John then brought his head back up out of the water again.

"Who is the leader of the dead man inside the shack?" asked John.

"His name is Black Hawk," Rito replied.

"How many are there of you fuckers around here?"

"We are many. Like a legion. We are going to take back what belongs to us, this land. It's ours," said Rowtag, gasping again to catch his breath.

John reared back his fist, striking Rowtag in the face. He then punched him again. Then again, and again. John then shoved his head back into the water and held it there until Rowtag stopped moving, drowning the Ute man there in the river.

"Fucking Indian! It's not gonna be yours because you're dead!" he yelled, as he shoved the body into the river, with no regard to his humanity.

John stood up and found a large rock resting on the bank of the river. He stood up, walked over and sat down on the rock, looking out into the river, and watched the lifeless body of the man floating down the stream. He saw the wounds he had caused on the man's face as he lifelessly floated away. He paused for a moment to catch his breath and to calm down from losing his temper. When he was finally calm, he stood up from the rock and turned to look to see that all his crewmen were standing there, watching him and waiting for him to say something to them.

"John," said Guadalupe. "Are you alright?"

"Fine," he replied. "Doing just fine, my friend."

"I don't mind you killing him, John. If you feel that's the best thing to do in the moment. But remember, he's a human too. We all respect you here, John, and look up to you."

"Did they show mercy to Domingo and Segundo? Or to Librada when they broke his head open like a god damn egg? Did they show mercy when they tried to take my land by sneaking onto it and killing you all?" asked John.

While John was talking, Rito and a couple of the men came back to the group after having walked upstream, searching the area.

"Guadalupe! We found canoes up the stream. Five of them. Not far from here, along the bank of the river."

"How many seats are in the canoes?" asked John.

"It looks like three seats per canoe, sir," said Rito.

"So, there are more of those fuckers out there somewhere, then. Scattered like goddamn roaches as soon as we figured out what was going on, didn't they?"

"What do you suggest we do?" asked Guadalupe.

"Pull the canoes from the river. Bring them back to the house. We'll burn them in a pile up by the house.

"And the dead Indian in the shack, John?"

"We'll burn him too. In fact, move the canoes and the dead Indian into the grove where the burial ground is. We're moving it all into the middle of their burial ground and setting it all on fire tonight," said John.

"Are you sure about that, John?"

"You're goddamn right, I'm sure. I'll go back up to the house and get the wagon to load the canoes up and the body. You all stay here," said John as he turned and walked back to the house in the dark.

"John, do you want a torch?" yelled Guadalupe.

"I'm fine," yelled John as the silhouette of his body disappeared into the darkness of the night.

"What do we do now?" asked Ramon.

"Go and grab the canoes from upriver. Bring them back here and when John brings the wagon, we can load them up along with the body in the back."

"What about Librada?" asked Rito.

"Not much can be down now for him. We'll bury him when we're finished with the Indian and the canoes."

"Guadalupe, I don't think it's a good idea to burn the burial ground and the trees around it. The canoes and body are one thing, but the grounds?" said Aniseto.

"It's not my choice, Aniseto. John controls what happens on this land. It's our job to help and support him in any way that we can. Roman, take the men with you back to the canoes. Take them off the bank of the river and bring them here."

Roman took the men with him downstream, along with the torches, leaving Guadalupe back at the shacks alone. He walked back into the shack with the dead Indian in it and sat down on the bed, watching the dead man on the floor of the shack, waiting for him to spring back to life again, but he never did. He lay on the floor, lifeless. His head resting still in a pool of blood.

"When it's my time one day, remember it wasn't I who decided to do this to you people," said Guadalupe.

Guadalupe sat on the corner of the bed, watching the body when he heard the wagon's wheels squeaking as they came down the road, approaching the shacks. John was back.

Guadalupe stood up and stepped over the dead Indian. He walked out of the shack, meeting John as he was pulling the wagon up to the door.

"Where are the men?" John asked him, as he was getting off the horse.

"They went to collect the canoes. John, are you sure it's a good idea to burn the burial ground?" asked Guadalupe.

"I'm fucking tired of the Indians already. They obviously have a problem with me, Guadalupe, if they went out and killed Segundo, Domingo, and now Librada, unprovoked. Trying to kill everyone here. I did nothing to them. I left their burial grounds alone on the corner of the property. For five years, I respected the area, and this is how I'm paid back for it. They come in the night, try to kill as many of you as they could, and do harm to my property."

"I understand, John. Just think about what you're doing. When you cross that line, there is no going back."

"You think I didn't think of that, Guadalupe? I know what is at stake and I'm willing to fight any invader that comes onto my land to do anyone or anything here harm."

At that moment, Roman and the men were bringing back the five canoes. One man carried from the front and one from the back, while one man carried from each side. They walked them up to the shacks and to John's wagon.

"Here are the canoes, sir," said Roman.

"Load them," said John.

One by one, the men loaded the canoes into the back of the wagon. When all five of the canoes were loaded, two of the men went back into the shack with the dead Indian in it. They picked up the body and put the dead man into the back of the wagon. The men helped load their friend, Librada, into the back of the wagon as well.

When everyone was loaded up into the wagon, John mounted Boone and steered the horse to the corner of the property where the burial ground was located. John stopped about a hundred feet away from the burial ground and ordered the men out of the wagon. They took the canoes and stacked them similar to a large campfire in the center of the burial ground. They then took the body of the deceased Indian, setting it on top of the canoes in the center of the pile.

John went back to the wagon and untied a clay jar from the back of the wagon. He walked the clay jar to the pile of canoes, throwing it into the canoes and breaking the jar. The smell of kerosene permeated the air around the men. John forcibly took the torch out of the hands from one of his men, who was standing nearby, and tossed it down onto the pile, igniting the kerosene.

The canoes went up in flames, catching the dead body that was now soaked in kerosene on fire, too. Some of the smaller trees and brush in the area also caught fire. The men evacuated the grove where the burial ground was located as the area heated up. John was the last man that walked out. In a short time, the fire burned the brush and smaller trees around the burial ground, then the long grass caught fire, and finally the larger pine trees, maple trees, and oak trees. Eventually, everything was on fire and the heat from the inferno was immense.

The men stepped back as the heat from the fire grew stronger and stronger until they were back next to the wagon and the horse. John, however, stood nearby, watching the grounds and the trees and brush burn. The wooden tombstones marking the graves burned, along with hidden Ute tribal artifacts.

John's silhouette was juxtaposed against the blazing background. His men saw the blaze expand and saw the faint shadow outline of John standing by, watching it all burn, refusing to walk away no matter how hot it got.

The fire could be seen for miles in the valley as it lit up the surrounding area. Along the hills on the other side of the river, Ignacio sat on a fallen tree that overlooked the valley and watched as his family's burial ground was burned. The sacred trees, the artifacts that belonged to his people, and the graves of his fathers and his men's fathers. The rest of the men stood by and watched as the burial site was engulfed in flames. Rage filled their hearts, and they thirsted for vengeance.

"Ahiga," said Ignacio, asking for his attention.

Ahiga didn't respond to him, but only stood next to Ignacio, watching his family's graves burn too.

"On my life, every one of the white and brown men will die," said Ignacio.

Chapter 11: Sheriff Walt Jones

The hinges on the front door to Hackenberry and Sanderlin Real Estate business squeaked as they opened in the morning hours. Stepping in through the front door was the sheriff of Montrose County, as he brushed rainwater off his black overcoat before taking it off and hanging it on the clothing hook on the wall by the front door. He then removed his black hat, set it on the same hook, and then shut the door behind him.

"Who is there?" asked a voice coming from inside the office area.

"Sheriff Walt Jones!" he yelled in reply to the question.

"Well, sheriff, it's a pleasure to see you come in today," said the voice as the Sheriff could hear a squeaking chair coming from the other room, then footsteps approach him there in the short hallway.

He was met by old man Charles Sanderlin, who shook the sheriff's hand.

"Please, do come in. We have some tea brewed on this cold and dreary day. You're welcome to have some. Unless, of course, you would like a drink of bourbon, then you are welcome to that as well," he said, leading the sheriff back into their office.

At one desk in the room was James Hackenberry, working on paperwork. James looked up and saw Charles and Walt walking into the office. He stood up from his chair and walked around the corner of it to greet Sheriff Jones.

"Sheriff, how are you doing today?" asked James.

"Just fine. Just came to stop by to let you know that I met Ashberger yesterday," said Sheriff Jones.

"Did you? What did you think about him?" asked Charles.

"He's a farmer. A hardened and stoic man," said Sheriff Jones, sitting down at a chair at James' desk.

Both James and Charles too sat in chairs next to the sheriff.

"I got a similar impression. A man that's not afraid to pull a trigger if he had to," said Charles.

"You may be more right than you think."

"What do you mean?"

"Last night, that fucking band of Indians that are camped out north of the town paid Ashberger a visit. Killed one of his crewmen before one of his men sent a bullet through the side of one of their heads, then another one of the men shot a second one. No idea what happened to that guy."

"Dear God."

"Indeed. A short time later, apparently, John went and torched the burial ground on his property there. Pissed those fuckin band of Utes off, I'm sure. So, we may just let them kill each other and when everyone is dead, then you two can take over the land there and I can get my property along the river there."

"Wait, how do you know this?"

"You don't need to concern yourselves with how I know shit around here. You just need to follow through with your promise to me."

"And indeed, we will, Sheriff Jones," said Charles. "However, I would like to know if you are doing business with anyone else. Just in case we have other interested parties in business."

"I know a couple of guys. Bounty hunters back east. They are experts in what they do. Indians don't even know these guys are around. They're good."

"How do you know them?" asked James.

"Two guys that owe me a favor. A little job I did for them about a year ago."

"Can we trust them too?" asked Charles.

"Of course. They owe me a favor."

"No honor amongst thieves, Sheriff Jones."

"And I suppose I walk out that door and end our business deal. Then what the fuck are you two gonna do? Wait until Ashberger is dead? Years from now?"

"You said it yourself. Just let the Indians and Ashberger kill each other. Then why don't we just let them do that and I keep that land for our business?" asked Charles.

"And when there are still men left behind, who will take that land for themselves. Then what? You two sons of bitches need me more than I need you."

"Alright, let's just calm down. Relax. No rash decisions here," said James.

"That's a good idea, James," said Sheriff Jones. "Now, like I said, I have two guys that owe me a favor. One man's name is Clarence, and the other is Harry. If you need to know more than that, I will respect our partnership and tell you. Until then, don't worry about it and trust that I know what I'm doing around this town."

"I really must say I'm not liking that—"

James cut Charles off mid-sentence and said, "That works for us just fine, sheriff."

"Good. I'm glad to hear that. Now regarding one of our tenants on the land. You got that tea after all?" asked the sheriff.

"Of course, help yourself," said James.

The sheriff stood up and walked over to the teapot by the fireplace, pouring himself a cup of tea. "I went by John Murdock's little hut down there south of Ashberger's place earlier this morning."

"And?"

"He's taken care of. He doesn't have any family living in the area, or anywhere, for that matter. As far as I know. He was rather easy to dispatch. There's nothing like burying a hatchet between someone's eyes, if you know what I mean," said the sheriff, as he turned around and walked back to his chair in the office.

"You killed him?"

"Of course, he's dead now."

"What did you do with the body?" asked James.

"Buried it on the property. Again, Clarence and Harry owe me a favor. They helped dig the hole, tossed old man Murdock into the pit and even poured the dirt right over the top of it. Only work I had to do was split his skull with that hatchet."

"Good. Now what about Ashberger?"

"He's going to be a bit more difficult to handle. He's armed. His work crew are armed. He's got a family. Men on the property. It's not going to be as easy as it was getting rid of Murdock. As in, I won't be able to just walk up to him and bury a hatchet in his head. That and Ashberger pissed that band of Utes off by incinerating their burial ground," said the sheriff as he took a drink from his tea.

"Have you heard if the Utes are going to retaliate for it?"

"Oh, you bet your ass they will. Ashberger started something that I don't think he may have thought about. Those Utes will die fighting for what they believe in and what they want, and they want that land."

"Fucking hell, so even if the Indians manage to successfully kill John and his family and those Mexicans, we would still have to deal with what is left of that group of indians."

"We would. Yes."

"Your two friends good with a rifle or pistol?"

"And a knife. And a bow and arrow. And a spear. They've used any kind of weapon at least once that you can think of. Killed a lot of men in their day, too."

"So, what do you suggest we do going forward then, Sheriff Jones?" said Charles, standing up from his seat and walking over to the fire to pour another cup of hot tea. He poured tea from the pot by the fire, then walked back, taking a sip from the cup.

"We kill whoever is left over. Utes. The Mexicans. Wife and children. We wipe his family out of existence from around here. Including his older daughter and husband, who live on the outskirts of town here on their own property. Everyone. Then we start with a clean slate on the property. It will go to auction with the state if there are no heirs to the estate."

"And what if he has family living outside of Colorado? Somewhere back east?"

"Like I said, there will be no heirs. I'll be sure of it. The job to find the heirs is mine. There will be no heirs found."

"Charles, I certainly do feel we found the right person to form a partnership with," said James.

"I certainly agree. Now, Sheriff Jones, what should we do now?" asked Charles.

"I take my guys. Find a few more. We keep an eye on the Indians and John, and once they are done killing themselves, then we kill the rest. That's it."

"I don't know if we have that much time," said James.

"What do you mean?" asked the sheriff.

"We have a crew coming to the property next week to work on building the plantation style resort and golf course there."

"A golf course?" asked the Sheriff.

"That's right. It is an outdoor game from Scotland. Then we're going to build a resort there too," said Charles.

"I suspect there's a purpose behind that?"

"There is," said James, standing up from his chair, and walking over to the window in the office, looking out on the street and watching passers walk by.

"Building a resort and having a golf course with it will help to modernize this primitive land. Not only that, but it will bring more elitists from the east coast out here to stay or vacation. It only makes sense, Walt. You know how much money is involved here? What we build here could sustain ourselves and our children and our children's children financially for lifetimes to come. And it could also benefit you. If we could come into possession of John's land, it would only make us even wealthier. The more land we have, the more opportunity we have to shape Montrose to the town we would like it to be."

"So, what is your plan? Create a new Montrose?" asked the sheriff.

"Precisely!" said Charles, taking a sip of his tea.

"Look at this street," said James, tapping on and pointing out the window. "This town is a disaster, sheriff. The streets are mud, there's horse shit all over the sidewalks, and piss in the alleys. Wouldn't it be better to live in a town with cobble streets? Or have more stores than just a couple of general stores? Maybe a couple of factories like lumber mills. Do you know what industrialization brings to an area, sheriff? Money. I think it's safe to say that the three of us like money, yes?"

"I certainly do. I also like gold," said the sheriff.

James smiled as he walked back to his desk, looking through some files on the top of his desk. He thumbed through a couple of folders until he found the one he wanted.

"So do I," James said. "Gold is a beautiful thing. So along with your property, sheriff, I also have this."

He handed the sheriff the folder. Walt promptly opened the folder and looked inside and saw the deeds to the San Juan Mountain gold claim numbers six, seven, and eight.

"These are the deeds to a gold claim up in the San Jaun Mountains," said the Sheriff.

"Three of the claims..." said James. "Are yours, if you get the job done and get Ashberger off that property and dispatch the natives promptly."

James took the file back with the gold claims in it, slipping the property deed of where the Sheriff would be living when the job was done into the folder as well.

"I may as well keep the home property in this folder, too. That's four land deeds for you, sheriff. Three of the four produce the most gold that has ever been found in the mountains around here. You can retire from being a sheriff, rest well, fish the river, mine the gold. You're taken care of for life," said James.

"I believe you have a job to do now, sheriff," said Charles.

"Gentlemen, I believe I do," said the sheriff, standing up from his seat.

"Good day to you both," he said as he turned and walked towards the front door. Putting his hat and jacket back on, he opened the door and stepped out into the rain and walked away.

"Are we really going to give him three gold mine claims?" asked Charles.

"We own fourteen of them now. I think we can afford to give three to get what we want here," said James, walking back to his desk and sitting in his office chair.

"You are right."

"Fourteen gold mine claims, most of the properties on the north side of town, including the housing development of Parker's Place out on the west side of town. And soon, my friend, you and I will own the only golf resort on this side of the Mississippi river. But before we get there, Asherberger and the natives need to be dispatched," said James. "They stand in the way of our wealth."

"Soon, my friend. All in due time."

Chapter 12: Economic Development

The work on the property started early on the east side of the river. Men with tools and equipment, clearing out the land and building a large foundation. Apart from building a foundation, trees were cleared out, laid in an enormous pile and burned to ash. Then they were disposed of and wasted rather than being turned it into lumber to use on the property, because it was pine and not cedar like the realtors had wanted. Bricks were also brought in by train from the east coast—a new material used in home building and popular on the east coast.

Grass and brush, and all living things were wiped out from the area, as the workers lay the golf course's foundation. It wouldn't take long for multiple shipments of lumber and bricks to arrive at the site with enough lumber and supplies to build a four level multi-room plantation style resort. James Hackenberry and Charles Sanderlin visited the site frequently, overseeing the building and development operation of their newest resort, claiming it to be the largest resort development on this side of the Mississippi river and enticing some of the elite class from the east coast to come and see for themselves.

On the opposite side of the San Juan River, John Ashberger and his men continued working on the root cellar. On their breaks, they watched as the land on the other side of the river was cleared out as many men came to work on it. John's crew was just about finished with the root cellar. They spent the whole last week working on it and clearing it out, developing a system where some men dug dirt out, while other men worked to build the interior structure of the cellar with the lumber.

The men worked and lived without any further incidents after what had happened in the night the prior week involving the Ute men. The burial site on the corner of John's land that was so precious to the Utes had been reduced to nothing but a burned-out area, charred black from the fire. Neither John, his family, nor his crew had gone to that part of the property since John set fire to it in the early hours of the morning the week before. The children were told not to play down there anymore, too.

Guadalupe walked out of the root cellar. John placed a lot of his trust into his experience and knowledge as he had worked many farms growing up in Mexico and when he had met John in Florida, he worked on his citrus farm for him. He walked up the dirt incline that the men had dug out for the root cellar. When he was out, he walked over to the wagon on the property and removed his hat. Wiping his brow of sweat and dirt with the back of his wrist, he put his hat back on and felt a hand pat him on the shoulder.

"How is the cellar coming?" asked John Ashberger.

"We're almost done, John. I checked out the apples this morning before we started working on the cellar here. They are starting to come in on the branches, too," replied Guadalupe.

"That is good to hear."

"What do you think is happening across the river?"

"Looks like something is going on over there. Something big. That hole in the ground looks to be large and deep enough for a foundation for a building."

"What kind of building would they be putting in out here? Town is ten minutes north of us, John."

"I know that. I'm not sure. They're clearing out the land around the area, too. Perhaps another house and orchard or farm? I'm going to go get the spyglass from inside the house to have a look and see what's going on over there. Let's see if we can finish this project up and then get back out into the orchard and thin some of the trees out. We need to do that either later today or tomorrow morning."

"We could probably start later today, John. I don't think we'll be here in the root cellar for much longer."

"How are we doing on lumber?"

"Just fine. We'll have a couple of railroad ties left over."

"Use them in there. Put it all to use, Guadalupe. Just helps to reinforce the cellar that much more."

"Alright, John. You got it."

"I'll be right back," said John, as he turned and walked away from the root cellar.

Walking back into the house, he went in through the back door to the living room. Martha Ashberger, was lying down on the couch, resting her head against a pillow and reading a book.

"Hey, how are things going out there?" she asked.

"They are going well. We're almost finished with the root cellar," replied John, walking into the living room and over to the bookshelf.

"What are you looking for?" she asked.

"The spyglass."

"Oh. Yes, it's in that decorative wooden box on the right side of the top shelf."

"Thank you, dear."

"What do you need that for?"

"There's some construction happening across the river."

"Oh?"

"Yes, it looks like they are digging a foundation of some kind close by the river. Cleared out the land too. I'm wondering if someone bought that land and are making some sort of farm out of it."

John stepped outside through the front door of his home, out onto the deck and raised the spyglass up to his eye and adjusted it for the distance.

He scanned the land on the opposite side of the river, watching men come and go. Wagons with material were being towed into the construction site by horses. Men were swinging axes and cutting down trees. Men were digging soil out of the ground with shovels. Other men were loading that soil onto more wagons and towing out the soil from the site. John watched the men work for another moment, when he saw a man through the spyglass that looked very familiar. The man stood back and watched as the foundation was being dug out, when he was accompanied by a second man whom John instantly recognized.

It was James Hackenberry and Charles Sanderlin.

John watched as the two realtors looked at the construction site from a safe distance. A third man approached them and spoke to them, pointing out something in the pit's foundation that was being dug out.

"Sons of bitches," said John. "Sons of bitches!"

John closed the spy glass and walked back into his home from the front door.

"What did you see?" asked Martha.

"Those fucking realtors!"

"From town?"

"Yes."

"What about them?"

"They're overseeing the construction over there. They lied to me. They own that god damn property."

"What do you mean, they lied to you?"

"Look. I met them a few weeks back. James Hackenberry and Charles Sanderlin. They're from the east coast; Baltimore, I think it was. Maybe Boston, I can't remember for sure. But they have an office back in town and when I asked them about who owns that land on the opposite side of the river, they told me they didn't know who owns it."

"Well, how do you know it's them who owns it?"

"Why else would they be there, Martha?"

"Maybe they are selling it to the new owner."

"Nonsense. If that were the case, then why are they overseeing construction on the land? Wouldn't they just sell the land as is and just leave it at that?"

"Maybe John Murdock down the way knows something about it?" asked Martha.

"Maybe. That's a good point. I'm going to go take Boone and go ride to Murdock's place and talk with him for a bit. How are the kids?"

"They're doing fine. Margaret went over to Anna's home to spend the day with them."

"Did she take a horse from the barn?"

"She took Lady from the barn a couple of hours back and rode to town."

"Do we trust her to do that?"

"She will be fine, John."

"How about Ida?"

"Ida is fine. She is playing with her dolls Ollie, Ellen, and Kelly in the apple orchard. Probably sitting under one of the apple trees as she likes to. Just living her best life."

"Sometimes I feel like a father that's nonexistent in her life."

"You have a busy job with that orchard and working with the crew out there. And yet you still find time to be a husband and a father. You are doing fine," said Martha, getting up from the couch.

She walked over and hugged John by the side.

"I love you," said John.

"And I love you," she replied.

He kissed her forehead and hugged her back.

"Alright, I'm going to go over to Murdock's place. I'll be back in about an hour, a couple hours tops."

"Alright. Be careful. Take your pistol with you."

"I will."

They kissed briefly and then John walked out of the living room, through the back door in the kitchen. Walking outside, he went out to the root cellar first as the men were working on finishing it up.

"Guadalupe!" he yelled for his foreman.

"Yes?" said a voice coming up from the pit.

"I'm going to take Boone, ride down to Murdock's property. I'll be back in about a couple of hours."

"You need me to tag along with you?"

"No. It's fine. Stay here with the men and finish up on the root cellar. If you finish before I get back, start working on thinning out the trees in the orchard. Start on the west side row first. We're going to work our way from the house to the river."

"You got it, John. Don't forget to take a pistol with you."

"I got one."

John then turned and left the edge of the pit, walking over to the barn. He walked in and got Boone out of his stall. Setting up the saddle on him, John mounted the horse and left the barn with him. He went south on his property, down to a small trail that led to John Murdock's property. On the way there, he passed the old burial ground that was charred black from when he burned it not that long ago. Trees had fallen and turned to ash, along with everything else in what used to be a beautiful, small forest grove. John passed the old burial ground and crossed the river over an old rickety bridge that was built years ago. The bridge, however, led to John Murdock's house. An older man who lived in the area and had lived at this home for several years now. He was one of the first settlers in the area.

Murdock had owned the small piece of land south of John for nearly twenty-five years now. John had the pleasure of meeting old man Murdock at Mary's Pub in town around the time he moved into the area when he and his crewmen went into town for drinks in the first season after they had finished planting all the apple saplings into the ground.

John rode slowly for about half an hour past the bridge when John Murdock's property came into view from a distance. A small home he had constructed himself by hand along the river front. When John approached the property, he called out to old man Murdock.

"John! Can you hear me in there? It's Ashberger from up the road!"

There was no response. John thought that was curious, but then again, Murdock always had a hard time hearing the older he got. He rode up to the front of the home, getting off Boone and tying the reins to the wooden fence in the front of the property.

"John!" he yelled again, but again, there was no response from John Murdock.

"John, are you home?" He yelled as he walked up to the front door of the home.

John looked up as he walked up the steps and noticed that the door was unlatched and cracked open.

"John, are you in there?"

John pushed the door open, and the door squeaked on its hinges as it slowly swung open, revealing the living room. Furniture was tipped over and lying on its side on the floor. Books were knocked off the bookshelf and had fallen on the floor. Wood that used to be neatly stacked by the fireplace was tipped over and small logs were scattered about the living room floor, too.

"John, are you in here?" said John, who pulled his pistol from the holster.

John walked into the kitchen area and noticed a dried red substance staining the floor. He bent down and took a closer look and noticed that he was looking at blood that had dried on the floor. John looked up and saw that it seemed as if something that had been bleeding was dragged out of the back of the home, through the opened back door.

John stood back up and walked to the back door, following the trail of dried blood to the back of the house. It appeared as if something had been dragged along the dirt ground, judging by the drag marks in the loose soil that led to a hole in the ground that appeared to have been freshly broken. He looked over and saw two shovels lying on the ground next to the pile of broken soil.

John placed his pistol back into the holster, then took one of the shovels and stuck it into the broken ground, digging dirt out of it. The soil was loose and easy to remove, and John dug and dug until he hit a solid object with the shovel. John set the shovel aside and got down on his knees and started moving soil away from the object.

It didn't take long for him to move enough soil by hand to find the deceased body of John Murdock. John pulled Murdock's body up out of the soil by grabbing hold of his blue plaid shirt that was now stained with blood and mud. He could see that John had a large gash between his eyes that had split his head open. The wound had split John's head in two from front to back, and it was clear that he had died from the trauma of the blow. John Murdock had been murdered.

When John saw the body and the wound on his head, he fell backwards into the shallow grave. Sitting at the feet of John Murdock with his back and shoulders propped up against the solid side of the shallow grave. He sat there for a moment, trying to sort things out and when the last time was that he had seen old man Murdock alive. It had been a while. However, because the body wasn't too decomposed, it looked as if old man Murdock was killed just recently. Based on the type of wound to his head, John suspected that he was killed by the Utes.

John got up and stepped out of the shallow grave and walked back into Murdock's house. John looked around the house to see if anything was missing from the home. All the valuables looked as if they were there, including the set of gold coins Murdock kept hidden behind some books on the shelf in the living room. Since Murdock wasn't going to be using these anymore, John pocketed the coins for himself and continued to walk around the home. His pistol was drawn again from his holster as he moved about the home.

There were, however, some things that were missing from the home. John knew Murdock had rifles and shotguns stored in the home that were no longer there.

"God damn it, now they have more weapons," said John, assuming the Utes had taken them.

He left the home through the front door and went back to his horse. Untying the animal from the wooden fence post, he mounted Boone and took off for the town as fast as he could. The dirt road leading from Murdock's place took John to the town of Montrose, coming into the town from the southwest side. John rode hard all the way to this point, entering the town in ten minutes' time from Murdock's property. He rode all the way to the Sheriff's office in town.

Once he got there, he got off his horse and tied the reins to the hitching post in front of the sheriff's office. John quickly walked into the office and saw Sheriff Walt Jones starting a fire in the fireplace of the main room that held his desk, next to the jail cells.

"Good evening, John. How are you doing?" said the sheriff, as he lit the fire and stood back up, walking over to his desk.

"Not good," replied John.

"What's wrong?"

"I just came from old man Murdock's place."

"What?" said the sheriff as he sat down at his desk.

"I said, I just came from old man Murdock's," said John, coming in and sitting in the chair on the opposite side of the sheriff's desk.

"Okay."

"He's dead."

"Who is dead?"

"John Murdock."

"He's dead?"

"Yes."

"How do you know?"

"I went there to talk to him about the construction that is going on at the property across the river from my place. If he knew anything about it. Went in and the front door of the house was opened slightly. I went inside his home, and there was blood on the floor inside the house. Looked like he was killed in the home, dragged to the back door, then dragged out of his house where he was buried in a shallow grave in the backyard."

"Interesting."

"It looks like it had just recently happened, too."

"How did he die?"

"I would guess a fucking hatchet to the forehead. Split his skull clean in two from front to back."

"What did you do with the body?"

"I left it there in the grave that was dug for him."

"Then what happened?"

"I went back inside and had a look around. Looks as if there were weapons stolen, too, rifles and shotguns."

"Indians then."

"How do you know?"

"That sounds like an Indian attack to me, John. They are getting bolder and more brazen these days around Montrose. The wound to the forehead probably was, in fact, a hatchet blow. I'm a bit surprised they didn't take his scalp, although from the sounds of it, it doesn't sound like a prized possession if his head was split in two from the blow."

"And what about the weapons?"

"What about them?" asked the sheriff.

"What do we do about them? I know for a fact he had two rifles and two shotguns in that house."

"They're gone, John. You're not gonna be able to retrieve those. I wouldn't worry about them."

"What the hell are you talking about?"

"The Indians probably have them. They're gone. You'll never see them again."

"And that's not a problem?"

"Well, of course it's a problem, John. But what are you going to do about it? Look, I told you to arm yourself and your men should arm themselves too. Those Indians are going to come back again. If I had to guess, they killed Murdock and now they are probably going to come for you and your family, too."

"So, help me then, goddamn it!"

"I can't just be at your place all the time, John. I have work to do for the citizens of Montrose County all over. If I spent all my time at your place, then it gives criminals free range to go where they please and do what they want. We live in a society of law and order, John."

"So, what do I do then?"

"Kill the Indians. Get them before they get you. Kill an Indian, save a man."

"It's not that easy. They come onto my property. Yes, I will kill them. But I'm not going to go out and hunt them down and start a fight."

"Even though they killed three of your guys so far, John?"

"We aren't the law or militia. We're farmers, sheriff. Yeah, if they come and start something, I'll kill as many of them as I can."

"Someday you're going to wake up, John, and not let those Indians push you around like that."

"I just want to run my farm with no trouble. For five years we've worked now and now we're close to a payday. I'm not here to start a war," said John, standing up from the chair and walking out of the sheriff's office.

"But the war is already here, John. You don't seem to understand that."

"Are you going to take care of John's body?"

"Why? Just leave the dead lay where they are. He's buried on the property. I'm sure that's where he wants to be, anyway."

"And you're not going to look into it?"

"I don't need to. It's obvious it was the Indians that did it. You said so yourself, John. He got his skull split open like a goddamn chicken egg with a hatchet. Sounds Indian to me."

John turned and left the Sheriff's office, disgusted and tired of dealing with Sheriff Jones. He walked up to his horse and untied the reins from the hitching post and was about to mount Boone when he looked up and saw the realtor's office, with the bright gold paint on the glass pane in the front of the office. John tied his horse back up to the hitching post and walked down to the realtor's office. Knocking on the front door of the office belonging to James Hackenberry and Charles Sanderlin. John waited for a moment when the door was answered by Charles.

"Oh, Mr. Ashberger. Can I help you with something?" asked Charles.

"Coming by to let you know that John Murdock is dead," said John.

"Dead?" replied Charles.

"Yes. Indians killed him, I think. Drove a hatchet between his eyes and split his skull in two."

"Did he own that small river front property just south of you?"

"He did."

"Oh yes. I know Murdock. Not a very big property he owned, but still a beautiful location. How unfortunate. He was a good man, too. He meant no harm to no one."

"I agree. He never did mean harm to anyone. But that's not all I'm here for. I have come to ask you a question. Who owns the land across the river from me?" asked John.

Charles looked back into the office, and then turned and looked at John again.

"We aren't sure who owns that property," replied Charles.

"Fucking bullshit. I saw you and your business partner there near the grounds, where they are digging a foundation out of the ground near the river. You two were overseeing the beginning of some construction and building."

"John, please come inside and let's talk about this like men. Come," said Charles, motioning with his hands and inviting John into the office.

John walked in with Charles and sat in a chair on the other side of Charle's desk. James was here at his desk, and he looked up and saw John there in the office.

"John, how are you doing?" he asked him.

"I'd be doing good if I get some god damn truthful answers from you two. I asked you a question, Charles, who is building on that piece of land across the river from me?"

"John, we don't know who is building on it. All we have been given was the task of overseeing the construction of a building there," said James.

"What kind of building?"

"A plantation resort."

"A fucking home, huh?"

"Not a home. A plantation resort. Something bigger than what you would call a home."

"Tell me, how do the realtors of the county not know who owns one of the largest pieces of land in the area? Let alone, who is building a plantation on it?"

"You ask a lot of questions, John, and I'm telling you, I don't know who owns that land. We were only asked to oversee the building site on the land."

"Who asked you to oversee it?"

"That's confidential, John."

"Confidential."

"Yes. That's right. I can't disclose that information. It's private."

"Why do I get the feeling I'm getting fucked over here?"

"No one is fucking you over, John. Trust me," said James.

"Mr. Ashberger, rest assured when I say this, I mean it. Your land is safe. Nothing will happen to it while you are there, and nothing will happen to you."

At that moment, the front door opened, and a young man ran into the office.

"Mr. Sanderlin, the Indians attacked us and killed three of our crewmen while we worked this morning!" said the young man.

"Oh, William. It's good to see you, son. We were just meeting with Mr. Ashberger. Now Mr. Ashberger owns the property across the river from where the crew is working."

"So, they're going to be like your neighbors, then?" asked the young man.

'What are you here for, William?" asked James.

"Just letting you know that Mack, Elmer, and Peter are dead. The Indians got them while they were clearing out trees from the land."

"Well, that is a shame."

"We killed one of them. Knocked him off his horse and smashed his head in with a hammer, sir."

"Good. An eye for an eye then," said Charles. "William, go back to the site and tell the men to continue working. James and I will be there soon to see how things are going, and to address any of the crew's concerns."

"What should I do with the dead Indian?" asked the young man.

"Just burn it. I don't have time to deal with Indians today."

"Yes sir," said William, as he turned and left the office.

"Now why would he ask if we were going to be neighbors?" asked John.

Charles laughed. "A confused young man, John. Probably the anxiety of the Indian attack had a lot to do with not thinking clearly. That's why James and I have to be out there constantly so that the boys stay on task. Now, if you don't mind Mr. Ashberger, James and I need to get out to that job site and see what is happening and what we are going to do with these three dead men. As you know, the Indians are turning into being a real problem around here."

"Yes, I understand," said John, skeptical of both Charles and James, but both the realtors had gotten up from their desks and were preparing to leave.

"I'm sorry for having to cut our visit so short, John. Please feel free to come back any time for a visit."

"Thank you," said John, standing up and leaving the office.

The two realtors watched from the office window as John walked back to his horse at the hitching post in front of the Sheriff's office and untied the animal. He mounted the horse and turned and rode through the town, down the road that led out of town to his property.

"That son of a bitch is asking too many questions," said James.

"I agree, James. God damn those Indians," said Charles.

"They are becoming a nuisance. But so is John now. It's fine if he just sticks to his apples, but with him nosing around the job site and keeping an eye on things... The one thing we can't let him know, Charles, is that we are the owners of that property, and we are building on that site. When he finds that out, there is no way we are going to obtain his property without killing him and everyone there on the land."

"Perhaps that is the way we must go anyway, James. Perhaps we don't have any other option. I'm just saying, it is something that we should seriously consider. John Ashberger is standing between us and a consistent healthy pay day."

Chapter 13: Taking a Prisoner

John rode back to his property after having visited the realtors in town. Getting no resolution from the sheriff regarding Murdock's death either and being shunned by the realtors in town put him in a bad mood. While John rode onto his property, on his way to the barn, he saw his youngest daughter Ida playing with her dolls. She was sitting under an apple tree in the orchard by the house, as she loved to do. John rode Boone over to her.

"Hi papa," said Ida, looking up from her dolls under the apple tree.

"Hi baby. How are you doing " replied John, as he got off his horse.

"I'm fine. Where did you go?"

"Oh, I went into town for a few things. But I'm back now. How are Ollie, Kelly, and Ellen doing here?"

"They're fine. We're all going to have apples for dessert after our dinner together. I made them chicken for their supper," she said.

"Great job cooking, baby. You did well. I'm sure Ollie, Kelly, and Ellen enjoyed it too," said John, coming over and sitting by her, propping his back up against the apple tree.

"Did you want some apple dessert too, papa?" asked Ida.

"I would love that, honey. Did Ollie, Kelly, and Ellen get enough apple too?"

"They did! Ollie always takes seconds, though," said Ida, picking up Ollie and taking a make-believe bite out of an apple, making chewing sounds for Ollie.

"Wow! Ollie takes big bites," said John.

Ida laughed. "He does."

John gave his youngest daughter a hug and a kiss on the head under the tree.

"How do you like living here, Ida, now that you've been here for a few years?" asked John.

"It's nice, papa. Pretty."

"Do you miss Florida at all?"

"I miss the oranges, but apples are pretty good, too."

"I just want you to know, and I don't know if I tell you guys this as much as I should, but I love you guys very much. Mom, Margaret, Anna. All of you guys mean a lot to me."

"Even Harry, papa?"

"Yes, even Harry."

"We love you too, papa."

"I appreciate hearing that. Sometimes my work and everything going on these days takes me away from what is most important. Which are you guys. And I'm sorry for that."

"It's okay, papa."

"Well, I gotta go meet with the Mexicans for a bit. Are you gonna be okay out here by yourself?"

"I'm not alone, papa. Ollie, Kelly, and Ellen are here with me."

"Of course. I'll see you at supper, baby. I love you," said John, standing up from the apple tree and walking back over to Boone.

"I love you too, papa. Ollie said he loves you, too," said Ida.

"What about Ellen and Kelly?"

Ida leaned into her stuffed animals as if they were whispering in her ear.

"They said they love you too," said Ida.

John smiled as he mounted Boone and took off for the root cellar. Riding on Boone, he got there as the men walked out of the root cellar through the ramp they had dug out. One of the last men that came out of the cellar was

Guadalupe. Dirt covered his exposed skin on his arms and face, and his shirt was covered in sweat and mud.

"I think we're all finished here, John," he said, walking up to him while John was still sitting on his horse.

"Did you end up using all the lumber?" asked John.

"Like you said, every last board and tie were used."

"Good," said John, dismounting Boone.

"Would you like to take a look with me?"

"Yes, show me how it turned out."

The two men walked down the dirt ramp into the root cellar. It was a warm day in Montrose. The thermometer back at the house read in the low 80s, but down in the root cellar it was cold.

"It is nice and cool down here. I would say twenty, maybe thirty degrees cooler than what it is up on the surface."

"It is. As you can see, we used the railroad ties to support the ceiling and used the river rocks to help keep the dirt compacted above us. All the four-by-four boards are used on the sides of the cellar. Some of the river rocks are also packed into the walls of the cellar, to help support as well. But all the lumber and all the river rocks were put to use, and we aren't leaving anything behind unused. This room should be able to store our harvest easily this fall."

"Great work, Guadalupe."

"Did you go into town, John?"

"After I left Murdock's place I did."

"How is Murdock doing?"

"He's dead," said John, resting his back up against one of the four by fours against the wall.

"I'm sorry. Did you say he's dead?" asked Guadalupe.

"He is. Found his body in a shallow grave on his property behind his home. Fucking hatchet buried between his eyes. His skull was split in half from front to back. Felt like if I moved him even an inch, his fucking brain was going to fall out of his head."

"My God."

"So, I went back inside and checked the house to see if anything was missing and all of his rifles and shotguns were gone."

"Did he have pistols too, John?"

"I never knew Murdock to use a pistol. I just remember seeing him with that rifle he carried around with him everywhere he went."

"Do you think it was the Indians, John?"

"I guess. I don't know, Guadalupe. The sheriff didn't seem interested in investigating the murder. If you don't mind, can you and Roman come with me? I'm going to get his body out of that grave and give him a proper burial in my family plot."

"I don't mind, John. I can tell Roman, and we can help load him up and bring him over. You gonna tie the wagon to your horse?"

"I am. But I'm not so convinced it was the Indians, Guadalupe. I think there is more to it than just that."

"What do you mean?"

"I think those realtors in town are up to something. I just don't know what yet. I stopped by their office after leaving the sheriff's office."

"Why?"

"I didn't tell you this before I left for Murdock's place earlier, but I had a look through the spyglass from the deck of the house and saw them both overseeing the job site across the river. Like how supervisors would."

"Are you serious?"

"I sure am. Went in their office and they are denying it, but I think they own that land, and I think they are building something big there."

"Those men who are digging and clearing out that land, they are staying on the land too, John. The men and I can hear them at night. Drinking, laughing, talking. While we sleep, they are drinking."

"I know those two fucking realtors own that land, Guadalupe. Feels like they are up to something. Between them and the goddamn Indians, I don't know who we should be watching our backs against."

"Both of them, John. It's us against all of them."

"Yeah, it's certainly starting to feel like that. Well, come on. Let's go get Murdock's body."

The two men left the root cellar together. John mounted his horse while Guadalupe walked over to Roman, pulling him aside and telling him what was going on. Both the men walked over to where the wagon was, and John joined them. They helped set the horse up to the wagon and then jumped onto the back of the wagon while John took off and rode to Murdock's property.

A short time later, they made it there and went to the back of the house, where Murdock's shallow grave was. They lifted his body from the ground and set it up on the wagon, taking it back to John's family grave site on his property. Before they left, they took the two shovels that were still lying on the ground with them. Once they got back to John's family grave site, both Guadalupe and Ramon jumped off the wagon and grabbed the shovels. John got off Boone and walked over to the corner of the plot, pointing to where he wanted John Murdock's body to go. The two men started digging, while John looked over the edge of the gravesite and watched as the men across the river kept working on the land, removing soil from the foundation they were digging up, and removing trees from the property and burning the brush.

"Guadalupe," said John.

"Yes?"

John turned around and looked at Guadalupe.

"I have an idea."

*   *   *   *

A large campfire was roaring in the camp on the opposite side of the river from John's property in the late evening hours. The men working for Hackenberry and Sanderlin were finished with their work for the day, and as true as Guadalupe had said the night before, most of them were drunk again tonight as they are most nights. They passed around bottles of whiskey while holding inappropriate conversations with one another. The only difference this evening was that John took notice and planned to finally find out who owned the property on the opposite side of the river from him.

"So, then I told the bitch, if you're not going to do it, then just get the fuck back to Tennessee!" said one of the men, as a group of them all laughed along with him around the fire.

"Boy Frank, you told her! What did she do then?" asked one of the younger men there.

"Well, the bitch left!" said Frank, taking another drink from the bottle of whiskey in his hand.

The group of drunk men erupted in laughter around the fire.

While the realtor's workers were drinking and enjoying their company, John Ashberger, along with Guadalupe and four of his crewmen, used the darkness of the night as a cover to cross the river quietly. They walked upstream a short distance and put the raft into the river. Using the current, they pushed themselves off into the water and crossed to the other side. Once on the side of the realtors, John and his men snuck up on the drunk workers around the campfire, careful not to expose themselves from the darkness into the light of the fire.

"Have you heard if she made it back to Tennessee?" asked one of the men.

"Nah, I ain't hear if she made it back yet or not. To be honest, I don't really give a shit either," said the drunk.

"What's back in Tennessee?"

"The hell if I know. She just always talked about Tennessee when she was around."

"How did you meet her in the first place, Frank?"

"We met at the tavern in town when we first got here a couple of weeks back."

"Frank, you're too much." Laughed one man. "There ain't no way you're bangin' a bitch after having just met her in two weeks' time."

"Well, she could have been a whore!" said Frank, debating his farfetched tale with the group.

"You're so full of shit, Frank. I'm gonna go take a piss. I'll be right back," said one of the younger men, as he stood up from the group. Turning around, he nearly lost his balance and fell over, when he gathered himself and started walking into the darkness.

"You need someone to hold your hand? Frank can help you out," said one of the men.

All the men around the fire laughed out loud, some falling down onto the ground and laughing in the dirt.

"You can eat shit, Martin!" yelled Frank.

The young man stopped and came back to one of the men by the fire, handing him the bottle of whiskey he had been drinking from. The man promptly grabbed the bottle from the younger man and took a long drink. The young man then walked over to just outside of the light of the campfire, around a large rock and was unbuttoning his trousers when he felt a blunt object strike him in the back of the head. His legs bent and his body went limp as he lost consciousness and tumbled to the ground. The sound of his grunt from the blow to the back of the head and his body falling onto the ground was masked by the laughter of the drunk men at the fire.

"Pick him up and bring him with us," said John to his men with him.

Guadalupe and Roman lifted the man up by the arms and carried his body back through the bushes in the darkness, quietly, back to the raft. They set him down on the raft and when everyone was on board, John pushed the raft off and crossed over the river back to his property. When they were across the river, the men carried the young man off the raft and up to the wagon that was ready to take him back to the house. After loading him up on the back of the wagon, John's crew jumped up and sat down on the wagon.

Guadalupe tied the young man's hands behind his back and then tied his feet together. He then used a towel to tie around the man's head, covering his mouth up to gag him. Not that the men from across the river would be able to hear him, anyway. When Guadalupe was finished tying the young man up, he sat down in the wagon too and John mounted the horse and quietly drove the wagon back to the house. Instead of going into the house, though, John directed the men to bring the young man into the root cellar to which they did. They carried him down the dug-out ramp and into the cellar underground. John lit a torch in the room that lit the cellar up with light while the men propped the young man up against the side of the wall.

"Guadalupe, get one jar of water up by the house and bring it down here," said John.

Guadalupe did what he was told and went back up to the house, grabbing one of the clay jars of fresh water and bringing it back down into the cellar. John took the jar from him, removed the lid, and poured cold water onto the young man, who moments later came to as the ice-cold water hit him in the face and chest, falling into his lap. The young man started moaning and shaking his head and body.

"Oh good, you're awake," said John.

The young man moaned some more. Gagged from speaking by the towel in his mouth.

"I'll make a deal with you. I just want to ask you a few questions and a young man such as yourself I figure, would probably know the answers to my questions. You see, I just want to know a couple of things. Answer my questions, then I'll take you back and everything will be okay. You don't answer my questions though, I'll be sure to just put a bullet between your eyes and use your body as fertilizer around here. You understand?"

The young man was wide eyed now, shaking his head up and down, indicating that he understood.

"Good," said John, as he reached around the young man's head and untied the gag, removing the towel from his mouth.

"Who are you?" asked the young man.

"I don't think you are the one to be asking me questions right now, you understand?"

"Yes, sir."

"Now, tell me, what is your name, young man?"

"Edward."

"Edward. That's a good name. I had a cousin named Edward before. Lives back in Philadelphia."

"Pennsylvania?" asked Edward, with fear and apprehension in his voice.

"No, Florida, you dumb fuck. Yes, Pennsylvania. Now, what are you working on at that property by the river?"

"Digging a foundation, sir."

"A foundation for what?"

"I don't know."

"How do you not know?"

"I just don't."

"You know what I don't know?" asked John.

"What?"

"Which one of these chambers in this pistol has a round in it?" he said, taking out his pistol from his holster. "Do you care to find out?"

John pointed the pistol down at the young man's knee and pulled the trigger.

Click! The gun didn't fire.

"Well then, looks like that chamber didn't have a round in it," said John.

"We're building a plantation resort, sir! Like a big building," said the young man, shivering from his wet clothes in the cold cellar.

"A plantation resort?"

"Yes, some sort of four leveled plantation that's supposed to be a resort, with a brothel inside and tavern and restaurant and a steam room."

"Why are you clearing out the other part of land there, then?"

"The land around the resort is supposed to be a golf course. I don't know what that is, but we were just told to clear out the land of trees, bushes, large rocks, just everything. Twenty thousand feet worth of land. Then plant some grass."

"Twenty thousand?" said one of John's crewmen unconsciously.

"You're doing good, Edward. I appreciate you answering questions for me like that. Now, if you know that much about the project that you're working on over there, then you surely know who owns that property too, yes?"

"I don't know who does, sir," said the young man.

John pointed the gun down at the young man's genitals and pulled the trigger.

Click! Nothing happened, and the man flinched in anticipation of being shot.

"Looks like there was nothing in that chamber, too. Want to see if there is anything in the third chamber?" asked John.

"Sir, I can't say!"

"Why can't you say?"

"They'll kill me."

"Who will?"

"The two."

"What two?

The young man grew more and more nervous while speaking with John, his breathing grew heavier as the anxiety took over his physical functions.

"James. And Charles."

"The realtors in town?"

"Yes."

"They own that property?"

"Yes."

"And they're the ones that are building a resort and golf course on the land?"

"Yes. They were telling Arthur, our foreman for our group, that they want to create a site that will draw more people out to the area. Famous people, sir. Like politicians and the rich. They're treating it like a vacation land here."

"Alright. When do they plan on being finished with their project?"

"I don't know. It sounds like it's a long-term project, but as soon as we're done digging into the ground, we're starting to build the plantation resort. They talked about buying out the land across the river from their land, and if they can't buy it out, then doing whatever they had to do to get the land."

"Whatever they had to do?" asked John.

"Yes, sir. I don't know what they meant by that, but I do know they talk about wanting all the land on each side of the river. They also talk about owning all the property in town, but the Indians keep getting in the way of them obtaining the land. There's also some farmer across the river that is in their way of getting that land, too. They already own most of the gold claims for the mining up in the mountains."

"How many men are working on the job site?"

"About thirty of us for now, but there will be more on the way. They're coming in from the east coast. With more supplies to build the resort."

"Alright. You did good, Edward. Do you have a family?"

"I have my momma back in Connecticut, sir."

"And your father?"

"He died in the war when I was a young boy."

"Sure, he did. And children of your own?"

"No, sir. No children."

"Wife?"

"No wife, sir."

"Anyone else other than your momma in your life?"

"No sir, it's just her."

"So why you come out here from Connecticut?"

"I knew a guy who knew the realtors. Promised me the pay was gonna be good, and that I could mine for gold up in the mountains in one of their mines for some extra income, too."

"How often do you drink and have a bonfire on the land?" asked John.

"Practically every night, sir."

"Aren't you afraid of Indians?"

"I suppose, but not too much. There aren't too many of them and they usually attack at night when we sleep. They scalped Louis and killed him while he slept last week. Then just recently they attacked during the day too, but they seem to enjoy attacking us at night. So, when the fire is put out and we go to bed, we always sleep with one eye open."

"That's a good idea. Speaking of one eye," said John, raising his pistol up to the young man's right eye and pulling the trigger.

The pistol fired, sending a round through the young man's eye, exiting out of the back of his head. The young man slouched over and died there in the cellar.

"Looked like that chamber had a round in it," said John as he stood up from his crouched stance. "Get rid of the body. I don't care where you dump him off. He told us everything we needed to know."

"Sounds like the Indians and the realtors are going to be a problem," said Guadalupe.

"I knew those goddamn realtors were lying to me, the sons of bitches. Roman scalp the boy and then dump his body off on the bank of the river on their side of the land. Make it look like the Indian's got him."

"Yes, sir," said Roman, as he took a knife out from his belt and slowly filleted the young man's scalp, revealing the red stained top half of his white skull.

"We only have one choice, it seems, Guadalupe. We're going to have to kill them before they kill us. I'll never sell this land. This land we worked so hard for... This land I will give to my daughters. And they to their sons and daughters. And then to their sons and daughters. I will die for this land if I must. I will never sell this land or let it fall into the hands of another. The land will not be sold in perpetuity, for the land is mine!"

Chapter 14: The Cat is Out of the Bag

In the early hours of the morning, the men of James and Charle's job site woke up in the first light of the new day. Some had headaches from drinking the night before, while others were still dizzy from drinking too much. One of the workers went to the edge of the river to relieve himself before starting his day. In the light of the early morning, he glanced upstream and saw the lifeless body of Edward, his colleague. He was lying face down in the water. His scalp was missing from the top of his head, and he had a hole through his right eye that ran through his head and out the back. The man turned and ran back to the camp, alerting the foreman of his discovery.

A group of the men who were awake ran to the edge of the river to have a look for themselves. Following them all was a tall man. The skin of his hands was dried and cracked from years of working construction. He had a long gray hair and a gray beard as well. Scars adorned the exposed skin on his face that wasn't covered with hair. He wore a large cowboy style hat, made of straw, with a brim that covered his face in the sunlight.

"What the fuck is the commotion over here?" said Robert Steele, the foreman.

"Edward, sir. He's dead. Looks like the Indians got him," said one of the men in the group, circling the body.

"Goddamn, I hate those Indians. When was the last time Edward was seen?"

"Last night, I guess. He got up to go piss, and I forgot about him. We all forgot about him, sir."

"Great. We're not going to have any men left over to work this job if you sons of bitches aren't more careful about the Indians around here. As bad as it is, now I need to go tell Hackenberry and Sanderlin that we lost another boy on the site."

"What do we do with him, sir?"

"Just push him into the river. Unless you want to take the time to bury his body, but I wouldn't waste the time digging a grave. We have work to do on that foundation, and I still have to clear most of the land."

"What are you going to do, sir?"

"I'm headed to town. Notify James and Charles. In the meantime, get back to work and kick that body into the river."

Robert turned around and walked back to the camp. A couple of the men helped pick Edward up and pushed his lifeless body out into the river. He floated lifelessly and slowly down the river. It was the last time anyone, including his momma back in Connecticut, would ever see Edward.

The men left the riverside, while some men relieved themselves in the river before they went back. They all eventually went back to their tents and got ready for the working day. Grabbing their shovels, the men went back to work on digging out the foundation of the resort. A couple of the men grabbed axes and went out into the field to continue cutting down trees for the future golf course, too.

Robert Steele mounted one of the horses at the job site and rode up to the men in the pit first before leaving the property to head into town.

"While I'm gone, David is in charge of the construction. Continue digging out the foundation and I'll be back later this morning after I'm finished talking with James and Charles. Watch out for the Indians around here, too. They're getting ballsier as each day goes by. Don't hesitate to kill them if you get the chance."

With that, Robert left the job site and rode into town to speak with James and Charles at their office. It didn't take him long until he rode into the southeastern part of the town. The streets were damaged from heavy rain a few days before, leaving large gashes from horse hooves and wagon wheels on the road. Robert slowed the horse down to a steady gallop into the town. Some of the townsfolk walking along the sidewalks and through the street stopped and kept an eye on him as he rode into town.

Robert had a reputation in Montrose. Often, he and some men that he worked with from the job site would get drunk at the local tavern and start fights unprovoked. One evening, just recently, they even held a man down on a table in the tavern and Robert used his knife to cut the man's tongue out. For some reason, the sheriff did nothing about it and the townsfolk never knew why, as there were at least a dozen witnesses to the assault. This wasn't the only thing that Robert had done that intimidated the town folk. There was another time that he and a couple of men from the job site took a woman to the top of a roof and threw her off the roof into an alley, killing her. The sheriff investigated that, but no arrests were ever made. Sheriff Jones always said there wasn't enough evidence to prove Robert, or his men had ever done such a thing, and the witnesses who saw them do these things were threatened by the work crew not to talk about it or else they too could find a knife jammed through their necks or a bullet in their heads.

Robert rode up to the office of Hackenberry and Sanderlin, where he dismounted his horse and tied the reins to the hitching post. He walked up to the office door and opened it, letting himself inside the office area. Inside was Charles Sanderlin, by himself, reading from his bible at his desk. Charles looked up, expecting to see James coming in the morning to the office, but instead saw Robert.

"Oh, Mr. Steele. To what do I owe this unexpected visit this morning?" said Charles, looking up and removing his glasses from his face.

"Fucking Indians killed another one of our boys. Edward, sir," said Robert.

"Oh, dear. I liked Edward as well. He was a young boy that showed a lot of promise. What happened?"

"Happened during the night again. The men think he went to go piss in the river but was jumped and killed by those goddamn savages. They found his body this morning. Scalp peeled off like a goddamn potato."

"What did you do with the body?"

"Told the men to just float it downstream and let the river take it away."

"And what am I to tell his mother now?"

"We don't have time to dig a grave, Charles," said Robert, sitting down in the chair opposite side of the desk to him. "We're already behind schedule in clearing out that land. You guys couldn't have picked an easier piece of land to build what you got in mind."

"The location is most ideal, my friend. And you are being paid handsomely. Now I suppose that the young boy is dead, you'll get a bigger portion for yourself, and flowers for his mother, who lost a son out here in the wild west."

"That's a reason why I'm not too upset about losing another worker, yes."

"Where are you at in breaking the ground for the foundation?"

"Close. Probably by the end of the week, we'll have all the soil removed and can start pouring cement to make a foundation."

"That is good news. I would like to get this resort built before the snow comes. At least the main structure and the walls up. We can work on the inside during the winter, but we certainly need the foundation poured, and the walls put up. This is going to be a four-level building, Robert. I should hope by next week we can start construction on the site."

"And what about the golf course?"

"The land is still to be cleared out of brush and wood. You're asking for a lot of land to be cleared out and I'm losing men on a day-to-day basis to Indian attacks."

"We need the resort built first. When the land is finally cleared out, spread the grass seed and then move those men to the construction of the building. We will deal with the golf course after its seed is planted."

"What would be helpful is if you could take care of the fucking Indians for us."

"Oh yes. The Indians. Aren't they just a nuisance? They will be dealt with. Sheriff Jones allegedly has a crew of men that are going to wipe them out and get them out of our way."

"Allegedly? You haven't met these men yet?"

"I have not, Robert."

"So, how do you trust him?"

"Because he is being paid handsomely, and if he wants what we are giving him, then he is going to do the job that we ask of him. Just like you and your crew."

"When will we get more men for the project?" asked Robert.

"James reached out to John at the office in Baltimore yesterday. We received a telegram back indicating that he had hired nearly twenty more men who are on their way as of this morning to participate in the festivities of building our resort."

"That's good to hear. And what about the farmer across the river?"

"A stubborn son of a bitch he is. James and I tried speaking with him a few times now, even offering to pay a decent price for his property, but alas, he and his family continue to live there," said Charles, getting up from his chair to go brew a pot of early morning tea.

"So, what are you going to do about that?"

"I'm afraid we must resort to what one would do if their pantry was raided by mice, Robert. You kill the mice."

"Whatever you two have to do, just as long as I get paid in the end."

"Oh, you will be. Everyone will be paid very well. This resort is going to change the west as we know it. It will no longer be known as a wild west, but a place for the elite and wealthy to go for a rest. We're going to change this town, Robert. Make it better. Look at the people in the street, wandering through mud and horse shit everywhere they go. We're going to colonize this town and make it something great. Everyone here will be rich. Because of us."

"So, is the sheriff going to handle the Indians, then?"

"He will, and you all have my permission to shoot them on sight," said Charles.

"Sounds good to me," said Robert.

"Is there anything more that I can help you with, or answer for you?" asked Charles.

"No, sir. Just thought I would let you know about Edward and see where we are with your plans."

"Well then, I will have John back in Baltimore send his mother in Connecticut some flowers then."

Robert stood up and walked back out of the realtor's office, out to his horse. He untied the animal from the hitching post, mounted it, and rode out of town. On the way out of the town, he passed the sheriff's office, observing the sheriff sitting in a chair outside along the sidewalk. As he rode by, he tipped his cap and greeted the sheriff with a stern look on his face. The sheriff, in return, tipped his hat back to him. Robert then rode out of the town, back to the job site, to resume working on the foundation of the plantation resort.

The sheriff continued rocking in a rocking chair there in front of his office, watching people wander to and from throughout the town. He reached into his jacket and took a cigar out from the inside pocket, sticking it into his mouth. He took a match from his pant pocket and struck it, igniting the match and lighting the cigar with it. He discarded the burned match on the ground, sat back and puffed on the cigar when four horses with riders on them rode up to the front of his office. All four men got off their horses and tied the reins to the hitching post, then walked up to the sheriff on the sidewalk to speak with him.

"You look like you got a pretty laid-back job here in Montrose?" said one man to him.

"It's not too bad," said Sheriff Jones, standing up from his rocking chair, still puffing on his cigar.

"I still can't believe they made you sheriff in this county. What a bunch of fuckin' idiots," said the man.

Sheriff Jones laughed. "You know, part of me always wished you had caught a musket ball between the eyes. Or a cannon ball. I still can't believe you made it out of the battle of Peach Tree Creek alive."

"Well, if it wasn't for you, sheriff, I probably wouldn't have."

"How are you doing, Harry?" asked the sheriff as he shook his hand.

"Doing just fine, Walt. Just fine. You were quick to cash in on these favors I owed you. I figured after we killed the old man down by the river, my debt was paid off to you."

"After what I went through to save your life from Admiral Porter at Peach Tree and then again at the Siege of Petersburg, I figure just one job isn't enough for a repayment. The same with you, Clarence."

"Well, that's why we're here. And Colorado is such a beautiful part of the country. So much out here has not been explored yet. God only knows what all there is to offer in this part of the country," said Harry.

"There's plenty to offer around these parts. Come sit with me inside my office, and I'll explain it all to you," said the sheriff, leading the four men into the office.

Once they were all inside, he sat at his desk while each man found a seat in the office. Clarence and Harry sat on the opposite side of the desk from Sheriff Jones, as their two friends stood up and stood against the wall by the door.

"Now, you two want the good news?"

"What is that, Walt?"

"I got you guys a deal."

"A deal?"

"That's right. You may be out here because you owe me a favor, but the realtors are also going to pay us handsomely."

"So, let me get this straight, Walt. Debts paid in full and we're getting money for it?"

"Now, I didn't say anything about money."

"What other kind of payment are you referring to then?"

"Gold."

"Gold?"

"That's right. For you two. For the two men you brought here today. A decent gold claim up in the San Juan Mountains for you to mine for all the gold you can get out of it."

"Yeah, but there's always a catch with you, you son of a bitch. What is it?" asked Clarence.

"Can't you just see that I'm trying to do something nice for you boys? After all, we've been through in the war together."

"He's right, Walt. There's always a catch with you. A god damn stipulation. What is it?" asked Harry.

"Alright, you two bastards know me too well. There is a catch. I need your help with more than just fulfilling a couple of favors."

"And when were you planning on telling us about that?"

"All in due time, the work is simple. Especially for guys like us."

"Alright, what is it?"

"A couple of things, actually."

"God damn you, Walt."

"Listen up. We have simple work. We're getting paid to hunt down the Indians up in the north. Apparently, they keep coming down here and fucking with those men at the job site. Killing one a day, it sounds like. The more men they manage to kill, the more time it's going to take to get this job done, which means those fuckers will take longer to pay us back for our services."

"So, we kill the Indians then?" asked Clarence.

"Precisely. I would like to think we know what we're doing when it comes to that."

"I have a few more men that I know I can talk them into coming up here from Oklahoma. You guys have a telegram service here?"

"Yeah, we do, over at the courthouse."

"Great, we'll send them a telegram and get them on their way. They don't live far from the Colorado border too, so they could easily be here in a day's time."

"You gonna let them pick from your gold claim?"

"It's fine, Walt. From what I hear, there is plenty of gold up in those mountains. We'll get our fair share out of the mine, too."

"That's great to hear. There is one other thing, however."

"What is that?" asked Harry.

"Across the river from the job site, there is an apple orchard. The farmer and his family live there. A man named John Ashberger. He has a wife, and two of his kids live there. Allegedly, he has another daughter that is married to some slum living in a different area around here. I don't know much about them. But he also has a crew of Mexicans working with him. We burn the apple orchard down. Kill the Mexicans. Then kill the farmer and his family. Wife, children, even their god damn dog or cat if they have one. Nothing can be left alive on that property."

"Seems a little extreme, Walt. What'd they ever do to deserve that?" asked Clarence.

"Not any issue with them specifically. It's strictly just business."

"Sounds like we're killing a lot of folks around here, Walt."

"Indeed. But the reward will be well worth it."

"I suppose so."

"It will be. You'll mine so much gold from that mountain you won't know what to do with it all."

"So, what do you suggest we do first?"

"We ride north, gentlemen."

"Now?"

The sheriff smiled at the men with the cigar in his mouth.

"Not just yet. First, we go to the courthouse and send your friends a telegram to Oklahoma. When they arrive, then we ride north," said the sheriff.

"So, you mean to kill the Indians first?" asked Harry.

"The sooner we kill those god damn savages, the sooner those boys finish up on that land, and the sooner we get paid. It just leaves John, his family, and the Mexicans, and they will be easy to put into a grave. They don't have very many weapons or resources available to them. The Indians will be the hardest part. They're the ones with the weapons and warriors."

"You happen to have one of those cigars with you by chance?" asked Clarence.

"For you gentlemen, I have a whole box of them here in my desk," said the sheriff, opening a drawer along the side and reaching into it.

He pulled out four cigars for the four men and handed them out. He reached into his pocket and took out a small box of matches, tossing it on the desk for the men to use.

"Thanks, Walt. So, do we have a plan or just go in blazing guns?" asked Clarence.

"We should do what they do. Attack at night. I'll hand it to those savages. They know when the right time is to attack who they want to attack."

"At night? If they attack that work crew at night, then if we attacked at night, then there'd be no Indians there to kill," said one of the two other men.

"Shut up, Ned. But he's right, Walt. If those fuckers aren't there at night, then what's the point in going there?" asked Clarence, striking his match and lighting his cigar.

"If they aren't there at their camp, then who else would be there?" asked the sheriff.

"Are you talking about their families?" asked Harry.

"I am. Their women. Their children. Their animals. We kill them all first. Then we piss in their drinking water too."

"I am impressed, Walt. I never knew you were this kind of guy."

"When there is money or something important to me involved, I'll do what I have to."

"Won't that make the Indians angry?" asked Ned from the back of the room.

"God damn it, Ned, I told you to shut up. Stop talking, you dumb son of a bitch! But he does have a point again, Walt. When the Indians return, won't they be upset?"

"Well, sure they will be. We had just slaughtered their families and destroyed what little they have. Wouldn't you be pissed off, too?"

"How do you plan to handle that then, Walt?"

The sheriff opened another drawer at his desk, taking out a sheet of paper with a handwritten message already on it. He handed the note to Harry, who took the note and read it out loud.

"You killed my Mexicans, now I killed your family. John."

"After we're done killing them all and burning their camp down, and killing their wives and children, and their animals, we leave the note there in the camp."

"So, you're going to frame the farmer and his men?"

"Precisely. We let them kill each other. Makes our jobs a lot easier. Then whoever is left over, we kill them."

"Well by god, Walt. That plan might just be effective."

"If you're good with it, Clarence, the courthouse is just down the road over by the church and cemetery. Why don't you send out a telegram to your friends in Oklahoma to come out and visit us here in Colorado?"

"I'll go tell them right now," he said, standing up and walking out of the sheriff's office.

"So, what do you boys think of the cigars?" asked Sheriff Jones.

"Rich. Tastes like vanilla, too."

"They came from the realtors here in town. The two men we're working for. They spare no expense."

Chapter 15: A Midnight Raid

It took two full days' time for the men to get to town from Taloga, in northern Oklahoma. By the time Clarence had made it to the courthouse, sent out the message to the courthouse in Taloga, and the men were served their message, it was already late afternoon. In total, eight men rode out from Taloga, Oklahoma, to Montrose, Colorado. Men better known to locals as the Holt Boys Gang.

George Holt, their leader, was a man whose violent and thieving reputation preceded him everywhere he went in the state of Oklahoma. A bounty of nearly five hundred dollars was set on his head by the Washita County Courts in Oklahoma, however no one had ever gone to collect it as George was a man with a vicious and intemperate disposition in all things he did. Riding with him were seven other men, known to the locals as "the boys."

They all had attitudes just as bad as George as well. There was Frank Noles, Edward Stokes, and his little brother, Joseph Stokes, Arthur Green, Oscar Robinson, Carl Wilson, and Peter Martin. The men would work jobs around the Oklahoma area together. Where one went, together they all went. Their last bank robbery from Beaver County in Oklahoma allotted them nearly two hundred pounds of silver, a deposit from some silver mines from the state of Nevada. The previous bank robbery, they got away with nearly one hundred pounds of placer gold in Logan County, freshly panned from California. Needless to say, money wasn't a driving force for them anymore. If they wanted money, they would just go to the bank and take a withdrawal out in their own special way. What drew them out to Montrose this day was the opportunity to kill Indians. Like their friends, George Holt and the boys hated Indians. Any chance they got where they could kill an Indian, they took it. They believed in a world free of them. It was never known where their hatred for the Indians came from, other than they just hated them.

Holt and the boys made it into Montrose in the early afternoon a couple of days after they had received the telegram message from Clarence. They rode in on the town's main road, being led in the front by George himself, when he stopped for a moment and spoke with a younger woman walking by the sidewalk.

"Excuse me, ma'am," he said to a woman passing by. "Where is your sheriff's office?"

The woman pointed over in the direction where the sheriff's office was located, but never made eye contact with George or any of his men. They looked down at her as if she was nothing more than a piece of meat.

"Much obliged to you, ma'am. Where do you live?" he asked, as he spat on the ground in front of her.

"Here in the town, just down the road from here with my husband," she said.

"What is your name, miss?" asked George.

"Anna," said the young woman.

"Anna. That's a pretty name. How do you like living here?"

"It's beautiful here, but I worry about the town and the people that live here."

"It's not the only thing that's beautiful around here," said George, looking at her aggressively, making her uncomfortable. "Where is your husband?"

"He's back home, waiting for me to come back home."

"I see. What does he do for work?"

"He doesn't work either. He farms the land. We eat vegetables and then hunt our food."

"Wouldn't it make it easier if he worked for the railroad? Or opened his own shop here? Did something with his life?"

"He does well with his life, and I am appreciative of how hard he farms the land for us, sir."

"With all due respect, ma'am. It sounds like he's a coffee boiler. A man who'd rather just stand around the coffee pot than do anything to help. You want to know how I know this?"

"Why do you think that, sir?"

"Because he'd send his young bitch to town to do man's business."

"With all due respect, sir. How do you know what I am doing here in town?"

"Well, I suspect you are either doing one of two things. You're here in town on business. Either personal business, or you're whoring yourself out for a few dollars. And if that's the case, why don't you come back around this evening around eight at the local tavern here and I'll meet you there?"

"I need to go," said Anna.

"Of course you do. I'll be sure and see you around then, Anna," said George, pulling his horse back out into the dirt street.

His men followed close behind him and Anna continued to walk back to her home, to the safety of her husband Harry.

Holt and the gang rode a short distance into the town when they came across the sheriff's office. Riding up to the hitching post, they dismounted their horses and tied the reins to the post, then went inside the office. Sitting at his desk was Sheriff Jones, along with his friend Clarence, looking over a map of the county together that the Sheriff had spread open on his desktop. The two men looked up and saw the group of men walking into the office.

Clarence laughed and stood up from his chair.

"I'll be goddamned! George and the boys!" said Clarence, walking over to the men and shaking George's hand.

"Clarence Bell. I gotta say, I'm a bit surprised to have heard from you. I thought for sure someone would have driven a foot up your ass by now. If not that, the barrel of a shotgun and pulled the trigger at least."

Clarence laughed again. "No, not yet. Come here, I'd like you boys to meet an old friend of mine back from the war. His name is Walt Jones. He's the sheriff here in this county now."

"Sheriff?" asked George.

"That's right," said Sheriff Jones, standing up from his seat. "I am the sheriff in this town."

"We kill sheriffs," said George.

"Good. I like to hear that. But I'm going to ask you boys to direct your animosities towards someone else before you try to send me to an early grave."

"Alright. I'm listening," said George, sitting in the chair on the opposite side of Sheriff Jones' desk, leaning back in the chair and putting his boots up, knocking mud on his map in the process.

"If you don't mind, Mr. Holt, get your fuckin feet off my desk, please," said Sheriff Jones.

"Or what?"

Sheriff Jones pulled his pistol, aiming it at George. This action caused George's men to pull their pistols and aim it at the sheriff. George sat back, smiling at the sheriff.

"They'll kill ya where you stand. I don't give a fuck if Clarence knows who you are or not," said George.

"They may get the drop on me, but not before I put a bullet in your head and turn your fuckin head into a canoe."

George laughed. "Goddamn, I'll tell you something. I like you Sheriff Jones." He continued to laugh as he took his feet off the desk and stood up. "And I fuckin hate you law men. So, forgive me, I'm a bit taken back for having a soft spot in my heart for a lawman all of a sudden."

George extended his hand out to the sheriff.

"I'm George Holt. These are my boys," said George as he pointed out and named each man.

After he finished naming each man off, the sheriff holstered his pistol. George directed his gang to holster theirs as well.

"Walt Jones," said the sheriff, extending his arm out and shaking hands with George.

"This sack of shit here," Walt said, pointing to Clarence. "Told me that you got some work for us to do here. Of course, he would send a message to us to come out and do his work for him."

"Indeed, I do. I can see about getting you boys paid for your service, too."

"I'll make a deal with you. If you turn a blind eye for a bit, allow my men and I to rob the local bank here in town before we leave back to Oklahoma, then we'll take that as our pay. But we're here to kill some Indians."

"I like the sound of that, but I'm still going to make sure you boys are taken care of. You're certainly welcome to kill some Indians and some Mexicans. As far as the bank is concerned, you feel free to do what you will. Just let me know so I can be out of town when you do your thing, which is all I ask. That way, these people won't expect me to do something about it."

"I can do that. So, what are you looking at here?" asked George, looking down at the sheriff's desk.

"What you see here is a map of the county of Montrose. Come, sit down with me," said the sheriff as he sat down in his chair.

George sat down in a chair and pulled it over to the desk.

"North of Montrose, there is a town called Olathe. There is a band of Ute Indians that are north of us, camping out along the road where the river meets the road maybe about twenty minutes from here. They are making my employers' lives a living hell. Attacking their work crew during all hours of the night. Killing a man a day practically."

"So? Why does that concern us?"

"So, this is a problem that needs to be addressed before my employer loses any more men on their job site. Which is where you boys come in. Now I need men who are fearless and want to kill some Indians during the night hours. Women. Children. Even their god damn animals."

"Forgive me for asking, but where will the men be?"

"If they are there, then we'll engage them and kill them, too. However, they are more than likely going to be attacking the job site during the night as they always do."

"Easy victims, it sounds like. Should be able to kill some Indians. No problem then."

"Indeed. We go this evening. Find their campsite. Kill anything that moves there. And then come home. It's simple as that."

"Seems simple enough."

"Are you boys up for it?"

"Oh yeah, we'll be up for it. So long as you leave that bank unguarded for a little while."

"I'll hand you the keys to the bank myself."

"My men are tired from riding and need rest. They need some food, too."

"Go to the inn here in town. Tell them that you are my guests and to give you some rooms there. Get some rest. I'll send you some food and drink. I want to ride out at midnight tonight. That will be plenty of time to let the Indian men go out and do what they've been doing for the last month now."

"Alright. Gentlemen, get back to your horses," said George to his men.

They all left the office, with Clarence following them close behind. George stood up from his chair and said, "Midnight, we ride out?"

"At midnight we ride out," said the sheriff.

"I will see you an hour before the midnight hour, then."

"Sounds good to me. And George, it was a pleasure meeting you today."

"The pleasure was all mine, sheriff."

George then turned and walked out of the office. The sheriff stood up and walked over to a wooden cabinet, and unlocked it. He reached inside, pulling out rifles from it. He set the rifles down on the top of the desk and then went back and got bullets out of the cabinet as well. After setting the bullets down, he went back to the cabinet and pulled a large knife out with a sheath. He set the knife down on his desk and then sat back in his chair and waited for the evening to come.

*   *   *   *

The sheriff's office door opened and in walked George and his men, followed by Harry, Clarence and their two men that accompanied them earlier.

"We have a decent sized group with us now. I'm glad you all could make it," said the sheriff. "Did you boys get yourselves a nice meal and some rest this afternoon?"

"The hospitality from the inn owner was top level. You folks here in Montrose really know how to take care of your guests," replied George.

"That makes me happy to hear. Are you boys ready now?"

"Oh, I think so," replied George, as he removed his pistol and checked to make sure it was loaded.

"Here are some extra rifles for you and your men. Clarence, Harry, here are a couple more rifles for you as well. Bullets are on the desk here, too."

"Thank you, Walt."

"Gentlemen, if you are prepared and ready to go, then follow me," said the sheriff, standing up from his desk and walking out.

The group followed the sheriff out to their horses and mounted up. Each man carried a rifle or a pistol with them. They took off, following the sheriff, who led them north through Montrose. In the buildings they passed by, the innocent citizens watched as they rode through the night. Their path was lit by torches that were burning on the sides of the street, hanging off the pillars of most buildings. When they got out of town, their path was lit by the light of a full moon as they rode north towards the town of Olathe. After riding north for about ten minutes, they came upon a dancing light in the distance—a bonfire that could be seen from where the men rode over the hill in the valley.

Sheriff Jones slowed his pace and galloped easily into the area, careful not to make too much noise as they drew closer. Once he was halfway down the trail along the hill, he stopped. George rode up to his side to have a conversation with him.

"Right there. That fire up ahead there. That's the Indian's camp."

"We should send in one of my boys first to have a look around. Make sure the men aren't there."

"They aren't there."

"How do you know?"

"Because those fuckin chickenshits do their work by night. Every night. They aren't there."

"Just like we are, I suppose?"

"If they did their work by day, we would be here at 1:00 PM as God is my witness, George. Not 1:00 AM."

"You're certain they aren't there."

"No, they won't be."

"You fuck us here, then it's your life, sheriff."

"If I fuck with you boys, then it's all our lives here. Believe me, those savages aren't there, and the bitches and children are the only ones to be concerned about this evening."

Sheriff Jones looked over at George, giving him a scowl as he started riding down the trail to the bottom of the hill. From there, it was maybe another five minutes of riding slowly in the night down the road. The men came across a fallen log, where they dismounted and strapped their horses with rope to their necks, hitching them to the log. With the horses secured, the men took their rifles and pistols out and held them in hand as they slowly slunk their way through the brush and tall grass towards the Utes camp.

Eventually, they snuck up on the camp but sat in the darkness just outside the light of the fire for a bit, observing the camp. No one was moving about the camp, with only the large bonfire burning in the center of the camp. Multiple wikiups surrounded the fire and were spread out across the area but set close to one another with little space between them. Sheep and goats, cows and dogs moved about the area.

One dog glanced over in their direction and started barking at the men, which alerted one woman in the camp. She left her wikiup to come out and see what the dog was barking at. However, Sheriff Jones and the men stayed motionless, and the woman couldn't see into the night beyond the bonfire's light. She scolded the dog and brought the animal back into the wikiup with her. Sheriff Jones and his men sat for a little longer watching the camp and were able to ascertain that, in fact, the men were not there.

"We go on your order, boss," said George to Sheriff Jones.

Sheriff Jones thought for just a moment and then spoke to George.

"Kill the animals first. Then take some of the logs from the bonfire and light the wikiups on fire with them in them."

"Understood."

"Go. Now."

With the sheriff's order, the men got up and slowly crept into the camp. Taking their knives out, they slaughtered the animals by slitting their throats where they stood and slept. The dogs barked until they, too, were killed. The commotion of the dogs woke some women, who got up and went outside to see what was happening. As soon as they took a couple steps out of their wikiups, the men jumped them and cut their throats as well. One man stabbed a woman in her torso with his knife, before making a slicing motion with the knife still lodged in her torso, opening her stomach. Her intestines spilled out onto the dirt ground as she slunk down and slowly died.

When some of the women and all the animals were quietly killed, the men went over to the bonfire. Taking lit logs out of the fire, they tossed them onto the wikiups. The dry hot summers caused most of the materials in the wikiups to dry out, making them very flammable, along with the wood that made up their structures. It was the Ute women's and children's undoing as the wikiups quickly went up in flames. Many of the women and children were still asleep while the flames from the fire spread across their shelters.

Sheriff Jones and his men stood back from a distance as the inferno grew bigger and hotter in the camp. The screaming of the women and children could be heard as they woke up. Most were burning alive. Some of the women and children who tried to flee were gunned down by the Holt boys. One teenage boy attempted to get to his weapon, a bow with arrows, and managed to fire one arrow at the men that fell short into the ground, hitting none of them. One of the Holt boys took aim and fired his rifle, striking the young boy in the head and killing him instantly, which caused the men to laugh after observing his death from a distance.

Sherrif Jones stood with a smile on his face, listening with delight as he heard the last bit of screaming from the women and children fade from the camp, leaving only the sound of the crackling fire as it continued to burn the wood of the wikiups and everything around them. The sheriff then walked back towards the small trail that led from the main road to the river where the camp was. He found an old wooden log there lying dead on the ground next to where the small trail left the main road. He reached into his black coat, pulling out the letter he wrote to frame John Ashberger, and pinned the note into the side of a log with his knife.

"What the fuck are you doing there?" asked George.

"Setting things in motion that will free us from any responsibility that ties us to the deaths of these bitch savages, George," replied the sheriff. "When those Indians come back, and see their families and homes destroyed along with this note, then we sit back and watch everything unfold."

George glanced at the note and read it, then looked back up at Sheriff Jones with a smile on his face.

"For a sheriff, you're not too stupid, you know that?" he said.

"I will take that as a compliment. Now, get back to the horses and let the fires destroy all that is left for them."

The men went back to their horses that weren't too far away, untied them from the log and mounted them, then took off into the night, riding north to Olathe to lie low for a few days to make it look like the sheriff wasn't even in town when this had all happened.

Chapter 16: The Siege at Mary's Tavern

During the early morning, Ignacio and his men rode back to their camp, after completing another successful raid at Hackenberry and Sanderlin's job site. They had successfully killed two more workers in the middle of the night, while the workers slept. With pride in their hearts, they rode some of the back trails around Montrose, and back to their camp, avoiding the town's population and staying hidden.

"Another successful evening, Ignacio," said Ahiga, to Ignacio.

The two men rode together up to the front of their pack, heading down some of the Indian riding trails.

"It was. I hope soon they get the idea that they aren't wanted here. I certainly don't mind killing more white men, though," replied Ignacio. "Whatever gets them off of our lands."

"We need to hunt this morning as well. My wife hasn't eaten meat in two days, and she is pregnant. She tires of eating blackberries and wild strawberries."

"Don't worry, my friend. We can go out this morning and find something for the women to clean and eat."

"Some of the men also shared with me that they feel we should move our camp again soon. They think some of the white men may have found out where we are staying along the river."

"We just moved our camp no more than one month ago, Ahiga. Remember why we do what we are doing. To have a permanent home and not be on the run so much."

"I understand. It's just what some men are saying," said Ahiga.

"I understand their concerns, but believe me, friend. It will be alright. If the men are still concerned in another month before the days get shorter than we can look at moving our camp again."

The men continued to ride until they got to the top of the hill, just before the valley where their camp was. They crested the top of the hill and looked down into their valley and saw a good majority of the area was burned down, leaving a charred black space across the land that was formerly their camp along the water. Plumes of smoke could be seen rising from the land around the camp as well. The men stopped riding and took a moment to take in what they were seeing.

"No," muttered Ignacio under his breath, as he kicked his horse and took off as fast as the animal could go with his men following closely behind him.

They slowed down as they turned down the small trail that led down to their camp from the main dirt road, riding hard until they reached the remains of their homes. Everything was burned to the ground and gone. Animals were lying dead in the area, their hairs charred, and skin melted. Ash covered the ground all around them. Inside, where the wikiups once stood, were the human remains of the women and children, completely burned down to the bones.

The men walked in through the camp, each man wailing in sorrow as the grim reality set in. Women, children, animals, their families, everything was gone. Some sat in the ashes with their loved ones and all that they had once owned, the very little they had, all taken away from them. Ignacio's heart sank when he found his wikiup, but he sunk to his knees and fell to the ground when he saw Ahiga's wikiup, the one next to the edge of the river with the burned bodies of his pregnant wife and three-year-old son, holding onto one another in their final moments as they were burned alive.

Ahiga was on his knees, in the ash next to his dead wife and child, as he looked up at Ignacio. The ash of his loved ones' bodies adorned his arms and face. He reached down into the ash and grabbed handfuls of what was left of his wife and child, bringing his face into the ashes as he sobbed.

"What did we do to deserve this, Ignacio? We lost our lands. And now our families. My child. My wife. The cost is more than I can bear," said Ahiga. "We have angered Senawahv and are being punished by the creator for what we have been doing."

"This is not punishment from Senawahv, Ahiga. There is only one reason why this happened. The white men."

Ahiga clutched the remains of his wife and son and screamed. His wail echoed, reverberating off the hills and into the valley.

"This is why we can't fail in taking back what is ours, Ahiga. Do you understand now?" said Ignacio.

Ahiga dropped the bones and ash on the ground and clutched his hair with both hands as he breathed harder and harder. Rage filled his heart.

"Ahiga, when you are ready, we need to bury our dead," said Ignacio.

"They have nothing to go with them into the afterlife."

"Unfortunately, they do not. But it doesn't mean that we leave what is left to be taken by the wind."

Ignacio stood up, walked over to Ahiga, and placed his hand on his shoulder. Ahiga broke down in tears again and he sat in the ashes of his family, picking them up with his hands and rubbing them onto his chest as he mourned. The rest of the men took time and sat with the bodies of their loved ones, rummaging through the burned materials to find small artifacts that were burned but not destroyed. Ignacio looked through the ashes of Ahiga's wikiup and found a small quartz crystal that his son wore as a pendant on a leather string in the fire. It had smoke damage, and the leather string had burned and dissolved, but the quartz stone was still intact. Ignacio wiped it clean with his fingers until the black soot was nearly completely removed. Ignacio stood up and walked over to Ahiga, who was sitting among the ashes, handing him the stone.

"This belongs to you now, my friend," he said, dropping the stone into his opened hand.

Ahiga took the stone and held it in the palm of his hand, staring at it.

"I think I have a leather string in my saddle. Let me go look," said Ignacio, standing up and walking over to his horse.

While he was looking through the saddle bags on his horse, one of his men walked up to him, with a piece of paper in his hand along with a knife.

"Ignacio," said Makya.

Ignacio turned and looked at him.

"Yes, my friend?" he replied.

"I found this note on the dead log by the road. It was pinned to the log with this knife," he said.

Makya handed him the note and Ignacio read it out loud.

"You killed my Mexicans, now I killed your family. John."

"The farmer," said Makya.

Ignacio crumpled up the paper, rage building in his body until he shook as he crumpled the paper and dropped it on the ground.

"The farmer and his Mexicans will pay. They will all die for what they did here," said Ignacio, as he turned and walked back to the burned down camp site.

He walked up to the men and to Ahiga and started talking aloud.

"My friends! My family! My people. You all want revenge just as much as the next man here. You all lost more than I will ever know. I will never feel what you all feel right now. But our time of mourning needs to cease, and our time of retribution needs to come to pass. The apple farmer is responsible for the loss of your wives and your children and your animals and all your possessions. Hear me well, my people, and understand this. We will not rest until the farmer, his family, and his workers are dead."

Every man there stood up among the ashes and screamed at the top of their lungs. Rage filled their hearts, and vengeance was on their minds. A slow, methodical, painful type of retaliation that would be swift, yet slow at the same time.

*   *   *   *

"I need four cervezas, sir," said Basidilio, one of the four men who decided that they would leave the farm for the evening for a bit and have a couple of drinks with his partners.

Joining Basidilio this evening was Eulatio, Romulado, and Rito. The four men had finished their work on the orchard for the day, pruning and thinning out some of the apples so that others could grow larger. It was tedious work that started at sunrise and ended just about an hour before sunset. The four men were exhausted, but wanted to do something different instead of just sitting around a fire and hearing stories from their co-workers all evening, only to get up the following morning to do it all over again.

"A cerveza? Here in Colorado, we call them beers. Now if I didn't know you boys, I wouldn't know what you are talking about and much rather tell you to go fuck yourselves and get out of my bar," said the bartender.

"But you know us, sir," said Basidilio.

"That I do. And that is the only reason why you're getting a beer this evening," said the bartender, pouring drafts into a mug for him while he laughed.

After the fourth mug was filled, Basadilo paid the man with a couple of silver coins and grabbed the mugs and took them back to where his friends were seated at a table in the bar. Setting the mugs down on the table, each man took their drink and drank from them simultaneously.

"So tomorrow we are pruning and thinning more of the trees in the second row from the river," said Eulatio, putting his beer down on the table.

"Si, we're going to be working on this project for a few weeks, it seems like," replied Basidilio, who took a second drink of beer from his mug before placing it down on the table too.

"I hate thinning out the trees," said Rito.

"This is only the second year you've thinned out the apples, you idiot. Last year wasn't so bad and took only a week to do."

The four men laughed together but sympathized with what Rito was feeling as well. The work was difficult. The bugs were terrible this summer. The god damned mosquitos were awful. If it wasn't for the cats out in the field, the mice would have also been terrible. The heat today had even been worse than it had been lately, and summer was just picking up steam for the season.

"How long are we gonna be here this evening?" asked Romulado.

"Oh, I figure we'll have a couple beers, then head back and get some rest before we get back to work at sunrise," said Basidilio. "We have an early morning ahead of us for at least the next couple of weeks. Probably longer."

All four men took another drink from their mugs of beer when the front door to the tavern opened and new patrons walked inside.

"Did you hear that Calixto is going to take Aniseto and Bartolome up to that mine they found in the hills and mine for some more gold this weekend?" asked Romulado.

"No, he hadn't told anything to us yet. We'll ask him tonight when we get back to the farm. I would like to get back into that cave and dig out some more gold. We found nearly a damn pound of gold in there the last time we went in," said Rito. "Hey, if we mine enough gold, then we won't have to work on the apple farm anymore. We could open our own mining business."

"Are you boys working for John, the farmer of apples?" a voice said from behind Romulado.

The men turned around and saw two Indian men standing by their table. It was Ignacio and Ahiga. Although the four men didn't recognize who they were, having never ever met them before.

"Yeah, we just got here a bit ago. Just going to have a couple of drinks and head back to the farm for the evening. We won't be here long.," said Basidilio.

"Can we join you for some drinks?" asked Ignacio.

"Of course, pull up a chair and seat yourselves," replied Romulado.

The door to the tavern opened and four more Indian men walked inside, sitting at a table close by the door. All four men who walked in were still covered in a gray and black ashlike substance.

"They friends of yours too?" asked Romulado, taking notice of the four Indians who walked into the tavern.

"We're all friends here in the area," said Ahiga.

"Looks like they were working out in the field. They looked like they're covered in dirt, too."

"What are you four drinking this evening?" asked Ignacio.

"Just beers. Would you like one?" asked Basidilio.

"Oh no, we're fine. I always enjoyed whiskey. There was a time before that I would sit in a building like this. Maybe not as nice as this, but I would sit at a corner table, like that one right over there in the darkness, with only a small candle to light my corner and just drink all day long. From sunup to sundown and even into the night. It was around the time that my family and my people were forced off our lands and onto what the white people called reservations. Land meant just for us. You four wouldn't know what that is. I'm assuming based on the color of your skin, you aren't from around these parts?"

"No, sir. We're from Sinaloa."

"Mexico?"

"Si."

"Either way, this land was maybe about five percent of what our people used to have for ourselves. There were buffalo that roamed freely, and all types of plants grew naturally. But when they came, they took everything from us. The animals and the fields. All they gave us was the land that was the most infertile, with no animals to hunt on it. But we somehow still survived through it all."

"I'm sorry to hear that. We experienced something like that back in Mexico. Our presidente would do things that would only benefit him and his wallet, at the expense of our families. They would also take our land and our homes, so I get where you are coming from," said Basidilio.

"It's something awful, isn't it? So ultimately some of our fathers and brothers rose up and fought back, but they considered it a war and brought in a cavalry of men armed with weapons from the east that killed most of our fathers and brothers. Then we were forced off the reservations they made for us, pushing us all around in small bands spread out wherever we could find a small part of the land to settle our families down, build some wikiups temporarily, and raise our families away from the white people who hate us so much and want everything that we have. We're always on the move to survive and not become prisoners on our own land."

"Senior, I'm not too sure where you are going with this conversation. We're just Mexicans. We don't mean no harm to your people, and yet a band of Utes had come during the night and killed one of our friends not too long ago. Before that, they killed two more of our friends who traveled home from town, and we still don't understand why. And even then, I still don't have any problems with you or your family or your people. No one here at this table does," said Rito.

"And we appreciate that. Believe me, my friends, we do. But then something happened that not even I had anticipated happening. Someone killed our women and our children, our families, and our animals last night. Everything we owned, gone. Burned in fire. Then this morning I found this knife nearby our homes."

Ahiga handed Ignacio the knife that was found in the log nearby their camp. Handing it to Basidilio to look at.

"A knife?" asked Basidilio.

"Yes, a knife. And it was holding this message," said Ignacio, reaching into his pocket and pulling out the folded paper that was found at their camp.

He handed it to Basidilio, who set the knife down on the table, grabbed the piece of paper and read it.

"You killed my Mexicans, now I killed your family. John," said Basidilio, reading the note out loud.

Before he could say another word, Ahiga quickly removed a smaller knife from his sleeve and jabbed the blade into Rito's throat. Blood quickly filled his windpipe as Ahiga made a second slashing motion, cutting his neck. Blood sprayed from the wound all over the table and across the ground as Rito helplessly grasped the gaping wound. The other three men stood up and backed away from the Indians, knocking their mugs off the table.

Ignacio stood up from his chair with his knife in his hand and jabbed Basidilio in the abdomen, knocking him down to the ground. He mounted the man and repeatedly jabbed Basidilio in the chest until he died.

Innocent patrons in the bar scattered as they ran out the door by the four Indians, who sat and watched as Ignacio and Ahiga continued their assault on John's men. Eulatio went for the knife on the table and grabbed it when Ahiga saw what he was doing and quickly jabbed his knife down through his hand, pinning it to the table.

Eulatio screamed in pain as Romulado turned to run out the door, only for an Indian to shoot an arrow into his chest, killing him instantly. Other patrons in the tavern who hadn't run out yet were hiding underneath their tables and behind the bar with the bartender, who also was ducked down, avoiding the attacking Indians.

Ahiga grabbed the knife that pinned Eulatio down to the table and pulled it out. Eulatio sunk down on his knees to the floor, holding his hand in pain.

Ignacio walked up to him and grabbed him by the hair, pulling his head up to speak to him.

"You, young man, you will live through all of this. Long enough to take a message back to the apple farmer and his family for me. Can you do this?" asked Ignacio.

"Si! Si!" yelled Eulatio.

"Good," said Ignacio, as he pulled out his knife and slowly filleted Eulatio's scalp from his head.

*　　　　*　　　　*　　　　*

"Well, another long day," said Guadalupe, who was sitting next to John on his deck as they both enjoyed a nice cigar after a long day of work out in the apple orchard.

"That was just a small amount of the work that we must do. We still need to prune a few hundred more trees out there. Sometimes I think we need more men, but these guys you got work so hard. Do you think we should see if we could find more men to work the apples?" asked John.

"I think it would be a good idea. We're down three men from our group and it's slowing us down significantly with only twenty-nine men. It'll take us at least a full month to get through the trees we need to thin out. By that time, we'll be getting closer to harvest. If we want to maximize our profits and our crop's yield, we may need to bring in more help."

"Where can I find it, though?"

"Look in the town. I'm sure there are some men who would be interested in working for us for an honest day's pay."

"I just don't know how I am going to pay for their work now. They would have to wait until we make profits from the harvest in the fall."

"I can see if there are any other men from Sinaloa who would be interested in coming up. But that takes me or one of the other men away from work around here until we get back from Mexico, and who knows if we even make it back alive with the Indians out there."

"Why don't you just send a telegram back to Sinaloa?"

"John, this is Mexico. Not the United States. You're lucky they even know how to write, let alone know what a goddamn telegram is."

Both men laughed, enjoying the moment of levity.

"Alright. So tomorrow I'll go into town and talk with Sam at the general store and see if he knows some guys that can come help on the land, too."

"Even if we could just get a couple more hands, it would help out in the long run, John."

John took a big puff of his cigar, exhaling smoke as he looked up into the starry night.

"It really is beautiful out here, Guadalupe. I never thought it would be, but I love this land. These moments. There is something different about the stars at night here in the mountains, as opposed to the beaches in Florida," he said.

A moment later, both men heard a horse galloping up their road towards the house.

"Do you hear that?" asked John.

"It sounds like a horse?" said Guadalupe. "Why is someone riding a horse here at night?"

The galloping sounds rode up to the side of the house. John and Guadalupe stood up from their rocking chairs and looked at the dark corner of the house when they heard something hitting the ground with a large thud. The galloping sounds started again, but in the opposite direction of the house, back out to the main road.

John took his pistol from his holster and aimed it at the corner of the house, where he heard something shuffling around. He was ready to shoot anything that moved around that corner when he saw a person stagger into view, using the wooden deck to hold himself up. Guadalupe recognized him instantly when he stepped into the moonlight.

"Eulatio!" he yelled, rushing over to his friend.

Eulatio collapsed on the corner of the deck as Guadalupe ran over with John.

"What happened to you?" asked Guadalupe, noticing that his scalp and hair were forcibly cut from his head. Blood had poured down his face and down the back of his neck, saturating the shoulders of his white shirt red.

"They did it," said Eulatio.

"Who did it?" asked John.

"Indians. They killed us," he said, struggling to breathe.

"Who is us?" asked John.

"Me," said Eulatio as he breathed his last and succumbed to his injuries.

John looked over his body and noticed that it looked like Eulatio had been physically beaten. Parts of his torso looked caved in, as if bones had broken inside and forced his body to take a new shape.

"What did he mean by us, Guadalupe?" asked John.

"I don't know. We need to ask the others. See if anyone else went into town with him."

"What is that in his hand?" asked John.

There was a piece of paper folded and stuffed into his hand. John reached over and opened his hand, taking the piece of folded paper out and unfolding it.

"You burned our burial ground. You burned our families. You burned our home. Now I will burn you and all you love," he said as he read the note in the moonlight.

"Those goddamn Indians!" said John.

"John, we need to find who all went to the town with him."

Both John and Guadalupe left Eulatio's body there on the deck as they ran through the backyard and into the apple orchard. They rushed between the trees to the river where the crew's shacks were. When they got there, they saw a few men sitting around a fire. They looked up and saw John and Guadalupe approaching, startled but with a dumbfounded look on their faces as they wondered why they were running down to the men's camp as quickly as they were.

"Verostico! Who went into town with Eulatio earlier this evening?" asked Guadalupe.

"Eulatio? He went to Mary's Tavern with Basidilio, Romulado, and Rito. Maybe a couple of hours ago. I'd think they would be getting back soon," replied Verostico.

"Eulatio's dead."

"What?"

"He's been scalped and looks like someone kicked the shit out of him. I would imagine Basadilio, Romulado and Rito are also dead," said John.

"Is that all who went to town with him?" asked Guadalupe.

"Si, as far as I know."

"Where is everyone?"

"It's just me and Calixto out here by the fire. Everyone else is in their beds asleep, sir."

"Did those four take any weapons with them in town when they left? Rifles? Pistols? Knives?" asked John.

"No, sir. All the weapons are still here in the shacks, and I have one of the rifles right here. Just in case."

"Where's Ramon?"

"He went to bed not too long ago."

"Wake him for me," said John.

Calixto stood up and went into the shack, while the three men stood out by the fire.

"I can't believe this is happening again," said John, grabbing the back of his head with both of his hands as he paced back and forth by the fire.

"John, that note. What did it say again?" asked Guadalupe.

John took the note out of his pocket, opening it and reading it aloud.

"You burned our burial ground. You burned our families. You burned our home. Now I will burn you and all you love."

"John, you burned their burial ground. But you didn't burn their family or their homes. Why would they think that?" asked Guadalupe.

"John, what is going on?" asked Ramon.

"More of our men are dead. Basadilio, Romulado, Eulatio, and Rito. Eulatio's body is up by the house. The other three, I don't know where they are yet."

"Oh my god," said Ramon,

"What were you saying, Guadalupe?" asked John.

"I'm saying it's interesting to me that they are saying you burned their burial ground, their families, and their homes."

"Maybe they feel that burial ground is their home and their family?" said John.

"Or maybe someone really killed their families, and now they think it's you who did it."

"Are you saying someone is trying to frame us for a crime?"

"I don't know all the facts. But it certainly seems like there is more destroyed than just a burial ground. That's what the note makes it sound like. If that is the case, and someone killed their families and destroyed their homes, then who really did it?"

"The fucking realtors," said John.

"How do you know?" asked Ramon.

"Who else could it be? If that is what happened and that's what they mean from this note, then who else in Montrose would do such a thing, if not us?"

"You think they know we killed the young worker the other night, so they're trying to frame us?" asked Guadalupe.

"They don't care about some dumb kid. They want our land, and it looks to me like they are going to turn the Indians on us to make it easier to get the land from me. I'll burn and rot in hell before they ever get this land from me."

"So, what do we do, John?"

"We're going to have to kill the Indians. Then we start killing the workers on the other side of the river. Then eventually, I'm going to kill the realtors if I must."

"That seems like a tall task with only a few rifles and pistols," said Ramon.

"Guadalupe, do you think it's possible to sneak into their camp and steal their weapons?"

"Tonight?"

"Yes."

"Well, it seems quiet over there right now. How many men do you want to risk sending over there, John? We're officially down to twenty-five men now and can't afford to lose another man."

"And we can't afford to just sit on our asses and let things happen the way they are happening. Or else we're going to lose more men."

"Ugh, fuck!" said Guadalupe.

"Can you do it?" asked John.

"I don't see what else we can do, other than abandon the land."

"There is no fucking way that is happening, Guadalupe."

"Then we don't have much choice."

"Take Ramon, Verostico, and Calixto with you to cross the river. Take the raft. Get as many rifles and pistols as you can. If you can get ammunition as well, grab what you can. Be careful and be quiet. If you wake a man up, use your knives to kill them quietly. Do you understand?"

"Yes, sir."

"Then go do it and come back alive," said John.

Chapter 17: Ladrón en la Noche

Ramon and Verostico walked around the corner of one of the shacks down by the river and found the raft they had used a few nights ago to kidnap the young man from the realtor's work site. Calixto and Guadalupe grabbed a couple of oars and helped the two men carry the raft upstream some, setting it into the water. The men got onto the raft and pushed themselves off the riverbank, using their oars.

The stream slowly took them downstream as they quietly paddled their way across the small river to the opposite side. Once they made it to the other side of the river, they beached the raft, and one by one, the men got off onto the bank and pulled the raft up onto the riverbank. John watched from the other side of the river, sitting on a rock, ensuring they got the job done from a distance. When they were all together on the bank of the river, they started whispering to one another.

"All's quiet in their camp tonight," said Ramon. "That's rather unusual."

"Don't kill any of the men unless you absolutely have to," whispered Guadalupe. "We're here just to get their guns. If they wake up, though, kill them to keep them quiet."

"You want to search in the tents on the north end of the camp? I'll take the tents at the south end of their camp. Calixto and Verostico, take the tents closest to the river here. Be quiet and be careful, you understand?" asked Ramon.

The four men each went their way. In one tent, Ramon accidentally woke one man from their slumber while he was grabbing a pistol from the ground. He quickly jumped onto the man, covered his mouth so he didn't make a sound, and jabbed him in the throat with his knife. Blood poured from the young man's neck, slowly killing him. More importantly, though, everything remained quiet while the men searched through their tents, grabbing rifles, pistols, and valuables.

Calixto and Verostico were the first of the men to make it back to the raft. They had managed to sneak out four rifles and six pistols, with a couple of boxes of bullets from the tents that they had checked. They also had to kill one man quietly as he had woken up in his tent while Calixto was looting. The next man back to the raft was Ramon. He brought back three rifles and three pistols, along with a box of bullets, too.

Guadalupe picked up a pistol off the ground in one of the men's tents, sticking it into the waistband of his pants. He grabbed two rifles and four pistols, stuffing bullets he found into his pockets. He slowly exited the tent and walked out. Looking up, he froze when he saw one of the Ute Indian men standing there, watching him from mere feet away. Both were equally surprised to see one another.

The Indian removed a knife from a sheath he kept on his belt and lunged at Guadalupe. Side stepping the attack, Guadalupe dropped the weapons and threw a punch, striking the Indian squarely in the face. The Indian staggered backwards, dropping his knife on the ground. When he went and bent over to pick it back up, Guadalupe delivered a knee firmly to his face, causing him to fall backward to his back, hitting his head on a rock on the ground.

A shot rang out and Guadalupe heard the sizzle of a bullet fly by him, striking something behind him. He turned to see another Indian there, with a hatchet raised in hand in mid swing as he was shot just before the Indian brought the sharp end of the hatchet down into Guadalupe's back. The bullet pierced through his eye socket, as he fell back to the ground, dead. In that moment, more Indians stepped out of the darkness and came into the light of the bonfire.

The sound of the shot woke the men in the camp and before the Indians could jump Guadalupe and kill him, some workers in the camp rushed out of their tents looking for their guns, but they couldn't find them. They grabbed knives from their tents and fought the Indians in a knife fight.

Turning around and looking back toward the river, Guadalupe saw Ramon with one of the rifles in his hand, discharging a shell from the barrel and loading another bullet into the rifle. He bent down and grabbed the rifle he had dropped on the ground. He picked up the Indian's knife as well and as the Indian was coming to; he jammed the knife into the man's face with all his might. The sound of cracking bone could be heard as the Indian fell back and flopped dead on the ground.

Guadalupe left the knife embedded in the Indian's face and ran out of the light as the Indians and the workers resumed fighting in close combat. Some of the Indians were killed while some crewmen were killed too. In the fight was the foreman, as well, Robert Steele. He killed two Indians before one invader struck him in the back of the head with a hatchet, splitting his skull open. Blood poured out of the open wound down his back as he slunk down to his knees. The Indian removed the hatchet from the back of his head, striking him repeatedly in the neck with it until his head was severed from his body.

The fighting continued for a short time before the Indians retreated into the night, taking their own wounded who survived the fight along with them. After the Indians were gone, the crewmen looked around for their rifles, but they could not find them. They assumed that the Indians had stolen them while they slept. In total, eight crewmen died, including their foreman, Robert Steele. The survivors counted that six Indian men were slaughtered tonight as well.

Not one Mexican died tonight.

The four Mexicans met back at the raft. Picking it up, they hurried it out into the river. They placed the weapons they had stolen on the center of the raft, then got on and pushed off into the river, using the paddles to paddle their way back to the other side of the river. The river's current took them downstream a bit, but with the oars, they paddled their way back to the other side of the river, beaching the raft onto John's side of the property.

John Ashberger met the men there on the riverbank.

"What the fuck happened over there? I heard a gunshot," asked John.

"The god damn Indians, sir. They did a sneak attack on the camp again tonight while we were getting rifles and pistols. We killed three of the crewmen as they slept. They woke up, and we killed them with our knives. But they were killing each other over there, John," said Guadalupe, as his adrenaline was pumping.

"Alright, Guadalupe. Calm down and relax. Did anyone see you over there?"

"No, I don't think so. The only person that did was the Indian, and I killed him with his own knife."

"Good. What did you guys get while you were over there?"

"Bullets. Rifles. Pistols," said Ramon, pointing out what they had stolen from the men that was in the center of the raft.

"Nine rifles, thirteen pistols, three boxes of bullets, and a handful of bullets that Guadalupe found," said John, counting out the guns.

"It's better than what we had before," said Ramon.

"A lot better. Are you boys good with a rifle?"

"The men know how to use rifles and pistols, John."

"Great. Arm them. Each man gets a rifle or a pistol. I feel that the Indians will be back. And at the rate we are going, so will those goddamn realtors and their men. I'll go into town and speak with Sam and see if I can get some more bullets from him. In the meantime, get some rest tonight and tomorrow I'll go into town," said John, as he turned and walked back to the house from the river and the apple orchard.

The men picked up the rifles and took them into one of the shacks. They secured them in the shack and then went to bed, getting some rest for the night.

*   *   *   *

A white horse rode into town from the southeastern road leading into Montrose in the early morning hours. A young man with dirt covering his exposed skin on his body, and covering his shirt and pants, galloped past the buildings and passed by some citizens of the town, walking along the street. The people watched as the horse stopped in front of Hackenberry and Sanderlin's real estate agency. The rider got off, tied his horse to the hitching post, and ran into the shop without even knocking first. Inside the shop was James Hackenberry, making a pot of tea for the morning. Charles Sanderlin had yet to arrive at the office. James looked up and saw the young man standing there in the office, breathing heavily. He recognized the young man as one of the workers from their building site.

"Young man, I'm sorry I don't know your name, but I recognize you from working our land. What is your name?"

"Charlie," said the young man as he tried catching his breath.

"Charlie. Great. What is it that you need?"

"We were attacked again last night."

"Shit."

"Sir, we lost eleven men. Our foreman, Robert, is dead as well. Fuckers cut his damn head off."

"Goddamn it," said James, shaking his head.

"Sir, there is something else."

"What is it?"

"Our weapons were stolen last night."

"By the Indians?"

"I don't know, sir. They were stolen while we slept. We heard some commotion outside. When we went to look for our guns, they were gone. So we grabbed our knives and went outside and we saw the Indians coming into the camp, but I don't think it was them who stole our guns."

"Then who else could it be if it wasn't the Indians?"

"I don't know, sir."

"John Ashberger."

"Who, sir?"

"John Ashberger. And his Mexicans from across the river. That fucking apple farmer. Would you care for a cup of tea?" asked James.

"Oh, no sir. But thank you."

"Well, if I had to guess, John probably had something to do with the weapons being stolen. But I can't prove that. Go to the sheriff's office, ask him to come here. I desire to speak with him."

"Yes, sir. After that, I'm going to go back to bury our dead."

"Don't bother. We don't have time to waste with burials. Especially with fewer hands helping on the land now and until reinforcements come in from the east coast, we don't have time for burials. Deposit their bodies into the river and let the animals eat them somewhere downstream."

"What about Robert Steele?" asked the young man.

"Dispose of all the bodies in the river," said James. "Then get back to work and hopefully John back in Baltimore was able to get the men sent on their way from the east coast sooner rather than later. Now, go fetch me the sheriff."

"Yes, sir," said Charlie, as he turned and left the office.

"John Ashberger, you sneaky son of a bitch," said James, pouring a cup of scalding hot tea into a cup.

He set the pot back down on the wood stove and walked over to his desk by the window with his tea. He took a sip from the cup and sat down in his chair, looking outside the window. While James was looking out the window, he noticed that the sheriff was walking over to the office. He walked up to the door, opened it, and came in.

"The boy told me what happened," said Sheriff Jones, walking into the room and sitting in the chair on the opposite side of James' desk.

"I suppose you have a plan for what you are going to do? This is quite a large setback for us, sheriff. Especially when the men from Baltimore are still in transit on the train here and won't be here for a couple more days still."

"I understand."

"So again, I ask you. What are you going to do about it?" said James, taking a bigger drink from his tea.

"Well, we can track down the Indians and kill them."

"What are we going to do about this!?" yelled James.

The room fell silent for a moment, the only sound emanating from a ticking grandfather clock in the corner of the office.

"James, I understand that you are upset. Trust me, we will hunt them down and kill them all."

"I hope so, sheriff. I wouldn't like to think that I paid for a service that I'm not getting my money's worth for," said James as he finished his tea.

"Their families are dead, their women, children, and even their animals."

"That's great, sheriff. And you framed John Ashberger and his band of Mexicans for doing it. But we don't have time to wait for things to play out. Now for you to get paid... For us to change this town for the better and turn a profit here, you need to kill those goddamned savages."

"Yes, sir."

James stood up and walked over to the fireplace with his cup of tea.

"Now, the young man also told me that their rifles, pistols, and bullets were taken from the tents as well."

"The Indians took them?" asked Sheriff Jones.

"No. I don't think so. What the boy was telling me didn't make sense. Said that the rifles were already gone when the Indians were sneaking into their camp."

"So, where did they go, James?"

"That is the question I would like for you to find an answer to, sheriff," said James, pouring another cup of tea and setting the pot down and walking back over to his desk.

He looked out the window and saw John Ashberger in the town, dismounting his horse and walking into the general store across the street from their office.

"I would imagine, though, sheriff, that I would start with that man right there," said James, pointing John out as he walked around his horse and up to the general store shop door.

The sheriff stood up and watched as John walked into the store too, shutting the door behind him.

"I'll go find out right now, James," said Sheriff Jones.

*   *   *   *

The shop door to the general store opened, letting in a gentle breeze from the outside. A man walked into the shop, as the shopkeeper sat in his chair behind a brand-new cash register that he was still trying to figure out how to use. He looked up and instantly recognized the man who had walked into the store.

"John! What a pleasure to see you again. It certainly has been a while," said Sam.

"Sam, I need your help," said John Ashberger, walking up to the counter by the register.

"John, you always know you can get help from me if you need it. What is it that I can do for you?"

"I need bullets."

"Bullets?"

"Yes, sir."

"What kind of bullets?"

".44-40 for rifle and .36 caliber for pistol."

"You are shooting with a Winchester rifle?"

"That's right."

"Well, I think I got cartridges in the back. How many do you need of them?"

"As many as you have."

"As many as I have?"

"You heard me right, Sam."

"So, I have two boxes in the back for the rifles. Each box contains 120 rounds."

"I'll take them both. And the pistol ammunition?"

"Pistol ammunition—I have three boxes in the back. They contain 60 rounds a piece."

"I'll take all three."

"John, what is going on? That's a decent amount of ammunition."

"Just fucking vermin, Sam."

"Vermin? You honestly need that big of a caliber rifle and pistol round?"

"Sure do."

"Alright, John. You're the boss. Give me a minute to go to the back and get the boxes out."

The moment Sam disappeared to the back in the storage area, the front door to the shop opened. John turned around and saw Sheriff Jones walk into the store. The two men made eye contact with one another and paused for a moment, saying nothing to one another.

"Good morning, John. What brings you into town today?" asked the Sheriff as he walked up to the counter, standing closer to John.

"Just coming by the shop to get some supplies is all."

"I see. What kind of supplies."

"It's not really any of your business what kind of supplies I'm getting."

"Now is that the way to talk to someone who is just looking to be friendly?"

"I question the friendly part."

"Now John, I'm not here to start any problems. I just happened to see you walk into the shop from across the street and thought I would be nice and come say hi and see how you are doing."

"Well, hi," said John.

"I hear those Indians killed some more of your Mexicans here at the tavern recently, didn't they?"

"Killed four of them."

"What did you do with the bodies?"

"Did what I did before, took the one that came back and buried him on my land. As far as the other three, I don't know what happened to their bodies," said John.

"Fucking savages probably took them with. Probably to cook and eat them, I would imagine."

"Sure."

"You know, I hear that there's a building project over by where you are, John. Indians attacked the workers there at the job site, allegedly stole their guns last night and killed some workers too. Not until some of those savages got what they deserved, though. You know what they say? Kill the Indian and save the man."

"Didn't hear anything about that happening. What is going on over on that side of the river is none of my business."

"Yeah, happened just last night. Stole a bunch of rifles and pistols. I think they even got away with some knives and tools, too."

"That sounds too bad," said John.

"Alright John, here are the bullets you were asking for. Oh, good morning, sheriff," said Sam, walking out front from the back storage room with boxes of ammunition in his arms.

"Morning, Sam. You are getting all this ammunition, John?"

"Stocking up for the fall and winter."

"That's a decent number of bullets. What kind you getting here?"

The sheriff looked over the boxes that Sam had set down on the glass countertop.

"Goddamn, John. That is a lot of bullets. 240 bullets for a rifle. And 180 for pistols?"

"Like I said, we're stocking up for the fall and winter months. Need to hunt to get food. Is it against the law to buy bullets to hunt meat and feed my family?"

"Oh no, not at all. It's a good idea, John. It's a good reason to get that much ammunition for that."

"Some of it is for home defense, too. Just in case the Indians attack us again. Don't want to be unprepared when the crazies come."

"Goddamn merciless Indian savages. Well, don't let me stand in your way of taking care of your business here, John. Like I said, I just wanted to come say hi," said the sheriff with a smile on his face, as he backed up and walked backwards towards the door, keeping his eyes on John the whole time.

When he got to the door, he laughed a little and turned, opening the door and walking out.

"What the hell was that all about, John?" asked Sam.

"I don't trust that son of a bitch," said John.

"Our sheriff of Montrose County?"

"That's right. I don't trust him, Sam."

"I don't see why not?"

"You need to get out of your own shop a bit more, Sam, and see what is going on out there."

"Well, nevertheless. How do you want to pay for it all?"

"Just cash."

John handed him sixty dollars for the ammunition, then turned around and left the general store. Walking outside with his cargo, John looked up and saw the sheriff walking into the realtor's office, shutting the door behind him. John packed the bullets up onto the back of his horse and untying the horse from the hitching post. He turned the horse around and started to leave the town when a couple of men stepped off the sidewalk and out in front of his horse on the road.

"Jonn Ashberger I take it?" said one of the men.

"I am. Who's asking?"

"My name's George Holt. This here is Frank Noles."

"What do you want?"

"Just wanted to say hi to you."

"Pleasure meeting you, but unfortunately I don't have time to speak and need to get back to my property."

"You own that apple orchard just out of town down this road here?"

"I do."

"You just about have a crop to harvest in a few months here?"

"I do. Colorado orange apples."

George looked at where John stored the ammunition on his horse, noticing all the ammunition John had with him.

"You got yourself a lot of ammunition there as well."

"I do. Stocking up for my property for the winter."

"What do you intend to do with it all?"

"That's none of your business, mister."

"Is that a fact?"

"Yeah. That's a fact. My business is my business."

"You know, that's a beautiful piece of land down that way, John. I hope you take real good care of it."

"I intend to."

George smiled and tipped his hat to John, then politely stepped aside. Frank Noles stood silent next to George, never taking his eyes off John.

John tipped his hat back to George and took off, leaving town and riding back to his property.

George and Frank watched as his horse left town down the dirt road towards his property.

"Frank. Go get the sheriff. I think we should go pay John and his family a visit this evening."

Chapter 18: A Red Sky in the Morning

Rain poured profusely at the property of John Ashberger this evening. A storm rolled in from the west through the town of Montrose and went southwest towards his property. The skies were dark, and it seemed like nightfall already by seven in the evening. John walked into his barn where his work crew were cleaning and looking over the rifles and pistols that they had stolen from the workers' camp from across the river, loading them and preparing them for use.

"How are the guns?" asked John, picking up a rifle that was leaning up against the wall.

"They're looking good," said Guadalupe. "Just dirty, but they are in good condition."

Ramon took one of the pistols that was cleaned and fired it at a target they had set up outside the barn.

"They're all accurate too," said Guadalupe.

"That's good to hear. You boys get dinner this evening?"

"A couple of the guys made menudo, John. You want some?"

"No, I just had some dinner. How are the apples?"

"Fucking rained all afternoon and this evening. Hoping that the ground doesn't get swamped."

"Shouldn't hurt the apples too much, you think?"

"No, shouldn't too much. As long as it doesn't rain for a couple days and saturates the ground like a swamp."

"It seems like everything is against us. Even God."

Another gun fired at the target outside.

"Rifle's good," said Ramon, handing the rifle to one of the men standing by him.

"I have a feeling that eventually something is going to happen. While I was in town getting bullets from the general store, as I was leaving, I saw the sheriff going into the realtor's office, too," said John.

"Think the sheriff is working for them?" asked Guadalupe.

"I think so. Then there was something else, too. A couple of men stopped me just before I left and took an interest in my business. Couple of guys I've never seen before. One man called himself George Holt. Can't remember the other man's name at the moment," said John, picking up another rifle and leaning up against the wall to check it out.

"George Holt, you say?"

"Yeah, that's right."

"I wonder if it's the same George Holt from Oklahoma."

"You know him?"

"The name sounds familiar, John. The guy I'm thinking of is a bandit. Has a gang of men that follow him around. They're bank robbers and thieves. Murderers and rapists."

"How do you know that?"

"I read the newspaper, John."

Another gun fired just outside the barn.

"This one is good too," said Ramon.

"Wait, we're missing a couple of pistols," said Guadalupe.

"Where are they?" asked John. "We had thirteen pistols, right?"

"And now we have ten."

"Where are the other three?"

Guadalupe looked at one of the men there in the barn.

"Refugio, did you pick up those pistols you left on the bed back in your shack?" asked Guadalupe.

"I thought Calixto was supposed to?" replied Refugio.

"Well, that must be where they are, then," said John.

"Go back and grab the pistols and bring them here to the barn. We need to make sure they are cleaned and ready to use," said Guadalupe.

Refugio left the barn and started walking back to the worker shacks out by the river. The men in the barn finished cleaning and testing the weapons, ensuring they functioned properly. John left the barn, walking back to his house and grabbing the ammunition he had got earlier in the day. He brought the bullets out to the men, who proceeded to make sure the rifles and pistols that they had were fully loaded and ready-to-use if needed. After the men finished loading the guns, Refugio came back into the barn without the pistols in his hands.

"Refugio, where are the three pistols?" asked Guadalupe.

Refugio had a blank stare on his face as he didn't respond to him, but fell face first onto the ground, dead. A large knife had been buried in his back. The back of his shirt was stained red with his blood.

Gunshots cracked as bullets hit the side of the barn. One bullet made its way into the barn, hitting one of the men inside in the torso, knocking him down to the ground as he clutched his stomach in pain. John and his men quickly shut the doors to the barn, boarding themselves inside as bullets plucked against the other side of the door. In the darkness, John heard a voice yelling out from outside the barn in the rain.

"Hey John! How the hell are ya?" said the man.

"Who is that?" asked John back.

"Names George Holt. I take it you and all your men are in that goddamn barn with ya right now, aren't they?"

"That's none of your fuckin business!" replied John, as he recognized the name from earlier in the day.

Thunder rumbled in the distance as the grounds lit up from lightning strikes in the area.

"Oh, but it is my fuckin business now, John!" yelled George as he started shooting the barn again.

The men from his gang surrounded the barn and started firing again, too. Bullets hit the wood on the sides of the barn, splintering some of the boards. The men inside the barn started loading the pistols and rifles as the man who was shot in the stomach bled out and died there on the ground in the barn.

"Why don't you come out and say hi, John? It's rude for you to leave your guests out in the rain like this!" said George, laughing menacingly.

"Are they still in there?" asked the sheriff, who stepped up to George.

"Yeah, they're in there."

"All of them?"

"Yeah, all of 'em."

"So that means his bitch wife and children are still in the house, then?" said the sheriff, turning to look at the house behind them.

"I would say so," said George, as more thunder cracked in the surrounding skies.

"I'll be right back," said the sheriff, as he turned and started walking towards the home.

He took a few steps back towards the home when he felt something move right by his head at a high rate of speed. He looked around himself and turned around to see that one of the men from George's group had an arrow sticking out of his right eye. Blood poured out of the wound and down the man's face before he slunk down to the ground and died.

The sheriff looked out in the direction from where the arrow was fired. At the same time, lightning struck, lighting up the area and revealing the silhouettes of men approaching Holt's group from the trees. The Utes had arrived.

"God fucking damn it!" yelled the sheriff as he took out a knife from his vest and slashed the torso of one of the attacking Indians, who were running out of the darkness and attacking George Holt and his gang.

The Indian slumped down to his knees, with his back towards the sheriff, who slashed through the back of the Indian's head with full force, cutting clean through the man's skull, exposing his brain to the elements.

"Kill those fucking savages!" yelled George to his men, who turned their focus on shooting the attacking the oncoming Ute men.

Some of the Utes were shot and killed before they got close enough to Holt's men, but some got past the guns and engaged the gang in combat with knives. Arthur Green was the first of Holt's men to be killed, as he was stabbed through the throat by one of the Ute warriors. Followed by Oscar Robinson, who was run through with a spear, then struck in the back of the head with a hatchet by one of the Ute men, splitting his skull clean in half.

George Holt shot at anything that moved that didn't look like one of his own men. It was hard to see in the rain and the darkness until lightning flashed, exposing the shadows.

John Ashberger and some of his men aimed their rifles out the open windows and fired, striking and killing three Utes. They also struck Carl Wilson in the side of the head as he turned to run away, killing him instantly. Another shot hit Joseph Stokes square in the chest, killing him before his body even hit the ground.

The rest of George Holts' men, along with George and the sheriff, turned and ran into the apple orchard. The Ute men gave chase, including Ignacio and Ahiga. George's men weaved in and out of the apple trees, trying to lose the Ute men until they met in the center of the large orchard.

"We aren't gonna lose those god damn Indians in here, George," said Sheriff Jones.

"We have an advantage, being ahead of them like this. Quickly, hide among the rows of trees, behind the tall grass. When they come by, spring up and attack them. We can kill them all in here," said George.

"No guns. Just knives," said the sheriff as Holt's men spread out, hiding among the tall grass and trees.

As Holt's men hunkered down and waited patiently, they heard the sounds of the Ute men running in from the distance. Their knives were drawn, ready to strike. When one of the Ute men finally broke through the trees in front of Harry Kilpatrick, he lunged out and plunged the knife into the man's chest. Clarence Bell also sprang out of hiding and jabbed his knife into the man's neck as well.

Another Ute man broke through the row of trees as George Holt came out of hiding and shoved the man into one of the apple trees. The man's hair got tangled in the branches, immobilizing him for a moment as he dropped his spear in the tall grass while his body was jerked back by the limb. George stepped up to the man and struck him in the face with the hilt of his knife, rendering him unconscious in the moment. More Ute men broke through the trees and one by one, George Holt and his men slaughtered them.

After the third Ute man was killed, Ignacio caught on to what was happening. He stopped the men around him and told them to retreat out of the orchard as it was too dark to engage men that were already set up and ready to strike as they came by. The rest of the Ute men turned and left the orchard. Ultimately leaving the property and Holt's men in the orchard alone, with some of their fallen Ute friend's dead bodies and the one unconscious man with his long black hair entangled in the tree.

"I think they are retreating," said the sheriff, using his wet black jacket to clean his bloodied knife.

"They're smart to do so. We would have killed them all," said George.

"What about the one whose hair is caught in the tree?" asked the sheriff.

"He's still here, unconscious unless I killed the motherfucker when I hit him in the face. Goddamn it, I lost so many men from my crew tonight! Fucking, Indians!" yelled George as he kicked the Ute prisoner with the heel of his boot in the face.

"Don't kill him yet," said the sheriff. "Wake him up if you can."

"He's out cold, Walt," said Harry, looking the Ute man over.

"Is he still breathing?"

"Yeah, barely. But he's still alive."

"Then wake the son of a bitch up," said the sheriff.

"How?"

The sheriff walked up to the Ute man, then knelt down by his side. Taking the pointed end of his knife, he proceeded to carve the man's face, digging out a piece of flesh. One of Holt's men held the Ute man's arms down when he started to stir awake from the pain. Blood poured down his face from the open wound, onto his chest.

"Wake up, wild man," said the sheriff, turning the back of his hand and slapping the man across the face onto the open wound, spraying blood onto his own face in the process.

"Well, there you are. How the hell are ya?" asked the sheriff.

The Ute man didn't respond to him.

"You too dumb to understand English, wild man?" asked Peter Martin, one of the last of George's crew who was still alive.

"I understand just fine," replied the Ute man.

"Well, I'll be goddamned, an educated wild man," said the sheriff. "What's your name, son?"

"Ahiga."

"Ahiga, pleased to meet you. I'm the sheriff of Montrose County, Walt Jones. This ruffian here to my left is a man named George Holt. He comes from Oklahoma and has a gang of men, well, had a gang of men, who wouldn't think twice to rob the federal reserve, or go after and kill the President of the United States if they wanted to, and I believe they could do it too. But as you can see, you and your friends killed several of their friends. Now the only reason why you're still alive here is because of me. Or else they would have put a bullet clean through your savage head by now, and used your brain as fertilizer for the apple trees here. And I don't want them to do that. You see, I've got a question for you that I suggest you answer for me. Can you answer a question for me?"

"Get fucked, white man," said Ahiga.

"Hmm, no. That's not the answer I was looking for," said the sheriff, who then took his knife out and buried it into Ahiga's thigh.

The Ute man howled in pain as the sheriff twisted the knife, burrowing out a hole into his thigh with the blade.

"Now, will you be willing to answer a question for me? And it's a simple question. Then all of this can be over, and you can be on your way to your next adventure. But my question is, where is your camp?"

Ahiga kept silent, refusing to answer the Sheriff's question.

"Come now, don't be worried about anything happening. I know you got a new camp where you are staying."

"How do you know that?" asked Ahiga.

"Oh, because we are the ones that killed your women and children and burned your last camp to the ground."

Ahiga's eyes filled with rage as he fought to free his arms from the men that were holding him down. Another man walked behind him, grabbed the part of his hair that wasn't caught in the ttree,and held his head back.

"You know there was one of your tents there specifically that I remember setting fire to myself. Over by the water next to the river. Young, beautiful squaw inside, pregnant. I think she was. Big belly. Looked like she was gonna pop any day now. Along with a young boy, no more than a few years old, you see. I made sure that the tent went up in flames, with them inside of it. I suppose they thought if they hugged it out, they would be okay inside, but you know how you Indians are goddamn stupid. Fire ain't gonna care one way or another if you hug it out. I watched as the skin melted off their bodies."

Ahiga started kicking at the sheriff, who was laughing along with some of the other men, too.

"Now calm down. I'm sure they're in a better place now. This world, as you can agree, is cruel, yes? Cold. Unsympathetic. Indifferent if you will. I've done my evil and I'm leaving it to that. My heart can only take so much bad. I don't want that anymore. So, if you just share with me where your camp is, then I'll free you."

"I will kill you, white man!" yelled Ahiga.

"You're not gonna get anything out of this savage, Walt," said Clarence Bell, as he held down Ahiga's right arm.

"You know what, Clarence? I think you're right. This is your last chance, savage. Tell me where your camp is, and I will set you free."

"And I will set your soul free from your body if you let me go, white man," said Ahiga.

The sheriff then stood up, grabbed Ahiga's spear that he had dropped and jabbed it firmly into Ahiga's chest, penetrating all the way through his body and out his back. He then moved the spear around, breaking ribs in the process as Ahiga slowly succumbed to the blunt force trauma caused by the sheriff of Montrose County. Before he died, the sheriff bent down and got up close to Ahiga's face.

"You see, I never lied to you. I kept my promise and set you free. Now you can be with your dead wife and child, in hell," said the sheriff.

*   *   *   *

"Where did they all go?" Asked Calixto.

"They all ran off into the orchard. Holt, his men, the Indians," said Ramon.

"Did you see the sheriff with them?" asked John.

"I didn't look out the window. I was too busy trying not to catch a bullet with my head," replied Guadalupe.

"I'm going out there," said John.

"John, give it a bit longer before you go out."

"No, my family is still in the house I need to check on them."

John turned around and looked back at his men, all armed with rifles and pistols, who were huddled in the center of the barn together. He looked down at the ground and noticed one of the men, lying in a pool of blood on the ground in the dirt.

"Who got shot?" asked John.

"Aniseto, John."

"He still alive?"

"No, he's dead."

John hung his head and shook it side to side in disgust.

"I'm losing more and more men as each day goes on. I lose anymore, Guadalupe, I won't have anyone left to work the god damn apples. Stay here, I'll be back."

John made sure his pistol was loaded, ready to fire if he needed, and then he opened the door to the barn. He stepped out into the darkness of the evening. The rain was pouring down on him as he looked around the area, seeing bodies strewn across the ground. Lightning stuck in the sky, momentarily lighting up the grounds around him just enough to see that no one was there but dead bodies. Ute men and some of Holt's men lay dead on the ground as he carefully walked past the bodies back to his home, careful to see if he could see anyone still alive around him. But there were none. John finally broke out into a run back to the home, rushing through the back door of the home.

"Martha!" he yelled in the home's darkness as he burst through the back door.

"John!" a reply from his wife came from the bedroom downstairs.

The door to the bedroom was closed, barricaded from the inside of the room.

"Martha, are you okay?" asked John as he ran to the bedroom to try to open the door. "The door is stuck!"

"Hold on, I have us barricaded in the room," said Martha, as she removed the bed from the door.

She opened the bedroom door, and John rushed in, hugging his wife in the room. Both children were inside the room with her.

"What happened out there?" asked his wife.

"The sheriff," replied John, letting go of her.

"What about him?"

"He brought some men out to kill us."

"That's impossible. He's the sheriff."

"He's not a good man, Martha. He has men here who Guadalupe thinks are a gang from Oklahoma. They were the ones shooting at the men and I in the barn."

"I don't believe it."

"Well do, because it's true."

"What do we do?"

"I think right now it's best if you and the children went back to stay with your brother in Philadelphia. I want you to be safe. Let Guadalupe and me handle what is going on here. When we get things cleaned up and safe around here again, then you and the kids can come back."

"What about Anna and Harry?"

"They'll be fine. The sheriff and his men don't know about them, and we need to keep it that way until I can get to them and tell them to leave and go back to Philadelphia, too."

"Okay, I'll trust you, John."

"Don't go outside for a little bit either," said John, turning around and leaving the room.

"Why?" asked Martha.

"There are dead men in the backyard that we need to clean up and get out of here."

Martha turned and grabbed her two children in the room and sat on the bed with them as John turned and walked out of the house. While he was walking outside, some of the Mexican men came out and met him in the yard, looking over the bodies. Thunder cracked in the distance again.

"Check and see what weapons or bullets you can get off them and then load the bodies up into the back of the wagon and get rid of them."

"Where do we take them, John?" asked Guadalupe.

"I don't care. Just get rid of them," said John, turning around to walk back inside the house when he stopped for a moment. He turned back around and spoke with the men. "You know what? We'll take the bodies to town. Drop them off in front of the realtor and sheriff's office."

John walked past the men and went into the barn to get his horse from the barn. The men grabbed the wagon nearby and pulled it over to the yard by hand, then loaded up Holt's dead men and the dead Ute men into the wagon. John came out of the barn with his horse, tying the animal to the front of the wagon. When his horse was secured to the wagon, John helped load up the dead bodies with the men.

"What about Aniseto and Refugio, John?" asked Guadalupe.

"Leave them here for now. They are like family to me. They will be given a proper burial in the family plot when we get back from town," said John.

The men finished loading the last of the bodies onto the wagon. In total, there were nine dead men in the yard, five of Holt's men and four of the Ute Indians. When the last dead man was placed on the wagon, John took off for town with some of his men sitting on the back of the wagon, making sure the bodies didn't fall off. When he arrived in town, it was nightfall already. Lightning continued to light up the night sky, and rolling thunder cracked in the distance.

Everyone in the town had returned to their homes for the evening, looking to escape the weather except for those citizens at Mary's Tavern getting their drinks in after a long day of work in the town. John pulled his wagon to the front doors of Hackenberry and Sanderlin Real Estate, where his men got off the back of the wagon and dumped some of Holt's dead men on the sidewalk by the front door of their business. The rest they dumped on the sidewalk by the front of the sheriff's office. When the last body was dumped on the sidewalk, they all jumped back onto the wagon and John left town, going back to his property under the cover of night in the middle of the storm.

Chapter 19: The Ides of August

The Ute men returned one by one to their camp in the San Juan mountains early in the morning hours just as the sun rose over the mountain. The storm from the night before moved out of the area, headed south to Texas. Sitting down on rocks and on the ground by their shelters, one by one, the men came back from their attack in the night. The grounds around their camp were muddied by the rainwater from the night before.

"There are so few of us returning to the camp. We lost men tonight," said Ignacio. "Where is Ahiga? He was in the apple trees with me."

"I don't know," said Ahote. "I lost track of him in the night."

"Who all hasn't returned?"

"Ahiga, Wanikiy, Utah, Tadi, Napayshni, Pallaton, Naakesh, and Makya," said Ahote.

"No wonder there are so few of us here," said Ignacio.

"I think everyone is here, Ignacio. The only man missing that I can't account for is Jaanesh."

"For all we know, he is dead, too."

"It's almost not worth fighting for anymore, Ignacio," said Ahote.

"It is always worth fighting for, Ahote. Until we get our lands back. We need to send a call for more Ute men to join us."

"From where? Where will they join us? The men we have left are all old, have seen many autumn moons rise and fall. There is no one left but us, Ignacio."

"Then we keep fighting until we succeed in our goals or join our fathers in death."

Footsteps sounded the side of the trail along the edge of the mountain. The men in the camp watched the trail as Jaanesh turned the corner and walked into the camp. Breathing heavily, he staggered into the camp and fell onto the ground by the men. His arm was stained with blood.

"Jaanesh! You're still alive!" said Ignacio.

"Bodies," said Jaanesh.

"What?"

"Bodies. Our people. Dumped in the streets of the town."

"What do you mean, Jaanesh?"

"The men that died last night, the apple farmer took them into town and dumped them in the streets like dead dogs. Their bodies rot in the town's mud."

Ignacio hung his head in frustration and anger. He shook with rage before tears of frustration poured out of his eyes. The thought of his family's burial plot being burned down by the apple farmer, his family and his men's families being burned alive along with all he had left, and now his dead men dumped off in the streets of the town was too much for him to take. With each fight he and his men took part in, and with each day that went by, Ignacio believed what the Pö' rat from his old camp told him more and more. Perhaps this was the beginning of his end, too.

"Did you see Ahiga among the dead in town?"

"No, I did not," replied Jaanesh.

"We must assume that he is dead, Ignacio," said Ahote.

"Jaanesh. Rest for a bit. Take one of the horses, and ride south along the river until you get to Nuche. When you reach their camp, ask for a man named Helushka Mountain Fire. Tell him that Ignacio Black Hawk needs help. I need more men. I need warriors. We are destined to die if we don't get more help to fight the white men."

"Ignacio, I will go right now."

"No, my friend. Rest, then ride. There is nothing we can do until we get more men to help in our cause."

Jaanesh understood and went and laid down in the mud around a large rock, where he rested for a short time along with the rest of the men. In total, they were five men now, after being a small band of nearly twenty Ute Indians. After Jaanesh had rested some, he got up and mounted a horse at their small camp. Then he rode south along the river, on his way to Nuche—another small Ute establishment, about a couple days' ride from them.

*   *   *   *

"How are we doing on lumber?" asked Charles Sanderlin, standing in the only piece of grass that was left in the area and careful not to dirty his clean business shoes.

He observed his construction site as the workers began building the large plantation resort building that was soon to be a high-class hotel for the elites from the east coast.

"We're doing good, Mr. Sanderlin. A shipment of lumber came in yesterday afternoon. Two by fours and more tools and supplies," said one of the workers.

"Yes, good. And the extra men from the east coast? How are they working out?"

"You see that we've got the foundation dug out, and the lower floor completely built, and we're starting work on the second floor. I would say they are working out well."

"Have you seen the Indians in the last week?" asked Charles.

"No, haven't seen anyone but workers around here. I heard they attacked that farmer across the river last week but haven't seen 'em for a while around here," said the man as he bent over, picked up more lumber and walked back to the construction area.

"Good. With any luck, they are all dead," said Charles.

"Mr. Sanderlin, will Mr. Hackenberry be out today?" asked another one of the men.

"No, he is working back at the office today."

"Okay, you can answer my question, too. When will we be paid next?"

"This Friday, gentlemen. And I tell you one thing, if you can have the second level built by then I'll throw in a twenty-dollar bonus into each of your paychecks, too."

The sound of this encouraged the men as they all hollered and went back to work feverishly. Charles smiled and turned around, walking back to his horse when he saw a familiar horse riding down the road to the construction site. The horseman rode up to where he stood along the side of the road and stopped next to him.

"Ahh, Mr. Hackenberry. What a pleasure to see you this morning," said Charles. "I wasn't expecting you to come out here this morning."

"How is the construction going, Charles?" asked James.

"I believe the men will be finished with the second level by this Friday. The construction, though, is coming along nicely. As you can see, my friend, the first level is completely constructed, and the men will start the second level soon."

"Any Indian attacks?"

"No, the men said they haven't seen any Indians for the last week now."

"Good. Perhaps the pile of dead bodies that ended up on our sidewalk last week was the last of them."

"Yes, but where did those bodies come from?" asked Charles.

"I don't know, and I don't care to be honest with you."

"Yes, but Walt nor George know where they came from."

"Like I said, Charles. All that matters is that they are dead. Perhaps it was a bounty hunter who wished to remain anonymous."

"Perhaps."

"Charles, walk with me," said James, as he dismounted his horse.

The two men walked away from the job site, out into the field where the grass for the golf course was being planted by some of the men working the grounds work. James and Charles stood on a hill that overlooked the open land and watched together as men spread grass seed about the ground.

"Walt is making a plan to kill Ashberger," said James.

"So, it has come to that, then?" asked Charles.

"John Ashberger will never sell that land to us, Charles. We've tried enough times now. He is hellbent on farming those god damn apples over there along with those Mexicans who look at him like a father."

"So, what is Walt planning?"

"We need everyone off that property. Everything, for that matter, his family, the Mexicans and their shacks by the river, his barn and animals, right down to his apple trees. The plan, Charles, is to burn the orchard. All of it. Burn his house, with his wife and children inside. Kill the Mexicans. Burn his barn to the ground, along with his animals in it. And then finally, according to Walt, slowly slide his knife into John's chest, cutting his heart in half and killing the great apple farmer of Montrose County."

"I take it George and what are left of his men are going to help do this too?"

"They are."

"It should be easy to do this with all the Indians dead. When do they plan on doing this?"

"Oh, any night now soon. Apparently, George Holt is seeing if he can recruit a few more men to come out from Oklahoma that are acquaintances of his."

"Family or friend?"

"Hell, I don't know, and does it really matter at this point?"

"Then we can pay them and be done with them. We need to be careful in the company we keep, James."

"Now don't be so quick to be finished with our people, Charles. We could use them after our tasks are finished and we come into possession of the land. We will need someone to provide some law and order for the town, and not just the town, but the surrounding county, too, should any other Indians come and try to ruin what we've built here and to keep the citizens under control."

"I will trust you, my friend. We are almost finished here, James. Soon we'll have control of everything and make a fortune off this land," said Charles, smiling as he looked over the future golf course.

"Indeed we will, my friend. Now come, we're to meet with Walt later this morning and discuss his plan with George Holt, too."

The two men walked off the hill and back to the construction site. When they arrived there, they observed the construction of their massive plantation resort. They then mounted their horses and rode back to town, back to their office. Charles followed behind James and when they arrived in town, they rode past the sheriff's office and saw Walt sitting in his rocking chair out in the front of his office, smoking a cigar.

"Good morning, Walt. Having a cigar for breakfast?" asked James.

"Is there any other kind of breakfast to have?" replied the sheriff.

"Are we still meeting this morning?"

"Yes, sir. Just waiting for Harry and Clarence to arrive. George is already inside the office resting," said the sheriff, sending a plume of smoke up into the air.

"Well, we will be waiting for you boys in our office," said Charles.

"You won't need to wait for long," said a voice coming from the street behind them."

"Well, Clarence. You're up early. Your night at the poker tables in the tavern end early last night?"

"You would think. Harry is on his way, too. Going to meet us at the realtor's office."

"Alright. You want to get George and bring him?" said James, dismounting from his horse and tying the animal to the hitching post.

Charles dismounted and tied his horse to the post as well. Walt got up, using the side of his fist, pounded on the door to his own office. He then walked with the two realtors over to their office. Clarence followed in right behind them. Charles started brewing some tea in the pot in the fireplace.

A few minutes later, the realtor's office door opened. George Holt and Harry Kilpatrick walked in. The realtors sat at their desks, while the men sat in chairs around the main office room. George Holt stood behind Charles, looking out through the glass out onto the street, watching the townsfolk walk to and from the different buildings. With all men present in the office now, James Hackenberry spoke to the group.

"Gentlemen, the time is coming for action. As many of you know, the resort has been under construction for the last two weeks now. I suspect that the resort will be in its final phase of construction by the beginning of autumn. Before the first snow falls here in the area. As you all know, John Ashberger and his family still reside on the twenty acres of apple land across the river from us."

"And we have a plan for that, James," said the sheriff. "The plan will be to burn the orchard. All twenty acres of it. Kill the Mexicans and burn their shacks down. Kill his horses and animals, burn his barn down. Kill his wife and children, burn their home down. Then finally, when John has seen he has lost it all, I will personally bury my knife in his chest and cleave his heart in two."

"How are you going to burn the orchard, though? Everything is wet. The small canals that run up and down the rows will make it difficult to catch anything on fire," said Harry.

"It'll be easy, my friend. There was a time when we would set fire to union soldiers back in the war. Now, what did we do first before dropping a match on them?" asked the sheriff.

"Camphene oil," replied Clarence.

"Indeed. Camphene oil. Insoluble in water."

"Where are we going to get camphene oil?" asked Charles.

"I know a guy in Oklahoma. Right now, he is sending a wagon to us with almost a hundred large clay jars of camphene oil. It should be here later today," said George.

"So, what are you proposing?" asked Charles.

"We are going to take the camphene oil and spread it around the orchard, on the trees, and into the small canals that run up and down the rows. Then one small match and poof. Twenty acres of a land will burst into flames just like that," said the sheriff.

"By god, that might just work," said Charles.

"It will work."

"Once the field is on fire, we can kill the Mexicans, then burn their shacks down before we fire to the orchard. Then we should be set up to gun the Mexicans down while they try to leave their shacks. The ones that wake up and try to leave, anyway."

"And once the Mexicans are all dead, it just leaves John, his wife, and two kids," said Clarence.

"Three kids," said the sheriff.

"Walt? I only know of the two."

"Oh, you didn't know he had a third?"

"I did not."

"Oh yes, she lives here in the town with her husband. It wouldn't be too difficult to kill them. In fact, you could probably do it right now and no one would notice. There's no way her bitch husband would be able to fight back. I don't think he could fight off a fly from his steak."

"All in due time, Walt," said James, as he reached into his desk and removed a file from one of the drawers. "Then finally, when he has lost it all, we kill John and the land will be ours. I have the paperwork right here, drafted already, for the new deed to the land, with our signatures on the title, ready to assume control."

Charles stood up and walked over to James's desk, grabbing the file from him and looking at the paperwork inside.

"This is genius, James. Well done. Soon, that property will be ours," said Charles.

"There is one more bit of business left to be tended to, however," said James, who stood up with his teacup in hand and walked over to the brewing tea in the fireplace.

Charles walked back over to his desk; his back turned to James as he looked over the paper documents in the file.

"Charles, would you like some tea?" asked James.

"Oh, yes, I would. James, this paperwork is perfect. You hit on every point needed to properly transfer the land out of John's name when he is dead."

James walked up to the mantle of the fireplace, quietly removing a knife from the mantle that was hidden behind some framed photographs.

"James, there's only one mistake on these documents, though, that I can see," said Charles.

"What is that, Charles?" asked James, as he turned around and walked up to Charles from behind.

"Well, it's only your name on the documents."

"Precisely," said James, raising the knife and driving the blade into the lower back of his business partner and long-time friend, Charles Sanderlin.

Charles let out a loud grunt as the knife penetrated his lower back. Blood stained the back of his white jacket as George pulled his knife out and jabbed it into Charles' chest. He fell to his knees when the sheriff, who was sitting nearby, quickly stood up, pulled out his knife, and slit Charles' neck. Blood gushed out of the wound. James retrieved the knife from his friend's back, then stabbed him again. Charles then fell face first onto the floor of the office, dying from his wounds, murdered by his friend and long-time business partner, James Hackenberry.

"Now then, with this piece of business having been addressed," said James, who bent over and picked up the paperwork that Charles had dropped.

"Oh good, he didn't bleed on the papers. This was my only copy I had made up, too."

"What do you want to do with his body?" asked the sheriff.

"Give him a proper burial. We were friends and business partners for years. The least I could do is give him a proper sendoff."

"Bury him tonight?" asked Clarence.

"No. Get rid of him now. I don't want to have to smell him throughout the day. Bury him in the town cemetery."

"In the daylight? People will see," said Harry.

"Let them see. It will remind them who looks over this town now," said James, as he turned and set the paperwork down on his desk.

Then he walked over to the mantle, placed the knife down, and carefully poured himself a cup of hot tea.

"Would anyone else like some tea?" asked James.

"Appreciate the offer, James, but I think the boys and I have work to do. You want us to clean up the blood, too?"

"No. No, it's fine. I can deal with that. Just please ensure Mr. Sanderlin gets a proper burial."

The sheriff and his men stooped down and picked Charles up. Each man took a limb, lifting him up, his white suit stained red with his own blood. The men took him outside, in front of the townsfolk. The citizens stopped and watched as they lifted his body up onto the back of a horse, then walked the animal over toward the cemetery through the town, where one of the pre-dug graves was waiting.

The citizens watched as they rode his body through the street to the cemetery. When they got there, some men went and fetched a pine casket from the carpenter's shop. They carried the flimsy casket back to the cemetery, where they set it down in the grave first, and they then lowered Charles' body down into the casket. Before covering it with the lid, the sheriff reached into Charles' pocket, pulling out his wallet and taking his money. He stuffed the money into his pocket and dropped the wallet back into the casket, and then they nailed the lid shut. When he finally crawled out of the grave, the men took shovels and buried Charles Sanderlin there in the cemetery of Montrose, Colorado. James had a tombstone specially made for Charles that was erected a short time later to mark the grave of Charles. The tombstone read:

"Here lies the body of our friend and colleague, Charles Sanderlin. Came from Baltimore to bring civility to a wild population, and received death from the Ute savages instead."

Chapter 20: George Holt the Ruthless Bastard

There was a loud knocking on the office door of Hackenberry and Sanderlin Realtor's Office. It was early morning, and a few days after "the Utes" managed to kill the business partner and close friend of James Hackenberry by driving their knives into his body. James, sitting at his desk in the office, stood up from his desk.

He took one last sip of herbal orange flavored tea from his cup before setting it back down on the desk and walking over to the front door. Grabbing the handle, he swung the door open to be greeted by a tall man with rough, dry skin. It appeared as if he had just ridden across the whole continental United States and back again. His clothing was dirty, and his belt that held a six shooter along with spare bullets was dry and cracked. His straw hat was worn and frayed. In his hand, he held a folded document.

"Are you Walt Jones or George Holt?" asked the man, extending his arm out to shake his hand.

"No, but they are acquaintances of mine," replied James.

"Oh, you must be James or Charles then, yes?"

"Yes, I am James Hackenberry. The realtor of this town," said James as he shook the man's hand.

"Oh yes, Hackenberry. I've seen your name on this list too. I have a delivery of eighty-five of these clay jars," said the man, pointing at the back of a wagon drawn by four large horses. "There's some kind of liquid inside of them, maybe wine. I don't know. I mean, that's a lot of wine, mister. Is someone getting married here in the town?"

"Oh. Yes, it's for a fall festival celebration for the next month," said James, as the two men walked over to where the wagon was parked in front of the realtor's office.

"Well, wine should be okay in these clay jars for storage. Just make sure you store it in a cool or shaded place. The wine should last for at least a couple months like this. Leave it out in the sun and it'll spoil in a couple of days, mister."

"I appreciate your concern and advice. I will ensure that it is stored in the safest of places," replied James.

"Alright, well, if you don't mind signing my paperwork, mister. Says I made my delivery, and you acknowledge that, and I can take this back to my boss."

"Of course," said James, taking a copy from the man.

"You're welcome to come in, get out of the wind out there. Would you like a cup of tea?" asked James.

"Oh, no thank you. I need to be on my way. My pay depends on how fast I complete deliveries and how much I can deliver in a month. So, coming from Oklahoma out here to Colorado is taking me away from my local deliveries."

"Well, I appreciate you taking the time and making the effort to deliver out here. The town folk do as well," said James, taking a quill from the ink jar and signing the rider's copy.

"It's certainly no problem, mister. Any time you need, my boss said that he'll get deliveries of whatever you want out here. It was a pretty ride too, so maybe I'll ask to be your delivery rider from now on, too," laughed the man.

"That sounds absolutely wonderful," said James, placing the quill back in the ink jar and handing the paper to the man.

"Thank you, sir. And you have your copy for your record as well?"

"Yes, you handed it to me."

"Good. Sometimes I forget if I do it or not. Well, I best be on my way now."

"Oh wait, what about the wagon?" asked James.

"Boss said for you to keep it. A favor he owes George he said? I'm not sure. I just do what I'm told, mister."

"What a nice gesture on your boss's part. And thank you for your efforts in delivering."

"Have a good day, Mr. Hackenberry."

The man tipped his worn hat to James, then walked out of the office. James took the paperwork, crumpled it into a ball and then tossed it onto the fire. He sat down at his desk when only a few minutes had passed, and Sheriff Walt Jones walked into the office.

"Oh, good. The oil arrived," said the sheriff.

"Oh no, that's wine, my dear friend," said James.

The sheriff laughed. "James, you drink that shit and you'll be dead in under a minute. It's very toxic. Yet very effective."

"Where's George at this morning?"

"Oh, he'll be on his way over here in a minute."

"I would say that tonight is the night that we execute what we have planned, Walt. We've waited quite long enough as it is. It's time. We can't wait any longer and we need to clear Ashberger's land out so we can plant grass before the fall and winter for the golf course there."

"Well, George will be happy to hear that we're ready for some action, too. Did he tell you the other night that he met John's oldest daughter and her husband out in the street?"

"No."

"Oh, yes. They were coming home from a play at the Stage West Theater."

"How'd he know who they are?"

"I pointed them out myself."

"What happened?"

"We found out where they live. Followed them to their home."

"Well, how about that?"

"I would suggest that we kill them first, James."

"Sounds fine by me."

The front door to the realtor's office opened and in walked George Holt, along with Edward Stokes.

"What did we miss?" asked George, as he and his man walked into the realtor's office.

"James wants to start killing John and his family and crew."

"Finally."

"Yes, and we need to make sure we kill every one of them. You understand?"

"Clearly."

"Good. Then tonight his oldest daughter, and son-in-law, will die."

"What do you want to do with the bodies?"

"I don't care. Leave them where they fall. We can blame it on the Indians again and the town can bury them if they wish. Just make sure you don't use guns. Use knives and hatchets, no projectiles."

"Alright James. Hell, why don't we go over now? Why wait?"

"I truly don't care when or how you men do it."

"Consider it done, James," said the sheriff as he stood up from his chair.

"Come on, you two," said the sheriff, as he walked by George and Edward, who followed him outside to the sheriff's office.

"This will be a good opportunity to show you just how well that oil works. We'll take a jar with us and pour it onto their home and then burn them dead while they're trapped inside. Like we did the Indians in their tents," said the sheriff.

"Sounds fine to me, Walt. Then we can let the town bury bones rather than bodies."

"Sure. To be honest, I don't care if those Mexicans are buried or not. Chances are no one around town will care if they are or not."

The sheriff reached out, grabbed the handle, and opened the door to his office, and inside, Harry and Clarence were sitting at his desk, both smoking cigars together.

"Who the fuck said you could smoke my cigars?" asked the sheriff.

"Oh, I just figured that you would be a man that wouldn't like to see a cigar sit around and go to waste," replied Harry.

"We got the word to move and kill Ashberger and his family."

"Good news. Then we can finally get this work done and be paid. We have an idea of how we want to do it?" asked Harry.

"We do. We're going to go kill the oldest daughter and her husband at their home first."

"When?"

"Now."

"In the daylight?"

"Yes."

"Won't that look bad for the county sheriff to be killing the townsfolk he's sworn to protect in broad daylight?"

"We're going to burn the home down with them in it."

"Well, I suppose that would be an efficient way of dispatching them."

"Then tonight, we're going to go after Ashberger and the rest of his family and kill his Mexicans, too."

"How do you propose we do that?"

"At night. We're going to take all of that camphene oil and pour it into the canals in the rows of the orchard. Then pour it all over the trees, too. The lands have dried out since the last rainfall a while back, so now is a good time to start a fire that will pick up fast and destroy the orchard."

"Okay, but what about the Mexicans?"

"We lock them into their shacks and burn them alive in them."

"And then his wife and kids at the home?"

"Kill them."

"Kill them too?"

"Yes. How yet I don't know. I would imagine we could use them as bait first and draw John out into the open if we must."

"So then, when he's out, just shoot them all?"

"Maybe. You know, back in the war, I sprayed a man with that oil and lit him on fire. No matter what he did, that oil adhered to his body like pitch from a pine tree. I watched as his skin melted off his body. So, I'm thinking maybe we will burn them, too," said the sheriff, as he reached into the drawer of his desk and pulled out a cigar, grabbing a match and lighting it.

"And Harry, let me tell you something. You haven't lived life yet until you seen this oil shit work and watched someone's skin dissolve into liquid as they burn alive. It's quite a spectacle."

"Sometimes, Walt, you can be a real sick bastard," said Clarence.

"Just the kind of man I like," said George, as he laughed behind them.

"But first thing is first, his oldest daughter and her husband," said the sheriff, drawing a puff from the cigar.

"We can handle it, Walt," said George.

"You want to see how that oil works, George?"

"No. We need to save it for the orchard. It's a big orchard."

"And it's a lot of dry land. This fire will probably be seen for miles, you guys. But in the meantime, go handle our business, George. Tell his oldest daughter and her husband that I give my regards too."

George turned to leave the office when the sheriff stopped him.

"George! Remember, make it look like the Indians did it."

George smiled, and then left the office, along with Edward, who followed close behind him.

"Gentlemen, by this time tomorrow, each one of you men will be rich. And you won't be smoking from my god damn box of cigars," said the sheriff.

*   *   *   *

"Anna! Did you go out and get the chicken eggs from the coop?" asked her husband, Harry, as he nailed another fresh board into the floor.

"Oh, no I did not yet. Do you want me to?" replied Anna.

"No, it's fine. I can run out there and do it too."

Harry picked himself up off the floor, setting the hammer down next to the nails. Anna walked into the room from the bedroom, carrying laundry with her.

"How is the floor coming along in this room?" asked Anna.

"It's just fine. You can walk on it now without falling through it," said Harry, as he used the back of his arm to wipe the sweat from his brow.

"Hey, that's a plus." Anna smiled as she leaned in and gave her husband a kiss.

"How is the laundry?" he asked.

"Ugh, still collecting. I just finished washing the bedsheets and now need to hang them up on the clothesline outside."

"Sounds like we both have a busy day ahead of us. I'll go out and get the eggs from the coop, then get back to working on the floor."

"Okay, sounds good to me."

"Love you."

"Love you, too."

Harry smiled and turned, leaving the house through the back door. He walked out into the backyard and saw that the chickens were scattered around the yard, pecking at the ground, as they normally do. Walking to the coop, he opened the door and walked in. Inside the coop, there were individual wooden boxes where the chickens would lie and lay eggs. He reached over and grabbed a bucket hanging by the door and went through each individual box, grabbing laid eggs and carefully placing them in the bucket, when he heard a noise come from behind him.

"Hey Anna, I can handle this. It's no problem, there aren't that many eggs today again," he said as he turned around, expecting to see his wife there.

Instead, there stood George Holt, with one hand behind his back.

"Who the hell are you and what are you doing on my property!?" yelled Harry, as George removed the hand from his back that held his knife, jabbing it into Harry's throat before Harry could react.

Harry dropped the bucket of eggs, breaking most of them on the ground as blood poured from his throat, stifling his breath as he staggered back with the blade still lodged in the front of his throat. He took two steps back, and then fell back into the chicken boxes, breaking some under his own body weight. By the time Harry's body hit the ground, though, he was dead. George walked up to his lifeless body and yanked the knife out of his throat, which caused spurts of blood to eject from the open wound.

"Good night, sweet prince," said George, as he wiped his knife clean using the front of his pants and sheathed it in the scabbard on his belt.

He looked around the coop and there he found another one of Harry's claw hammers, hanging up on the wall being supported by nails in the wall.

Inside the house, Anna finished grabbing dirty clothes from the last room of the home—the baby's room that the couple was working on after Anna found out recently that she was three months pregnant. Before leaving the room, she turned and smiled in anticipation of this time next year.

She walked outside and set the basket of dirty clothes by the wash bucket and grabbed the clean bed sheets. She rang out the bedsheets, then walked over to the clothesline in the backyard and hung up the bed sheets one by one. As Anna hung the second set of sheets, she noticed a shadow on the ground approaching her from behind.

"Harry, how many eggs were there in the coop today?" she asked as she held some clothespins in her mouth.

But Harry didn't respond to her.

Instead, George raised the hammer and struck Anna will full force in the back of her head, rendering her unconscious. She slumped to the ground in front of the clothesline of bed sheets, lifeless. George swung the hammer six more times, splattering the clean sheets with blood as Anna died there in the yard under the hand of Oklahoma's infamous gangster, George Holt.

*   *   *   *

The sheriff reached back into his desk, pulling his second cigar out for the day, along with a match. Striking the match on the side of his desk, he lit the cigar and started smoking. He shook the match out, walked outside of his office and tossed the burned match into the dirt street. Sitting down in the rocking chair on the sidewalk by the front door, he leaned back and exhaled a plume of smoke from his mouth.

"What a goddamn beautiful day," he said to himself, as the sun was out and not a cloud was in the sky.

For being early afternoon, it was getting warmer out—a true Colorado late summer day. He was grateful that his rocking chair was in a shaded area and the back of the office was catching more sun than the front. He was still sweating, just sitting in the shade, though, as beads of sweat ran down his neck and face. Sheriff Jones exhaled another puff of smoke from the cigar when he saw George Holt walking across the street over to the office, followed by one of his men.

"George, how did it go?"

"The job is done. They're both dead," he said.

"Good, well done. Then what has been done has set future events in motion that cannot be undone now."

"Indeed. We need to act tonight on the rest of the Ashbergers. I would assume John wouldn't be too happy finding out that his oldest daughter and her husband are dead as well. You got a cigar for me?" asked George.

The sheriff reached into his coat pocket and pulled out a cigar, along with a match. George sat down in the rocking chair next to him and lit the match, then his cigar, and tossed the match out into the street.

"What time do you think we should start heading out to their property this evening?"

"Oh hell, I would say at dusk. We can hook up a couple of the horses to the wagon and haul it out there. Then take some ladles and start spreading that oil over as many trees as we can. Some men can pour some of the oil into the canals that run through the orchard too. We'll let the canals carry the oil down for us. Then one match later and everything will be ablaze. The long dry grass in between the rows will also help the fire spread through the orchard quicker."

"I suppose you're doing this at a good time of the year, with everything so dry and before the autumn rains come."

"Like I said, George. It's now or never," said the sheriff, exhaling another plume of smoke from his cigar.

"I'll be sure and go tell the men what we're doing. It might take a while without too many men to just get the oil poured."

"It will. Which is why you all should get some rest. What did you do with his daughter's body?"

"Left it. Made it look like the Indians got them."

"No guns?"

"No guns."

"Good. Go get some rest, George. Meet back here by sunset. I'm going to ride out here in a bit and check out the progress of the resort. I'll also look for a way to get into that orchard without having to go down their main road."

"Why don't you take the old bridge to the south of the property?" asked George.

"Because that's where the god damn Mexicans are," replied the sheriff.

"So, you take your time, move slowly, use the sound of the rushing river water to mask your sounds. Or kill them before getting onto the property, and then set fire to the orchard."

"Or you could take the other bridge to cross the river down there by the burial ground?" said George, taking a puff from the cigar.

"What other bridge?" asked the sheriff.

"The Indians constructed another bridge over in the corner of the property where the burial ground is. I would imagine that's where they came in the other night when we caught Ashberger and his guys in their barn."

"Even if they made a bridge there, do you think it's strong enough to get horses and a wagon full of that oil across it? Or even stable enough?"

"Utes do everything twice as hard as most other Indians. It probably can. While you're out, why don't you check it out and have a look?" said George.

"Alright, I will."

"Well, with all due respect, sheriff, I am going to go speak with the boys and then get some rest. I appreciate the cigar, as always. Maybe I'll even get a good meal in. There's nothing like a good meal and a good cigar after killing someone."

"You're welcome," said the sheriff, thinking about this bridge that allegedly the Utes had built the previous night.

He thought about it and began to believe that it must be true. The only way the Indians could have attacked them the other night from the direction that they came from was swimming over the river or crossing a bridge. The sheriff stood up from his rocking chair, checked his pistol to ensure that it was loaded, then mounted his horse and, with his cigar in mouth, took off for the realtor's property.

It didn't take him long to ride out of town, down to the construction site. When he arrived there, he saw the men were already halfway finished on the second level of the plantation style resort. One man working on the ground noticed the sheriff and came over to speak with him.

"Good afternoon, sheriff," said the young man.

"Afternoon. How are you boys doing out here today?" asked the sheriff.

"Oh, fine. Everything is going fine. Just working on the second level here. Grass seed is being planted in the field right now."

"Good. Sounds like you all are making some progress. Savages give you any more trouble lately?"

"None since the other day when they were here, sir. Been quiet out here for a while."

The sheriff looked across the river, over onto John Ashberger's property. He saw some smoke billowing up into the sky as if he were burning a pile of brush.

"Any of you boys know of any way across this river to the other side of the land?"

"Well, there's a bridge down the way that leads to a small shack down there. Indians killed the old man that was living there, we heard."

"Is that it?"

"Well, we haven't had time to wander too far around the river, sir."

"You got a horse?"

"Yes, sir. I do. I have her tied up to the tree in the shade on the other side of the job site here."

"Get it. You're coming with me."

"Where are we going?"

"Down the river to see if there is another bridge."

The young man hurried off and retrieved his horse from the shade before they took off down the riverbank until they came up to the bridge that the young man had mentioned.

"There, that bridge, sir," said the young man, as they approached the bridge.

"This the one that leads to the road down to the shack where the old man lived, yes?"

"Yes, sir."

"I hear there is potentially another one just up ahead."

"No, I wouldn't know anything about that, sir. I just know of this one."

"Well, come ride with me and let's have a look up ahead."

"Yes, sir."

The two men rode ahead for five minutes beyond the first bridge they came across, when they came across a shallow point in the water. The sheriff looked over when he noticed the riverbed was only inches below the top surface of the water and saw footsteps in the mud leading down to the water along the bank.

"Stop!" yelled the sheriff.

The two horses stopped abruptly, and the sheriff dismounted his horse. He walked a slight decline down into the river, stepping out into the water. The water level barely covered the toe of his boots. He stepped out further into the water and the ground was solid rock.

"Ride your horse down here," said the sheriff.

The young man rode down the embankment and took his horse into the shallow section of the water. The ground held the weight of the horse with ease.

"It wasn't a goddamn bridge they used to cross over the water. It's just a shallow section of the river."

"I'm sorry, sir, but what are you talking about?"

"Nothing. Head back to your work site. I've seen all I need to see here. Thank you for your help."

"Alright, anytime, sheriff. Have a good day."

The young man turned the horse around and galloped out of the river, up the embankment and back towards his job site. The sheriff stood in the middle of the river as the water rushed around his feet, examining the embankments on each side of the river. It seemed very possible to cross the river and the embankment on the other side. He found exactly what he was looking for—a solid crossing point onto Ashberger's property without being detected.

The sheriff walked out of the river, back to his horse. He reached into his satchel and removed a red cloth from it and tied the cloth around the limb of a fallen tree, marking the location. Finally, the sheriff mounted his horse and rode back to the work site and then back into town, resting at his office for the long night he and his men had ahead of them.

Chapter 21: The Dark Night of the Souls

The door to the sheriff's office squeaked open, while the sheriff was lighting a lamp at his desk for some more light in the late evening. He shook the match until the flame was extinguished and then looked up, expecting to see George Holt or one of the other men, but instead he saw James Hackenberry.

"James, what are you doing here?" asked the sheriff.

"I'm coming out with you this time to help," said James.

The sheriff laughed but then realized that James was serious.

"You're serious, aren't you?"

"I am."

"Well, James, you're welcome to come along, but it will not be pretty tonight."

"With all due respect, Walt, I stuck a knife into my friend's back earlier today, then buried his body in a rather uncivilized way. I think I can handle not pretty."

The door opened to the sheriff's office again, and George Holt and the rest of the men walked in with him.

"What the hell is he doing here?" asked George.

"He's coming with us tonight. All hands on deck, George. I need every swingin' dick in the field right now because we have a lot of work to do this evening. Are you boys ready?"

"Ready as we'll ever be," said George.

"You ever use a gun, James?" asked the sheriff.

"Once before I have," replied James.

"Well then, take one of the pistols from the gun cabinet by the door and let's go. Earlier today, I found a section in the river where it is shallow enough to take the wagon and horses across. The ground there is solid. We'll get through easy enough."

"So, this route that you are planning to use, will we stay undetected once we're on John's side of the river?"

"With ease, under cover of the night," said the sheriff.

"And I see you have the horses hooked up and ready to ride already."

"I do."

"Everyone's pistols loaded?"

Everyone checked their weapons and acknowledged that their pistols were loaded and ready to use.

"James, how is your pistol?"

"Seems loaded."

"Looks like it is to me, too. I suggest you strap the holster to your belt as well."

The sheriff reached into his desk and took out a holster and belt and tossed it towards James, who took it and tied it to his waist.

"I think we're ready," said Clarence.

"Then, gentlemen, let's go," Walt said as he walked around the corner of his desk and left the office.

Night had just fallen, and the sun was completely set. The sheriff mounted the seat on the wagon that carried the clay jars of oil. George and another one of his men mounted their own horses, while the rest of the men got into the back of the wagon with the oil. The sheriff then shook the reins, and the wagon started to move.

They slowly rode out of the town, towards the resort's construction site, passing through the camp where some workers were still awake and sitting around a large campfire. They continued riding along the side of the river until they passed the bridge that led to old man John Murdock's place. The sheriff focused, using the light of the lamps held by George and his man up in the front of their horses until they came up to the red cloth he had tied on the fallen tree earlier in the day.

"Here," said the sheriff, as he held back the horses and wagon.

George and his man stopped their horses as well.

"What do you mean here?" asked George.

"This is the spot. Walk down the embankment and test it out for yourself."

George cautiously rode his horse down to the river and went in and realized the sheriff wasn't lying about the shallow stretch of river.

"We're lucky it's late summer and we're in a drought right now. The ground is firm enough for the wagon to get across."

"This is how the Indians crossed the river the other day and attacked us," said the sheriff.

"Indeed, it is."

"I'll get back up to the wagon, bring it down here, and cross. When we get to the other side, extinguish our torches and follow me. We need to be careful and quiet. I will take us down to the orchard first. We'll spend most of our time there tonight. Then we'll deal with the Mexicans. Then I'll handle Ashberger and his family myself."

The sheriff walked out of the river and back up to the wagon, informing the men of his plan. He carefully navigated the horses and wagon down the embankment, trekking across the river to Ashberger's property. George and Frank dropped their torches into the water and followed the wagon as the sheriff steered the horses towards the orchard.

They quietly rode and pulled the wagon until a short time later they came across the first set of rows. Apple trees stretched on for what seemed like forever, and the canals were filled with water that flowed down the rows and back into the river.

"George," whispered the sheriff, looking back in his direction.

George quietly rode up to him on the wagon.

"We need to dam this spot in the canals where the water goes back out to the river. We need to keep the oil in the canals in the orchard. If we don't clog this spot, then the oil will just flow back out into the river," said the sheriff.

George looked down and saw the point where the trenches were dug and came together into one larger canal that led back to the river. George got off his horse and found a rock that was close to the size of the canal resting right by the connecting point where the trenches came together to form a larger canal. Getting some help from the men, they pushed the rock down into the canal, effectively blocking the flow of water.

"Now, we have limited time to get up to the top of the orchard where the water is coming in from the river and dump all the oil into the trenches and canals. The sheriff took the wagon and steered the horses carefully up to the other side of the orchard while George and Frank mounted their horses and rode behind the wagon. A short time later, they reached the top of the hill in the orchard and found the canal where the water flowed in from and filled the trenches that ran between the rows of apple trees.

"This is it," said the sheriff. "We dump all the oil here into this canal and the flow will carry it throughout the orchard for us, but we need to hurry. That dammed canal down at the bottom of the hill is no doubt holding the water back and going to flood soon."

The men jumped out of the back of the wagon, while two men stayed in the wagon. Some men grabbed the smaller jars of oil, tossing it onto the apple trees of the orchard. The two men in the back lifted the larger, heavier clay jars down to the ground where the sheriff, George, James, and the rest of the men opened the lids and poured the oil into the canal. The oil flowed into the river water and moved out into all the trenches that ran between every row of apple trees in the orchard.

The men spent nearly all-night dumping large clay jars and smaller clay jars, one by one, into the canal, spreading oil around some trees, until they were down to just a few jars left in the wagon.

"That's it. Save the rest for the Mexicans and their shacks," said the sheriff, who got back into the wagon driver's seat and kicked the horses back around, steering the wagon out of the orchard.

The men carefully walked behind as George and Frank mounted their horses again and rode behind the men. They worked their way over to the farm hands shacks, and when they got there, they noticed that all the men were asleep inside still. Not one person was out of bed.

The men slowly took more clay jars of the oil out, spreading it onto the shacks one by one until the sides of all the shacks were covered. The sheriff then took one of the clay jars and poured a trail of oil on the ground, connecting each shack to one another. When the jars were exhausted of their contents, he took a cigar from the inside of his black jacket and stuck it in his mouth. He then removed a match from his jacket pocket, struck it against a stone on the ground, and lit his cigar. With the match still lit, he dropped it down into the trail of oil and it instantly ignited in flame.

The trail of fire ran across the ground until it got to the first shack. The first shack then burst into flames with men sleeping inside. The flames from the first shack reached the next shack, followed shortly by the next shack in the same manner, until all the shacks were in flames.

Inside, the men could be heard waking up and screaming for help, as the sheriff and his men stood back and watched the shacks burn. The shack doors opened, and some men ran out of them, trying to avoid the fire, only to be shot and killed by George Holt and his men.

Back at the barn on the property, John Ashberger was still working with Guadalupe, Ramon, and Roman. Ramon saw the shacks burning at the edge of their property. They all ran down to the shacks by the river to see what was happening when suddenly they saw their entire orchard bursting into flames as each row lit up on fire. Fire quickly spread from one side of the orchard to the other, up the rows and igniting the trees. The men stopped running and looked at the orchard in shock, watching as their livelihoods burned right before their eyes. All they had worked for over the last five years was being destroyed by fire.

John sank to the ground on his knees, watching his crop burn. The other three men continued to run towards the shacks to check on the men. John came to and then got to his feet and ran down towards the shacks as well. When they got there, they saw the shacks were completely engulfed in fire.

The heat from the fire in the orchard was immense, and they couldn't get close to it. John tried getting close to the shacks to see if he could help anyone, but he saw that there was no one to help anymore. His men lay dead on the ground by the shack doors, and inside the burning inferno he saw that some men didn't get out of the shacks alive either. John then heard something else—popping sounds coming from the direction of his house.

"What is that?" asked Guadalupe as the four men turned and looked back at the house.

A couple more popping sounds could be heard coming from the house again, followed by flashes of light with each pop.

"Gunshots," said John, who started running back up to the house.

The other three men who were still alive followed him up to the house, but John ran faster than they did and made it to the home first. He kicked the back door in and ran inside the home.

"Martha!" he yelled for his wife as he frantically ran around the first level of the home.

It was quiet in the home. John drew his pistol as he cleared each room frantically. John eventually made his way into the bedroom, where he found the body of his wife, Martha, dead in bed with gunshot wounds across her chest. Blood covered the bedsheet and her nightgown.

John dropped his pistol on the floor. His world collapsed around him as he walked over to the bed, staring at the lifeless body of his wife. Guadalupe was the first of the Mexicans to enter the home, followed by Ramon and Roman. The three men made their way to John's bedroom as well and saw the lifeless body of his wife, along with John kneeling against the side of the bed. His breathing intensified as he grabbed the sides of his head and wept.

"Ramon, go upstairs and check if the children are still alive," said Guadalupe.

Ramon turned and went up the stairs to the children's room as John wept at the bedside. A short time later, Ramon came back downstairs.

"Well?" asked Guadalupe.

"There's only one up there in bed. She is dead too. She was shot," said Ramon.

"Jesus. Jesus have mercy," said Guadalupe, making the sign of the cross on his chest with his hand. "Did you not see the youngest, Ida?"

"I did not."

"Did they take her?"

"I don't know."

Guadalupe walked over to John, who was still on his knees by the side of the bed, weeping over her deceased body.

"John, I know this is hard. But you need to find your youngest daughter."

John ignored him. His thoughts were completely disoriented, running in all directions.

"John, listen to me," said Guadalupe, grabbing his shoulders to get John to look at him. "Ida is missing. Martha is dead. Margaret is dead too. You need to focus for a minute. There will be time to mourn. But right now, you need to find Ida. Do you understand, John?"

John wiped tears from his face with the back of his shirt sleeve. Then he tried to pick himself up off the ground. Guadalupe helped him up to his feet as John staggered from the bedroom. Passing the other two men, John made his way to the staircase and walked up the stairs to Margaret's room. There, he found the body of his deceased daughter as well. She, too, had bullet wounds in her chest.

He started to turn and leave the room when he heard a sound come from behind him from the closet. John turned around and noticed the closet door opening slightly. He raised his pistol and aimed it at the closet door when he saw it was Ida opening the door. She had hidden in the closet and in her arms were her stuffed dolls Ollie, Ellen and Kelly.

"Papa?" said Ida, as she stepped out of the closet.

John holstered his pistol and ran over to his youngest daughter. Kneeling down, he grabbed onto her and gave her a hug.

"Baby, are you okay? Are you hurt?" asked John as he looked over her body for wounds.

"What happened?" she asked him. "Why would the sheriff come into our home and do this?"

John boiled with rage, hearing his daughter say this.

"Did you see who did this, Ida?" he asked.

"Yeah, the sheriff came inside Margaret's room and hurt her," she said, tearing up.

Guadalupe, Roman and Ramon came up the stairs and into the bedroom.

"Baby, how do you know it was the sheriff?" asked John.

"I saw his badge through the crack in the closet. He used his gun, and he shot Margaret, and she fell backwards onto the bed."

"Was there anyone else you saw?"

"I heard a bunch of footsteps, but I only saw the sheriff come into the bedroom. Margaret told me to hide in the closet and that she would talk to the sheriff and make everything okay."

"John, what about your oldest daughter and her husband?" asked Guadalupe.

John never had thought about them until Guadalupe just asked that.

"Ida, you need to come with me. We're going to check on your sister and Harry."

"I don't want to leave, papa."

"We're going to."

"Where are we going, papa?"

"Going to go into town, to your sisters. Then we'll figure out what to do from there."

"Are we going to go see the puppy?" asked Ida.

"Yes, now get your jacket on and let's go see the puppy."

"Okay, papa."

John walked out into the hallway with the three men, speaking to Guadalupe.

"Guadalupe, please stay here. Take care of the home until I sort things out with my oldest daughter."

"John, what about Martha and your daughter?" asked Guadalupe.

"Leave them for me. I will take care of them both when I come back. Let me bury my blood."

"We'll be here to help, John. Any way that we can."

"Thank you, Guadalupe. You've always been a good friend," said John.

"Okay papa, I'm ready," said Ida as she walked out of the bedroom.

"Okay, let's go to the barn and get my horse and we'll ride into town together."

"Be safe, John," said Guadalupe.

"We will. Come on, Ida."

John and his youngest daughter went outside to the barn. John wasn't sure how he was going to explain to Ida just yet about what happened to her mother, but the only thing on his mind now was to get to his oldest daughter and her husband. Instinct told him that something didn't feel right if all this damage happened to his property.

The two went into the barn and got John's horse out. John helped Ida up onto the back of the animal while he got into the saddle.

"Hold on tight, Ida. We're going to ride fast," said John.

"Okay, papa."

John shook the reins, and the horse took off, sprinting out of the barn and up the road towards Montrose. As dawn broke through the darkness, John made it into town. He rode through the town to his daughter and her husband's home, just on the outskirts of the town. Riding up to the property, John dismounted his horse.

"Ida, wait here. I'll be right back, okay?"

"Why can't I come in, papa?" she asked him.

"I just want to make sure everything is safe, is all, okay? So do papa a favor and just stay here for a few minutes. I'll be right back, okay?"

"Okay, papa."

John forced a smile on his face for Ida to reassure her. He then turned and walked towards the front door of his oldest daughter's home. Stepping up onto the front doorstep, he knocked on the front door and on the third knock; the door opened of its own accord.

Removing his pistol from the holster, John pushed the door open with the barrel of the gun and walked inside.

"Anna! Harry!" he yelled in the house.

But there was no reply.

John walked through the house and there appeared to be no one home. Nothing had been knocked over or damaged, as if there had been a physical altercation there. John walked towards the back of the house, through the kitchen and dining room area where he looked up and noticed that the back door to the home was wide open. He walked outside, into the backyard and saw some laundry still hanging up, when he heard a dog coming from the chicken coop. The door to the coop was wide open, too.

John walked over to the door of the chicken coop where he found the body of his son-in-law being eaten by a coyote that paid no attention to his presence. John raised his gun and shot the coyote, killing it instantly. He holstered his gun and walked up to Harry, bending down to have a look at him. He noticed he had a large stab wound through the side of his throat.

"Oh God, no," said John.

He quickly stood up straight and ran out of the chicken coop and looked around the yard, when he noticed the sun peaking over the San Juan Mountain range and lighting up the area where the laundry was hanging up. He saw crimson splotches on the white sheet, then a basket of clothing resting on the ground, still waiting to be hung up on the lines. John walked over to the clothesline, moving some clothes out of the way. As he walked through the hung-up laundry, he glanced down at the ground, where he saw his youngest daughter Ida, in tears, standing over the dead body of his oldest daughter Anna.

John screamed out loud. He quickly grabbed Ida and turned her face away from the gory scene where the back of his oldest daughter's head was completely caved in, exposing brain matter from the open wound. John looked around and found the murder weapon lying on the ground—a hammer stained with his daughter's blood. He picked up his daughter and walked back into the house, sitting her down at the dining room table on one of the chairs there. He sat down with her in another chair.

"I don't know what to do," said John.

Ida looked up at him, tears falling out of her eyes and down the side of her rosy and innocent cheeks.

"I knew this day would come. I knew it. I was anticipating this day to happen. I'm paying for the sins of my past, and the cost is more than I can bear," said John.

John took a deep breath, fighting back tears himself and trying to stay strong for his daughter, the last of his bloodline.

"Ida, I need to send you back to Philadelphia. I want you to go to your aunt and uncles, and I want you to stay there for now."

"I don't want to leave you, papa," she said, crying more.

"I don't want you to worry about me. I will meet you there. But for one, I need to keep you safe and two, there are some things I need to do before I can come out to Philadelphia with you. Can you be strong for me and travel on your own if I send a telegram out to your aunt and uncle?"

"Okay, papa. I'll try."

"Thank you, baby. We need to leave here, though. This is no home for us anymore."

"Okay, papa," said Ida, wiping tears from her face with her shirtsleeve.

"We need to go back home, pack some of your things, and then I will take you to the train terminal and get you a ticket for Philadelphia."

"Can I bring Ollie, Ellen and Kelly too?" asked Ida.

"Of course, you can," said John, forcing another smile through his tears.

The two got up from the table and walked out the front door of the home. John helped her up onto the back of his horse, then mounted the horse himself. He then turned and rode the short distance into town and stopped at the courthouse, as it had just opened for the morning. John got off his horse and helped Ida off as well and together they walked inside.

"Mr. Ashberger, good morning. How are you doing this morning?" asked the clerk.

"It's been a hell of a night to tell you the truth," replied John. "I need to send a telegram out this morning, please."

"Okay, I can do that. Hey, did you see all that smoke coming from the south part of town there?"

"Yes, I did."

"I wonder what is being burned?"

"I'm not sure, but can we hurry up and send the telegram?"

"Oh, sure. Who am I sending to?"

"Robert and Mary Rogers, Philadelphia, Pennsylvania," said John.

"And the message you want to send them?" asked the clerk.

"Ida is coming to stay with you for a few days, end sentence. Please pick her up from the train depot, end sentence. She will be leaving Montrose today, end sentence. Be arriving in Philadelphia in two days' time, end sentence. Please pick her up and keep her with you until I can come too, end telegram."

"Got it. I'll be sending to Philadelphia's clerk's office, and they will relay the message to Mr. and Mrs. Rogers, John."

"How much is it?"

"Twenty cents today, John."

John reached into his pocket, paying the twenty cents to the clerk.

"You want a written receipt, John?" asked the clerk.

"No, it's fine."

"Well, thanks for stopping by John. I'll send the message out right now. Hope you have a good day."

"Thank you," said John, turning around to leave the courthouse.

He opened the door to step outside, to be met face to face with the sheriff of Montrose County.

"Oh, John. Good morning to you," said the sheriff.

John gritted his teeth. The thought of pulling his pistol out and gunning this bastard down right here in the courthouse crossed his mind, but the time wasn't right yet. Not now. Not in front of the people of the town. Killing the sheriff now in cold blood here in the streets of Montrose would be a sure way to the hangman's noose.

"It's fine, sheriff. A good morning," replied John.

"That's really good. Is this your youngest daughter?" asked the sheriff, surprised to see her with John.

"It is," said John.

"What a sweet little girl. You really do have a beautiful family, John. Someday if I ever have a family myself, I'd hope they are just like yours. Wife and all."

"That's great."

"Well, don't let me stop you from getting on with your day."

John grabbed his daughter's hand and walked out the door, dragging her out the door with him. The sheriff smiled, closing the door behind them.

"Well, it has been a busy morning already. What brings you in today, sheriff?" asked the clerk.

"Just coming in to see what John Ashberger wanted is all."

"Well, he's having a telegram to family in Philadelphia."

"What did it say?"

"Well, you can see the copy for the county record here, sheriff, but I don't know why you gotta see that."

The clerk handed the copy of the telegram to the sheriff, who looked it over.

"The train to Philadelphia today, huh?" asked the sheriff, handing back the copy to the clerk.

He thanked the clerk for her time and, with a smile on his face, turned and left the courthouse.

Chapter 22: On Their Wrongs Swift Vengeance Waits

"Alright Ida, pack what you can and don't forget your dolls too. Make haste," said John, as he held the back door to his home open.

The orchard out in the field was still burning in some places and the workers' shacks were completely burned down to the ground. Only bones and some charred remains of his men were left in the rubble.

Ida ran past her Papa and up to her room to pack her clothing and stuffed dolls in a bag. John walked back out onto the deck and looked over the orchard when he saw Guadalupe walking up from the field. His face and arms were covered in ash and soot.

"The whole fucking thing is a loss, John. It's all gone. Every god damn tree is either on fire or burned down," he said.

"Where are Ramon and Roman?" asked John.

"Inside, resting in the barn on some piles of hay. They've been up all night, John."

"You should have got some rest as well, Guadalupe."

"I kept an eye on your wife and daughter, making sure nothing more happened to them."

"Thank you, Guadalupe. I've always been able to count on you," said John as he sat in a rocking chair on the deck and buried his face in his hands.

"What do we do now, John? Everything we've worked for in the last five years is gone up in smoke," said Guadalupe.

"I'm sending Ida to Philadelphia to stay with Martha's in-laws. If we live after what we must do, I'll go and join her there. I don't really care where you go from here, though, Guadalupe. You or Roman and Ramon certainly don't have to be a part of this, and the three of you can leave back to your families in Mexico if you want. There's nothing more for you boys here. In fact, I'd rather you boys leave. I don't want you getting caught up in this mess."

"John, we've been caught up in it for months now. The Indians, the sheriff and his men, the realtors... They killed all our friends too, John."

"Which is why I can't have you boys getting mixed up in this even more than you already are and getting killed for it."

"And what about you?"

"What about me?"

"You going to get killed yourself? Will that justify your feelings? Then what about Ida? What happens to her?"

"She'll be fine in Philadelphia with her aunt and uncle. Even if something happens to me. I just need to make sure she gets on that train and on her way back to the east coast."

John stood up and walked away from Guadalupe, back toward the back door of the home.

"You boys get out of here, Guadalupe. Save yourselves," he said, as he stood up and walked back into the house, calling for Ida to come downstairs.

Guadalupe sat in the rocking chair, watching as the field continued to burn.

"Ida, are you ready to go?" asked John.

"Yes, Papa. I'm just grabbing Ollie, Ellen and Kelly."

"Hold on to them tight, baby," said John.

He picked up her bag of clothing, then ushered her out the back door and back to his horse in the backyard. Helping her back up on the horse, he handed her the bag of clothing and instructed her to stuff her dolls into the bag so that they weren't dropped on the ride to the train station. Ida stuffed the dolls into the bag and held on tight to her father. John then shook the reins and spurred the horse and the animal took off, headed for town. Guadalupe watched as the horse disappeared down the road in the distance.

After riding for a short time, John made his way to the train terminal in Montrose, where he tied his horse to a hitching post and went inside the terminal to check the departure times for Philadelphia. The train to Philadelphia was leaving in about twenty minutes and was now boarding passengers. It was the last train to leave for Philadelphia for the next couple of days. He walked his daughter up to the ticket counter, paid nearly forty dollars for the one-way ticket to Philadelphia, and hurried her out the terminal doors and out onto the passenger dock.

"Papa, I don't want to leave you," said Ida, with tears in her eyes again.

"Honey, listen to me. I know you're scared. But it's all going to be okay. Uncle Rob and Aunt Mary are going to pick you up in Philadelphia and then when I'm finished handling a few things here in town, then I will be right there, and we'll be together forever, okay?"

Ida sniffled, then wiped tears from her face with the back of her hand.

"Okay, papa. I love you," she said.

"I love you too, honey. Don't worry because everything is going to be okay. I promise that."

"Okay," she said, picking up her bag from off the passenger dock.

She gave her father a hug and then turned and walked onto the train, where the conductor assisted her with finding her seat.

"Okay, there she is," said the sheriff to Clarence and Harry, who were standing inside the terminal, watching through the glass and out of sight from John.

"When you get going, see if you can sweet talk her and then coax her to a private place to kill her. Then from there you can go wherever you decide you want to retire, I suppose. You can dump the body off along the tracks somewhere and no one will ever know."

"Not a problem at all, Walt. We'll telegram you on where to send our pay, but I think we'll go to Florida after all of this is finished. Maybe retire somewhere on the west coast down there."

"That sounds delightful, gentlemen. Maybe one day our paths will cross again. But for now, get your asses on that train and remember, no guns. Keep it quiet. Use a knife."

"No problem," said Harry, as the two men boarded the boxcar behind the one Ida walked into.

John watched his youngest daughter, his last, turn in the window seat and wave goodbye. The train blew its horn, and the conductor added coal to the fire, propelling the train forward along the tracks. John watched the train disappear in the distance from the dock, leaving him feeling very much alone.

"Excuse me, miss," said Harry as he walked past a female passenger and sat down in seat 9A onboard the train to Philadelphia, Pennsylvania.

His friend and colleague, Clarence Bell, sat down in seat 9B.

"Would you gentlemen like something to drink?" asked the car attendant.

"No, ma'am. We're fine for now," said Harry.

The car attendant carried on as Harry looked outside the window. The train was picking up speed, and they were well on their way to Philadelphia now.

"So, when do you want to do it?" asked Clarence. "I don't want to take forever to do this."

"We need to be careful how we do this, Clarence. There are a lot of witnesses on this train. We aren't in Montrose anymore, after all."

"So do we wait until we're in Philadelphia, then?"

"The thought did cross my mind, but no. I think we wait until she gets up to use the toilet."

"How will we know when she gets up if we aren't in her car?"

"We'll need to make our way up there; find some empty seats and just wait there, I think."

"Why doesn't one of us just sit in the empty seat next to her? Talk to her a little bit."

"That's not a bad idea," said Harry. "Can you see her through the windows in the door?"

"I can."

"You gentlemen look like you're well off," said a man sitting across the aisle from them.

Both Harry and Clarence looked over, noticing a younger man in a straw cowboy hat looking at them, along with one of his friends, in the seat next to him.

"What? Is it any of your business how well off we are?" said Clarence.

"Sorry, mister. Just looking to make small chat. We have a long train ride ahead of us, after all."

"You know what? We're sorry. My friend here gets nervous on trains. Leaves him short-tempered. My name is Harry. This is Clarence."

"No problem at all, misters. Pleased to meet you both. I'm Billy and this here is Thomas."

"Pleasure to meet the two of you," said Harry.

"I should apologize. He's right. I do get a little nervous on trains," said Clarence.

"Don't worry about it at all, mister. So, what takes you two to Philadelphia?" asked Billy.

"Business," replied Harry.

"Oh? What kind of business?"

"Just personal business is all. Won't be there for too long."

"Oh, gotcha. Yeah, Tom here is going back to see his momma back home. Ain't been home for nearly three years now."

"That's right, three years," said Thomas with a blank expression on his face.

"Three years is a long time," said Clarence.

"You gentlemen have mommas too?"

Harry laughed. "Oh, Billy, sure, maybe twenty years ago. They're long dead now."

"Well, I'm sorry to hear that."

"So, what brought you two young men out west in the first place?" asked Harry.

"Business."

"What kind of business?"

"Just personal is all," said Billy.

"How long will you be in Philadelphia for?"

"Oh, however long it takes for business to calm down out here, you know?"

"Calm down?"

"That's right, mister."

"What kind of business requires you to leave your work in order for it to calm down?"

"Let's just say fighting."

"Like boxing?"

"Sure." Billy laughed.

Thomas never broke his gaze from Harry or Clarence.

"Well, we all need a break from time to time. Hey, listen, as much as we'd still like to talk with you young men, we see a girl in the car up from us that we'd like to visit with. We know her father from Montrose and haven't seen her for a long time now and we noticed that she's traveling alone. Thought we would keep her company."

"Oh? That's too bad. Not good to travel alone. Very dangerous. Well, it was a pleasure chatting with you gentlemen. Perhaps we'll find time to talk some more on the trip to Philadelphia."

"Absolutely, we'd love to," said Harry as he stood up from his seat.

Clarence stood up when Harry did as well, and the two men walked to the door to move up cars.

"Oh, hold on gentlemen. It looks like you left your wallet behind on the seat," said Billy, as he bounced up out of his seat, followed by Thomas.

He leaned over, picked something up from the seat as Harry and Clarence stopped to see what he was doing. Both men were checking their pockets when Billy walked up to them both with a knife drawn in his hand while Thomas held his pistol.

"Like I said, you gentlemen forgot something," said Billy.

"Who the hell do you think you are?" asked Harry.

"Well, my momma calls me Harry. Some friends call me William. Most folk know me as Billy the kid."

"Who?"

"You two never hear of Billy the Kid?"

"And you two boys never hear of Clarence Bell and Harry Kilpatrick? War heroes from the South?" said Clarence.

"Who?"

"Fuck you!" said Clarence.

"No, I don't think so. Step outside the car for a minute, or else Thomas here got a couple of spare bullets with your names on it, you see?"

"You insolent little fucks!"

"Just move, old man."

The two bandits pushed Harry and Clarence out of the car, outside on the gangway between the two cars. The sound of the train roaring by on the tracks was loud, and the men had to yell to be heard.

"Stop right there," said Billy.

"What the hell do you want from us? Leave us be so we can conduct our business."

"You see, my partner Tom and I here, we don't mind leaving you be, but first we want your wallets."

"Look, you want some money? I don't give a shit. Take what we have. Our business is more important than a few dollars."

"You men made the right decision," said Billy, sheathing the knife into his pocket.

He extended his hand out as Harry and Clarence both handed him their wallets. Billy took the wallets, removed the money from them, and stuffed the money into his pocket.

"It was absolutely a pleasure doing business with you two gentlemen. You know something? It's always polite to give a proper handshake after doing business with fine gentlemen such as yourselves. Even out here in the wild west."

Billy extended his hand out to shake Harry's hand.

"Like I said, we don't want no trouble. And our business is more important than just a few dollars. The best of luck to you boys," said Harry, extending his hand out and shaking Billy's.

Billy and Harry shook hands, but the gesture was a trap. Billy shoved Harry backward, sending him tumbling off the gangway and onto the tracks, where he was instantly crushed by the train. Clarence, witnessing his friend's horrific death, barely registered Thomas's knife plunging into his own side. Then came Billy's brutal punch, sending Clarence to the same gruesome fate. Billy and Thomas watched with chilling laughter as Clarence was also run over by the train.

"Well, that's one hell of a way to go," said Billy. "I must say, I don't think any one of us has ever killed a man like that before."

"Kinda fun, wasn't it?" said Thomas.

"Ya. It was. Come on, fuck 'em. Let's get some drinks and enjoy the ride."

"What about the girl they said they saw up in the car? Maybe she's waiting for them?" asked Thomas.

"Tom, you fuckin idiot. Did you not hear him before?"

"No, what'd they say?"

"They said they hadn't seen her for a long time, so she ain't know they were on this train, anyway. Besides, we don't kill no woman, Tom. There ain't honor in that."

"Oh, well, okay then."

"Come on, dipshit. Let's go get some drinks."

The two young gunfighters walked back into the car they had come from, ordering whiskey drinks from the car attendants. The bodies of Harry Kilpatrick and Clarence Bell were never recovered.

Meanwhile, young Ida Ashberger sat comfortably in her seat, crying herself to sleep, completely unaware of the danger that was merely just a few feet behind her, saved by the infamous gunslinger of the west, Billy the Kid and his colleague Thomas.

Chapter 23: Saying Goodbye is Hard to Do

"Alright, John. Just one more grave to dig," said Guadalupe, sticking his shovel into the dirt of the family plot on the small hillside overlooking John's land and the San Juan Mountain range.

He crawled out of the grave he and Ramon had just dug and sat down on a rock in the middle of the midday sun.

It was another hot late summer day in the Montrose area. All morning long, he and the last two Mexicans dug graves for some men whose bodies weren't incinerated in the fires caused by the sheriff and his men, then also graves for John's daughter Margaret, and his wife, Martha. John returned late in the morning after dropping off his youngest daughter, Ida, at the train terminal. Before he came home, he gathered the bodies of his daughter and her husband from their home in the town, took them through the town with their bodies wrapped in the white bed sheets stained in their own blood. Citizens of the town watched as he slowly rode through the town with the bodies on the back of his horse, headed to his property. The people stared at John as he rode by with blood-soaked sheets on the back of his horse.

The sheriff also watched as he sat in his rocking chair, smoking his cigar as John slowly left town. He came back to his property, the apple orchard still burning in some places where the oil wasn't completely burned out yet, but most everything else was smoldering. Smoke rolled into the clear blue sky, signaling the destruction that had occurred the night before.

When he had dropped off the bodies of his oldest daughter and her husband at the burial plot, he rode back to his house and went inside. Gathering the bodies of his second daughter and his wife from their rooms, he placed them on his horse and then walked the animal to their graves in the family plot. When he arrived there, the first body that he laid to rest was his son-in-law, Harry. Covering his body with dirt, the next body he laid to rest was his oldest daughter, Anna. Before covering her body with dirt, he reached into his pocket and laid a gold cross pendant on her chest. Leaning down, he kissed her check, getting some of her blood on his lips in the process. He then crawled out of the grave, and with his own hands, buried his oldest daughter.

In the same manner, John buried his second daughter in her grave. Before covering her with dirt, he laid a small gold rose pendant on her chest, kissing her goodbye as well. He crawled out of the grave, and with the help of the Mexicans, buried her.

Finally, John had worked his way to the last grave, where he laid his wife to rest. He went down into the grave, placing his wedding ring onto her chest. Then leaned down and kissed her for the last time, uttering the words, "I'm sorry," to her.

"I can't do this anymore, Guadalupe," said John as he stood in the grave, over the top of his deceased wife. "I don't deserve this. No husband or father deserves this."

"No man deserves to have their family taken from them like this, John. What you do now, though, will define the man that you will become for the last of your days," said Guadalupe.

"I don't want to live anymore," said John.

"But you still serve a purpose, John. What about Ida?"

"Everything I had is gone. My family. My farm. My friends. I have nothing left but Ida."

"Job had nothing left either, but he didn't give up, John. And he lost everything. You at least still have your youngest daughter, and that is worth fighting for."

"I'm not Job, Guadalupe. And God has forsaken me this day. I knew there was going to come a day that I would pay for my sins," said John, looking down at his wife's lifeless body.

"We're all going to pay for our sins, John. You think you're the only one that lost something here?" asked Guadalupe.

"Once my wife is buried, you don't have to stay any longer. You and your two friends may as well save yourselves and go back to Mexico."

"And do what, John? I told you already, John. What are we to do when we're back in Mexico? Just wait for our next hope to come live here in America? Even now, on the edge of a knife and the end of a gun, life is better for us right here. There is nothing for us in Mexico anymore."

"All we have, John, is you and us, here," said Roman.

"We're not going anywhere, John. We're here with you until the end," said Ramon.

"I appreciate you, boys. I won't force you to do something you don't want to do. If you want to stay and die with me, then stay and die with me," said John. "But know this, as God is my witness, I won't stop fighting until they are all dead or until I am."

"John, that's fine, but you need to be careful. Starting a fight is like breaching a dam. We need to gain the upper hand. Especially with only four of us. What can we do if we fight the realtor, the sheriff, and their man's head on with only four of us?"

"Help me out of the ground," said John, extending his hand out to Guadalupe.

Reaching down, Guadalupe grabbed his hand and pulled him up and out.

John turned and looked one last time at his wife, before pushing dirt into the grave, covering her body with the earth. The Mexicans helped bury her body in the ground. When the grave was filled in, John set the shovel on the ground. He then set the tombstones up at the head of each grave and at his wife's grave, he draped a cross pendant necklace over the top of it. He then went down to a knee, placing his forehead on the tombstone and quietly cried.

"John, what do we do now?" asked Guadalupe as the Mexicans set their shovels on the ground by the graves.

John stood up and turned to look at the three men.

"We take everything from them, too," said John, a man with nothing more to lose.

*   *   *   *

James Hackenberry reached out and grabbed the doorknob to the sheriff's office. Opening the door, he walked inside and shut the door, and took a seat across from the sheriff at his desk. Walt Jones smiled as James set down a couple of folders on his desk.

"Well," said the sheriff, looking over across from him at his desk.

"Well, what?" asked James, smiling.

"How are things going?"

"Things are going swimmingly. The crew is working on the third level of the resort. The grass seed is spread and growing already. I received a telegram from John Rockefeller, Cornelius Vanderbilt, and even Andrew Carnegie, inquiring about the resort and when it would be ready to use."

"Well goddamn, James. Isn't that something?"

"It certainly is. These are some of the richest men in America, Walt. It's a good start to building what I feel this town could potentially be."

"Sounds like you got everything planned out."

"I do. Have you heard from Harry or Clarence yet?"

"I have not, but I would imagine that train is still on its way to Philadelphia and won't arrive until tomorrow in the evening. I don't think I'll hear from them until then, but don't you worry, James. They'll finish the job."

"Oh, I'm not worried at all, Walt. Things are going very well. In fact, I'm on my way over to submit the paperwork to obtain Ashberger's property."

"Oh, you are? Where is Ashberger?"

"Gone. He abandoned the property. Last I heard, he's taking what little he has left and is starting his ride back to Philadelphia, too."

"Well, good riddance to him."

"That brings me to your situation, Walt. You've done well for me," said James, as he picked up one folder from the desk and opened it. "And as promised, I have the deed to a piece of property for you, as well as the claim to a couple of gold mines up in the San Juan Mountains."

"Well, goddamn again, James. You're an honest realtor. Never thought I'd ever say that about a realtor before."

"You do good work for me, then I'll make sure you're taken care of. If you'd just sign these documents, we'll take these over to the courthouse right now and file them along with my paperwork, make it legal and the deal will be settled."

James slid the folder with documents into it to the sheriff. He opened the folder and looked at the papers carefully.

"Five acres?" asked the sheriff, surprised.

"I know I didn't offer much at the beginning, but I appreciate all you've done, so yes, five acres."

"How generous. Along with the gold claims."

The sheriff picked up the quill from his ink jar on the desk, signed the documents in the folder, closed the folder, and slid it back to James, who grabbed the file and picked up the second file on his desk.

"If you would be so kind to follow me to the courthouse, Walt. We'll get this settled and make it official," said James, standing up from his chair.

"I suppose I could spare a few minutes," said the sheriff, standing up from his desk.

The two men walked out of the office and down the road to the courthouse, where they entered and filed the paperwork with the county clerk, who notarized and finalized the paperwork for the realtor.

"Do you need copies, Mr. Hackenberry?" asked the clerk.

"Yes, please. Can you have them made up before the end of the day so that I can pick them up tomorrow morning, please?" asked James.

"No problem."

The two men then turned and walked out of the courthouse, walking down the street together, back to their respective offices.

"Walt, this calls for a celebration. Would you and your friends care to join me at the resort this evening? I'll bring some drinks out and we'll celebrate with the workers there, too."

"That sounds like a great plan, James. It has been an absolute pleasure doing business with you, too. I'll be sure and tell George and his men."

"Good. Very good. I would love for them to join us, too. There will be drinks and food. I'd say women too, but as you can see, there are none here in town who are worth the effort." James laughed.

"Whatever you say, James."

"I'll head down there here in a couple hours, meet me at dusk there and I'll make sure a fire is going and ready to cook, too," said James, patting the sheriff on the back.

"Thanks James."

James then broke away from the sheriff and turned down the street, heading back to his office for a little bit before going down to the job site. The sheriff stopped for a moment along the sidewalk and looked around the town, watching some of the townsfolks walking back and forth, completely unaware of the deal the sheriff had made with the devil not that long ago. Turning to walk to the hotel in the town, the sheriff crossed the street and continued for a few minutes to the hotel. Walking inside, he approached the front desk.

"Excuse me, I'm here to see George Holt," said the sheriff.

"Oh, hello Walt. Good to see you. Yes, George is here now. He is in room seven. His friends are also checked into rooms three and four."

"That's fine. I'll go pay him a visit in his room."

"Okay, sheriff."

"Does he have any company?"

"Not this evening, no."

The sheriff walked down a long hallway, away from the front desk towards room seven. When he got there, he faced the door and knocked.

"Who is it?" asked the man inside.

"It's Walt. Open the door, George."

"It's open. Come on in."

Walt pushed the door open and saw George sitting in an old wicker chair by the fireplace, writing a letter in silence.

"James is calling for us to come with him to the job site this evening. Wants to celebrate with all of us. Said that Ashberger abandoned the property today and took off for Pennsylvania."

"Abandoned the property?"

"That's right. I guess he's gone back to Philadelphia."

"Well, that's a problem, Walt. Did anyone see him go?"

"No, damn idea," said the sheriff, sitting on the edge of the bed. "I certainly didn't. And I'm going to say you didn't either."

"If we didn't watch him leave, then how do we know he really went back to Philadelphia?"

"Can't say with certainty that he did."

"Walt, if your wife got killed, along with your daughters, your son-in-law, and had your livelihood burned to the ground, do you think you would just walk away from it all without getting revenge?"

"No."

"No, indeed. Walt, there is nothing more dangerous than a man with nothing to lose. And John Ashberger is now a man with nothing to lose. Hell, we even killed his fuckin' Mexicans. And he's not the kind of man that would leave it to God to get his vengeance either."

"What are you thinking?" asked the sheriff.

"He didn't go back to Philadelphia. At least not yet. He's still around. And I'll bet my last dollar that we'll find out tonight for sure."

"So, what do you suggest, then?"

"Well, I suggest we be ready for him. He's the last man standing. Once he's dead, then it really is over. And we can all get our pay and go our separate ways."

"I respect that."

"What time are we meeting him over at that work site?" asked George.

"Here in an hour."

"Well, I suppose I should get ready. I'll go tell the men."

"No, it's fine. I can tell them on my way out. I'm heading back to my office. I'm going to make sure I got enough bullets."

"Now that sounds like a good plan to me."

The sheriff stood up from the side of the bed and walked out the door, leaving George sitting in the old wicker chair by the fireplace. On the way out, he stopped and spoke with George's men in their rooms, letting them all know what was going on and to be on guard for John Ashberger this evening. After briefing the men, he left the hotel and walked out into the street.

The sun was starting to set behind the hills as he walked back to his office. Walking inside, he went to his chair and sat at his desk. Pulling open the drawer to his desk, he reached in and grabbed a box of bullets for his pistol and loaded the bullet holders on his belt with fresh rounds. While he was doing this, James Hackenberry was leaving his office, locking the door to his office behind him. He walked past the sheriff's office and looked through the window, seeing Walt loading his pistol and belt with ammunition. James stopped, turned around, and walked inside the sheriff's office.

"Hey Walt. I'm heading out to the job site now. I had some of the workers come up and grab the boxes of whiskey and take them back down to the campsite for the evening."

"That sounds good to me. I told George and his men about this evening, too," said the sheriff.

"Why are you loading your pistol like that?"

"You can never be too careful, James. There are still Indians out there."

"Oh, I suppose you're right. Do you want to follow me over right now?"

"I think that's a good idea, James," said the sheriff, stuffing the last bullet into his belt.

The sheriff and the realtor left their office and mounted their horses, which were tied to the hitching post. As they rode through town at sunset, citizens watched them pass, noting their destination: the plantation resort. Even now, some townspeople worked on its construction, planting grass for the golf course. The ride to the site was short. Dismounting, they tethered their horses to some lumber. A few workers approached them and began a conversation.

"Mr. Hackenberry, thank you for coming out and throwing this celebration," said one of the two men.

"Well, you guys deserve it. You all have worked very hard to get to this point, and the fact that we have three levels done already is a testament to your hard work."

"Thank you, sir. Something that Mr. Sanderlin would have been proud of."

"Indeed, Mr. Sanderlin would have been proud. What did you do with the drinks and meat for barbecue?"

"The meat is over by the fire and the drinks are in Ted's tent for now."

"Fetch the drinks from the tent and prepare the fire for cooking the meat. We will have more guests soon."

"You got it, Mr. Hackenberry," said the two men as they turned and walked towards the worker's campsite.

"Come, Mr. Jones. Come see the golf course with me."

The two men walked away from the resort, out to the hill overlooking the beautiful flat land with freshly planted grass that was just starting to break the soil with small spears of grass. The two men got to the top of the hill just in time to see the last bit of sun disappearing in the west, behind the Uncompahgre Peak. Beautiful colors of purple, orange and red colored the evening sky.

"Look at it all, sheriff. You know you're going to have a nice view like this on your new property. Even up at your gold claims up in the San Juans," said James, with a smile on his face again.

"It all was certainly worth the effort, James," replied the sheriff.

"Well, I appreciate your help. I don't know if I could have done it all by myself."

James paused and looked over in the direction of Ashberger's property. The trees in the orchard were still smoldering as white smoke rose into the sky.

"Where do you suppose John Ashberger went? Now that his wife and kids are dead?" asked James.

"I don't know, and that's also another part of the problem."

"What do you mean?"

"Well, last we heard, he had left after he found out that all his Mexicans were dead, along with his family and livelihood. But here's the thing, James. Did he really leave? Or is he just waiting for the right time now to do something? Then, on top of that, what about those fuckin Indians? We can celebrate this evening, but let's not get carried away because we won the battle but haven't won the war yet."

"I suppose that's why you loaded your belt up this evening, isn't it?"

"The most dangerous men are men who have nothing to lose, James. There was a Union man in the war that lost his whole company, and that motherfucker charged the field and slaughtered three Confederate soldiers before one of my friends was able to launch a cannon ball through his stomach. You know why he was superhuman for that brief moment? Because he had nothing to lose. He wasn't afraid of dying. In fact, he wanted to die. Just like John Ashberger now. And since we don't know if he's dead or taken off for Philadelphia, yes. I, as well as we all, need to be on guard."

"God damn it, you're right. Okay. Do you mind if one of you doesn't celebrate with us, Walt?"

"Not only am I not celebrating and drinking my ass off, but George isn't either. I can't say the same for his men, but fuck 'em either way."

"Thank you, Walt."

"However, I will enjoy some of that barbecue that you brought here this evening."

"That's fine. Just as long as you stay sober."

"You don't worry about that."

The two men walked down from the hill, back down to their horses at the job-site. As they were walking back, George Holt and the rest of his men, William Brewer, Frank Noles, Edward Stokes and Peter Martin, all rode in on their horses.

"Gentlemen!" yelled James, as he waved at them.

"James. Walt," said George as he got off his horse. "I figured you all started. I saw two smoke clouds rising in the sky instead of just the one out in John's orchard."

"Pleased that you could join us in our celebration and your efforts won't go unrewarded. Aside from the food and drinks, I have decided to pay you gentlemen each three hundred dollars for your troubles."

"Well, that sounds very nice indeed," said George.

James turned around and yelled into the field of tents.

"Matthew!"

A young man ran up from a large fire that was started in the camp.

"Yes, Mr. Hackenberry?" said Matthew.

"How are things progressing?"

"The drink is out for everyone to enjoy, and the meat is cooking on the fire, sir."

"Good. Gentlemen, would you care to join me by the fire as we toast to our success?"

The group of men walked together into the camp, to the large bonfire in the center of the tents where they met up with the work crew who were already participating in drink and food.

"Please, help yourselves, gentlemen. The best cow meat here in the western states and the finest whiskey, imported directly from Ireland. Only the best for you men," said James.

George's four men grabbed bottles of whiskey from wooden crates, neglecting to grab a glass and opting to drink just straight from the bottles. However, George and Walt refused to drink.

"You gentlemen make sure you get yourselves something to eat, at least. Then take a couple of bottles back to town with you after this evening for later."

"Thank you, James. We will," said the sheriff.

James went back to visiting with workers around the fire, while George and Walt kept a vigilant eye on the night.

For hours into the evening, the men ate and drank and made merry with one another, laughing and singing together. One man from the work crew stood up from the fire and went and grabbed a couple of bottles of whiskey from the wooden crate. He then wandered off into the darkness, unbeknownst to the rest of the crew.

A short time later, he returned without the bottles of whiskey in hand. He walked back over to another wooden crate filled with glass bottles of whiskey imported from Ireland and grabbed two more bottles. He staggered about the campsite, appearing completely drunk. Another one of the work crew stood up to go relieve himself when the man grabbed him by the shoulder.

"Hey," he said to him.

The man tried to acknowledge him but couldn't.

"You lookin' to go piss now?" said the drunk man with the two whiskey bottles.

The man let out a grunt that indicated yes, he was.

"Come, I'll help you out there. But I won't hold it for you!"

The men around the fire laughed at the drunk man's joke, as he held the second drunk man up and they staggered off together into the darkness. Once they had walked out in the field alone together, John Ashberger walked up behind the second drunk man relieving himself, and struck him in the back of the head with a hatchet, splitting his skull open as his body collapsed and slunk down to the ground.

"Nice swing, John," said Roman, who was acting drunk and dressed in the workers' clothing.

He set down the bottles of whiskey on the ground, intending to use them later.

"Quickly, take his clothes, give them to Ramon. This one is about the same size body shape that Ramon is," said John.

While they were removing clothes, the man moaned as he wasn't dead just yet. John took the hatchet, swung and buried it into the back of the man's neck, efficiently killing him this time. The men finished removing his clothing and Ramon quickly put them on. The button-up shirt was a tight fit, but the jacket the man wore hid the fact that the shirt didn't fit Ramon very well.

Now two of John's men were disguised as workers, entering the camp. When they walked back into the camp, they again headed back over to the wooden crate filled with bottles of whiskey and took two more bottles each. They acted as if they were drunk and staggered around the men. They watched as another man stood up from the fire, walking off into the distance to relieve himself. When the man went and did this, Ramon and Roman stood up and walked out into the darkness together as well with their knives drawn.

They found the man in the darkness and grabbed him from behind. Ramon covered the man's mouth, then jabbed his knife into the man's neck. They removed his jacket before it became too bloody, left the shirt, and took his pants. Guadalupe changed into his clothing.

They each left the four whiskey bottles with John and now the three Mexicans, dressed as workers from the job site walked back one by one into the camp. Each man again walked over to the crate and took a couple bottles of whiskey and, as before, they intermingled with the drunk men of the worksite who didn't recognize them, nor remembered the other men walking off in the night. Because of this, neither Walt nor George paid any attention to the men and only saw the same number that went out and came back in each time.

One of the workers around the fire happened to notice though, that Ramon was Mexican and made a joke about it, but he was too drunk to remember that James didn't have any Mexicans working for him. A short time later, another man got up from the fire and walked out into the field to relieve himself. This time, only Roman and Guadalupe followed him out, leaving Ramon behind around the fire. They again took their whiskey bottles out with them and found the man in the field and greeted him. In the darkness, John Ashberger walked up to the men and swung his hatchet, striking the man and burying the hatchet in his face.

While John was taking the man's clothing off, Ramon walked out into the field to meet them.

"Jesus Christ, Ramon. You scared the hell out of me," said Guadalupe as he turned around with a knife ready to lunge at him.

"How many bottles of whiskey did we get?" asked John.

The men counted the bottles they gathered from the camp.

"It looks like we have twelve bottles," said Guadalupe.

"Good. That'll get a fire started. Come, grab the bottles and follow me," said John as he leaned down and picked up four of the bottles.

The Mexicans picked up the rest of the bottles and followed John. They snuck around the campsite in the darkness, out of sight. They approached the building and walked through a door into the first floor of the structure. There, they opened the bottles of whiskey and poured them onto the wooden floor of the building. They poured whiskey everywhere: the walls, the floor, and even the ceiling.

They went up to the second level floor and poured the rest of what they had on the floor there, too. They then walked back down to the first level of the resort building and when they did, the Mexicans walked out the back of the building, leaving John alone in the room that now reeked of alcohol. John took a match from his pocket, lit it, and dropped it onto the floor. The whiskey ignited and in a moment, the floor burst into flames. John turned around to walk out when he was abruptly met with a fist in his face, knocking him back down to the ground.

"Son of a goddamn bitch!" yelled George Holt as he stood over the top of John.

George took his knife out and went down to stab John with it, but John dodged to the side as George plunged his knife into the wooden floor.

John turned around, kicking George in the face with the heel of his boot. The blow staggered him, allowing John to get back up on his feet. The fire engulfed the whole room in flames, as John and George engaged in a fistfight.

"John, get the hell out of there!" yelled Guadalupe.

John took a moment and looked around the room. The heat was intense, and the structure was starting to get weak as boards cracked and collapsed around the two men. George swung and connected with the side of John's head, knocking him back down to the ground.

"I knew you'd come back here, you dirty son of a bitch! Now I can send you to hell to go see your dead wife and kids, you worthless piece of shit!"

George mounted John while he lay on the floor and choked him, tightening his grip on his throat.

"You and I, we can die together in here. How does that sound, John?"

John looked around as he struggled to break George's grip when he noticed George's knife still stuck in the floorboard next to them. He reached over and grabbed the knife from the floor and plunged the blade into the side of George's stomach.

George grunted as the knife sank into the side of his body. John made a slashing motion with the knife, slicing George's belly open as he fell to the side. George then turned around with his back on the floor as John stood up. With the little time he had left to escape the burning room, John quickly leaped out the open window just as the structure crashed down on George, killing him.

The disturbance of the falling structure got the attention of the crew around the campfire, as well as the attention of James and the sheriff.

"What the hell was that?" asked James, as he looked over toward the sound.

The sheriff stood up from the log he was sitting on and looked over, noticing that there was now a familiar glow in the night coming from the direction of the resort building.

Before the sheriff could speak, though, an arrow shot through the night, sailing by his head and found its target in the chest of one crewman at the camp. Ignacio and the Ute men with him then charged into the camp from the darkness. The sheriff and Holt's men that were left took aim with their pistols and rifles, shooting and killing multiple Indians.

One of the Ute men shot an arrow, striking Peter Martin in the stomach. Peter shot a couple more of the charging Ute men when a second arrow struck him in the face, killing him before he hit the ground. The Ute successfully charged the camp and killed many of the workers with hatchets and knives, while some workers who weren't too drunk pulled their pistols from their tents. They aimed and shot at the Utes, killing some of them in the camp. One of the workers who was drunk and unable to see clearly, had shot and accidentally killed Edward Stokes, another one of George Holt's men, striking him firmly in the chest.

James noticed that Edward had fallen and died right next to him. He leaned down and grabbed Edward's pistol and took aim and started shooting the Ute men as well.

John and his men sat back and took aim with some rifles at everyone who moved into the camp, Ute or worker. Guadalupe successfully shot Frank Noles in the back of the head, killing him.

"I'm going after that goddamn sheriff," said John, as he got up from behind the hill and charged into the camp.

Guadalupe, Ramon and Roman charged into the camp with him, shooting at anything that moved with their pistols. Ramon fired his last bullet from his pistol and attempted to reload his weapon when one of the Ute men stabbed him in the back with a knife, then bludgeoned him in the top of the head with a hatchet.

While the sheriff was reloading, one of the Ute men named Liwanu jumped on him with his knife drawn. The sheriff, however, overpowered him and took his knife from him while they wrestled on the ground, then pushed the sharp end of the blade into his throat, pushing the knife through to the back of his neck. Blood erupted from the dead Ute man's neck until he stopped moving. The sheriff pulled the knife out of the side of Liwanu's neck and just in time plunged it into the chest of Jaanesh, who had attempted to jump on top of him.

The sheriff pushed Jaanesh, who fell on top of him, then rolled him onto his back while he was still alive and pulled the knife out of his chest. The sheriff then jabbed the knife up through the bottom of his mouth into his head. The sheriff then reached over, grabbed his gun, loaded it, and fired at the Utes again.

James Hackenberry quickly ran out of the area and up onto the hill with a pistol in his hand, seeking shelter for himself. He looked over the large fight going on in the camp and then saw where his resort used to stand. Now it was nothing more than a smoldering pile of burning lumber.

"Look what your greed got you," said a voice behind James as he watched his plantation burn.

James turned and saw John Ashberger walking up from behind.

"You let greed kill your friend and colleague. You let greed get a bunch of men killed here this evening. You let greed put a lot of innocent citizens of the town in danger. And most of all, you let greed kill my family and my livelihood," said John.

"Greed never ruled me, John! I wanted a better life for these people! Industrializing this area, putting it on the map—they would have prospered, and flourished under my leadership! They wouldn't have had to debate amongst themselves, working for miners and trappers along the stagecoach routes and railroads. But, John, I'm glad you're here at the end. It's fitting that you destroy my future, as I destroyed yours." said James as he raised his pistol and pulled the trigger.

The gun clicked, but didn't fire.

James pulled the trigger again and again with the same result each time, an empty clicking sound coming from the cylinder.

"It appears you are out of ammunition, James," said John, walking up to him and drawing his knife out.

He jabbed the blade deep into James' chest. The sound of James' ribs cracking could be heard as James let out a loud moan and fell backwards with the knife still plunged into his chest.

"Judas sold Jesus for thirty pieces of silver, but you betrayed your friend Charles with your greed. The only sad thing is, Charles would have done it to you if you didn't do it to him first. Burn in hell, James Hackenberry. Charles is holding a special place in hell for you now," said John, as he watched James breath his last breath there on the hill overlooking what would have been his golf course and the plantation resort building, now turning to ash.

The Ute men continued their assault, killing more and more of the crewmen. The sheriff and William Brewer kept gunning them down one by one. While reloading his pistol, William was attacked from behind by Ahote who knocked William down to the ground. The sheriff saw this and saw Ahote mount William as he raised a knife up over his head to plunge down into his chest. Before Ahote could do this, though, the sheriff kicked him in the face, stunning the Ute, while William pulled out his knife and stuck it into Ahote's throat. Blood poured out the wound onto William as Ahote fell to the ground and died.

The sheriff looked up and saw another Ute indian bearing down on his position. The Ute man aimed and threw his hatchet at the sheriff. It missed, striking William in the side of his head, effectively killing him. The sheriff took aim with his pistol and shot the Ute in the chest and killed him.

John walked down from the hill after killing James. Piles of the dead lay everywhere, and the ground was stained red with blood. He looked around and found the bodies of Ramon and Roman, both men killed by Ute men with a hatchet. However, he looked everywhere and could not find the body of his closest friend, Guadalupe.

"Guadalupe!" he yelled out loud, but he got no response.

He tried yelling for him again, as he searched among the piles of the dead around the camp, when he heard a faint voice from behind one tent. John turned around to see Guadalupe stagger around the corner of the tent, out into the open.

"Guadalupe!" he yelled as he rushed over to him.

"John, you're still alive," he said.

"And so are you."

"Where are Roman and Ramon?"

"I found them. They are dead. The Indians killed them both. Are you alright?"

"I suppose. How are you?"

"Sore. But still alive, I guess," said John, holstering his gun.

Guadalupe groaned, all the air leaving his body as John watched a metal object burst out of his chest. The sheriff then walked around the side of Guadalupe from the darkness with his face stained with blood that shimmered in the campfire's light.

"Hello, John," said the sheriff as he pulled his knife back out of the back of Guadalupe.

"Goddamn you!" said John as he pulled out his pistol and fired at the sheriff, who quickly ducked back behind the tents and hid as John fired the last of his bullets into the tent.

When he had run out of bullets, the sheriff re-emerged from behind the tent and ducked behind.

"I knew you would be here tonight," said the sheriff. "I'm not stupid. You have too much pride to run away. Or you're just too stupid to know when you should leave."

John dropped his gun on the ground and reached over to his side, pulling his knife from the sheath as the two men circled each other.

"Maybe I should have left while I could, but you took everything from me and for what? You killed my wife, my children, my workers, my friends. You took my property, my livelihood. You took everything from me," said John.

"John, please. You would have done the same thing if you were in my position. You're just as much of a cold-blooded killer as I am. The only difference is that you have a wife and children. Well, you had a wife and children."

"You're right. I had a wife and children and a future. But now I don't. Which means I have nothing to lose anymore."

"That makes a man dangerous," said the sheriff, pointing his knife at John. "And you're right. You have nothing left. By now, you don't even have your youngest daughter left."

"She's safe and you don't mention her!"

"You think she's safe, John? But right now, I would speculate that my two friends have already taken her life, too. I hope they enjoy Philadelphia just as much as your youngest daughter would have," said the sheriff, laughing.

John yelled and then charged the sheriff, taking a swipe at him with his knife. The sheriff avoided the slash and responded by slashing at John himself, missing him, too. The two men sized each other up, each taking swipes at one another.

"I'm going to kill you, John," said the sheriff. "Tonight, the bloodline of Ashberger ends and when it does, I will hang my knife up on the mantle of my fireplace and every time I see it, I will smile, knowing the man's life it had taken."

"Why don't you do it already, then?" said John, lunging at the sheriff again.

The slash struck the sheriff's blade, causing a metallic clanking sound. The two men exchanged slashes with their knives once again. On occasion one man would cut the arms or chest of the other, but not deep enough to cause any serious damage.

The sheriff eventually knocked the knife out of the grip of John's hand and knocked him down to the ground. The sheriff leaped in and attempted to cut John's throat, but John reached over and grabbed a small piece of lumber and hit the sheriff's wrist as he leaned in with the weapon, knocking the knife out of his hand, too.

John got back to his feet as the two men engaged in a fistfight. They fought for minutes, with each man landing blows to one another until the sheriff landed a blow that knocked John down to the ground, stunning him. He mounted John and landed multiple punches into John's torso and face. Finally, the sheriff stopped as John was breathing heavily lying on the ground.

"I have something for you, John. You son of a bitch," said the sheriff, picking him up by the shirt and carrying his body over to the fire.

"It ends here, John. A knife or a gun is too good for you."

The sheriff dropped him on the ground by the fire, then walked over to one of the tents. He walked into the tent as John came to and pull himself away from the fire. After a minute, the sheriff came out of the tent with a clay jar in his hands. Setting it down on the ground by John, he reared back and kicked John in the ribs while he was crawling away, knocking the wind out of his lungs. Then he kneeled down next to John.

"You see this clay jar, John? There's some serious shit in there. You see, I discovered this stuff back in the Civil War. It's called camphene oil. This is the same shit I used to burn your Mexicans to death and your apples down to the ground. And now, I'm going to watch as it helps to melt the skin off your body."

The sheriff then stood up, turned around, and walked over to the jar next to the fire as John turned over and pushed himself up to his knees. As the sheriff bent down to pick up the clay jar to pour the oil onto John's body, he felt something sharp penetrate his back with force. He quickly shot up and turned around to see Ignacio, the last of the Ute men, with a bow in his hand. The Ute man had shot him in the back with an arrow from close range.

"You goddamn, Indians. You shot me pretty good," said the sheriff, laughing.

John stood up and grabbed the clay jar from off the ground, then hurled the jar at the sheriff from close range. The jar burst, covering the sheriff in camphene oil and knocking him back into the large campfire. The sheriff instantly burst into flames and the burning oil melted the skin from his bones as he painfully burned to death.

John turned around and saw Ignacio, reaching for another arrow from a quiver lying close by on the ground. He quickly walked over to one of the dead crewmen and leaned down, grabbing a pistol from the ground and took aim at Ignacio. The Ute leader took aim with an arrow and fired, striking John in the abdomen just as John pulled the trigger, shooting Ignacio between the eyes. Ignacio staggered back as blood poured down his face from the bullet hole in his head. He instantly fell and died there on the field.

In the flood of morning light, John was the last man standing there in the field.

He slowly staggered over to his friend, Guadalupe, who was lying on the ground with the arrow stuck in his belly. He kneeled next to his friend and examined him, but Guadalupe was dead from the wound inflicted by the sheriff. John hung his head in sadness as he stood back up and left the campsite. He walked to the edge of the river and into the water, as he slowly swam across the river and onto the other side. Pulling himself up onto the bank with the arrow still lodged in his abdomen, he staggered up onto his property and forced himself up to the burial plot on the hill where his wife, two daughters, and son-in-law rested. He felt numb, cold, and disoriented in that moment.

Reaching the hilltop, where his family was buried, he collapsed onto a large rock. Each breath was a struggle, shallow and painful. Silently, he watched the sunrise over the San Juan Mountains, a familiar pleasure, as the sky blazed with orange, yellow, and red. A cool morning breeze blew up the side of the hill, cooling his sweat soaked face. The sunlight touched his blood-streaked face, and a single tear rolled down his cheek. He smiled, drew a final breath, and his chin fell to his chest. He died there, among his family, in the most beloved place on his property.

Chapter 24: The Final Chapter

In the late 1800s, Philadelphia led the nation in industrial production, especially in manufacturing. This position not only defined the city's economic status but also shaped many of the international connections and helped to carve out neighborhoods in the city. It was a manufacturing leader in America, a diverse city with many ethnic groups, and a city where the upper-class lived in mansions and the poor lacked access to baths and functioning toilets. Here in the suburbs of Philadelphia lived Martha's family, her brother and Ida's uncle, Robert and her aunt Mary.

The day started off normal for Robert and Mary, as they had Martha's daughter Ida for the past week now with no word from Martha or John Ashberger until a post delivery service delivered a telegram to their front door one day. Robert answered the door and read the note, then read it out loud to his wife, Mary.

"Telegram from Montrose, Colorado. The county clerk of Montrose. Says that we are the only found family to John Ashberger, who was found dead on his property a week ago. The county took the liberty of burying him in the town cemetery."

"Well, that is that for the family, then," said Mary.

"Where is Ida?" asked Robert.

"She went into the backyard to play with her dolls this morning."

"I don't know what to tell her."

"Perhaps the right thing to do is to say nothing for now?"

"And lie to her? What happens when she asks where John is and when he's coming home?"

"Let's just hope she doesn't ask that for quite some time, Robert."

Robert hung his head, disheartened.

"I don't know if I can lie to her, Mary. I don't know if I can hold that back from her."

"You need to do what is right, Robert. Maybe what is right is telling the truth about what happened, and maybe it's not. You'll feel what is right when the time is right and that might be now, or tomorrow, or years from now."

"I'll be right back," said Robert, as he turned and left the living room.

He walked through the kitchen and out the back door, stepping outside into the yard where he saw Ida, with her dolls Ollie, Ellen and Kelly, sitting under the apple tree they had grown in the backyard. It looked as if she was playing with her dolls, but her face told a different story of worry and despair.

"Ida?" said Robert, as he watched her.

Ida looked up and saw her uncle standing there by the tree with her. She then looked down at her three dolls, gathering them close to her and clutching them as she leaned back against the trunk of the apple tree.

Robert walked over and sat down with her next to the tree.

"You know something?" asked Robert.

Ida didn't respond to him.

"I planted this apple tree when your mom left Philadelphia to go live down in Florida. It's been planted back here for over a decade now and for years it's produced some of the sweetest red delicious apples in the whole area!"

Robert reached up and pulled one of the red apples from off the tree, wiped it on the sleeve of his shirt, and then took a bite from it.

"Sweet and juicy, just as I expected. Would you care to take a bite and find out too?" said Robert, offering Ida a bite.

She quickly took her doll, Ollie, and put his mouth up to the apple and imitated a biting sound.

"Woah, Ollie took a big bite!" said Robert.

Ida then clutched her doll to her chest, with a blank expression on her face.

Robert put his arm around her and sat there under the apple tree with her.

"Ida, I don't know how to tell you this, other than I want to be honest and truthful with you."

Ida looked up at her uncle, tears forming in her eyes.

"I want you to know that your father loves you very much. So did your mother. And your sisters, too. As well as your aunt Mary and I. You will always have a family. Here with us and here in your heart," said Robert, pointing at her chest.

"I know," said Ida, as she went back to playing with her dolls.

Robert stood up from the ground and reached up into the tree and picked a second ripe apple, handing it to her.

"Here's an apple all for yourself. Make sure Ollie doesn't get any more, okay?" Robert smiled.

"Okay uncle Rob."

He turned around and walked away, leaving Ida to play under the apple tree with her dolls. Walking back inside, he saw Mary standing by the kitchen window, looking out and watching Ida play.

"Did you tell her?" she asked Robert.

"Not really. I don't know how to say it, but I think she already knows it somehow."

Mary turned around and walked back to the living room, while Robert stood by the window, watching Ida in the backyard.

Ida sat innocently with her stuffed dolls Ollie, Ellen and Kelly in her arm underneath the apple tree alone. Just as she did back at the house in Montrose, Colorado all those summer days ago. The calm, cool wind blew her hair back as a single tear rolled down her rosy, red cheek and falling into her lap. She palmed the apple in her hand and examined it closely before taking a bite.

www.ingramcontent.com/pod-product-compliance
Lightning Source LLC
Chambersburg PA
CBHW022027260626
47156CB00017B/429